A Sporting Marrying

Jon Rosebank

Copyright © 2025 Jon Rosebank

The moral right of Jon Rosebank to be identified as the creator of this original work is hereby asserted. All rights reserved. No part of this publication may be reproduced, distributed, or transmitted in any form or by any means, including photocopying, recording, or other electronic or mechanical methods, without the prior written permission of the author or the publisher, except in the case of brief quotations embodied in critical reviews, and certain other non-commercial uses where permitted by local legislation.

No AI training: Without in any way limiting the author's exclusive rights under copyright, any use of this publication to "train" generative artificial intelligence (AI) technologies to generate text is expressly prohibited. The author reserves all rights to license uses of this work for generative AI training and development of machine learning language models.

This is a work of fiction. Most characters, places, and entities are fictional. Where real-life historical figures appear, the situations, incidents, and dialogues concerning those persons are entirely fictional and are not intended to depict actual events or to change the entirely fictional nature of the work. In all other respects, any resemblance to actual persons, living or dead, is entirely coincidental.

Trigger warning. May contain spoilers.

Some passages in this book deal with assault. While the author has taken great lengths to ensure the subject matter is dealt with in a compassionate and respectful manner, it may be troubling for some readers. Discretion is advised.

Edited by Helen Baggott
Design and layout by Oliver Tooley

Published 2025 by Blue Poppy Publishing,
87 High Street, Ilfracombe, Devon EX34 9NH

ISBN: 987-1-83778-054-9

For the smacksmen
and the community in which they lived

A note on Devon dialect

The Devon dialect I have used mostly comes from *Seems So! A Working-Class View of Politics* written in 1911 by the journalist Stephen Reynolds. He wrote it with Bob and Tom Woolley, two fishermen from Sidmouth, twenty miles across Lyme Bay from Brixham. I have drawn some expressions also from Francis Brett Young's *Deep Sea*, a novel set in Brixham, written by one of the town's doctors and published in 1914. These are as close to authentic sources from the period and location of this book as we are likely to discover. One or two additional words come from Clement Marten, *The Devonshire Dialect* (Newton Abbot 2002).

I once wrote a narrative partly in the authentic dialect I remembered from my childhood. I sent it to an expensive literary consultancy. The consultant wrote back that he could not take it seriously since it was 'written in pirate-speak'. It was an annoying response, but it highlighted a genuine problem. Dialect is distracting if it gets in the way of our characters and their meaning. But nor is it convincing for the working poor of Edwardian Brixham to speak with middle-class voices from a century later.

So I have compromised. I have used the Woolleys' dialect, and some expressions reported by Brett Young and Marten, but neither completely nor consistently. Instead I have tried to allow characters to have authentic voices, and at the same time to allow what they say to be clear and fluent. The purists will have to forgive me. I hope other readers will allow the dialect to be a kind of poetry.

You can find more about the research I have done at the end of the book. The sailing terms from the sailing trawlers, or 'smacks', come mainly from Edgar March's *Sailing Trawlers*, a deeply researched study, written in 1953, and drawing on surviving boats and smacksmen, including many from Brixham. While sailors tell me that what I have written is technically correct, the reader needs to know none of the jargon to follow the story. It too is a sort of poetry.

Chapter 1

Jimmy was thinking only of Alice. *Maryann* was lifting in the swell, rounding the new breakwater and Jimmy scanned ashore and there were a hundred other trawling smacks already home, some berthed on the inner mud but most further out at their chains. He could see the red brown of canvas ripped and whipping and knew the stories would even now have started of the storm. But the truth was that he had thought of Alice Rogers every moment for two years. He had explained everything to her a hundred times, swigging up the topsail and sheeting it home, warning her clear as the after shoe of the trawl beam came shouldering ill-tempered and untrustworthy alongside. Together they had topped the booms as a breeze had smartened, and lowered main and mizzen halyards to put in a reef. In reality, Alice, of course, had never sailed aboard *Maryann*. No smack ever allowed a woman to kill its luck. She had never been gripped with small hours cold, ghosts under the careering naptha, as you untied the net and the silver living slid dying at your feet, nor reeled into the stink and heat of the cabin when the last survivor was gutted and the baskets in ice. But in Jimmy's imagination she had been with him every single hour, on every trip blessed and unblessed since they had met all those months before, when *Maryann* had been alongside, the gorgeous red of her sails just a crumple and the running gear all uncoiled.

Now he knew she would be waiting on the quayside and the certainty suffocated him. He looked for her, frail among the smacksmen, the buffs and blacks of caps and oilskins, the heavy dealers bidding at the fish market and the lads who ran to tell your people when you came in. He imagined the drawn haunting of her face and the blonde curls pinned up into the bonnet, the skirt so full you would never believe it of a shop girl. This time Jimmy did not know what to expect except days of hopelessness. He did not even know if she had heard.

They reached level with Upham's yard and prepared to luff up for a mooring and Jimmy could see the middle harbour was packed already, at least seventy smacks riding there at their chains. Twice that number must still have been out and it would be hours before they knew if any had been lost. It had been worse than anything since the three evil days just before Christmas 1910, when four of the Brixham smacks had gone down, three men and a boy on each, and two men also lost from *Friendship*. Then they had raised £6000 and said they would support the widows and their children until the end of their life. Jimmy could think of half a dozen men gone over in the thirty months since, exhausted, deaf to shouting crew, sometimes only heartless yards away when they vanished. Each time it happened it was a son, a father. They said there were more orphans for every man in Brixham than anywhere else in the kingdom. The mourning lasted for ever and yet was quickly over, another man in your berth and the bowsprit run out for another trip. This time Jimmy knew it would be the same but that it was also entirely different.

The mainsail clattered on its ashen hoops and Jimmy made his way to the port rail where Eb, *Maryann*'s mate, was heaving it down, thick canvas stinking still fresh of the new cutch they had painted to waterproof it. They hauled the foresail aback and dropped her as the chains approached, lowering the anchor away to dredge the last few yards, security against a last kick of the storm. Eb said nothing and Jimmy left him to stow the canvas and climbed down into the fish hold, unable to bear the watching of the quayside any longer. He felt the stillness that told him the news had landed, that Alice must already know and his face fell into frozen hardness. It was not the stiffness of salt or the mask of wind and sun, but the heaviness that was the ice cold of coming in a man down. Below, he was glad of the damp pine around him and heaved the fish trunks for lifting out. They had taken three dozen pair of soles in the four days but none of them was hurrying to make the market, the ship's boat still on its slide, even its gangway yet to be opened. No-one wanted to walk the sympathetic rows.

Someone would have to collect the boy's possessions, his scant rig of life. Jimmy supposed it would usually be the skipper's job to return it to the family but knew in this case it was his. He climbed out of the hold and called over to Henry from the hoodway.

'I'll get his things.'

'I piled 'em up in his locker.'

'Will you tell them, Skip?'

'Reckon they know.'

'They'll want to hear, exactly.'

'I'll do it. But you'll go there now anyway?'

'Yes.'

The cabin was clear, scrubbed, ordered because Henry ran the best smack in the port. But this time everything was stinking damp from the sea that had come over and taken the boy. Jimmy opened his low locker and found the spare guernsey, the kind of luxury a thirteen-year-old cookie would beg from a father after his first trip. They said you had your own pattern knitted against the day you were found on the rocks bloated beyond recognising, but now only the old men had them and they would die in their beds. They would only see Billie Rogers again if he came up in a trawl. There was a bar of chocolate half eaten and Jimmy wondered if Alice had begged it for her brother from Farley's shop where she worked. Little chance from George Farley. There was also a Bible and Jimmy opened the cover and found it had belonged to the boy's grandfather, its tissue-yellow pages rounded and smudged, the Gospels black frayed with turning. Jimmy remembered lying in his bunk two days before, opening his eyes and seeing Billie stuffing the Bible into the locker as Eb came clattering down the companion, the beef the boy was supposed to be cooking burned dry and ruined. He had never seen him open the book before. Perhaps he had somehow known he did not have long. For a hundredth time Jimmy prayed he had gone in peace, as the wind shrieked its hullabaloo and the main boom bent and the foresail screamed on its iron horse and *Maryann* had bucked and rolled. She was a good one and they had laughed with her as they battened her hatches. But then the sea had come over and they had got back to the cabin and discovered with a shout that the boy was gone. Now Jimmy was putting the objects on the cabin table, feeling them under his fingers like touching dead hands. He bundled it all in the guernsey and tied up the arms. It was not much. Billie must have been wearing every other single thing he owned. At least he could tell Alice it would have been quick.

She was alone on the middle pier. As Eb brought *Maryann*'s boat to the wooden steps Jimmy looked for her father, for Farley, for anyone to stand by her. But Alice was alone, her lips full to cry, the wind bullying her curls across her eyes, tugging at the cambric she wore for work. The boys would have run from the quayside as *Maryann* broached the harbour and brought her straight from the shop. How much had they said? Her eyes were set beyond the breakwater, her face white taut as if anger could make the elements own their guilt. Jimmy climbed up awkwardly with the bundle. It would have been impossible to find the words even if things were still as they had been, five days before, when they had raised *Maryann*'s mainsail into the breeze and the boy had climbed down to stow his cookie's stores. With things as they were Jimmy was unable to imagine what Alice was capable of doing. He put out his arm and she turned away.

'Jimmy, don't.'

Already she was walking. Jimmy followed, carrying the eyes of the whole quay. What he had seen in her expression was confusion and guilt. Her voice, however, was sharp and bloody.

'You were going to make it right for him.'

'Alice, I'm sorry.'

She was walking more quickly. Jimmy did not know his own voice.

'We went up. We had to, for the storm jib, the stay foresail. I left him in the galley. Alice, I told him not to move. Billie didn't know what to do. *I told him to stay below*. But a sea came right over. It filled the cabin.'

It was not the moment. It should be in the quiet of the house, as he had imagined it. Alice was heading back along the pier, turning into the town and the market and the crowded street between the pubs and the fish market where it was impossible to say anything with honesty, where her tears were a condemnation for everyone to see and Jimmy's could not be allowed. She was holding herself tightly away from him as if everything was already clear. They had apprenticed Billie Rogers to *Maryann* ten, twelve weeks before. *He'll be safer than ashore.* Jimmy remembered saying it and how he had wanted to believe it. Billie had been a disgraceful cookie, lazy and useless, and the sea had never broken his arrogance. He had given not one ounce of his soul, never pretended to be part of the crew. Henry and Eb had stood by him out of regard for his father Pentecost, one of the finest shipwrights in town and, in a port where church and chapel drew almost the entire fleet in every Sunday, as mordant and two-fisted a preacher as any had heard. And also for Jimmy because, if she ever consented, marrying Alice Rogers would be a lifelong trial and he would need all the hitching a crew could muster.

'The sea came right over, Alice. Eb was strung up in the shrouds. I catch'd the forestay. We were lucky. When we went below the cabin was water everywhere, and in the hold and in the sail locker. It took him, Alice. *It took him.*'

Alice at last looked round. They were at the end of the fish market, where the quay turned and the road ran on into Middle Street. Her voice was thick with crying but her mouth was disfigured with scorn.

'He went overboard, Jimmy. Didn't you see him? Didn't you see *what he was doing*?'

'Alice, anything happens in a blow. The rope locker turned upside down... the coal everywhere. I was six hours at the pump...'

'But he jumped.'

The silence between them was suddenly without beginning or end. It strangled the crying of the market traders and the racket of boots on the wet granite street. Alice held his eye with a level bitterness.

'Billie jumped, Jimmy. He killed himself.'

Jimmy stopped. Started again after her, wanted to pull her back, stop her in the street. But she was hunched against him, carried along by the anger she always carried, but now blacker than he had ever seen.

'*Jumped?* Alice, you weren't there. How do you know?'

'*They told me.*'

CHAPTER 2

'Alice.'

There was no reply. She was striding on, towards the steps that let up to Higher Street. Jimmy caught up, ignoring the men with the baskets, stepping around them in the road, and the girls with their white aprons looking from one to the other.

'If Billie'd jumped I'd have gone after him.'

It was a pointless exaggeration and Alice turned again and at last raised her hazel eyes to his.

'Don't be bloody ridiculous. There's no chance once you're over in your boots. 'Tis what you always said.'

Her square jawed face was now a chalk mask and the black around her eyes and high on her cheeks said she had not eaten or slept for twenty-four hours. Her voice was bled white except for confusion and the guilt Jimmy heard but could not quite catch. She shook her head and turned and began climbing the steps, shoulders round hunched with the effort, suddenly old.

'You didn't know about Billie. There's so much you don't know, Jimmy. You don't know about me. About what 'tis like for us, about how hard 'tis for us. How hard 'tis for me.'

'I know you better than anyone. You've told me…'

'I haven't told thee naught.'

Jimmy had expected there to be anger because there always was with Alice. She seemed to live by the conviction that the world was harder for her than for anyone, that nothing could be expected of her, that anything she gave was generous and she expected you to be grateful. And Jimmy knew that what had happened would make her convictions impossible to pierce. For how long, he could not bear to think.

'Don't do this on your own, Alice.'

'Six days of the week I have to do everything on my own.'

'Somebody has to earn a living. Somebody'd have to…'

Jimmy could not go on. The words he had said so often were dead on his tongue, the future lost in a whitened wake. Alice was walking on, not looking back.

''Tis not a living for two, a deckie's share.'

For weeks Jimmy had known that this was coming. Now she was saying the words that would finish it, at the moment it was impossible for him to say the hard things that needed saying. They climbed into Higher Street without any more words, granite setts shining hard with the rain, the shouts of the harbour dying to a memory. Alice reached the little house she now occupied only with her father and the door under the low arch was open and the place was empty. They stood lost in the tiny living room, the range barely warm, thin yellow curtains drawn across the window to the yard behind. He put the lad's things down on one of the two heavy armchairs and took her firmly into his arms and waited the wordless minutes as boots clacked past in the street and the range ticked the adjustments of its warmth, until at last her face lifted a fraction to his and she closed her wet eyes and he could kiss her. Her lips were ungiving but she stood, her head buried in his shoulder, and he felt the squalls thrashing through her until in the end she gave in to the gusts of loss. It was something shared but still stony cold and still it seemed she could not speak. She was withdrawing from him further with each beat.

'There's not a smacksman born who would jump, Alice. There's no pain in the world would push you onto the rail and make you look into the black and go over.'

Even as Jimmy said the words he knew they were pointless. Billie had never been a smacksman with the rest of them. He had never stowed his soul. Aboard had been imprisonment, the huge horizon a horror, and the time that passed, two gutting hours by two sleeping hours, day after bitter day until the death in your hold drove you home. Even so, Jimmy could not imagine the boy's arrogance so cowed he would turn his face to the water and welcome it, and in a storm so violent every human sinew screamed for safety.

'Even Billie, Alice. Even Billie couldn't have done it. Whatever they told you.'

'I know you hated Billie…'

'Alice, we didn't…'

'He was doing the best he could. Everything was wrong for him from the time he was born and there was no-one he could tell except me, and I couldn't help. I tried so hard, Jimmy. I tried. He sobbed so you thought he couldn't breathe and he wouldn't be held and I just said, Billie, Billie … I *know*, Billie. And I used to take him up on Berry Head and try to talk but all he ever did was throw stones and swear 'cause up there his father couldn't hear him. Swear at his *bloody* father and his *fucking* religion. And his *fucking* mam and her *fucking* affairs. And everybody else. Swear nobody had ever wanted him. And I told him I loved him and he said it was no use 'cause I was one of them. He said it was my fault, I could make it stop, they would listen to me. But I couldn't do naught. I had everything of my own to cope with. I tried. I tried so hard to make it right for Billie. I'd have done anything for him to have a life to live.'

'We tried too, Alice.'

She pulled away and when she looked back he could see her face filled with an anger too much for him to fight. They were locked in the fire-cracked silence when they heard her father's footsteps from the top of the steps, echoing in the narrowness, his stride deliberate and unchanged. When Jimmy went to the door the man was walking briskly, oddly hatless, eyes fixed on the road, a firm handshake. Alice looked up but without feeling. Pentecost sat in his tall chair at the table and quietly praised the Lord for his ways and for bringing Jimmy safe home and Alice knelt on the floor by his chair but was far away. Jimmy brought him tea and sat across the table and looked into his preacher's face and tried to tell him what had happened, his words intended for Alice to hear. Pentecost accepted everything without tears and without blame. Jimmy thought all the time the man had little idea what he was saying. At last Pentecost hesitated.

'Roddy Farley came to tell us. *Coronet* tied up last night. They'd heard it from the *Sanspareil*. Then they came straight in. Roddy ran here.'

Pentecost's words hit Jimmy like a squall. As the storm had died, the crew of *Maryann* had seen the little *Sanspareil*, mainsail ripped, topsails both away, and gone to offer help. Of course they had told them about Billie. Farley and the men on *Coronet* must have come by after and heard the story and then set every inch of her canvas and bent their spars for port. Jimmy, Eb and Henry had been hours at *Maryann*'s pumps before they could pull everything out of the sodden cabin and the lockers. And then they had not pushed fast for home, labouring with the heaviness they carried, the rain still puckering the grey, glad for the smack, none of them ready for other faces.

That was not what hammered Jimmy. They had known the news would come in before them. But Farley. *Bloody Roddy Farley.* Alice worked in George Farley's shop and Jimmy had known his son since before he had known Alice, since before they had both become third hands – deckies – on the trawling smacks. But Roddy and Alice had in some way been thrown together as children and whenever Alice said his name, and Roddy said her name, it was as if they belonged together. Alice told Jimmy they had never been lovers and he believed her. But in all these months he had known, in the quietness that was himself alone, that she kept something apart. She had never been entirely his.

'What did Roddy tell you?'

Jimmy could hardly bear to hear what would come next but when Pentecost raised his red eyes they were lined with acceptance.

'He told us as you told us. The seas were over the gunwales, masts fit to crack. Said they'd not seen a sea like it since 1910 and any one of them could have lost a man. *Coronet* had her trawl beam down as an anchor. There'll be more lost, may the grace of the Lord Jesus Christ be upon them.'

Jimmy looked to Alice but she turned away. There was no clue to what Roddy had said to her.

'That's all?'

'You always did everything you could for the boy, Jimmy. He always know'd better and there was never no telling 'en. The Lord's will be done. Job did not raise his voice in his tribulation and nor shan't I.'

'Amen.'

Jimmy found the room diminishing and unreal. He knew Alice too well to think she had lied, but what she had said made no sense. *He jumped. They told me.* Jimmy had expected Alice's anger but not this. From Pentecost he had imagined there might be disgust at the God he doggedly proclaimed but who took back everything he gave. He had supposed the man might find some gentleness towards his son now that he was gone and would remember his dead wife and what she would have said. He had thought there would be guilt, talk about the years of bitterness and blame. The smacksmen spent their days in the face of death and when it came it was recognisable, even familiar. The people who kept these little stone ranked cottages talked about it often but knew it less. But now there was just piety and silence and it was impossible to find a hold. He guessed the loss of a child and a brother was a grief beyond numbness and everything would take its turn over the days, the ordeal of meeting the skipper, a memorial service at the big Methodist chapel on Fore Street, the worst of a drowning that there was no body to lay down.

Pentecost shook his head and the room fell into a rigid silence. Jimmy found he was grateful. Alice shook as she cooked, refusing help, unable or unwilling to say a word. Finally she stood with him at the foot of the steps that led up the rough stone alleyway to Prospect Road where he lodged, the eighty-three rough stone slabs, each the size of a small coffin. Jimmy could not read her, did not know whether she had at last decided to do this difficult thing together. And now Roddy was between them, almost as never before.

'Alice – what did Roddy Farley say?'

'He told me Billie jumped.'

''Tis stupid, Alice. Cruel. Billie was down below. What does Roddy Farley know?'

'Roddy knows about Billie. He knows what it was like for him.'

'What *it was like for him*? He was a cookie, Alice. Everyone knows what 'tis like.'

'That's not what he meant. You don't know what it was like for Billie. I loved him. I knew. Roddy knew.'

'Alice – why don't you believe me? I was with Billie all day. Every day. I know'd him too. We know'd him. Henry's the best skip in Brixham and *Maryann*...'

'You just hate the Farleys.'

Jimmy's anger now began to take his breath. This was about a storm and a dead child, not about the bloody Farleys.

'*Coronet* wasn't within a mile of us. You couldn't see more 'n a few yards. Roddy doesn't know naught about what happened. You know what Roddy wants.'

Jimmy would have said that the Farleys said and did anything to get what they wanted. He wanted to say that the poor looked after each other in this cradle of granite streets and embraced the helpless, and the orphan like him, in their humanity of courtesy and fairness and time. But the Farleys needed no-one, expected nothing and gave nothing. Whatever Roddy had said about Billie, it wasn't difficult to guess what he wanted. Alice was wilfully blind.

'What do you want, Alice? Why don't thee just say what 'ee want?'

'Perhaps I will, Jimmy. You could give me some time. My brother's just been drowned. You don't understand it but I loved him. And I know'd what it was happening to him.'

Jimmy could see her face was stone and there was no touching her.

'Don't listen to Roddy, Alice.'

'You don't know about me.'

Chapter 3

The rain had massed from spit to downpour and Jimmy pushed himself up Fore Street towards the Methodist chapel, head down and numb. The sympathy would be well meant and it had to be got through but there would not be many in the pews today who had limped home with an empty berth, only the possessions left and the family to tell and that for a child. He was aware of the other people hurrying around him, couples pulled tight against the wet, nothing said, the closed shops sending back the clack of boots in chorus, and he kept his face down, cap pulled, unwilling to attempt some expression to suit their expectation. They were good people and wrapped in a Sunday calm but they would be in a hurry to get this thing through and to make some good appear to come out of it. Jimmy had played the game himself in the past and recalled the bruise it left. He only wanted it over.

It had rained most of Sunday and it had shut Jimmy in, the wearied walls and rough wooden gear in his Prospect Road room strange as if dreamed. The roiling of emotions and words baffled and sank him. He had walked with Alice and her father to chapel at ten-thirty, the still formality of the morning service imposing a decent space between them. Afterwards Alice's tears were relentless and her father's silence impenetrable and, once they had eaten, Pentecost slept, mouth open, guttering and disturbing. Then Alice's anger flared unreasoning, Jimmy asking only for her to explain, Alice saying and sobbing over and over that Billie had jumped but making no sense of it. Finally her father opened his eyes and told her to take thought for the Sabbath and she went silently to her room. Jimmy stood at the door.

It was the room she had shared with Billie and his bed was still made, his Sunday boots underneath, the effigy of his feet. There were two small cream-painted cupboards, Alice's few things spilling from the drawers of the taller, the smaller closed, Billie's. Jimmy wondered how long it would be before they could open it. Alice lay on the bed, eyes black against wasted white, at an infinite distance. Jimmy said they could meet at chapel in the evening if she were well enough, or he would call at her house afterwards. There was only silence. He told her that the skip, Henry Buckley, would come as he had promised but still she said nothing. He edged down the staircase, found Pentecost again still, eyes closed, Bible open in his lap in front of the range, and let himself out.

He had lain on his bed unable to tame the storm in his head. Alice's anger was not anything like he had foreseen. *You don't know me.* It was as if her brother's death had carried her over an uncrossable sea. He watched her walking away from a far shore, stripping off the brittle, edgy intelligence she showed to the world, the Alice he had loved, and then disappearing alone into a dark interior where she was a small child and where the only person who knew her was Roddy Farley. All that Pentecost had done was to daub on his preacher's face, a heartless, spiritless ritual and Jimmy turned away. Faith without charity was sour and offensive.

By six the rain had claimed the streets once more and Jimmy hesitated outside the door of his lodgings, torn for a moment between the dim damp of his rooms and the ordeal of a crowded, insistent evening service. As the afternoon had gone on Billie had begun to haunt him. He could not escape the boy's face, his voice, the stink of the alcohol on his breath. Jimmy demanded, relentlessly, and pacing up and down his room out loud, *what could we have done?* But the faded, dirtied paper of the walls said nothing back. In the end he dropped down the steps to the quay and set off for the chapel, no longer able to trust his own company. The more Fore Street filled with people, the more he doubted his decision.

The chapel was always noisy full for the evening service. The gas hissed its own damp into the dripping air and the wooden floors reeked of wet where the boards had worn. Jackets stank from the rain, the cracked varnish of the pews sweetening the air with its incense. Jimmy sat in his usual place, with the other unmarried men, towards the front of the gallery. The pews below filled with couples, men stiff in Sunday collars, wives hidden under their feathers. Their conversations flickered briefly under the bleating of the organ. Jimmy was acutely uncomfortable, hunted by every eye and whisper and by the accusing space below, where Alice usually sat with Billie and Pentecost. It was impossible to banish the howl of the storm and the shouting for the lad who had already gone and his mind now began to pulse with an image of Billie coming on deck and climbing over the rail. He barely noticed as the minister began up the steps to the pulpit and the organ died. Neither Alice nor her father had come.

'Jimmy.'

It was a voice he knew but for a moment could not place. He turned and found Edward Beaton, Alice's uncle, married to her dead mother's sister. The man usually sat downstairs, but was now leaning over his shoulder from the pew behind, eyes mournful as a beagle. He took Jimmy's arm with his great sea-swollen hand as if he were a child. Jimmy noticed the scented oil on his remaining hair and his skin soft as a girl's.

'You don't need to be here, Jimmy. Not this evening.'

Beaton was a short, graceless man, his expression concealed behind a black moustache that made the pink sag of his face ridiculous. Everyone called him Flush and not one of them could remember why. Jimmy saw him every week in his usual pew below, shiny baldness inclined in attention, or extravagantly bowed, an effort of meekness it was hard to credit. It was, they said, the only way to duck the spitting acidity of his wife. Fanny Beaton, Alice's aunt, was the younger of the two sisters, childless and embittered, outspoken in her dislike of almost everyone in the town and Pentecost Rogers more than all the rest. Normally on Sundays Jimmy felt only pity for her stooping husband. This evening Beaton had apparently come alone. He pulled at Jimmy's arm.

'We'll go somewhere 'til they're finished. They don't know about losing a man. We'll come back in 'fore they're done.'

Jimmy turned and looked properly into Beaton's dark pupils for the first time. He saw what seemed to be a kindling of warmth and steeled himself for the man's crooning, grating piety. The last thing he wanted was to relive the awfulness in the eye of this man's pity. The worst was that Flush Beaton was mate aboard *Coronet*, the same smack as Roddy Farley. The organ rose into life again and they were hoisting the first hymn into the whiteness above. Beaton's grip was iron on Jimmy's elbow and he found himself being edged along the pew and climbing the awkward steps to the door at the back of the gallery, grateful at least for heads hidden in hymn books and voices that covered their steps.

Jimmy followed Beaton through the half dark to a schoolroom. At least, he told himself, he might discover what story Roddy had told Alice. A smell of recent paint thickened the air and a feeble light struggled through rain-greyed windows. Jimmy leaned against the dark, matchboard dado, the harmony of the congregation now a dull rumble as they sang their Amen and sat for the first prayers. He waited for Beaton to speak but he was apparently expecting Jimmy to begin.

'We had to douse the foresail before we cracked our mainmast. We were swept clean over and it took him. You were out in it. You know.'

'Yes, we were out in it.'

Again there was silence. If the man had nothing to say Jimmy decided he might as well go back to the gallery.

'Thee's know what Roddy Farley told Alice?'

'Yes I do. I went with 'en.'

'You were at her house?'

'I'm the girl's uncle.'

Still the man was offering nothing to help. Jimmy wondered what he was keeping from him.

'Roddy told Alice Billie jumped. What does he know?'

'That's what he were going to do, Jimmy. Jump.'

'What he were going to do?'

Beaton had not raised his eyes and it was hard to continue talking to him without sounding like a preacher. When at last the man looked up his eyes were colder. There was not a sliver of sympathy.

''Tis what Billie said, Jimmy. He was going to jump. 'Tis why I have to tell you.'

'Billie said? When did he say? What was he talking about?'

'Before you sailed. He said it Sunday last. He said it was your fault, Jimmy.'

Beaton's voice was low, expressionless. Jimmy was utterly stalled. He had to listen again to the man's words in his head, a prickling crackling up his legs and his back as if the man were about to gut him like a sole. It was *his* fault?

'He was kid. What's it about, Flush?'

Beaton's face was shifting. In place of sympathy there was now a kind of anxiety, as if the man were about to clinch a deal. Jimmy had never seen him like it, almost ready to stand up for himself. He looked more closely into the black eyes, barely discoverable in the growing dark. They were steady and steeled in a way he would never have supposed in the man. He guessed he was under pressure, forced into a task he would never have attempted. Another hymn was rising dully beyond the wall.

'I want thee to understand me, Jimmy. I don't know if the boy was telling the truth and I don't care. But you need to know 'cause it'd make your life in this port difficult if it gets around. I'm telling 'ee 'cause happens I've always thought 'ee were a decent man and you don't deserve less.'

There was a long silence, the singing muffled, familiar enough to be mocking. Finally there was the rumble of the congregation sitting again, the preacher's voice distantly announcing the Old Testament. Beaton reached out and touched Jimmy's arm.

'Billie Rogers said he was going to take his life 'cause you wouldn't leave 'en alone.'

'*Wouldn't leave him alone?*'

Jimmy searched his head for what the man meant. But the wincing crease of Beaton's face told him most.

'Don't make me tell you the rest of what he said, Jimmy. You understand what I'm saying. He said you wanted him to...'

Suddenly the room was spinning in black idiocy. Jimmy found his hand at Beaton's throat, his face an inch from the other man, breathing his tobacco, the oil on his hair, the stench of the fish market that nothing ever purged. It was not Beaton he was pounding with his fist, it was Billie. The boy had lived in a bitter and imagined world in which everyone persecuted him with bloody singlemindedness. Billie believed nobody had a right to expect anything from him, that he was accountable for nothing. Of course Jimmy had never touched the boy. But there was no knowing what he had gone round saying, and there was now no making him deny it or take it back.

In a moment Jimmy found himself on his back, a heavy knee in his chest, another on his right arm, Beaton's fist hoisted and about to crash into his mouth. In the hesitation Jimmy's voice came strangled but calm.

'I never went near the boy, Flush. Except when he poured lamp oil all over the galley and when he left the warp knotting itself all over the locker floor. *And all the other times I giv'd him a clip* 'cause he was a fucking idiot and he hadn't listened to a living word since he took his bloody berth. I wouldn't go near a boy. An' Billie Rogers was a two-faced, foul-mouthed git.'

At last Beaton grunted and lowered his fist and took his weight off Jimmy's chest and stood, eyes tight. Jimmy vaguely supposed he should be surprised the man had fought back so easily. But nobody walked the quays for forty years without a fight and this new, unrecognisable Flush Beaton was obviously, surprisingly, at ease with violence. The man was *enjoying* himself.

'I always thought you were a decent man, Blackbridge, and I don't know the truth of what the boy said and he's dead and I don't care.'

Beaton dropped his voice and stepped closer, grasping Jimmy's arm as he got to his feet. Another stifled hymn rose around them. Beaton's breath smelled of whisky.

'But if Billie Rogers said it to Roddy Farley he'll have said it to others. And there'll be men tonight who'll be saying you've got blood on your hands. And worse.'

'*'Tis a fucking lie. 'Tis a fucking invention...*'

'*Jimmy*. I'm telling thee 'cause 'ee have to know. For if it gets around.'

Beaton paused and for a moment Jimmy wondered if the man's habitual chapel anxiety was about to come panting pink to the surface, a mumbled apology that he had only said what he had to and they would not speak about it again. But then he realised that the cold had not gone from Beaton's eyes. They were sharp and steady as his breathing. It was the slight, lifting smile of the moustache told Jimmy that Flush was not warning him of a rumour that might spread. He was *threatening to spread it himself.* Jimmy braced himself for what it was the man wanted. He found himself pulled once again close to the face, now creasing into a grin.

'So. Now you keep your hands off Alice Rogers, Jimmy Blackbridge.'

For a second Jimmy thought he was going to smash the man's face through the darkening window. He could see the wet, the blood and the cold rainwater, mingling down the pink jowls as he slid. But Beaton's grip was iron and his body beginning to swivel, winding up for the punch.

'And if I don't? You and Roddy Farley are going to spread this crap around the harbour? No-one in this port cares about dead fucking Billie Rogers.'

Jimmy's voice was hoarse, weighed down by the heavy silence that was now coming from the chapel. Beaton also dropped his voice again.

'All Alice Rogers's got left is a Bible-thumping, hellfire-spouting pulpit puritan of a father and somebody's got to watch out for her. We told her what Billie said and the girl blames 'ee for what happened. She wants a fresh start. Maybe you don't. But if you touch Alice Rogers again, there's others are going to hear what the boy said.'

Jimmy did not believe there was a skipper who cared about a dead cookie if it came to hiring an able hand. He was good at what he did and knew it. Beaton was a blustering fool, a bumbling husband, a baldy pushed about by his stone-faced wife. But he had already made it cold clear he would deliver on a threat. Jimmy was struck by an image of Alice, grief torn up and scattered by the confusion this bastard was brutally pushing into her face. *We told her what Billie said.* Jimmy pulled away again but the grip was merciless.

'I'm a reasonable man, Jimmy. I believe in thee. You're a decent lad. So I'm making you an offer. A way out of your present difficulties. Until everyone forgets about Billie Rogers.'

'The answer's no.'

'I'll offer you a berth, Jimmy, a place on a new smack. It'll be the fastest ketch in the town. I'll even make you its mate if you like. I'll give 'ee time to get your ticket. I'll lend 'ee the cash if that's what it takes 'cause you're a good smacksman and you deserve better than this.'

'Let me guess who else.'

'You, me and a cookie.'

'Who's her master?'

Jimmy already knew.

'Roddy Farley'll be her master.'

There were two new smacks on the town slips. Most, like *Maryann*, were owned by their skippers. But everyone knew that one of the new boats belonged to George Farley.

'Forget it.'

'You're a fool, Jimmy Blackbridge.'

Beaton pulled him closer. There was still silence from the chapel. Prayers, long silent pauses.

"Tis better money than you'll get anywhere. Mr Farley an't asking for his whole three and three-quarters. He'll take one and a half and if your calculations are as good as mine are, that's two for the master and one and three-quarters share for each man.'

'I'll never work for George Farley.'

'Except you'll have noticed he's Alice Rogers's employer. So let's say you're a good lad and we give it a year and the happy day comes when we can ask Mr Farley to have a word in his employee's ear. By then you'll have a tidy sum in the Co-operative. And maybe us can all be happy ever after.'

For a moment Jimmy found himself sliding into the man's hands. The schoolroom had grown dark, wax wan light coming from a gas lamp in the street. There was no sound from the service. Jimmy guessed that Beaton had lied about Billie and about the shares and about the mate's berth. It was inconceivable Farley would make Jimmy mate if his son was master and Flush Beaton aboard. But to work on Farley's new smack would be a thread, a fragile line connecting him to Alice and for a second he imagined himself accepting.

The moment died, cold as the air, and Jimmy's breathing came in a hiss. *He would never work for Farley*. He would never sleep in a cabin with Roddy Farley and Flush Beaton, every trip five endless days for them to taunt him with what Billie Rogers was supposed to have said. Every return a chance to throw him to their thugs on the quayside.

'Tell Farley to stuff his bloody berth.'

Beaton released his grip a little and stood back.

'I understand, Jimmy.'

That, Jimmy guessed, was the first honest thing he had said. The man's voice was again cursedly gentle, the pink-faced pew voice, the buffoon squeak of the concerned uncle. The real Flush Beaton was a shadow again.

'I'd say the same in your place, Jimmy. Aye, 'tis going to be very hard for you these weeks, without anyone to stand by. Just Henry Buckley and Eb Mutch. Old men. Let's say the offer's between us. You'll think about it for a trip or two, let a bit of salt air in.'

'So you've had a chance to spread your shit around the quay.'

The man smiled, barely visible in the dark.

'Seems so. I asked Roddy to go and take care of Alice. Tell her what I've offered you.'

It was the man's accursed smile that lived in Jimmy's eyes as he pulled himself free and made for the door to the street, his footsteps painfully loud as the singing began again. The dusk cold hit his face like reality and he ran unsteadily towards the quay, a man throwing off bandages and emerging from a grave. His was only thinking of Alice. If it was going to end between them, it must not end like this. He had reached the corner of the quay when he saw her. She was across by the fish market, yellowed by the light from the window of the *Rising Sun* that should not have been open but probably was. She was arm in arm with Roddy Farley. Jimmy began to run again. The bastard was leading Alice towards the steps that led up to Higher Street and her house. Jimmy wondered if Beaton was following him and slammed his mind on the man's face. He heard a shout and realised it had come from his own lungs, a blinding roar as Alice disappeared. He was about to shout again when there was the clatter of footsteps and his head exploded. He was headlong in the black wet filth of the quay, sprawled grazing along the setts, pain in his hands, knees, chin, skull.

When he opened his eyes it took him a moment to realise that it was not Beaton over him but a face he did not know, except that it belonged to one of the men whose life was spent on the quayside outside the *Rising Sun*.

'Hands off, Blackbridge.'

Jimmy tried to get to his feet, to shout for Alice, but a boot winded him and sent him rolling, doubled up, vomit rising in his throat, unable to speak.

'You're finished, fag.'

Chapter 4

Jimmy barely needed to be on deck. There is a stillness about a smack with her trawl down. She makes slow progress, her bow turned slightly to port under jib-headed topsail and single-reefed mainsail, the strain of the great towing rope warp over her quarter transferring its energy to everything above deck. Even after years at sea you are aware of a kind of waiting, not so much for the time to haul, but of the possibility of the net snagging and fouling, the sudden grinding, groaning as it pulls the stern counter down to the sea and then the flimsy safety stopper rope around the dummy post parting with a whipping crack and the heavy trawl rope flying over the side, wrenching the bow around and halting the smack shockingly, head to wind, every foot of canvas pounding in protest against its hoops and ties.

They had cast off under a razor sharp May sky, blood along the horizon and streaking down the swell under blue and green and amber. Eb had loaded stores before dawn and they agreed they would share the cookie's duties between them until Henry could find another. Jimmy ached to be alone, one eye black sore from his attacker's boot and his right ankle so swollen he could barely pull on a leather sea boot. He had sat, writing to Alice, the business with Beaton, the assault in the street. He had set off in the cold and silent black before dawn, meaning to push the paper under her door. Now he stood on the grating at the tiller and the letter was still in his pocket. He had imagined Roddy Farley holding it, tossing it to his mates, mocking all that was tender and warm and generous. Alice he could not picture at all. She had become a raw weal that Jimmy was afraid to go near. The

Alice he had imagined with him each time he sailed was a ghost, soft, laughing, asking after the smack, a figment of his need for someone who wanted him, wanted to know about him, a weightless child.

Billie's shadow clung to every stanchion and spar and below filled the cabin with cold. Jimmy was glad he was gone and that made it worse. He had been truculent in the galley, obstructive over the lights, a hindrance with mallet and marlinspike on the ice. They had had to yell again and again for him to take the tiller when they shot the trawl or to coil the warp when they hauled it in. Billie had made it clear he would not stay, from the day he first fumbled his way awkwardly aboard and refused to stow his bag below. Every day he whined he was going to college, into the bank, away with the Army, as if these were the callings of men and not the drudgery of creatures. He regarded learning anything as a criticism, as if all that was worth mastering should be obvious. The skill that shaped a course by smell and taste, the calculation of time and tide that got the trawling gear travelling along the bed and knew when to haul, the power of the smack at full cry under a new suit of sails, the things that still moved Jimmy, Billie mistook for a simple old lore and waved them away. To Jimmy, *Maryann* was seventy foot of gorgeous gold-lined black, her two masts raked forward optimistic and strong, her deck confusion unless you knew. Billie compared her with the grubby steam trawlers that came grinding out of Hull and Grimsby, swearing the sail smacksmen were all dead men now. Jimmy told himself he had ignored the boy's bitter carping when he was alive and he would face him down now he was gone. He knew neither was true.

The wide openness was a comfort and Jimmy lashed the tiller and stood by the rail, cradled by a moody sky and letting himself be rocked. It eased the stiffness a little from his back and hips. Loose ties were clattering on the mainsail and the canvas was not drawing all it might. But relacing could wait so long as the breeze did not freshen. He was grateful they would only be out three days. Some weeks they trawled off Ireland, loading two and a half tons of ice and staying at sea until late on Saturday. Or they worked the Bristol Channel, landing catches at Swansea or in the bleak, green vastness of Milford Haven. Or they shot their gear off the Cornish coast and sold over the quays of Padstow or Newlyn. Then they might stay out a second week entirely. In those weeks Jimmy loved making the long passages, *Maryann* heeling over, a whole night flying through the white tops, long hours of rolling sleep. Today they were all numb and Henry had set a course for the local grounds, between the Start and the north of Torbay, no more than eight or ten miles off the land. The gear was down early in the morning. If the fishing was good enough they would slip quietly home for Wednesday night.

But for the first time since he had joined her, Jimmy found that *Maryann* had become a wooden cage. He felt isolated, suffocating, struggling all the time not to think of Alice. There was a man on one of the smacks who had taken the swinging mizzen boom full in the face. He would not have survived had they not already been tacking into harbour and they carried him ashore. His face was pulp, bloody bone and viscera. It was months before they saw him again. He had the same body, the same shaped head, but where his face should have been was grotesque, a bony hole where his nose had stood. His lips were beaded and twisted, his eyes deep in the ruin. You got used to it. But he would only ever be the man without a face. Jimmy told himself what was happening to him was nothing in comparison. Yet he felt like a man without a face, a wound where he met the world.

He had given everything to make it work with Alice but in the last twelve hours he had lost his bearing. On board time and tide were the masters and you knew your bearings. On shore you were adrift. There was no almanac for the currents that ran through the town and when you ran foul they broke you. The truth was that neither Beaton nor Roddy had taken her from him. There had been months of drift and dark until they had reached the place where there was nothing left to do or say. Jimmy realised he had made a decision. He would act for himself before anyone else did. When *Maryann* came in on Wednesday he would go up and finish it. Alice would not be expecting him and would not have her marble mask ready. He sat heavily on the rail and looked down into the water shouldering past and could think of nothing but the injustice of the accusation cooked up against him, the odds stacked always and ultimately in the Farleys' favour. Suddenly he found the blackness below was drawing him, like a voice he had never heard before, and he thought it would be a comfort to drop quietly over and away, to leave the bruising, day-by-day, defeating drudgery and breathe it out into a cool deepening end. And for a moment he pictured Billie, almost as if they were sitting side by side, with an understanding for the first time between them. But it was Henry's voice that was calling, quiet as his shadow. Jimmy looked round to find the skipper, woollen cap slanted over the sharpness of his grey eyes, watching the wake's finger across the swell, ready to haul. Without a word Jimmy went forward and took the foresail sheet and hauled it across. *Maryann* came gently to a stop.

They slipped in at dawn on Wednesday, shipping three trunks of soles over the quay. Along with the cod, haddock and whiting it made nearly £6 before the first London train and they counted themselves lucky enough. By ten they had washed out the fish lockers, swabbed the decks and got *Maryann* in shape to sail again. They agreed to ship out on the four-thirty tide. Henry put on his shore clothes and set off up the hill. Eb elected to stay aboard.

Jimmy put on the cleaner of his guernseys and set off for Alice's house, numb with what was coming, grateful for a deserted fish market and the empty streets. None of the lads were about who would usually run up to warn that they were in. He thought it possible that Pentecost might still be at home, perhaps even Alice herself. But the place was dark when he went in. No-one locked doors in these streets. He stood under the weight of the parlour stillness, filled with a scent of their lives and nothing more. A mess of crockery filled the sink and its washboard, and washing littered the little table along the wall. Alice had let it all get ahead of her and Jimmy made himself remember how utterly lost she had been. It was already the house of a stranger. He called and climbed the steep wooden stairs, dado rubbed brown with the passing of its people, paper above blackened with condensation. Alice's door was open and her room comfortless and bare. Jimmy went and sat on her bed, her form printed roughly in the sheets as if she were still struggling to sleep. Then he asked himself if he was able to complete what he had come to do and reached out for a moment to order the rumpled linen. It was foreign, rough to his fingers. The odour that drifted for a moment made him wince and then he knew he had decided. He got up and pushed the door on the other side of the landing and met the stench of sweat and sickness. But Pentecost was not there.

Jimmy looked in at the parlour and told himself it would be the last time. He walked along Higher Street towards the church, to Farley's shop, heart hammering, feet without feeling. The shop was barely a couple of minutes but he was out of breath by the time he looked through the glass of the door and saw the place empty and Alice alone behind the counter. She glanced only briefly as he went in and he knew from the angle of her shoulders and of her head that she was going to make him bear all the risk of what they needed to get through.

PART I

Chapter 5

From the day she had jumped down into *Maryann* and they carried Eb barely alive to the cottage hospital, Jimmy had spent most of his time ashore with Alice Rogers.

He had imagined he was in love with the tall girl with the blonde curls since he was fifteen, cookie aboard his first smack, *Deliverance*. He saw her, legs swinging on the frame of a sloop at Upham's shipyard, head back, reflecting the thin gold of the late spring. Suddenly her eyes had snapped open as *Deliverance* beat out, hearing the shouting aboard, thinking perhaps the men were yelling at her. She had waved to the lad as he stood clinging to the topsail sheet, supposedly ready to haul, in truth hiding in the lee of the mainmast, dreading the thumping he knew he could not avoid from the skipper. Her look was shy as a fourteen-year-old, yet framed with a knowing that made him think she might understand what it was to be a cookie with a broken, violent, crew. Her golden halo and the conspiracy of her quiet half-laugh had stayed, his star to steer in the impossible days and nights that came after. He understood that her father must work on the smacks at Uphams and he had looked for her each time he had come to the narrows off the slip. And very often she was sitting atop a smack in frame or on the cradle ready to launch and if the skipper was not on deck he had won a look and a smile and the following of her eyes as they passed.

One Friday evening the mate caught him and blew his moustache and told Jimmy who she was and that he had better be careful because she worked behind the counter at Farley's. And then for months Jimmy spent the little money he had there, hoping she would be the one behind the high, flaming mahogany counter, her hair tugged into a shaggy, complaining bun, her thin hands awkward among the jars, leaving them open or half closed or on the counter, laughing self-consciously at her mistakes but never hesitating with the money. And he discovered that her voice had a lilt and cadence that came from self-assurance when they were alone and vanished when the other girls were there or when George Farley came in with his schoolmasterly way of speaking.

One gusty morning, late in May 1912, not long after Jimmy had joined *Maryann*, Eb fell as they hauled the trawl beam alongside, breaking his thighbone on the aft winch with a terrifying crack. He had lost plenty of blood. Jimmy and the cookie scrambled the net inboard and set every inch of canvas they dared for home, Eb sinking into and out of life and Henry by his side willing him to make it home. It was the first time Jimmy had taken the helm and brought her in, and by the time she was approaching the middle pier, in the early light, the cookie letting the canvas drop, the drogue at last bringing her up, he was flying with exhilaration and relief. And then he saw Alice at the end of Upham's slip, arms outstretched in the wind and he yelled to her and made her run for Dr Brett Young. She was astonishingly quick, hair suddenly a flash in the grey. The doctor was at the inner quay only minutes after they brought *Maryann* alongside, Jimmy grateful for a tide to get her in so far. That was the only time Alice had ever gone aboard, jumping down completely out of breath, her chest heaving, unable to speak, trying to do as Jimmy told her, clinging to the sodden ropes as he and the cookie sorted sheets and halyards while Henry lifted Eb in his great bear's arms and carried him ashore. And when they were gone she stood by him as he finished.

'I was watching 'ee come round the breakwater. I saw you were at the tiller. I'd never seen that before.'

'Do you think I did it alright?'

'I think you were perfect. My father says *Maryann* is one of the best smacks in the harbour. He says you're lucky to be aboard.'

'What else does your father say about me?'

'That he doesn't see thee in chapel. He says that about everybody.'

'I come sometimes.'

'I know you do. T'would be easier if he saw 'ee every week.'

'T'would be easier?'

'Easier for me.'

'Easier if I were ever to ask 'ee to walk out with me?'

'I don't know why you don't, Jimmy Blackbridge. I've been waving at 'ee for months. And you come to the shop even when you don't need naught.'

'Then you would come with me on Saturday if I walked to Berry Head? *Maryann* won't be going out until Eb begins to mend. I should be here a few days.'

'I've got to work on Saturday. Let me come in the afternoon, later, when Mr Farley has finished with me.'

Jimmy was pushing the hoodway shut and turned a smile to Alice to agree. For a moment he caught an uncertainty in her expression. And then the smile returned.

From that time Jimmy knew he was alive when he was with Alice and also that his life hung in the balance. She was four inches short of him, ridiculously curly blonde hair impossible to tame. She was from the start his friend and his sister, someone whose words he could guess. Nothing needed explaining except that they were nineteen and twenty and there was so much of the story to catch up. But she was also unpredictable, hiding in a haze of resentment if Jimmy asked too much or wanted too much of her approval. Sometimes she was inexplicably angry and Jimmy had to learn that reason was then pointless, her eyes quick hazel in a face so sharply alert you never stopped wondering where her mind was. It was hard to tell, but she appeared to be building their life together in a way that would last. The first time they kissed they were sitting above the lifeboat house, looking along the unfinished breakwater. That was even before Jimmy had gone back to sea on the Monday.

That summer of 1912 was relentless, cold and incessant rain, the worst anyone could remember, a bewildering wrench from the year before when the heat was so heavy old people had died in their armchairs. A German company set up a factory in the town to make cattle feed and glue from the fish offal and filled the place with a breathtaking stench. Jimmy put on his oilies and bought an old set for Alice. When she put them on she was a ridiculous, crumpled and shabby figure and turned up her nose at the clinging stink of fish oil. But at least they could escape the town and she took his hand and they walked out up and out, their oilies rain-jewelled. They crossed the bridge that spanned the quarries and the railway that carried the stone out along the wall that was still edging out across the harbour. Then they took the shingle way past the tidy row of lifeguard cottages and up through the trees out onto Berry Head common, its bright clarity, and its short-tufted turf a world lifted apart. Jimmy took Alice to the strange new lighthouse on the headland. Its stunted lantern was barely six feet off the ground. But it was two hundred rocky feet above the shore and he told her he would see its flash twenty miles out and imagine her awake, waiting for him. And after he had said it, it was true.

Most often Alice took Jimmy in to Upham's boatyard where her father worked as a shipwright. The men were entitled to Saturday afternoon off and then the place was still and swept silent. Sometimes one or two of them had stayed on to make a stool or a skiff for themselves but they ignored the young couple because she was the preacher's girl and he was Henry Buckley's deckie. They only wanted to cling to each other and to talk. So they spent the saturated summer afternoons watching the rain dripping down the workshop windows and when it was dry sitting in the ribs of a smack on the slip. Even though he was all week aboard, Jimmy loved this growing, thickening frame, honey-smelling still and straw-toned, the sweet strength of scarph and tenon, the architecture of quarter, horn and cant, the framing of a fanning stern from the fashion timber. You glimpsed under bulkhead and keelson, into the splintered marrow, and admired the men who spoke and smoked quietly and moulded soft curves that would last two generations. To each vessel they gave a soul, headstrong and resilient.

'No wonder then.'

Alice was leaning back against him, deep in the stern of the growing smack, so close that through the rich scents of the yard he could smell the varnish of Farley's shop, the prickle of the spice and the waxy freshness of cloth starch. He squeezed her more tightly.

'No wonder what?'

'You don't trust a single person, seems so, Jimmy Blackbridge.'

Jimmy had found, in these moments when she would listen, he had scripted his life into words so for the first time it fell into place. He had told her how his mother was dead before he was a week old and how his father had been unable to make a home in the moorland schoolhouse. He had left the baby for hours at the rectory or with a neighbour and fell asleep over the table in the evening with the toddler still clattering awake. Later there were eighteen children crammed into the school, all of them from labouring families and only one other a boy of Jimmy's age, a wee-stinking thug who treated the master's son with covert and vindictive rage. Jimmy learned to calculate and to think, mostly after the other children had drifted home and his father would tell him about the school in Tavistock where he would win a scholarship that would carry him to university. The pneumonia that killed his father was over in a week. Jimmy was eleven and discovered he was without a relative in the world.

'They a-shut me away with my panic in a cold attic at the rectory, pushing down meals I didn't want with a housemaid who shook and didn't speak. The parish wrote out an apprenticeship. They told me I was lucky that the trawlers were still taking poor country boys and I believed 'em. So I stood on the quayside, my father dead a fortnight, sails a-stretching out to where they were starting to build the breakwater. I saw the ropes and baskets and oilies, and held a parish indenture that was the only thing that told me I was alive. I was a child, lost in the rain. I'd already discovered that nothing is fair and nothing lasts.'

'You survived. You're still here.'

'I saw a face, a-looking down at me with a smile. Then the woman took my hand and put her arm round me and breathed the life back. Her name was May Grant.'

'Kitty Grant's mam?'

'Kitty's mam. She asked me why I was lost and took me to her home in Overgang and fed me. For the first few days I slept on the rug in front of the Grants' range. They only had Kitty, who was seven or eight then. Kitty asked if I was a pickpocket. Her mam told her I was a gentleman on important business. Then she led me down to the harbourmaster's to arrange everything with the apprenticeship. I've hardly seen 'em since, the Grants.'

'They don't go to chapel. They're Catholic. My father says they're going to hell.'

'They were the first people I trusted. And later Henry and Eb. And now you.'

He was unable to go on. He had supposed it was the same for everyone, this finding the balance of things relentlessly against you. Alice was the first person who had broken the spell and he was not yet even sure if he trusted her. He knew it but would not say it, even to himself.

'Sometimes, Jimmy, I think you don't decide things, you just wait for them to decide theirselves, seems so. And I think 'tis 'cause your mam and your pa died and you don't know when the next wave is going to hit you. I don't wonder thee trusts no-one.'

'Who do you trust, Alice? Your parents? Do you trust Mr Farley?'

'Mr Farley's kind to me. 'Tis you I trust, Jimmy.'

From their first hours together Jimmy noticed that Alice would allow no discussion of her employer. He asked what it was like in the shop. He tried imitating old Farley's pretentious way of asking smiling questions he knew you could not answer, making him seem capable, better than you. It was a trick Jimmy had seen doctors and lawyers and vicars pull, a privilege the rich gave themselves, a shortcut to shoddy superiority. But Alice's face shut completely when Jimmy said it. George Farley employed her. He was kind to her. That was all.

For a long minute she traced the lines on Jimmy's hand with her finger.

'You're such a little boy.'

'You make me.'

Alice turned and kissed him.

'Always about to be sunk, drowned by the next wave. 'Tis why you need me, to tell 'ee you're safe home.'

Jimmy could not tell whether Alice loved or despised him for it, nor how she managed to shift the sand under his feet so easily. Instead he could feel her breathing, bewitching and baffling. She had turned him away from the Farleys again but he was content to give up. He knew how much he needed Alice and wondered whether it might be too much for her to carry. She seemed to think much more about herself than about him, but Jimmy took it for granted that it was impossible for people to do anything else and was grateful for a scrap of affection and even a fraction of a moment when she put him first.

'Where's home?'

'People who love you.'

'Do you love me, Alice?'

'I think I do.'

'You *think*?'

Alice sat up, away from him.

'I have a brother who hates everyone and a father who reads and talks all the time about love but doesn't know what it means and a mam…'

She seemed unwilling to finish.

'She loves you.'

'You're your father's an' I can't be expected to listen to you. Every day. Jimmy, she says it every day.'

Jimmy could not answer because he had heard it himself. It was as meaningless as all the other weeping wounds he saw people inflict on each other, day after suffering day. These smack-framed confessions taught him that Alice too was orphaned, even though her parents were then both still alive. She was unable to grasp the love her parents might once have had for her. It made him think how ill-made and adrift they both were, incomprehensibly floundering and he wondered if the lines between them would part because they had nothing to hold, nothing solid of their own.

'You've had a boy before.'

Alice took a long time to answer.

'Not that it meant naught.'

'Does this mean anything?'

'I love you, Jimmy, whatever it means.'

He believed her when she said it but the moment was flown as quickly as it had come. Already Alice was standing and away to the next thing, unwilling to let the thought pool enough to seep down. Jimmy both loved and mistrusted her mercurial lostness. He asked himself if he would ever want to contain it.

June 1912 ended wet and August was no better and by its end the heartless rain had stiffened into iron cold. Simply to escape the house and the freezing, streaming streets Jimmy parted with the money and they joined the Excelsior dancing classes. They found themselves eyeing a dozen other couples in the gaslight of the town hall, all of them there to learn the new tango that had swept in from Paris. Jimmy and Alice were soon laughing hoarse through the rain on the headland and shouting, 'no twist' and 'point, point' and *'your chest, what are you doing with your chest?*' Jimmy turned out to have the rhythm and the lightness while Alice was slower. So she shrugged and her face shut against him and she found excuses to be half-hearted. The instructor, her perfume as thick and insincere as the French accent, insisted the tango was a *milonga*, very private, and Jimmy held Alice closer to him until one Saturday for a moment she forgot her defiance and they were one in the rise and fall, over and over, dazed in the lightness, and when it was over were clinging to each other, dizzy and breathless. Alice pressed her face into Jimmy's neck, her voice fragile, smaller and closer to him than he had yet known.

'Is that what it really should be like?'

Chapter 6

The last Sunday in August they took the road south towards Upton and then out to the fields where the guillemots dived bolt-straight over the cliff. They walked down the steep oozing drop to the sand and on past the overgrown quarries, climbing, inventing obscene private names for the endless flowers. Then with the wind at their backs they traced the rabbit runs through the fields and dropped to the little sodden valley and the heavy old limekiln. Here they could take the road to Woodhuish where they would be able to cut back to town or go on into Kingswear, so long as they could reach it before the Sunday afternoon bus had gone.

'There's another cove. With its own beach.'

Jimmy was sitting on top of a gate and looking out towards the line of the cliff. The rain had held off for nearly two hours and they were carrying the stiff oilies.

'We see it when we come round from Start, just behind Scabbacombe Head.'

'Next time jump over and swim ashore and tell me what 'tis like.'

'I casn't swim.'

'You casn't swim?'

'None of the smacksmen swim. 'Tis quicker that way.'

''Tis a beach in its own cove?'

'Looks like it from the water. No houses, nothing at all.'

Cutting out through the fields was like running away from school, climbing one slimy waterlogged gate after another until at last they made it to a sunken lane that led down between high hedges. And then they walked out onto the long sweeping green hillsides of a valley that curved until the sea was rolling silver in the sudden sun. The path brought them down to a stream deep in leafy rocks and stepping through they could hear the sea on the shingle. They ran out at last with the stream into a perfect inlet, unwatched unless from the sloping grass above. Far out a lone smack was tacking east. Almost all the boats would have been in for Sunday and she was maybe late after a good week in the Cornish waters, or perhaps delayed by fouled gear or split canvas, and now slowed by the awkward easterly.

They were as alone as they had ever been, and they stood in the strong salt breeze and kissed for long minutes before Alice untied her boots and pulled off her woollen stockings. Jimmy yelled, stepping after her and stopping in disbelief as she hitched up her skirt and waded screaming into the biting cold water until all her clothes were wet from the knee and the drizzle began again but not cold and the wet did not seem to matter any more. Jimmy was shaking off his boots and socks and rolling up his trousers, wondering at the madness of it when Alice marched solemnly up the beach and unbuttoned her narrow skirt and blouse and dropped them in the shelter of the low crumbling rock wall and walked back through the rain into the jumping water in nothing but her linen bloomers and camisole. She was suddenly frail, curls spray-buffeted, legs wet, sleek, more slender than Jimmy had imagined possible, arms thrashing chaotically as she tumbled and staggered across the sharp shingle and on into the low pushing breakers. Jimmy was transfixed by the spreading dark of the linen and the soft breasts and beautiful, pale arms so long and slight he could not believe they had held him so firmly so often. He supposed he should run and throw his arms around this extraordinary girl or crash into the water behind her but he hesitated for fear of chasing the magnificence away.

Then Alice was standing in front of him again, looking up into his eyes, wet spreading across her clothes, taking his hands and unbuttoning his shirt and unbuckling his trousers and he too was screaming in his grey flannel drawers, suffocated by the cold and by the risk of it all and Alice was grinning beside him and shouting over the waves.

'I'll teach 'ee to swim.'

'You can swim?'

'I fell into the harbour when I was four. I was running along the edge. And I came up from the water and saw twenty faces pointing and shouting and cheering and I never imagined there was anyone couldn't swim. And then my father took me to Fishcombe and taught me properly. He never told my mam. He rowed me back across the harbour and dried the things at his workshop. That's when I used to watch 'ee coming in on *Deliverance* and thought you'd see I was sometime soaking and laughing like an idiot.'

But Jimmy was shying and swaying as Alice tugged at his arm and they waded deeper and the water welled up at his waist and he could not breathe with the cold and his smacksman's horror of the water.

'Alice, I don't think so.'

But suddenly she pulled him over backwards, spluttering and panic kicking as the water closed over his face and then looking up into Alice's elated scream, her arms under his shoulders, and shouting, though his head was too full of water to hear, steel cold clamping his skull, lungs paralysed. He had heard of men who went over and were pulled in dead, not from drowning but killed by the cold, suffocated, their lungs empty. Alice pulled him back through the water and the terror took him completely and he doubled up, disappearing under the surface and struggling to his feet, hands waving wildly and the water surging up his nose like a spike. He rounded on her, hands to his salt-stinging face, but his anger died in his throat at the triumph in her eyes and her arms held out to take him and she was perfect and wild and sea-soaked. Jimmy was more or less naked too and in the swelling pushing water they held each other and kissed with an intensity that Jimmy thought he would never be able to contain until Alice pushed him away and clapped her arms across her chest and struggled, screaming through the heavy water and ran up the beach, her wet clothes clinging, and sat shivering, knees hunched up, pounding the shingle with her feet and whooping as Jimmy dragged himself behind, still unable to speak, shaking every inch and coughing like a horse. They sat a little apart, laughing in their unbelief and shyness and the unspoken but iron conviction that they could not touch each other. That was something that could not happen without being intended.

Jimmy's head never left the little beach at Scabbacombe during the grey, storm-clogged days at sea that followed, its friendly stone and closeness and the dead, complicit quiet of the grass where you walked leaden after. But mostly he imagined the cold and forbidden-ness of the sea and Alice soaked through and refusing any guilt and laughing and her eyes radiant. She was reaching her hands out and holding him and he was a child in her arms and yet also a man as he had never been before and their friendship was now between equals and the strongest thing he had ever known.

They went to the cove whenever they could slip away from Alice's parents, keeping the towels and wet clothes at Jimmy's lodgings. Each time Alice fell shrieking into the water, spinning easily over and over, disappearing and flying up yards away. With a patience he had not yet seen in her she taught him to reach out and finally to make a desperate, gasping thrash with his arms and to float a yard and then two until he was finally crashing towards her, feet an inch from the sand, arms pushing rigidly at the treacherous water. All the time he was less aware of his own fear and cold than of his intoxication with Alice undressed in her waterlogged linen but not caring and watching him, only him. Finally, as a cloudy, thundery September at last grew warmer Jimmy found he was swimming, half a dozen strokes at first and at last for a minute at a time.

The first October Sunday in 1912 was warm and windless, the water as calm and warm as they had yet known it. This time Alice disappeared under the water and reappeared naked, hurling the dripping underclothes to the shore and Jimmy nearly drowned, suddenly suffocated by the flawless soft of her skin and its dark and light, and the roundedness and fullness and the confidence in her eyes. She sat shivering naked after on the stones and was suddenly a stranger once again. It was as if everything had started over, this time with the air headier and his pulse pushing more urgently and their voices quieter and adult. That week Jimmy found he could not look down into the blue green as the net came alongside and the catch sparkled silver and grey without seeing Alice, twisting, rolling, lithe and white and wonderful. But he found also that her nakedness was now a question hanging between them.

Chapter 7

Without ever meaning to they had found themselves at a moment when something had to be decided. Jimmy struggled to think, at the tiller and casting the lead and now in his turning, tilting bunk where he could not sleep for his pounding heart.

He found that the decision he had to make was snagged and tangled. His share as a deckie aboard *Maryann* would keep Alice in nothing but dark cold and poverty. If he wanted to ask Alice to marry him he would have to move on. But he understood with painful keenness that he had no home except *Maryann*. Henry was a mountainous silence who missed nothing. He was a lifetime ahead of his crew. Eb had an angry silence that told you of a past he would not be drawn into discussing. It left him generous because he appreciated the company of those who had no interest in remembering. Jimmy also watched his own hands, rough swollen and browned, and was aware he already understood every mood of boat and sea, enough to be mate and even master as soon as he had his Board of Trade tickets. It was a mistake to stand still, like the old smacks rotting at Galmpton, timbers slime-blackening, strength trickling and crumbling into oily water as their spirit fled. The peace he had found this summer signified only that the tide was turning. But if he quit *Maryann* it would be against a hope of a girl still lost in her own traces, hidden in the simple complexity of being young.

He knew it was no easier for Alice. The first weekend, as they stood above the lifeboat house and kissed, she told him how she would escape the grey streets and her parents' bickering and the little harbour turned in on itself. She was saving to go to college and train to teach. They both knew she would not be accepted unless she were single but then it had not mattered. Now each time Jimmy tried to frame the question in his mind and find her in his imagination, he found he had no idea what she would say. Yes, or no or not yet. Jimmy's guts lurched at the prospect of three or four years' waiting, perhaps longer, while Alice saved and took the express up to the college in London and found a position somewhere and resolved her ambition, hoping every time he came in and tied up those quick eyes had stayed on her smacksman and a townie had not caught her away. It was impossible. He believed it could not be done.

He heard the skipper call his haul-oh and climbed on deck and took up his position at the foresail sheets, the rope familiar and tough in his fingers and suddenly knew with complete clarity that the moment would not return. His decision had already been taken. He had no idea what Alice would say.

The next Saturday when they came in she was waiting for him. The barrow boys had run up to the shop and Farley was now unable in law to deny her the afternoon. Henry and Eb nodded when Jimmy asked if they would see to his share and he took Alice by the arm and together they walked up through the streets. Alice was bubbling.

'I've started teaching and you won't guess who.'

'Billie?'

'*No*. Nobody could teach Billie. Eb Much's lad, Harry – the one everybody calls 'Boy'. He's Billie's age but he's funny. And he wants to get on, get a job.'

Jimmy guessed that her excitement was as much about putting off talk that was more difficult as it was about teaching Boy Mutch.

'Does Eb know?'

''Tis only just started. He's going to come for lessons in book-keeping. Accounting – '*counting* he calls it. *Are us going to count more Williams?*'

'Williams?'

'Bills. And *oops I discounted*, when he means *miscounted* and *is this a crossed cheque or a happy 'un?* You casn't teach someone when he makes you laugh. He comes to the shop for lessons.'

'Does Mr Farley know?'

''Tis Mr Farley suggested it. He said it was to give me experience, afore I go to college.'

Now the quiet fell between them. Jimmy could tell from Alice's deepening silence and the way she walked with care as if she did not want to leave any footprints, that they both knew why they had come. They walked out onto Durl Head and looked over the long sands, the moments weighing more and more. Jimmy's heart was beating quickly, and he supposed Alice could hear it when he spoke.

'Why don't thee go as a pupil teacher, Alice? Learn on the job, like I had to, on the smacks... 'Tis quicker and you'll be teaching straightaway. Like Boy.'

'I should do the proper training. Go to college. Get a better job.'

'But what then if ...'

'Mr Farley says I deserve it...'

''Tis a long time.'

''Tis four years to save enough from what Mr Farley pays. Then the training and school for a year.'

'Seven years, Alice.'

She was smiling but the tears were beginning to spill over the brown of her cheeks because they had suddenly reached the most difficult part without any warning at all. Her hazel eyes blinked, unsteady, asking him whether he still wanted to do it, whether he would still dare to ask.

'We've got forever, Alice.'

He knew already he did not believe it. Alice held him tightly to her but it was unimaginable. Her wildness had bewitched him and it was not to be contained now.

'Seven years ago I was running the track with my father to watch the men at the hedging and the cows down for tagging. He died a few weeks later. No smacksman knows if he will be alive in seven days. In seven years you'll have forgotten today, and its westerly and the haze and the skylarks. You're like water in my hands, Alice. Like the sun on a swell. I never know you.'

He gripped her tighter but she was looking away. Their poverty was a chill between them just when they had seemed so rich.

'I'll do the ticket. I'll be mate in six months. Then we'll have enough. You won't need to wait. You won't need to go away.'

Then, after an infinity of time Alice turned.

'You'll be skipper and we'll use my savings to buy our own smack and you'll fish the rest of 'em out of the town, Jimmy Blackbridge.'

'You'll do it?'

'I don't know. I don't want to say, until we've decided.'

And he looked expecting it to be nothing but words and saw instead that she was in this moment utterly with him. He kissed her again and held her without speaking because it was the biggest thing she could have said. It was a decision they would *make*, a choice they could take together. In that moment he believed their love would go on, exactly because they would choose and never wait for things to happen. Then at last he looked down into the face that seemed so close it was inside and so far it was impossible to distinguish, and heard his voice from a thousand imagined moments, the words that had been the belaying of his whole life until now. And in the moment that came after and had been dreamed a million times and yet never finished, and when it came was infinitely long and unreal, she simply said yes.

They lay on the wet grass and held each other and forgot about the impossibility of what they were setting out to do, and about being two people, and knew by the words they had said they had already made themselves one person. It was as if something very deep inside her had let go, something precious and guarded with jealousy and secrecy all her life that had suddenly dissolved and let loose a torrent, a haemorrhage. She could not stop herself from laughing, wiping the tears thoughtlessly from her eyes, holding Jimmy's face in her hands, her look distracted and fairy light and curiously private. Later they walked back from Durl Head still dazed and wrapped in each other, Jimmy unable to believe the sudden, impossible October brightness of things. They came clattering, laughing through the narrow fields and down past Redhill House and stopped at the junction, at the back of the first houses, where the town lay out in front of them. Jimmy held Alice again and they kissed and then held each other, unable for a long time to go on into the streets and breach the moment.

'Alice. Shall I ask your father?'

It took Alice a moment. Both her arms were around Jimmy and her head was in his shoulder. But she turned her fragile face and let him go.

'Jimmy – my father will say I'm saving for college and I can't if I'm engaged to be married. He'll say I'm young and college comes first.'

'I'll just tell 'en we'll wait.'

'Yes.'

This time there had been no hesitation.

'And we will, if we have to.'

'Yes.'

Alice kissed him again and again until they walked on down through the town, Jimmy numb with what had to be done, his head reeling with the words. He knew from the brittle tension in Alice's hands that she did not know what would happen when they reached home and how this thing could be explained to her father. He was convinced they had been joined together in a way that must be visibly obvious to everyone who saw them. But he wondered if her father would launch into one of his heartless sermons.

They kissed each other briefly and awkwardly at the top of the steps into Higher Street and stepped gingerly into the house. Pentecost and his wife were waiting for them, on their feet as they came in and for a moment Jimmy had the notion Alice must already have told them what they were going to do. Perhaps all they needed to do was to shake hands and kiss and everything would be agreed. Then he could see Alice was unsure, looking from face to face, about to tell them even though he was supposed to ask first. Already her mother was taking her hand, speaking with a kind of uncertain quiet.

'Alice. 'Tis going to be alright. Mr Farley was here.'

Chapter 8

Alice looked from one parent to the other, her father half smiling, half shaking his head, her mother flushed and talking as if out of breath. She had taken one of Alice's hands in each of hers.

'Mr Farley was here after dinner. He came to see you.'

Alice pulled herself away and stepped back towards Jimmy.

'Why did he come here? What did he tell you?'

Her mother looked around at her husband and he held out his hands for Alice to take.

'He came here after dinner. He sat in the chair, by the range. Thee's know I haven't always been able to agree with George Farley. But he sat in the chair and said he wanted to pay for 'ee to go away to college. No need for thee to save up all those years.'

There was the silence of breath held, not one of them moving. Then Alice's hands were suddenly in her hair, the curls everywhere. She was shaking her head.

'He says he'll *pay for me?*'

'He said he will pay your college fees, if 'ee save for your keep.'

Alice was shaking her head and saying only 'no, he can't' over and over and looking up at Jimmy, lost as if mad. He smiled because it had all happened so quickly it seemed as if it must be a seal on their secret. She would go to college straight away and it would only be three years to wait. But he could see already it was not like that. Alice was looking back at her mother and then her father, and Jimmy saw they were both waiting for her to laugh and accept but the fine skin was drawing tighter on the square of her jaw and her lips were growing full for the crying that was coming. The silence grew heavy.

'He can't.'

Alice's parents both smiled as if from relief, as if it did not matter if that was all it was. Jimmy could see from the horror in Alice's face that they had not understood. Her father put his arm around her shoulders. Jimmy noticed the glance the man threw in his direction as if it was time he was gone.

'He said it was 'cause you'm doing so well for 'en, at the shop. He said if he had a daughter of his own he would to do it for her.'

Alice shook herself free and sat down by the range, blinking, trembling looking from her father to her mother but her face closed to them. Jimmy realised he was not simply there now.

'You don't understand. Mr Farley won't ever just pay for me to go away to college. I'll have to earn the money so I can go.'

Alice had spoken clearly and deliberately and her mother slipped silently into the scullery. Pentecost sat in the other chair by the range. Jimmy noticed he was sitting on its very edge, and wondered if it was because the man was thrilled or unnerved with what was happening. He saw Pentecost's hands tighten around each other, white showing through the heavy cracked brown. Alice did not look up at him.

'Mr Farley hasn't got enough money to pay for me to go to college.'

'Alice. How could thee's know?'

''Cause I do his books. Every week. Every Saturday after the shop closes. He's lying. He's only saying it 'cause, 'cause…'

Alice looked at Jimmy and he thought she was looking for help. But then he realised it was because she didn't want him to hear. He sat at the table, heavy, as small as possible. Alice collected herself.

'What does he want me to do?'

Tightness pinched her father's face. His voice was louder, quicker.

'He said you would work extra hours for the money and at the end of two years, maybe three, you would have seventy-five pounds put aside, enough to keep 'ee 'til 'ee get a teaching position. And he would pay the college fees. I said it would be Southlands College and he said you could go wherever you wanted.'

Alice's eyes were now blank, lost in the range. Jimmy could see her spirit had flown and he was sinking, unable to accommodate his emotions. It was not just the time that counted. It was the ruin in Alice's face. Then, unexpectedly, she nodded and found a smile and Jimmy knew it was completely empty, intended only to end the conversation. Pentecost's voice was as near to gentle as he had never heard it. He guessed it was more like relief.

'Good girl.'

Pentecost reached over to his daughter and she touched his hand but only for a moment. He stood, back to the range, everything about the lifting of his head and the clasping of his hands as if a sentence had been lifted. Jimmy was aware that they were talking now about the yard and the smack they had begun but he could not take his eyes from Alice, the girl who had said yes to him an hour before and was now tissue frail, crumpled, colourless and gone.

It was more than two hours before they were alone again, the corner street lamp gas yellow with late lighting, the October sun long cold below the ridge of the bay.

'Farley don't even have the money to keep his shop open for much longer.'

'Alice, that's good. 'Cause then you can leave. Be a pupil teacher. Become my wife. I'll have my skipper's ticket. We just have to wait. 'Tis not long. And if I ask your father now…'

'No! Jimmy, thee casn't. He always does what Mr Farley tells 'en and he'll turn you down.'

'This is about Roddy Farley isn't it?'

'Leave Roddy out of this, Jimmy. You wouldn't want a father like Mr Farley…'

'My father's dead.'

Alice looked up, her face suddenly filled with affection.

'Jimmy… I shouldn't have said it. This is horrible for you too. You don't have anyone 'cept Henry and Eb…'

'And you.'

'And me. And if I could just run away I'd do it now. Right now…'

'Are you serious, Alice?'

'Jimmy! We casn't. We haven't naught, and if you lose your place 'tis even worse. I've – us – just got to wait 'til this is over. Mr Farley has calculated. He can make me do whatever he wants, put up with whatever he bloody chooses to do to me. He can pay me nothing at all if he wants. All he has to do is to make a promise and my bloody parents will make me go and suffer whatever he wants me to do 'cause they haven't never got a farthing, and there's Billie to look after. And now Mr Farley has said one day he'll pay up and they're too scared of him to say no. If us want to marry and live in this town, I have to let him do whatever he fucking wants for another three years.'

Jimmy had never heard her use the language before then and now her voice disappeared into her sobs and she was not talking to him but to herself and to a bitterness that strangled her.

'He'll do what he wants and throw me out with nothing anyway. And my fucking parents will let 'en 'cause... 'cause...'

Jimmy held Alice because there was nothing else he could do. She was cold, hard as a coffin. He pressed his face to hers.

'I don't care. I love you, Alice, and I love you and I want you to marry me. And then fuck 'em – they won't matter, none of 'em.'

'And I love you and love you and I want to marry you. I want to.'

She had not hesitated and suddenly she was kissing him as tightly as she ever had and her eyes were full of burning and then closed and she was lost in him but he could feel the hardness gaining control in her body. He knew that he understood only a fraction of what was happening and that he would have to wait until Alice was able to tell him.

Chapter 9

After that the light that had flooded Jimmy's hours for these months guttered and slowly died and there was nothing he was able to do. When he called for her the following morning, Alice had taken a step inside herself. He felt her hand gripping his, urgency tight in her fingers and saw her skin stretch tight, colour sapped and thinned as if by a sickness. The longer he thought about it, the less Jimmy was unable to explain to himself why Farley's offer could have breathed such deathly cold into their love. The man had made an empty gesture, the kind of pompous showmanship Jimmy associated with councillors and politicians. Yet it seemed to Alice to have been a sentence, hard labour, solitary confinement. It was a door bolted between them.

In the first weeks after Farley made his offer they stole hours together late on Saturday afternoons, after she had finished the books and given Boy Mutch his lesson. They climbed the wide wooden stairs over the harbour commissioner's office and slid in to the new Electric Theatre. Alice loved the fantasy so that she laughed and gasped without believing any of it. Jimmy fell for the magic of its flickering window. It was black and white and stilted, but it was astonishing to see in the news reels through another eye, a privileged eye, observing a society wedding or a varsity rugby match. You shared its quavering secrets. Then there were the dramas and comedies, *Dr Pellie and the Secret Despatch*, *The Child Detective*, *The Stolen Picture*, something new every week. Burglaries and murders, affairs and chases came scrambling across the screen and it was all absurd and unaccountably moving. When they left Jimmy was exhausted with the novelty and brilliance of it all. More than that, Alice had put her head on his shoulder and everyone had seen they were a couple.

But their hours grew rarer and dimmer. Farley was driving his bargain like a stake. Now she worked late into every evening and all through Saturday afternoon. By the middle of November they only had Sunday afternoons. They slipped out of the starched silence of Alice's parents' house and sat in their uncomfortable best on the quayside or the grass above the quarries until the cold and the early dark shut them in. Alice let him touch her less and less. A paleness began to thin her skin until it was transparent, shivering to his fingers. She was shrinking visibly, bleached by the pitiless weeks, the blackness of her days imprinted around her eyes. He began to doubt she could any longer remember what she meant to do, what she had hoped for, who she had meant to be.

When it came to her pay Farley handed her only four shillings, sometimes less. The other ten he said she had earned he had her write in the ledger as money saved towards her keep during the teaching course. Twenty-five pounds and ten shillings a year, counting one week of holiday. He told her she could have the cash now if she wanted, but that then he would not pay her fees. Her parents would not hear of it. Every evening, she said, she hauled herself home from the shop in the dark and shouted at her father, putting her hands over her face and weeping that Mr Farley would never honour his pledge. But her father pointed a finger into her face and told her she was ungrateful and should think of others.

Alice told Jimmy that when the shop was empty Farley made her work in his house. Boy Mutch came there for lessons. Billie often turned up too. He would walk the few yards home with her in the dark without speaking, showing off the money he said Farley had given him and stinking of the drink Farley had poured into him, even though he was only a boy. On those days, Alice said, Farley would yell at her that she was worthless and that when the time came he would throw her out with nothing. Jimmy could not understand why she could never bring herself to walk out, whatever her parents said.

'Is Roddy still in love with you?'

They were sitting in the unfinished smack at Upham's again.

'Of course. Ever since he was at school. Ro-ddy.'

They were wrapped in their oilies, the Sunday rain dripping around them through the open frame. Alice was again far away, as she usually was when he mentioned Roddy. She always said his name slowly, because, she said, that's the way he spoke when he was boy and she had never taken him seriously. But Jimmy heard in her voice something complicated, impatient and yet tolerant, knowing and blunt and he understood that they had somehow grown up together, and that something she had never explained bound her to the Farleys. Jimmy waited for her while the swell gnawed the slip. Eventually he broke the spell himself.

'Did you ever go with 'en?'

'Roddy? He's just a boy.'

Jimmy ran his fingers through the silken hair at the back of her neck, the soft down where her skin was finest. Then Alice was talking again, and he could feel her voice beneath his fingers.

'Mr Farley says I was meant for Roddy. 'Cause of my mam.'

'Your mam?'

Alice took a long time to answer and Jimmy wondered whether she did not want to tell him or did not know how.

'Mr Farley was in love with my mam, afore she married. And afterwards. She took us up to Mr Farley's house, several days each week, when my father was at work. From afore I was too small to know. When I was a child I could hear the way he talked when we were there, too fast, too loud, ignoring me, trying to find something common with my mam when there was nothing.'

Alice shifted and Jimmy could look into her face. Now she was pushing her words out as if they were heavy, difficult to manage. But he could see she very much wanted to tell him.

'Mr Farley used to say I was *his* daughter now. I thought I was just another poor girl, the preacher's daughter. There was always some poor kid at his house. He used to take clothes out of the shop, make me dress in 'em, walk about in 'em, take 'em off afore I went home. I was ashamed, as I got older, in my dirty drawers, undressing and dressing and Mrs Farley coming in and shouting at 'en about it, especially when Billie was there. She hated it when Billie was there.'

'What happened to her? Mrs Farley?'

'She suddenly went away, eight, nine years ago. Everyone said she had been taken to a sanatorium. Nobody missed her. Mr Farley says the bills are breaking his heart. Roddy never says a word about her.'

'Did she leave 'cause Farley was having an affair with your mam?'

'Partly.'

'Is he still?'

Once more Alice took a long time to answer, as if resolving a calculation.

'They only argue.'

'Is that the real reason he's going to pay for you?'

There was silence.

'Or 'cause of Roddy?'

Still nothing.

'Farley wants you for Roddy? Is that what this is about? That's what he wants?'

'I don't want to talk about it no more, Jimmy.'

Suddenly she took his face in her hands. Too roughly.

'Jimmy, 'tis not about Roddy. I don't want him. I love you. I want to marry you.'

'I believe you. I love you too.'

But when Alice talked about Roddy, Jimmy heard the many voices that spoke together, contradictory, secret and frightened, calling distantly for help, crying for somebody to understand. Yet also telling him he had reached a door through which he would not be permitted.

Chapter 10

You could not help liking Roddy Farley when you met him, however superficial he later came to seem. The first time Jimmy met him was when Roddy saved his life.

Jimmy had first been apprenticed aboard *Deliverance,* a fetid old hulk where he was apprenticed as the cookie, its skipper so sunk in drink they returned week after week with hardly a basket. For six years they beat their young cookie and defrauded him so he could barely keep his lodgings or find clothes. One grey, gusty Saturday in the spring of 1910 they were limping in with their mainsail ripped on the skipper's watch. The truth, Jimmy guessed, was that he had been drunk at the helm, tiller lashed, head down in the ship's boat, but there was not a man aboard with the courage to say it. *Deliverance* had spent the afternoon lashed alongside a Dutch coper, a heavily repainted old fishing ketch that had begun turning up in the Channel, its hold turned into a saloon for cheap drink and tobacco.

This particular afternoon they had tacked across the outer harbour and come about off Fishcombe. Now they were reaching back for the New Pier, the skipper in the cabin yelling for Jimmy in a blue fury. Jimmy jammed himself forward of the bow winch, ready to drop into the sail locker if the man made it up the companion, praying they would by then be in sight of the crowded quay. Only another twelve months and he'd be clear of the bastard for good. He heard boots coming forward but knew the tread was too sober for the skipper's. Looking up saw the mate carrying a wooden crate.

'You lie low.'

'What's the box?'

'Something for someone what needs it. No need for 'ee to say naught.'

The man was watching forward, and Jimmy looked and saw a ship's boat coming out, a lad of his age at the oars. The mate waved, signalling the boat alongside. But as they approached they heard a wild roar from the hoodway behind and the skipper almost on deck.

'You'd best 'op over too, Jimmy.'

Jimmy turned and realised the mate was completely serious. He was lifting the crate onto the bowsprit so that it was some kind of barrier between the two of them and the skipper. Without being able to think Jimmy heaved himself up and crouched on the rail, deep black water now rushing at him below. He saw the lad bringing the boat on a course almost under *Deliverance*'s bows and for a moment was sure they would run him down. Then in an instant the crate was in the air and a hand pushed Jimmy over and he was falling and flailing into the water, the sudden cold a winding punch, sea filling his boots and starting to drag him down as he thrashed and broke the surface and sank again, his mouth full of salt. There would only be seconds before his oily lost its buoyancy and everything would be over. For a moment he was bursting into the air again and there was a hand at his collar and the darkness of the smack was passing far above and the rough varnished wood of the little rowing boat was pushing into his face. Then he was being piled over, retching, coughing and crumpling in a gasping heap.

The lad was hauling the box over and scrambling for his oars, hissing at Jimmy to shut the shit up and pulling hard as the wake from *Deliverance* sent them rolling, the skipper's yells carrying away and the mate's curses in return.

'Fuck me and the duchess. You need bloody practice if you're going to get that right.'

Jimmy opened his eyes and the lad was looking over his shoulder at the smack. When he turned back he was grinning. Jimmy pulled himself up.

'You need to bloody row faster. What the fuck was I supposed to do? Fly?'

'Jump properly, idiot. That was bloody hopeless.'

'Fuck 'ee... and your bloody duchess.'

Now most weeks Roddy would row out in the boat, collecting a box or a crate from the mate. Jimmy took to dropping over as well. He guessed the mate was probably helping himself to the best of the catch but he could not have cared less. Petty theft was worth the moment of winking conspiracy between them whenever they broached harbour, and the satisfaction of slipping out of the skipper's reach. It also turned out that Roddy was collecting sixpence a week for the job. He gave a penny of it to one of the quayside lads, who would load the box into his homemade barrow and grind along out of breath behind them, as King Street rose steeply above the spreading ochre chaos of the Saturday harbour, the smacks trailing in and spreading their sails to dry. When they reached the ice factory they always sent the boy back to Jimmy's lodgings with his bag and carried the box themselves the last hundred yards to the sheds that stood behind the general stores on the corner. There it was easy to hide among the spewing rubbish that poured out of every door. Everybody knew the place as Old Aggie's. The old girl herself sat on the shop step, lifting her cold eyes with a wave of crooked blue fingers through the cigarette smoke. The boys still had five pence left, enough for two pints of beer at O'Connor's, if you knew who to ask.

The *Rising Sun* was on the quayside behind the fish market. O'Connor, its Irish landlord, was a man whose calm willingness to use violence haunted the streets. Everyone assumed he was running rackets, probably petty theft and protection and evading the men from the Customs House. Nobody thought it worth the risk to interfere. Jimmy met O'Connor the first time he went with Roddy. He was tall, grey, with a square Irish head and steady eyes, and he looked more like a town councillor than a criminal. Jimmy laughed to himself that the difference between the two was probably not much. Now he was trapped by O'Connor's half-amused look.

'You'll be here with someone I know?'

O'Connor's soft Irish accent was polite and precise. It froze your senses.

'I'm here with Roddy Farley.'

'You are? And your name would be?'

'Jimmy Blackbridge.'

'You'd be the cookie aboard the *Deliverance*. A good *Methodist* lad?'

Jimmy was amazed. What else did the man know? Roddy must have talked about him.

'You'd be welcome at the *Sun*, Mr Blackbridge, even if you are a Methodist. So long as you'd do a good job and keep your mouth shut. You'd see nothing, and you'd hear nothing.'

Jimmy looked for a trace of humour, a quayside joke, but there was not a flicker. The shapes around the bar shifted and sniggered and Jimmy knew they were watching for what he would do.

'I'll keep my mouth shut, Mr O'Connor.'

The man shook his hand and that was all.

Jimmy discovered that everyone knew Roddy, because he had that hair that was almost white in the sun and because he had a voice to shake your guts. And he behaved as if his father owned the entire town, not just a general shop in a back street. There was nowhere Roddy went that he was not treated with a kind of deference that at first intrigued Jimmy and later disgusted him. They spent Saturday nights at the *Sun*, in the back room because they were too young. Jimmy began to detest the way the beers stacked up while Roddy and his mates made a show of emptying them, stumbling out onto the quayside to throw up and pissing in the harbour like a barber's cat. He also hated the drunken shouting, especially O'Connor's cursing hatred of the English that was so open and loud the men called him a Fenian bastard to his face and he laughed his acid laugh, a stink of violence that hung in the smoke. Under the bench in the back room was a collection of greasy cards, girls in a photographer's garret, nude on velvet couches they could never have owned, large painted canvases behind them. The other lads whistled and pointed their fish blood fingers but Jimmy was only able to think about the girls who had not been able to pay the rent and wondered if any of them were orphans like him. He imagined what it was like after the crack of the flash, the grubby coins left on a chair, patched clothes pulled tight as the girl fumbled down some dark hallway and into the cold, eyes down, away from the stares. Or maybe it was worse. Then his attention would snap back into the room, Roddy shouting about a girl he had bought with his father's money and the other lads tipping their glasses and cheering. 'Waste of piss,' was always Roddy's verdict. Jimmy guessed he was not the only one in the room who did not believe a word of it.

He told Roddy about Alice as soon as they started together. The business with the boxes had finished and Jimmy had got his deckie's birth aboard *Maryann*. He had gone on spending time with Roddy, less and less willingly. He wished he had other friends to pass the hours on shore with but found himself falling into the same habit each time he was in port. When he told Roddy about Alice, Roddy's voice was suddenly hoarse, his smirk condescending in a way that was meant to threaten.

'I know'd Alice when you were still up on that bloody moor, dribbling on your bloody father's knee, God rest his schoolmaster's pocket book. And I know'd her windbag of a father and her pathetic squat-to-pee brother. She's got the finest bloody legs up to her bum in the town and the smartest head for figures since there were seven days to count. When she goes with anyone, Jimmy Blackbridge, 'tis my bed her shoes are under.'

Jimmy almost laughed out loud. Roddy was a child stamping, shouting out into the adult world, frightened by the sound of his own voice. He imagined Alice then, so quick, laughing at Roddy and treating him with pity because he would never be able to keep pace.

'Roddy – I just see her on the slip, and up at your father's shop. She's a good girl.'

'Too fucking right, Blackbridge. You mess with her and I'll have your balls for a necktie.'

Jimmy bought Roddy another pint and left the pub. He never went back. Over the months he got to know Alice better he noticed the way she spoke about Roddy Farley. It was, he later realised, as a sister would a brother. He told himself it did not matter because Alice told him dozens, hundreds of times, *'tis not about Roddy. I don't want him.* But as the autumn of 1912 went on, and George Farley's bargain began to steal the oxygen from their love, Jimmy once more could not keep his doubts down. Whatever they had agreed and she had wanted, Alice would surely never end up as a mate's drudge, a wife who scrubbed a little house and worked long hours for children's clothes. She would be a Farley because in the end they would make her choose it. Was that not what her own parents always intended? And knowing that Alice's mother had had – perhaps was still having – an affair with Farley made it all the more certain.

One weekend in November Alice told Jimmy that Roddy had barged into the shop, stuttering and mumbling that he had started classes with Schjonemann, the retired Danish sea captain who lived at the top of St Peter's Hill and made a living getting lads through the Board of Trade examinations. He would be mate in a couple of months, master in a year. Jimmy could see the Farleys' trap closing. They could snap it shut whenever they chose and on whatever terms. By the time November sank into dark December Jimmy could no longer bring himself even to recall the agreement he and Alice had made two months before, with the skylarks calling above Durl Head.

CHAPTER 11

December 1912 had been crisp, damp, the water blue with the sky, nights bitter and the sun cold burning by day when the rain held off. The twentieth was Friday and *Maryann* flung herself into the harbour early in the afternoon, running on mainsail and foresail with two reefs down on a strong easterly, fish hold topped out with cases. They were early, Friday, and he knew Alice would be at the shop, not expecting him till tomorrow lunchtime. Henry had decided they had done enough not to go out on the Monday or Tuesday and there was a decent chance they might not even fight out through the press of smacks on Boxing Day, nor any day until the Monday after. Six months before Jimmy would have shouted out in excitement at the white topped water. Now he no longer knew what he expected. He could not remember ten days tied up since he had started on the smacks, nor a moment when he more needed the time. It was a lifting of the cloud, hope in the grey.

Over the last weeks Alice had steadily withdrawn, from Jimmy, from her parents and her brother, from the whole task of living outside her own body. She would not let Jimmy speak about the Farleys and wept about the life that was being taken from her. She talked endlessly about her mother, returning always to her bitterness that her mother would not take her away, spitting the justice she imagined when the woman would watch her daughter die from her neglect. But Alice's mother seemed as lost as her daughter, her face as shadow scarred and her skin as drawn. She had wept openly one Sunday when Alice had screamed at her, making no attempt to wipe her face or turn her eyes. Pentecost stood, limp and defeated, just a bystander.

Jimmy set about the long stowing of the boat's rig for the ten days of Christmas and let himself believe it might be time enough for her to begin to be his again, however far away, hidden behind her curtains of mist and rain. Even Farley would not be able to shackle every dark-filled hour of the holiday. He saw Henry sculling back to *Maryann* and wondered how the fish auction could be done so quickly. Then Henry was calling over the water.

'Leave the rest, Jimmy. I'll do it.'

'There's time, Henry. I'll manage.'

'You're needed, Jimmy. Ashore.'

Jimmy went below and threw his sea guernsey and trousers into his canvas bag so they could be washed and took his oily because it needed new cutch and there would be time for it to dry before they were out again. Coming back on deck he found Henry waiting, still in the boat, and climbed down. Henry pulled away powerfully in a moment.

'Bad news, Jimmy.'

'What?'

'Mrs Rogers.'

'Alice's mam?'

'Pentecost came home from the shipyard, Wednesday evening. Found her in the scullery. She'd been dead hours.'

Jimmy found Alice scouring the house, her mother's body gone to the chapel of rest, the funeral set for Tuesday, Christmas Eve. He stood uncertain in the parlour, bag bulky and stinking by the door. He did not know what to do. He was numbed by the certainty that Alice would turn her guilt and her anger on him, somehow blame him for this new abandonment. But he was also humiliated by his own cynicism, the thought he could not put down, that now at last something might shift. If Farley and Alice's mother were no longer together there might at last be an opening through which light would reach them. But Alice completely ignored him until he spoke.

'Alice, I'm sorry.'

'Everyone says that. I'm not.'

'What do you want me to do?'

'Nothing. She never cared. Now I've got everything to do.'

'Alice. We'll help.'

'*We?*'

'I'll help… Billie…'

'*Billie?*'

Jimmy had said it because he had no idea what else to say. Alice was grey, her face shockingly old. Jimmy now saw that her mother's death had stolen her last shred of freedom, the possibility of walking away from the house and its two useless men. He too was part of what she was losing. He held out his hand for the broom and Alice looked up accusingly and let him take it and crashed away into the scullery. Jimmy saw the brown of blood still in the roughness of the scullery tiles.

'What happened? Alice, what happened?'

Alice was not looking, at him or the discolouration. She was slamming the metal pots into the sink, pouring cold water uselessly over them, spilling it onto the floor, herself.

''Tis what she wanted. She didn't care.'

'Did she fall?'

Alice was motionless for a long moment, gazing into the pots as if looking for an answer.

'I expect she did. He'd cleared most of it up afore I got home. Ask him.'

'*Alice.*'

Jimmy stepped into the tiny space and held her, ignoring the blackness of the recent weeks and for a few moments she stopped struggling and hid herself in him with her sobs. Then she pulled away and smashed into the sink once more, scattering the pots deafeningly on the floor, bouncing in the mess. Jimmy bent and picked them up. He saw there had been blood everywhere, under the sink, on the wall opposite. He could not imagine what the woman had done to herself.

'I'll do it, Alice. Thee casn't be here.'

'I live here, Jimmy. Nobody else is going to clean it up. You're a smacksman. You get out of this fucking hole every week.'

'I'll do it now.'

"Tis probably my fault.'

'How can it be your fault, Alice?'

Alice did not answer. Jimmy held out his hand to hold her but she moved away. His voice seemed loud now.

'I've got ten days. I'm here until New Year…'

'I can't cope with thee as well. Now I've got everything to do. For *those two*.'

'Let me help. I'm here for thee, Alice.'

'There's no time for me. Not for months. Never again.'

'What does your father say?'

She looked up at him again, an expression of complete scorn, and he realised he already knew the answer.

'He says the Lord will provide. He sits like he always sat, clinging to his Bible, while the Lord provides. The Lord provides his meals and his clothes, and the Lord washes and darns and cleans. My mam hates 'en. She tells Mr Farley every time she goes to his house. I always thought all men and women hated each other 'cause my parents do and the Farleys did. I wondered why my mam talks to the man until I saw they were having an affair and they always had. I even felt sorry for my father. But he does nothing. 'Tis always someone else. The Lord will provide. Well now 'tis me. Now I have to do everything for him so he can sit there and preach.'

For a wild moment it came into Jimmy's head to take the girl away. To take her upstairs and pull her clothes out of the chest and together walk out of the door and up the short streets, and buy the tickets and take the train to Exeter. Or to go down to the harbour and find a Plymouth smack that was making for home. And he imagined them in the December crowd around Plymouth's smack-jammed Sutton Pool, hurrying, rain soaked and trying doors for somewhere to stay and holding each other shivering with the cold and what they had done. And he would find a position and so would she and everything would work out.

'Let's go, Alice. Let's just walk out. Leave your bloody father and Billie to fight it out.'

'Fuck off, Jimmy. Say something worth my listening to.'

He looked down at the dull tangle of hair and saw she did not have the spirit. She was driven by some tyranny of duty just as strongly as her father. In the next months they were going to drown and their love would not survive. Again he took her in her arms and she let him, though she stood unbending and when she finally took her hands from her face it was lined red and blue with exhaustion, and filled with anger that would not let him close.

He went back into the parlour, meeting the room as if he had never seen it before. It took him some seconds to realise Alice had not been cleaning but removing every trace of the dead woman, the painted plates that had stood on the dresser, the sampler she had made as a girl and which had hung in the darkness beside the window, its absence now pale and accusing; the rough cambrics she had embroidered for the chairs when she was first married. Fanny Beaton, Alice's aunt, had apparently been each day, ordering Pentecost out and holding Alice while she cried. She had already taken most of her sister's possessions away. Jimmy thudded the broom into the dustless corners, thankful for the comforting wood in his hands, and then swept up the stairs and found a pile of clothes at the top, the smell of mothballs conjuring the dead woman with the sharpness of a knife. They pushed it all into a pile of pillowcases because Alice insisted she had kept them to pawn.

Pentecost came home at the end of the afternoon and Jimmy listened to his meagre, pious talk and heard in it a thin epitaph for an arrangement that had come to an end and had, it was now clear, never even been satisfactory. Billie appeared at supper time, stinking of spirits and refusing to eat and saying only that his mother had just been a housekeeper and now she had fucked them all by dying. The funeral was on Christmas Eve and healed nothing, a wreath from Farley too expensive, Fanny holding Alice and warning Pentecost away with her bitter eyes, the hymns of the faithful and their conventional comfort broaching awkward in the white cold of the chapel. Then came the rain-green burial, the space for the stone that would have to be bought and paid for and honest words somehow found to leave. Finally there was the knot of mourners who came back to the empty parlour and talked to each other about their ordinary lives. Billie was not there. Pentecost hid behind his pulpit face while the church women rustled stiffly and Alice stood in the scullery unable to speak. On Christmas Day the relentless rain was the only comfort, a veil across the face of things, the death inside too much even to name. Jimmy was relieved to be back at sea when at last they untied, and hated himself for it. He had wanted to love the hope and faith back into life, but he knew Alice's father had taken possession of those words and she would not even hear them.

Something completely broke in Billie after his mother died. Now he spent most of his time at Farley's, using the money he somehow acquired to buy drink in the back yard of O'Connor's, vomiting in the house, unable or unwilling to speak, dishonest and blind. He was thirteen. That was when Pentecost took the decision to send him to sea. He would be under Henry Buckley, such an extraordinary giant of a man, who knew the score and agreed when Jimmy asked. But there were no papers signed and they all understood they were putting the boy on trial and would only do what they could. Jimmy wondered how long Henry would let it go on. The only reason he suffered the lad himself was because it bought Alice days rid of him. It was something he could offer, whether or not she knew it.

Jimmy had never seen the winter seas more gorgeous than they seemed as January passed into February. The sudden, luminous green of the lifting waves took turns with the retreating, darkening purples that chased into the distance. A lace-backed swell lifted them into skies of red gold and indigo, shot with arrowed clouds of pure-spun white. The blue cutting clarity was joy Jimmy could compare with almost nothing else. But the cold of the openness froze your blood and lashed steel-bladed into your face.

Alice had apparently set herself to create at least the brittle shell of a home. But each time Jimmy came back into port he found in her face a shabby grey of lost trust, and her curls a mocking straw. She was, he thought, confronting the numb not-thinking of the working girl, the mask of disappointment they all wore. It was too cold to take her to the yard and there was never the time. Nor would she tell him what happened in the days he was gone, except that there was nothing for her, that they did what they wanted with her, that she no longer mattered. He listened to her, standing in the awkward scullery where her mother had died her messy, complicating death, while her father sat reading, dozing, dribbling until Alice began clattering out a bitter meal. Then Jimmy would tighten his fists and give Pentecost his attention. But the preacher was too closed in on himself to notice.

March of 1913 was cool and wet and April no better and the start of May was only ordinary. The second Saturday Jimmy returned to port with the familiar dull dread, relieved that he would be rid of Billie for a day. He was almost unable to lift himself up the steps from the quayside to Alice's stony voice. He persuaded her to go with him to the little beach at Scabbacombe and they set off early on Sunday afternoon, under an exhausted sun that laboured through the grey. By the time they had come wet-foot down to the beach Alice had fallen silent and Jimmy understood it was useless. They sat where they had been so happy, and watched the swell, a feeble, useless affair. Alice's arms were around her legs. For a moment she almost smiled.

'Roddy came to the shop. He's such a child. His knuckles were white and you could see he had something he had to say.'

'What was it?'

'He went round picking up brushes and pots and cloths and things he wouldn't know how to use. In the end he told me his father had signed the contracts on the new smack, and it was already started on the slip and it would be built in time for the August Regatta. And he was going to be its master.'

Jimmy tried to look into her eyes. There was no scorn nor humour, only resignation.

'So Farley's got money from somewhere?'

'I don't know where from. He's told t'other girl in the shop he can't keep her on. He's hardly paid me naught for weeks. I have to put it all on account.'

'He's borrowed it. He's gambling on the fishing. As if his Roddy is going to make 'en a fortune.'

'I don't care.'

'So you believe Roddy'll make the money and they'll pay your fees?'

Now Alice looked into Jimmy's eyes in a way she had less and less and Jimmy searched again for the soft, quick intelligence, the way she had of understanding what was in his mind. He found mist, hopeless and weary, a complicatedness that he could not pierce.

'How did we lose it, Jimmy?'

'We didn't lose it. It was stolen.'

'You just never knew what was happening.'

'Do you trust me, Alice?'

She did not reply and Jimmy gave her credit for not lying. Perhaps she no longer knew. Jimmy saw there was no way to persuade her since she had stopped looking at him and listening to his voice or noticing the struggle that he too was facing. The next week Billie died in the storm and on Sunday Flush Beaton gripped Jimmy by the arm in the chapel schoolroom and explained his terms. Then Roddy Farley walked into Alice's house and took her.

Part II

Chapter 12

The following Saturday, having found the house empty, Jimmy went straight to the shop and Alice got her coat and called for the housekeeper to stand behind the counter. It was not yet quite time to close for dinner but Jimmy spoke with a calm and a cold that surprised and frightened him and he saw, as from a distance, the alarm that completely took Alice's confidence. Jimmy had decided he did not want to return to her house because Pentecost would by now be back for dinner and they walked past it in silence and on to Upham's, the yard emptying for the afternoon and the man in the office used enough to Alice to let them.

They climbed the rough wooden scaffolding into Farley's new smack on the slip. It was shockingly far on, hull planking complete from topside to bilge and now edging up from her garboard. Heads of frames were cut down and the beams all bolted with carlings for hatches and masts. At her stern a section of pine decking had already been laid and a pile of rails and cleats was building up. Jimmy took Alice by the hand and gently perched her on the transit rail that ran around the stern. They had not sat in the smack before but Jimmy felt he already knew every inch. She would be a sister to every vessel in the harbour. Her timbers were still pale naked, her hull open to the sky and without bulkheads and she appeared tender, frail. Looking forward he knew she was already strong, her structure complete, the architecture that would give her solidity in a blow and fine lines for speed in a breeze. Sitting as he would on watch, Jimmy almost felt an affection for her, as for a small child, picturing her finished and underway. But every line, every deceitful splinter pricked his flesh with Roddy Farley.

'They beat me up last Sunday. Left me bleeding on the quay. That's why I couldn't come.'

'I didn't see you. I walked down to the quay.'

Her voice was calm. It was a conversation between strangers.

'Your uncle, Flush Beaton, pushed me into the bloody schoolroom, told me to leave you alone. He *threatened me*. He wouldn't let me out until Roddy had time to go and get you. I saw you. *I ran after you.* That's when they hit me. The man nearly cracked my skull.'

'Roddy Farley took me home.'

'I know.'

Silence.

'Alice. They'd made an agreement. Beaton bullied me out of sight while Roddy picked 'ee up. It was a deal.'

'No it wasn't. I was upset and you were nowhere. Roddy came to see if I was alright.'

'Roddy came for to take thee for himself. He also came to accuse me. He said, 'bout Billie...'

'Roddy knew about Billie. He waited for you to come to the house. He stood in the street for an hour after he left me. He came again on Monday. I didn't know what had happened to thee...'

'One of Roddy's mates from the *Sun* kicked me in the head. He was standing there a'make sure I couldn't follow.'

'I thought...'

'You thought?'

'I thought you'd left me. 'Cause of Billie.'

Jimmy took some seconds to calculate the meaning of Alice's words. She had blamed him for Billie's death and now she was accusing him of deserting her.

'You thought I walked away 'cause of Billie? Did Roddy Farley tell you that as well?'

'Leave Roddy alone.'

'Why do you believe what the Farleys say?'

'The job is all I have.'

'So you'll do whatever they want you to do?'

Alice turned her face fully towards him for the first time.

'*You bastard*. What do you know? You get into a fight and you do nothing. Nothing for me, nothing to get yourself a mate's ticket, nothing to change naught. And Billie…'

'*It wasn't my fault.*'

'I've got enough without 'ee and your quarrel with Roddy. Why can't you leave anyone alone?'

Her voice was broken as glass and Jimmy was unable to go on. He looked away, through the timber, along the graceful curves collecting at the bow as if they had always grown that way. But what he saw was the smack smashed around them, robbed of her timbers by a storm driven sea, masts and spars and rails carried away, crew clambering, hands trembling as they struggled to loose the ship's boat, slipping, staggering on the sea-slimed pine. And he felt through his skin the force of the current that was running, out of control. On land, in the streets, there was no master, just the fortunate who were carried along faster than the rest. And the wounded helpless like Alice who were taken and carried away. Jimmy was hopeless against the dead logic of the storm. He would cast the last lead, a final throw for the deeps.

'I love you, Alice.'

'I don't know what it means.'

'It's something you say 'cause you think 'tis true and you want it to be.'

'I don't think no more.'

'Hold on, to what we have, to love and hope.'

'I haven't got naught. No past, no future.'

'We've a year of living done together.'

'We've never been *together*, Jimmy. You've never known me.'

'I've known 'ee as well as anybody knows anybody. You casn't do more 'til you die.'

'I need someone who will love me the way I am.'

'What way? *Which* way are you, Alice?'

There was no answer and Jimmy wondered for a moment if he should shut up, wait until the shock of Billie's death had drifted further. But he knew by the eddies in Alice's voice it was not going to clear.

'Alice. Everyone changes, hour by hour. Us don't know ourselves.'

'Someone who doesn't always want more.'

'You want more, Alice.'

'You never give me naught.'

'Patience and time and loyalty and understanding and wisdom and support and forbearance. Do you want me to go on?'

'No.'

'*Why hast thou cast our lot in the same age and place, and why together brought to see each other's face? To join with loving sympathy and mix our friendly souls in thee?*'

It was Wesley's wedding hymn and Jimmy heard it as if from far away, a memory, carried on a gale. They had said it many times together, coy and uncertain of its significance.

But this time he knew the words did not contain them. Alice still had not looked up. He went on, his tongue growing thick and numb.

'Didst thou not make us one that we might one remain, together travel on and bear each other's pain?'

This time Alice put her hand on Jimmy's but without looking up, her voice barely rising above the shush of water on the slip.

'Till all thy utmost goodness prove and rise renewed in perfect love?'

At last she turned and lifted her face and Jimmy closed his eyes to time and tide and kissed her and had only the moment that should never end, yet was brief and had to end and that was why two people could never be one and would always wonder about each other and could always mistrust each other if they chose. Alice looked away.

'You didn't come back for me.'

'I was beaten bloody unconscious, Alice. Roddy always threatened…'

'Shut up 'bout Roddy. I expect he had a reason.'

'Roddy made this happen, Alice.'

'I don't want to hear.'

Then in the closed face and the hardness of the silence and the pale tightness of the hands Jimmy saw that the black breakers had rolled in. He was asking Alice to trust him when he no longer had a shred of trust in her.

'We're sailing in two hours. Back Saturday.'

Alice said nothing. Her face was now contorted, ugly with the tears and Jimmy found he was angry. He knew, even if she didn't, that Alice used her tears as a tool, allowing herself unreason, giving up responsibility. He stood, numb, and clambered across the beams to the square space where the binnacle would soon be and looked down into the cabin and galley, a mess of shavings and wasted ends. Then he turned and the girl was wracked with sobs.

'Don't trust the likes of them, Alice. They'll hurt you.'

He considered stepping over and sitting and putting his arm round her shoulders again and trying to smooth the crying. But it would have been an act between strangers.

Chapter 13

Jimmy walked towards the quay, setting out into a new and unfamiliar country, the grey blue, grey white of the clouds hard edged, their movement contradictory, rapid, the uprights and diagonals of masts and spars in the harbour cold etched in the damp air. The ground was moving too fast, his feet too noisily, the grey sandstone unforgiving. At the same time he was moving under water, everything drugged, leaden, his senses confused, unsympathetic to his need not to be living this moment.

He could see the shops along the quayside but they were a blank, their closed faces turned away for the dinner hour. The streets leading back behind were magnified by quiet and the air coloured by cooking. He scanned between the buildings to his right, the shipyards, the ice factory and the warehouses and knew he was looking for *Coronet*. She was lying just beyond the middle harbour. Let Alice dredge Roddy's shallowness if that was what she was set on doing. Without intending it, Jimmy turned and headed up towards Old Aggie's shop, not hungry except for some scrap of company. She would be sitting on the step and she would open up for him.

Aggie was watching, smoking as she always was, watching lives aboard and lives ashore passing her like a carnival. You wanted to like Aggie because she never changed and was always sitting in the same place, as if she were in some way older and more fixed than the rest of the world. But she was a lying cheat who stole from her customers and circulated vicious rumours when it suited her. You kept in with her because that way she might charge you less and spare you her tongue. She smiled at Jimmy through the hanging cigarette blue, her hooded eyes calculating.

'Hold on, Jimmy Blackbridge. Alice Rogers'll be yours.'

Jimmy wondered whether she knew nothing or everything.

'You make it happen, Aggie.'

'You don't need me. You just watch and see the way things work. Do what 'ee have to.'

'What do I have to do, then?'

Aggie coughed her phlegmy laugh. All that was left of her voice was a choke. It wreathed her words in obscurity.

'You keep the line. Farley'll sink without help. A spring marrying.'

Her words stalled Jimmy like a trawl caught, wrenching him to a stop with everything lost. He dimly hoped the woman would not have noticed. Aggie only grinned and climbed to her feet and shuffled inside, saying nothing at all but emerging, smiling again, a brown tooth on her crumpled lip. She sent him towards the harbour with a paper bag from her back room and refused to be paid. It was a pie and stank of her cigarettes and sweat. But the old witch possessed some kind of magic. Jimmy noticed as he set off for the town that the street condemned him less, its shades less brutally black and grey, its sound suddenly enlivened as the gulls shouted their arguments around the harbour's broken bowl. It was as if Aggie had conjured the soul of the place with a flick of her ash.

Jimmy found he was carrying her tobacco scratch in his mind and by the time he was at the end of Fore Street he was lightheaded and threw most of the pie to the birds. He felt for the courage to face the crowd around the fish market before finding a lad to row him back out to *Maryann*. But by the time he reached the crown of the harbour he was frozen, unable to take the next steps, and looked blindly out to the harbour entrance without any idea what he was looking for. He covered his burning face with his sleeve, lost and drowned.

'Marry me, Jimmy Blackbridge.'

Jimmy struggled back towards the afternoon, dizzy, wondering how long he had stood, and what he had imagined. A girl was standing by him on the quayside. She was a little taller than Alice, seventeen or eighteen, her eyes clear, grey-blue, searching and waiting, her hair a frizzy crown of mousy brown in the sun. She was pale, plain, yet animated with a sure confidence Jimmy found hard to recognise after all the months in which Alice had grown cold and unreachable. He heard the voice again. He was looking into a face, almost as if he was unable to understand what it was.

Jimmy was eleven again, an orphan, on the quayside almost exactly where he stood now, bewildered by the hurry and hardness, embarrassed by his tears. Then too he had seen a face. It was this face, except it was older. Now it made sense. That time it was May Grant, who had taken him in her arm, walked him home. Now it was little awkward Kitty, May's daughter, standing on the quay beside him, not little any more, but lit with the same complete, uncomplicated calm as her mother, the same gift of complete attention.

He struggled to find words he could speak but Kitty was already talking again, and Jimmy screwed up his eyes as if she were too bright to look at.

'I said hello, and then I thought it wasn't Jimmy Blackbridge but somebody who looked like you, and couldn't see nor hear.'

Jimmy wiped his face with his hands and tried again to look. The wind had given Kitty's face an apple bloom and Jimmy was taken aback by the sudden laugh which leaped from her lips into her eyes and made her shine brighter still. He was struggling to the surface from the drowning cold.

'*Kitty*. I don't know what I was doing. I wasn't looking at thee or listening. I was all eye and elbow.'

The words were just making themselves up while he watched.

'Did 'ee ask me to marry thee?'

'Yes.'

'Why not? Are you in love with anyone?'

Kitty's look shifted but barely a fraction. The smile was still bright.

'Yes, but the man I'm in love with has never asked me.'

'He's a bastard and I hate 'en. Can't he see you're perfect?'

'He's after another girl. I can't understand why.'

Jimmy was struck then that Kitty was looking at him, him alone and it had been months since Alice had. He did not know whether he wanted to be alone or to put up with her chatter. A handful of times in those first couple of years he had gone back to their little home next to the Customs House in Overgang and told Kitty sea stories, looking over the harbour from the window, until her father had come wheezing and coughing in. Jimmy could see in her grin she had inherited her father's quickness and irony. It was also obvious that, if he had hardly noticed her all these years, she had noticed him. He told himself he must not hurt her. He found himself lifting his hands in mock blessing.

'From this moment let him be yours.'

Kitty's brilliant smile faltered a point.

'Jimmy?'

'Kitty?'

'What's happened?'

Jimmy thought for a second but no answer came. Kitty took a step.

'Where be Alice to?'

'I left her at Upham's. Billie died, in the storm.'

'I heard. I'm sorry.'

'Alice blames me.'

'She doesn't, Jimmy. She blames herself.'

'I don't understand. But she doesn't want to see me.'

'She's confused, Jimmy, about Billie, about her mam.'

'She may be. But she doesn't tell me naught.'

Why was he saying all this to Kitty Grant? He had enough of his own emotions to carry without her childish crush.

'Let her take time, Jimmy.'

'Things get better or they get worse, Kitty. Do nothing and the time comes when you stop trusting. Then you casn't go back.'

Jimmy decided he did not want to talk, to Kitty or to anyone, about this or anything else. He did not have the strength to put everything into this girl's language. He pressed his fingers to his eyes. When he opened them Kitty was brushing crumbs from his guernsey, looking into his face.

'What can I do?'

'Do? Kitty? Nothing.'

'I'll say Hail Marys. For Alice and for you. Our Lady'll pray for 'ee.'

Jimmy smiled. He remembered that the Grants were Catholic and how it had seemed to him another new strangeness when he had first arrived. For a few days he had vaguely supposed the town people all said Hail Marys along with everything else that was confusing. *Hail Mary*. It was a simple thing for little Kitty to say, standing on the quayside, gulls strutting, shops starting to stir. And yet the love to say a prayer was more than Alice had offered for months.

'Thank you, Kitty.'

''Tis what friends do.'

Again the girl had reached straight in and touched the thing that mattered. She held out her hand and without any thought Jimmy took it and pulled her closer. He was for a moment overcome with the loneliness he had been carrying, when nobody waits for you or thinks the best of you or finds a way to bring you back when you are drowning. When he opened his eyes again the air was clearer, the space around him bigger. He found Kitty holding him awkwardly and he thought he had frightened her. But when he stood back she reached up and wiped a tear from his face with her fingers. Jimmy said what came into his head, words once again he had not made for himself.

'Maybe, I shall see you, Kitty?'

'When?'

Jimmy had no answer. Time seemed to have stopped in its ebbing and he was unmoored. But the silence was heavy and he longed for a voice to lift it, his own or hers. Something spoke in him.

'Saturday?'

Jimmy was astonished, guilty, half-laughing at himself once more from a great distance. He told himself to wake up. It was only Kitty Grant. But Henry and Eb had their own families and affairs and the chapel people were wrapped up with Pentecost and Alice. He was in no condition for the *Sun*, even if bloody Roddy Farley weren't holding court and spreading his lying bile about Billie. He was an orphan again in the blank streets. At least Kitty and her parents would have time for him. It would be a kind of going back home.

'Dinner time.'

Kitty smiled her brilliant smile.

'I'll be here, on this spot. And if you come for me, you do. And if you don't...'

Kitty stood on her toes and kissed him on the cheek.

'You don't know what you want just now, Jimmy Blackbridge. But if you need someone, I'll do.'

'Say some Hail Marys for me.'

Chapter 14

The wind was on the starboard quarter so they had heaved the gear around outside the rigging and shot from the starboard rail, streaming the net over, skittering like sardine. They paid out sixty fathoms of the warp, feeling for the bottom as it went. The last haul had been decent, cascading sole and plaice, turbot, cod, two hours of cleaning and gutting. They had reached the fishing ground around midnight. But the sun was now high and they had shot for the third time. Once they had hauled again they reckoned on a decent passage to regain position for the next tide. That at least would be a break. Henry had talked old Horace Johns out of port as cookie. They could have gone with three but the fishing had been lucky and Henry wanted all hands. You guessed Horace was in his seventies, face hidden in a frizz of wrinkles, one black survivor all that remained of his teeth. Mostly he sat on the quayside hoisting a crooked finger at your rig, always right. But then, Horace had been a smacksman since the beginning. Now he sat on the hoodway watching Jimmy.

'They'll stink 'ee out the scuppers.'

Jimmy looked down into the basket and saw old Horace was right. He was making a wretched job of the fish. You wanted it done quickly to win the next two hours of kip before you hauled again. But you had to get the gutting right or your fish rotted before you got in.

'I was asleep, Horace.'

'Thinkin' about a lass.'

"Course not.'

But he was thinking about Kitty. He took the fish back from the basket and went through them again and washed them in the bucket and threw it back over to refill. He was trying to imagine her, decent little Kitty Grant, trying to recall the times he had seen her. She was clumping down steep steps, her coat too big, hair cut short by parents who babied their only child when she was already twelve or perhaps thirteen. She was holding the hands of the two tiny twins who lived above the chandler's near Upham's, solemnly telling them the boarded-up house was not haunted any longer because she had said her prayers and old Knapman's ghost had gone to heaven. He was sure Kitty would be waiting for him on Saturday. He was awkwardly conscious that she would seem like a child, out of her depth, but he longed not to spend the weekend alone with the suffocating coldness and he told himself it need not matter if he spent an hour with her. Her parents were infinitely kind. It would be good to see them again and they would understand.

He slept heavily when the fish were finally done and it was ten before the next haul and then they were on the long run back. At midday Horace turned out the usual boiled beef and suet and they sat at the cabin table, Horace taking his turn on deck. They usually ate without talk because most things had been said. But Eb and Henry wanted to know from Jimmy about Farley's new smack. He ran his mind along its lines, oak frame and planking, pitch pine decks, teak in the cabin and they laughed that Upham's yard had been charging £560 for years, and Farley's boat would cost him all of that and at least half as much again for spars, rigging and canvas. Eb barely nodded, mouth full, eyes laughing at Henry.

'Farley hasn't got sixpence to scratch his arse. Must've mortgaged the shop. And the smack.'

'He'll need a decent skipper then.'

The grin was all round the table. It was laughable to imagine Roddy Farley working off £800 of mortgage. They would sink shamefully in debt, the pretentious young git and the pompous old man. Jimmy was laughing with them. But inwardly he was drowning, choked by the realisation he would never sit in a smack's frame with Alice again nor hear about a boat's progress from Pentecost. He was beginning to long for the others to shut up when there was a shout from Horace and Henry was on his feet. Neither Jimmy nor Eb moved a muscle because the smack had not shifted. It could not be anything serious. The sound of Henry's boots climbed the companion and crossed to the starboard rail. A moment later Eb was on his feet and Jimmy was climbing on deck behind him. *Maryann* had veered eight or ten points to starboard and they were all at the rail to see what was on.

Jimmy saw a boat was laying a couple of miles off, apparently at anchor, not much larger than *Maryann*. Horace pointed.

'Coper. Dutch. Rum, bum and bacca.'

Jimmy looked again and recognised the Dutchman from his days with *Deliverance*, and remembered its cargo of cheap oblivion and smut. The memory made him wince, not for the waste and stupidity, but for the foul-breathed violence of the *Deliverance*'s crew when they came back and the drifting twenty-four hours or more with a puking crew and no notion where they were.

Eb was pointing. There was a smack lashed alongside.

'*Coronet*. And I wouldn't bet against her bloody cookie being three sheets to a north-easter.'

'Her cookie?'

'Boy.'

'*Boy?* Aboard *Coronet*?'

Eb could barely speak and Jimmy could see he was fighting his anger, not at Boy but at himself.

'George Bloody Farley, talked the lad into it. We've always told 'en not to go near the man. But 'ee can't watch over a child every hour, can't keep 'en in the house. First it was sweets, then it was lessons with your Alice Rogers. And then it was *Mr Farley has promised me this* and *Mr Farley will give me that*. He's a bright child but he trusts everyone. Never has a bad word. But I'll have 'en make his way ashore, not risk his bloody life so people can have their bloody fish and chips and their bloody lemon sole in some fucking fancy London restaurant.'

Maryann was cutting her way beautifully through the swell and Jimmy understood that Eb loved the smacksman's life as he did, but that the times were shifting. And Jimmy remembered his own father. Every man wanted better for his son. Eb looked up into the rigging.

'He said he just wanted to know what 'tis like. Of course he did. He can see 'tis in your soul. I said I would bring him, one day, maybe soon. But yesterday morning he was gone, out of the house afore us were up. And down at the quayside they were saying Beaton'd taken 'en out on *Coronet*. *Just to see*, is what they said Beaton told 'em. The bastard, the *bastard*. He's just a kid.'

Eb was straining his eyes towards the coper as if he could skip the distance and jump aboard. Henry was forward, sheeting the mainsail to get the last inch and Jimmy went to the foresail for the same. It took less than twenty minutes to come up and Jimmy threw the fender over and called for *Coronet*'s crew to take a line but there was no answer. Eb was already over, climbing across *Coronet* and onto the coper, his hands and shoulders clenched. He flung back the green painted hoodway door and pounded down the companion bellowing his son's name and the sound of laughter died below. Jimmy looked over to Henry and they made fast and followed.

Everything was as Jimmy remembered it, the same stale light and dense stink. They had taken out the bulkhead between hold and galley and made a bar, lined at one end with shelves, bottles crowded behind its batons. There was a table bolted in the centre, thickly varnished wooden benches along each side, dull with spilled liquid, the hatch above a grime-streaked skylight, its glass brown with tobacco, light struggling down through the lingering pall of stale smoke. In the greyness Jimmy saw Roddy Farley in one corner, crumpled on the floor, his head lolling hopelessly as the boat rose and fell, a dead cigarette hanging from his mouth. Eb stood at the table, breathing hard and heavy, too angry to speak, gripping his son by the collar. Boy was half standing, half sitting, the glass in front of him emptying itself over the table and onto the floor. A barman stood uncertainly with a bottle in each hand and another of the Dutch was emerging from the cabin behind them, a cigar in his lips. Jimmy guessed from the naval cap he had pushed over his eyes that he was the skipper. The man gestured widely, his face a mask of mock seriousness, and made his way across the heavy space to the bar and picked up a bottle.

'Schnapps, gentlemen? A drink before we fight?'

His laugh fell dead against the men from *Maryann*, filling the centre of the saloon. The barman retreated to the far corner, put his bottles up into the shelves and took the greasy towel from his waist, busying himself at the counter. He had seen it all plenty of times. Eb heaved Boy to his feet but the lad crumpled hopelessly on the floor. The Dutch skipper smiled at Eb and corked the schnapps, his round Dutch vowels comical and yet unsettling. He took a slow drag at the cigar.

'Give him a while. Please. Your crew will take some tea?'

'My crew will take the lad.'

Eb hoisted Boy up again. He was a bear of a man. There was a grunt from the end of the saloon, Roddy now on one knee. He fell heavily back on the deck, a finger pointing unsteadily at Eb.

'Put 'en down, skipper. Not fit.'

Jimmy imagined Alice at this moment, sitting on one of the benches in the half light, watching Roddy and the wet spreading on his shirt from his drool, a patch of dark beer on his trousers, his legs, tongue and head all useless. A seagull alighted on the skylight overhead and loosed its ugly shriek, its claws scratching, screeching. Jimmy imagined Roddy dying in a hole like this. Roddy grinned.

'I told her what Billie did.'

He was wagging his head at his audience, raising his glass, no more than half an inch of cloudy liquid left.

'I told Alice. Billie jumped over, Henry. He finished it.'

'You bastard.'

Henry was over Roddy, hands seizing his oily and lifting him off the floor, spitting his words into his face.

'Whatever 'ee say, skipper. Billie Bloody Rogers stepped over your rail. And if 'ee don't believe me, thee can fish and find out.'

'You're pissed and perjured, Farley. You were nowhere near and 'ee bloody knows it same as I do.'

'He said he was going to do it. He said it was 'cause of Jimmy, and us know'd it was 'cause of...'

'*Shut up*, Roddy. You're embarrassing.'

It was Flush Beaton, standing in the doorway to the aft cabin, his voice steady and sober in the thick air, the chapel voice that made Jimmy's skin scream. Henry dumped Roddy on the floor with a snarl. Roddy struggled to stand, his face fogged. Then he looked away as if he had taken a decision. Beaton took a step into the saloon and was once again the dealer, steel and ice.

'I'm sorry, Henry, Eb, Jimmy. 'Twas my idea to come over and I took my eye off the lads. Should've known better and I'll see no harm's done. Boy won't do it again.'

Boy struggled to speak but nothing came except a gob of dribble. Eb gripped him like a doll.

'Too bloody right, Beaton. He won't set foot with 'ee again. You bastard. You'll piss when you casn't whistle.'

Eb and Henry lifted Boy over towards the companion, the Dutch skipper turning his back. Beaton blocked the way.

'Give Boy a chance, Eb.'

'I just did.'

'We'll talk about it, the end of the week.'

'I'll fill your bloody face, the end of the week.'

'Mr Farley speaks well of 'en. And Mr O'Connor'll see he's looked after.'

There was a new note in Beaton's voice. Perhaps it was uncertainty. But it contained a note of threat. Eb dropped the lad and pushed Beaton back towards the cabin.

'Let's hear what my son has to say about you first. And about your bloody Fenian boss.'

Beaton made a grab for Boy but Eb pushed him first with huge force to the cabin door. Beaton slid to the deck and Jimmy watched Eb calmly place a boot on his chest, reach over and open the door. Then he lifted Beaton by his lapels and threw him into the cabin, crashing into a large wooden crate that lay on the cabin table and sending it into the chaos that lay across the bench beyond. Henry was already heaving Boy up the companion and Eb began to climb, laughing grimly. Jimmy went to go up.

'I can help 'ee, Jimmy. We're family. You, me, Fanny, Alice.'

Beaton was sprawled across the table, blood beginning to seep heavily from a cut on his right hand.

'I'm done with Alice Rogers.'

Jimmy sensed his voice giving him strength. Flush was sliding awkwardly off the table to his feet, holding out his hands, the blood now running.

'I'll do 'ee a deal.'

'Fuck your deals. Tell me what you think you've got against me. Tell me thee's know 'tis all a fucking lie.'

'No deal. Have the girl if 'ee wants her.'

'Fuck you.'

'Billie's story'll get around. You'll never find another berth.'

Jimmy was already halfway up the companion.

Eb put Boy in his own bunk on *Maryann* and took the tiller while he slept. Jimmy sat silent on the forward winch, glad of the cold and the air. After two hours he saw the lad struggle silently on deck and, without looking back at his father, grip the mizzen halyards and throw up over the rail. Then he slumped limp by the gangway. Jimmy went aft and offered to take the tiller but Eb shook his head.

'Got to learn.'

'Talk to 'en.'

'I'm a useless father, Jimmy.'

Chapter 15

They shot at four and hauled in the bitter dusk at eight, Eb calling to his son to stand by and earn his keep. And Boy clawed the net over the rail with the rest of them and once it was hoisted up over the deck he was in again, his father showing him how to untie it, the catch streaming, struggling across the deck. He was enjoying himself and doing his best to impress. Within half an hour they had put about and the gear was down again. Henry took the tiller and Jimmy finished his share of the gutting and went down hoping to find something to eat. He found he was alone in the cabin with Boy.

Jimmy took the square brass shoe kettle from the boiler, filled it with fresh water from the tank and dropped in some dry tea. Scraping it back on its shelf in the boiler would have it scalding in a minute. All Jimmy needed was half an inch of condensed milk in the bottom of a mug and some spoonfuls of sugar. Boy watched everything.

'Can I have some?'

''Tis dangerous stuff, Boy. Turn 'ee into a smacksman.'

'Better'n beer though. Turns 'ee into a Dutchman.'

'Should have said no.'

'I did. But they said it'd turn me into a smacksman.'

Jimmy could see the lad coming to life again. More than that, he wanted to talk.

'You should listen to your dad, Boy.'

'Why does Flush hate you, Jimmy?'

'Does Flush hate me?'

'He doesn't trust you. That's what he tells Roddy.'

'And what does Roddy say?'

'Roddy says nobody knows as much as you do.'

'That's nonsense. Your dad knows more than I do. So does the skipper.'

'We'll never know how much Mr Buckley knows. He talks a foreign language. "Lee ho the scupper sheet".'

Jimmy laughed. *Lee ho the scupper sheet* made no sense at all, but sounded as if it should.

'Ah, Boy, you see, all that's a kind of *magic*.'

Jimmy gave him a mug of the tea and the lad pulled a face.

'You could have *tried* to make tea, Jimmy. That's fish soup.'

''Tis *cavil rail topping* tea, Boy. Special. To test whether you'll ever be a smacksman.'

Boy looked down into his mug, as if trying to read a message.

'My dad wants me to do something better. He says, look what happened to Billie Rogers. But Roddy says Billie jumped and killed hisself.'

'Don't listen to Roddy Farley, Boy. I was there. Billie was washed over in the storm. It was the most terrible thing could have happened.'

'They beat Billie up, the night afore thee sailed.'

'Who did?'

'Flush and Roddy. They were talking about it on *Coronet*.'

'Why did they beat Billie up?'

'They said Billie was shouting he would tell everyone. Flush said he was all wind and no piss and he would see to 'en. Then Roddy said *he said he'd jump, but how were us to know he'd go and do it?*'

'*What* was Billie going to tell everyone?'

'Billie told me they bullied 'en, making 'en tell 'em about Mr Farley.'

107

'Tell what about Mr Farley?'

Boy tried the tea again and pulled a face. But Jimmy could see that the conversation was becoming difficult.

'Maybe about you and Alice.'

Jimmy took a step into the cabin, as if to see the lad more clearly, but in fact to look into his eyes. It was clear that, for once, Boy was completely serious.

'And what was Billie telling 'em?'

'I think he told 'em about Mr Farley... About what he did. But... I can't tell 'ee no more.'

'Why can't 'ee?'

'And get mysel' beaten up too?'

Jimmy hesitated. Whatever scam it was that Farley had going, Billie had been disgusted enough to tell his story to Beaton's thugs and to get himself a beating. And then perhaps he really had pulled on almost everything he owned and climbed out into the storm and jumped. No wonder, if that was true, that Beaton had thrown on every inch of canvas to get home before *Maryann* and break the news to Alice and her father in a way of his own choosing. And then he had made it his task to pick Jimmy off because there was no knowing what Billie might have told him on that last trip. And perhaps that was why he had talked Boy Mutch aboard *Coronet* and clear of the town before he could tell anyone what he knew. Beaton's plan had run foul the moment Eb had crashed into the coper's hold. Jimmy put his boot again on the companion step.

'I watched Billie every day, aboard and ashore. I don't think he jumped.'

'Well I think I would jump...'

Boy considered for a long moment, emotions fighting for his expression.

'I might jump if I had to drink your tea, Jimmy. Anyway, I reckon us have to reef warp the mizzen winch, or something.'

'I'll *reef warp your mizzen winch* if 'ee say aught more about my tea.'

Despite what the lad had said about Billie, Jimmy could not help laughing at the *crams* he talked. He climbed on deck and pulled himself forward to where Eb was at the foresail horse. They exchanged a head-shaking smile as Boy scrambled along behind. He told himself he should let the lad's rattling chatter heal his own hurt. Billie was gone and his agony with Alice was cooling. So be it. They shared the four bunks between five, with one on watch. Despite himself, Jimmy tried again to make Boy talk, to find out what else had been said. But the lad clung to his father, watching the rest of them with a kind of wry wonder, talking more of his mock smacksman's nonsense, making them all laugh. They shot again at midnight on the Friday, a last trawl before running for home. Jimmy took his turn above deck after Henry and found *Maryann* cutting quiet and steady through a broken sea, held firm on the port tack by her trawl and a decent breeze.

Jimmy loved the quiet watches with the gear down. The swell was running ghostly, cloudy moonlight silver veins in its blue. *Maryann*'s mainsail sheet creaked as it always did, the old girl singing quietly to herself. After an hour a mist had clouded the moon and Jimmy checked the lights on their stanchions in the shrouds, their pulsing glow leaching uselessly into the quickly closing whiteness around them. The air was taking on the chill of a fog and Jimmy pulled the horn from the hoodway and settled back into the tiller.

He found he was listening to another sound. It was the deep, mechanical throb and the soft sluicing crash that came from a big powered ship. He swung the rope lashing around the tiller and stood at the aft rail, concentrating head-tight to find the direction. Sounds travel at sea and the fog echoes and confuses. Every two or three weeks a smack came limping into the harbour, planking stove in or gear ripped away, victim of the belching monsters bound for New York or the smutty coasters working the coal ports. Sometimes it was the freighters bound for the near Continent. The smacks' crews said they were on you in a second and gone without even a yell. Then there would be the days without money and the long, ragged wrangling over compensation with office men who could not care because they had it easy and earned more than you. It had been getting worse since the early months of 1912 because Royal Navy ships had been gathering in Portsmouth and Devonport, hammering fast through the trawling grounds on their way to the war they quietly said was coming and also loudly said would never happen.

Jimmy scanned the blankness. He could hear the engines more clearly and cursed the breeze that had shifted a fraction and was lifting spray from *Maryann*'s foot. Again he checked his lights. If one of the new Dreadnoughts was about she would slice through them almost before he had seen her. With her trawl down *Maryann* could barely shift a point. The moon was now completely gone and Jimmy could see nothing beyond the rail and felt for the foghorn, dropping its clumsy box on the deck, pointing its stubby brass trumpet aft and winding the handle to give the long blast and the two short ones that meant he was towing. The sound died mocking on the wall of damp and Jimmy guessed it was anyway useless over the ringing din of the engines, the clank and hiss of pistons now clear and grisly. Whatever was bearing down on them was huge and hidden. He could see not a single light.

Jimmy took the foghorn again and gave the four short blasts that meant he could not manoeuvre, yelling to the others as he did. At that moment the fog parted and he saw her. She was an immense black shadow, the angry jutting profile of a warship, forward guns silhouetted by lights so far above his head he would never have seen them in the murk. She was headed just to starboard, no more than thirty yards, plunging through at twenty knots or more, water curling silver at her foot, the air filled with oily, coal-sweet smoke and the pounding of her engines at full cry. Henry was now at the taffrail and Jimmy turned to grin with relief. Then he heard the skipper curse and saw him throw the tiller hard across, though they both knew it was hopeless against the pull of the trawl. Dead aft, bearing down on them out of the blackness, was another immense hulk, its sharply pointed steel bow towering high as their mizzen mast, slicing directly towards them at impossible speed, utterly unlit and silent. Henry yelled and pointed and Jimmy saw the huge wire cable, running bolt rigid forward from her prow. The thing was under tow, and would barely have a crew and a useless helm. *Maryann* came round a point towards her trawling gear and then lost all steerage, her canvas shaking as the lowering warship stole her wind. Jimmy felt the smack shudder to a stop as her trawl dug in, the rush of the oncoming bow now suddenly deafening. Two immense funnels steepled above, side by side in the sudden moonlight.

Then Henry's mouth opened and his inarticulate fury hit the confusion as *Maryann* lifted and rolled and the second ship hammered merciless through just feet to starboard. A massive hawser hole swung through at the height of the smack's topsail and empty lifeboat gantries rattled past far above, one after another, cables swinging, jolting, rattling, the hulk's two empty masts leaping far into the black. *Maryann*'s whole crew was now desperately hauling on the sheets to bring her booms inboard. The endless wall of riveted iron edged steadily closer as she thundered through, four hundred feet or more, on and on, throwing *Maryann* over on her beam ends, sea sluicing into her port scuppers. Jimmy could see that the old warship on tow was riding high out of the water, a rusting shell, superstructure gaping, canvas-covered barrels of guns pointing useless into the sky. Then with a furious white churning crash she was through and Jimmy looked up from the pitching deck and saw far above in the dim grey iron the name, *Empress of India*, a machine from another world, terrifying, pitiful, retreating, thrashing and dying. He too felt a shout bellowing up from his chest, though what he was shouting and why he had no idea, overwhelmed by the sense that the world was becoming too fast to encompass.

Then the *Empress* had gone into the black and *Maryann* was yawing uncertainly and turning, her warp slack amidships, her net inside out and catch gone. Jimmy suddenly found he was shaking with the shock of it and he saw Eb had Boy in his arms, head bowed, his face in the lad's hair.

Chapter 16

Jimmy left the Saturday fish market and rowed back to *Maryann* with Henry. They raised the foresail to dry and refurled the main and let Eb go up the hill with his son. Jimmy found himself work to do, lacing the new flappers that Horace had insisted on making inside the net. He had said it was cookie's work and long overdue, which none of them could contradict. Even so, at eleven-thirty, when they finally took the ship's boat back to the quay, Jimmy had still not made up his mind what to do about Kitty.

He could not shake off his disgust at the scene on the coper, Beaton sulphurous, sham, snide, shying at deals like a fish trader. He thought of going to Farley's and confronting Alice with the mess that was entangling itself around her. But even if she heard, it would not be an hour before she would begin to tear at him, ripping again at their intimacy, bludgeoning him with accusations. He knew he had himself passed from grief to anger. He let the thought fall. Instead, he found himself filling with a freshness of life and the possibility of belief. It had somehow begun in the encounter with the *Empress*. In the churning, choking black something exhausted had passed and something new had begun. The life he was now living was unexpected and unwritten, clear and light, still to be stirred.

Just before noon Jimmy came down the steps to the quayside, catching sight of Kitty, feeling from yards away the fear and innocence that were fighting for her expression. She had put on a straw bonnet he had never seen before and a woollen coat he had only seen her wear on the way to Mass. Bless her, she had turned out in her very best and it made

Jimmy smile because it was a long time since anyone had done so much for him. Her face lifted with apprehension and delight as she saw him and he saw the specks of salt on her cheek, wondering whether it was the sea or a tear.

'Well?'

'Well yourself.'

Kitty's voice was too loud, her body rigid as a lamppost and Jimmy understood she had no idea what to do.

'You've had dinner?'

She shook her head, unable to find the words. Jimmy tried again.

'Kitty, how's about dinner?'

'Yes, but where?'

'We'll take a risk.'

'Already?'

'Buy a *pie*.'

At last she was laughing and he offered his arm and she took it and they were walking unsteadily towards Shinner's Bakery, along Fore Street from the quay and Jimmy was saying whatever came into his head, waiting for Kitty to catch up.

'We could of course buy a pie from Old Aggie. Last one I bought from her had died long before. I fed it to the gulls.'

'I saw Old Aggie this morning. I expect she had been waiting for me.'

'She was on the step of her shop, smoking.'

'Do thee know everything as well, Jimmy?'

'And she said, Kitty Grant, marry that boy Blackbridge.'

'Yes, and I agreed. Actually she said you were a good lad and I was to keep 'ee out of mischief for a while. I said you weren't up to no mischief and I'd make sure 'ee didn't start.'

'I bain't up to no mischief when I'm with you, Kitty Grant.'

The bakery wrapped you in a glow so golden you wondered how you had lived without madeleines or pies turned over and crimped like a pasty and laughing, as Frank Shinner said, till their sides burst. They climbed up to eat on Rea Hill, looking down over the roofs to the grey blue of the harbour. Smacks were straggling in, tying up, jostling in rows along the chains and Jimmy told Kitty their names were a kind of poetry. *Valerian* and *Vigilance*, *Replete* and *Revive*, *Compeer*, *May Queen* and *Fern Leaf*, *Guess Again*, *Toreador*, *Lucetta*. Then there was *Sanspareil* with her new mainsail and Upham's sloop *Ibex*, which had won the Regatta every year until they refused to allow her to enter. He told Kitty about the *Empress of India* and she laughed that her pa waved the *Western Guardian* in his hand every Thursday and said the world was about to end.

'He laughs at the way the newspapermen write. *The muttering of unrest*. But he mutters a lot himself.'

'Best thing in a newspaper…'

'…is fish and chips.'

When they walked back into the town Jimmy kissed Kitty as he had seen people kiss aunts and grandmothers and watched the red discs in her cheeks as she blurted a goodbye and was hurrying away to her parents and the needlework she had taken home from the dressmaker's to finish before Monday. He walked home with her smile in his eyes, her tea and twine smell on his hands, telling himself that he had let her grow an inch, gently, quietly and that it had healed something to give himself to another's good for an hour. He had suggested they meet again in the same way the following weekend. That too would be good so long as it was uncomplicated. She had nodded and thanked him and accepted and you could see she could barely breathe.

The next Saturday Jimmy collected Kitty from the house where she worked in New Road and where Miss Wills had run a dressmaking business for twenty years. He had pictured Kitty in the week with the fondness you have for a child. He found Miss Wills's workroom suffused with softness, the sweet smell of the fabric and the deadness it gave to the air. Two girls were finishing up, Kitty's age, and they hid their faces and giggled together. A mannequin stood in the centre, a yellow and white dress half constructed and the two girls pointed out the feather stitching, graceful crossing, curving wreaths in beautiful even silk, dropping from the waist. And then he had to see the tuck shirring over the shoulders and they asked him what he thought of it all. And he guessed the game and told them it reminded him of Kitty, knowing all along that she must have done it. She finally came down from the upstairs room with Miss Wills, who tilted her head in acknowledgment and told Jimmy there was not a better needlewoman than Kitty Grant and that he was not to stop her working on Saturday afternoons because her parents depended on the income. Then Kitty was protesting and Jimmy heard in the laughter between them that this was a conversation they had often had in the last fortnight. And Jimmy was stopped short by finding that Kitty was not a child but a woman, capable and with burdens already to carry. And Miss Wills was now holding up a finger and commanding Jimmy to be as thoughtful as Kitty had assured them all he could be, and was being drowned by the squealing from the workbench.

Kitty had not yet been to the Electric Theatre and the following week Jimmy took her and felt her flutter as soon as the piano began and the pictures climbed into the frame and he remembered what it was like to discover for the first time the jerking, uncertain world. Even the abrupt and hectoring newsreels seemed novel again. *Gaumont Gazette* followed *Topical Budget* and Jimmy felt a bitter satisfaction in overlaying the remembered anxiety of watching with Alice. The bird man of Manhattan swooped and two men flattened themselves on the grass. Young men in whites shambled through a gate for a hockey match, eyeing the camera with disdain and uncertainty. Before you saw anything of the match, Lady Edwina Roberts was being married to a scowling man in a ferocious moustache. Other couples were sniggering and ignoring the screen but Kitty had not yet taken her eyes from it.

''Tis Earl Roberts' daughter. The man who won the Boer War. Except my pa says...'

'Mutter, mutter.'

Kitty laughed but did not look round. She was spellbound and Jimmy wondered if he was charmed or embarrassed. Since February they had been showing *What Happened to Mary?* with a new instalment every month. Jimmy whispered to Kitty what had happened in the first one, the only instalment he had seen with Alice. It had followed a poor young American orphan girl who left home rather than marry the man her foster father had chosen for her. Now the piano played its hackneyed, quavering chords and the images span into life once more, the projectionist putting in the colours for each scene. Jimmy looked again into the dark-rimmed eyes of Mary, wondering if he was the same person or someone he had only just met, and tried not to compare Kitty and Alice, the one delighted attention and laughing where you should and the other a cynical step ahead and watching only with acid eyes.

Mary reached New York. Jimmy had never seen anything like it. You glimpsed London in the newsreels, a choked, black, crawling mess of horses and umbrellas, always hurrying and still crushed to a stop. New York disappeared silver and giddy into the sky and the streets were crazy with trucks, its people absurdly confident. Jimmy began to wonder, as he used to long before, if it was time to throw in the fishing, with the gentle old smacks and the weekly struggle for a few shillings and try for a place on a liner. He imagined himself with Mary, searching for a place and a position and he wondered what colour her long dark hair really was and those immense eyes and how her voice might sound. He looked sideways at Kitty, her profile lit in the beam, pale, her chin perhaps too prominent to be pretty, and he wondered whether he would want to put his arm round her and whether, if he did, she would expect to be kissed. He also wondered if he would ever share with her what was inside him.

Kitty insisted Jimmy come back to the house.

Chapter 17

They found Kitty's pa at the doorway, looking out across the harbour. It really was one of the finest views in the place, next door to the Customs House. Kitty took her arm from Jimmy's and hurried on and kissed him. Jimmy found himself in their little parlour again, where he had slept in those first days. Kitty disappeared into the scullery with her ma and Jimmy felt awkward, thinking her pa was watching him through Kitty's eyes. It was a living room like any other, its fireplace with its dated, tasselled cloth and a clutter of brass and cheap cards; wire-scrubbed pans on the chipped Raeburn, a thin rug wearing threadbare, black-painted boards, deal table and unmatched chairs, the Catholic print, Jesus hand on chest, heart glistening like a star. Yet this room was different from the others. The paper and ceiling were brown from coal and cigarettes and its two armchairs wore thick, dark green, an aged velvet Kitty or her ma must have begged from the dressmaker's where they worked. One of the chairs was moulded and slumped, holed with cigarette burns, feet buried in a litter of newspapers, stacked in slithering heaps. This was an intimate cell and it was filled by Kitty's pa.

Jimmy had never had a conversation with William Grant. When he had been at the house before, Grant's bald head had been hidden behind a newspaper or slumped on his chest. He knew that the man had for years been too sick to work, but he had no idea how he had earned a living before. This time Grant had shaken Jimmy's hand, but it was not the firm grip that stayed with him, as the man sat back deep in his chair and waved Jimmy into the other. Nor was it the chest heaving with the effort to breathe, each lungful of air hauled as if it were against a rip, pushed out whistling and through gritted teeth. It was the eyes that were keen grey blue, watching with a quickness and a rogue intelligence Jimmy had not seen before.

'Good picture?'

Jimmy tried to remember the newsreels. Grant was a man who read newspapers.

'There was the Oxford and Cambridge hockey match and Lady Roberts getting married…'

Grant rolled his eyes.

'Do you mind the likes of them?'

'Kitty said Earl Roberts won the Boer War.'

'That's what Roberts says. 'Twas men like you and me who won it. Not that we *won* it at all.'

Jimmy saw the liveliness jumping in the man's eyes and felt himself picking up, like a smack when you put on more canvas.

'Then we saw *What happened to Mary?*.'

'And what happened to Mary?'

'We don't know yet. Eight more films to come.'

'Clever people the Americans.'

''Twas New York. It looked like a place you could make your way.'

'*Land of the free.*'

'You don't think so, Mr Grant?'

'Well, you get to vote. The rest of the time it's guns and corruption. What did Roosevelt say – "without force, fair dealing usually amounts to nothing"? But when there's a war the Americans'll do nothing except make money.'

'Let's not go to America, then.'

'It's no better here, Jimmy, except they're cleverer at keeping a secret.'

'Kitty said…'

Jimmy stopped and Mr Grant laughed and coughed, a hacking, spitting wrench that convulsed him. Jimmy liked him more and more, a mind that danced like a boxer. Grant's voice croaked through the phlegm.

'What did Kitty say?'

'She said you're always muttering.'

'I'll give her a thick ear. Every man needs a mutter. Don't you mutter?'

'As good a mutterer as the next man.'

'Let me guess…'

But Mrs Grant was breezing noisily back into the room and there were plates clattering over the old brown canvas cloth and Jimmy was helping Grant to his feet and steadying him as he swayed. He could see he had been a strong, athletic man before his lungs had given up. Now his face was crisscrossed with scarlet, his mouth under the trimmed moustache half open as his chest laboured. They sat and the three of them crossed themselves and recited their Latin and Jimmy felt suddenly like a boy caught in the neighbour's orchard. The preaching and the plainness of the chapel had instilled in him that Popery was shameful. Grant caught his eye, his laugh rumbling, congested.

'Don't mind us, Jimmy. We're not *killing* each other, like they do in Ireland.'

Kitty was pushing the plates in front of them all. Her face said that this was a game she had played a hundred times before.

'They're not *killing* each other either, Pa.'

'Not much, and not yet. Though if enough men like O'Connor get their way, it won't be long.'

'Yes, and I bought a large loaf from Symons's, a pint of milk, a pound of sugar, a quarter of tea and half a dozen eggs from Mr Youlden *and* a pound of good beef from Tully's.'

Mrs Grant's voice tinkled with laughter. She had not taken her eyes off her husband. Kitty was smiling broadly too, spooning steaming potatoes onto Jimmy's plate.

'And you still had change from half a crown?'

Grant was grinning, winking at Jimmy.

'Half a day's wages for a skilled man and that only after last year's strikes. Can't blame Asquith for trying to buy votes with welfare...'

But Kitty and her ma were already off once more, drowning him in their mocking, affectionate talk and he grinned again at Jimmy and cut his meal into neat packages before eating, stopping to lean back and heave more oxygen into his blood. Jimmy had the sensation of flying. The shrewdness of the smacksmen could be astonishing, but none had this man's presence, his intimidating, absorbing capacity to get to the next thought so long before you that your mind went speeding more quickly than you believed possible. Jimmy realised that Grant was the only man who had ever reminded him of his own father.

Long before the others had finished Grant was standing by the range, cigarette lit and coughing till his face was blood red. Jimmy remembered the cough from before, but now it had become a curdling, shocking bark and he longed for it to subside so he could hear the man talk some more.

'Sit with 'en, Jimmy, while we clear away. He'll be alright in a minute.'

Kitty and her ma shut the kitchen door and the man rocked in his chair, chest labouring, apparently half asleep. Then his eyes cracked open, startling once more.

'The Farleys.'

'What?'

''Tis what you mutter about, Jimmy. The Farleys.'

Jimmy guessed that Kitty had probably been chattering about him all week. He liked the man's directness but wondered what he was trying to find out. He shrugged, cautious, his mind again moving much quicker than usual.

'I used to spend my time with Roddy Farley, but no more. He's too important for the rest of us, now his father's building 'en a smack.'

'Any other lad in the town and I'd say good luck to him, show a decent working man's as good as anyone. But *Farley*.'

Jimmy recognised the momentary arch of the eyebrow. He was getting better at this game.

'What do thee know about the Farleys, Mr Grant?'

'Don't get 'en started.'

Mrs Grant was shouting from the scullery but it was obviously too late and equally obvious she knew it. Grant struggled forward in his chair.

'I was a policeman, Jimmy, the sergeant at the station by the town hall. We lived there when Kitty was born and I had four men. I also had the reputation as a bit of a detective. Thinking man.'

His wife's voice came again through the door, singing this time.

'*It started when I got on to O'Connor...*'

Grant's smile glittered but he was intent on his story.

'It started when I got on to O'Connor.'

'The landlord at the *Rising Sun*?'

'Morgan O'Connor, or Sean Morgan O'Ryan's his real name. He turned up ten, eleven years ago. Gossip was he was an aristocrat on the run, or a businessman who'd gone off with the takings. You've been in the *Rising Sun*. Cheap drinks and tobacco, anything from marbles to manslaughter if you know who to ask. You see him some occasions at Mass. Plays the sacristan, pious look on his face, sorting the things the priest needs, sounding the Mass bell. Out in the street he's all Irish nationalism and shooting the British out. None of it smelled right to me and I made it my business to be on the quay in the evenings. Of course, they saw the uniform and were good boys. So one Saturday I shut myself away after my shift and put on every stitch of black I could find.'

'You had a woollen hat of mine over your head.'

Kitty's ma was wiping her hands in the scullery doorway. She was enjoying the story now, her round face lit with the same sharp light as her husband's. Kitty was still busy behind her but Jimmy knew she was keeping as quiet as she could. He could hear Grant's breathing getting easier. Now there was no stopping. He was like a smack on a beam reach.

'Picture me, then, creeping out the back of the station, through the yard and up the alleys like I was spying for the Kaiser. There used to be a shed behind the *Rising Sun* and inside there was a stack of pallets and I climbed down from Higher Street and looked out where the boards had lifted. Closing time came and there was a crowd still in, round in the back room. I could have hauled O'Connor in for that. But I guessed there would be more. And then, strolling into the yard comes... well you can guess.'

'Farley.'

'Dressed up like a pox doctor's clerk. And Roddy is with him, couldn't have been more than twelve, carrying a box big as himself. A man comes out from the pub and money changes hands. My brain goes *click*.'

'What?'

'Tobacco.'

'Tobacco?'

'Not hard to work out. General shop, big box, light enough for a small boy, late at night, back of the pub, money.'

'Smuggling?'

Grant laughed.

'Well, there wasn't an eye patch in sight, nor a parrot. Trading without paying the legal duty.'

'You arrested Mr Farley?'

'I did not. Farley's a councillor. He could line up half the solicitors in town and they'd swear he'd been at dinner with them that night. I was on private property without a witness or a warrant and wearing my wife's hat. But it was the lead I needed.'

The man stopped as if suddenly uncertain whether to go on. He looked up at his wife, still leaning in the doorway and Jimmy saw the momentary flicker as he asked the question and she considered and gave her answer. She turned into the scullery.

'Kitty, can we trust your boyfriend?'

Now Kitty was in the doorway too, red jumping to her face.

'Jimmy? I didn't say he was my…'

Jimmy joined in the laughter and would have hugged Kitty in her confusion. He anyway had the sense that this was the story Grant had intended to tell him ever since he stepped into the house, maybe ever since he had set a time to meet Kitty. Grant had lived this episode a thousand times. He gave Kitty his best grin.

'Let's pretend. I'd like that.'

Grant's smile was a compliment. Now it was Jimmy who was coming up to speed.

'I didn't get very far with O'Connor. Night after night I watched 'em. There were more barrels and boxes and I watched 'em drinking at one o'clock, two o'clock. But I never saw O'Connor himself, nor anything taken into the pub. You could see O'Connor was a professional and you couldn't lay a finger on him. Anyway, he wasn't doing much more than any of the other petty racketeers who hang around the harbour. It was just a question of scale. I had too few men to police them all.'

Jimmy was struck by the guttering world that Grant was conjuring. He himself must have drunk past dozens of midnights at O'Connor's, under age, thick with Roddy Farley. How many times had Grant watched them?

'Anyway, 'twas Farley you were after?'

'It was obvious that Farley was the *fork*. He was the middle man, the one who passed the goods on. It looked to me as though he was new to the game, but you could see why O'Connor had chosen him. He was perfect for the part. Farley'd be the one who was caught but he had friends who would make sure nobody came to harm.'

'What happened in the end? Did thee ever arrest them?'

The man paused and both Kitty and her ma were quietly laughing as they came and sat in the parlour, Kitty in the darkest corner, her attention torn between Jimmy and her pa. Jimmy understood from their faces and the way they watched him that the story was going to get better and better.

'After a time this particular business must have got too big for the back of the pub. They left their goods in other places.'

Now Jimmy knew what was coming, or some of it.

'Like Old Aggie's?'

'Some of it went up to Old Aggie's, dumped in her stores at the back of the shop.'

'I'd bet she know'd all about it. Old Aggie knows everything.'

'Seems so. But there's not a copper in England insane enough to pull Old Aggie in. She was just as likely to blow the gaffe on me and tell O'Connor or Farley. I was much more interested in the likes of them and how they were getting their material in. It had to be one of the smacks. But in those days there were over two hundred and I needed a place to start. So I looked up my man at the Fishing Smack Insurance Society. It turned out Farley had held shares in one of the smacks but had sold them eighteen months before. 'Twas a grim old tub and Farley was over his head in debt.'

'Which is why he started the business with O'Connor?'

''Twas also a decent hunch Farley had in fact sold his boat to a friend of O'Connor's and together they were using the old girl to do their little bit of *smuggling*. So I set up to watch this particular smack coming and going. Rum crew she had.'

Something in the nod of Grant's head, the too long interval between the blinking of his eyes, told Jimmy he knew he had made the connection.

'*Deliverance.*'

'As well-named a boat, Jimmy, as you could wish for.'

'And the goods were in wooden boxes?'

'Sometimes. It was a professional job and they transhipped their *slock* before landing, pushing it out onto a little skiff.'

'Rowed out by Roddy Farley and a brainless lad who had no idea what he was doing.'

'Nor did Roddy. There was no need for Farley to tell his young sonny boy or his bright new friend.'

Jimmy could not help laughing out loud. It had taken Grant only a few seconds to flip his life over, spinning it like a sampler and pulling the loose threads behind. For a moment he pictured himself running out into the street, yelling that nothing was ever what it seemed, that respectable George Farley was a small-time crook and Jimmy Blackbridge was the idiot who had carried his stolen goods. It was a monstrous joke. Jimmy felt understood as never since he had been torn terrified from the schoolhouse. He wanted to hug Grant as his own father. He began to register the change in his world, as if he were standing in a different place, seeing himself from a different angle. He searched for words, some new footing from which to begin. All those years since he had sat in this room as a little boy, Grant had been watching, registering the alterations in his course, the way his luck and his life had shifted. He wondered for a wild moment whether Grant had even sent little Kitty to haul him in. But the girl was obviously in love and Grant's own affection for him self-evidently real. He floated back to the little parlour, to the man's eyes that were locked on his, watching his confusion. He saw that Kitty and her ma were waiting. Grant's face was now sallow, the coughing blood drained. Jimmy's voice came much quieter than he expected.

'What did 'ee do, Mr Grant?'

Grant leaned back a moment and smiled. Jimmy saw with relief that it was clear he did not blame him. His story was not meant to catch him.

'I made a mistake. I decided to go on alone. I reckoned if I made it official it would sooner or later get out, and then either Farley or O'Connor would head me off. One of them would call in his solicitor friends and the other would put me at the bottom of the harbour. So I would collect my evidence alone, and then blow the whistle. I also took a gamble. 'Twas going to be too difficult to nail O'Connor directly. But Farley was a weak link. If I could make some sort of case against him, enough to pull him in, I would have him across a table. And I calculated I could get enough out of him to put the rest of them away, maybe including O'Connor himself.'

'So you arrested Farley?'

'When I was sure I had it sewn up, I put my evidence in a file and marched it up to my superior officer, the inspector himself, and asked for the warrant. He was a Welshman. I stood in front of his desk like a schoolboy with a prize essay. So much empty leather on that desk, Jimmy. Not a paper in sight. What did the man do with his time?'

'What did he do with your evidence?'

'He looked down at the first paragraph. Read a few words. Then he closed the file. He told me I was a bloody fool and I should go home to my wife and little girl. I was a good policeman and he didn't want to lose me. He told me I was not to be concerned. He would make sure nobody ever got to hear about it.'

'But what did 'ee do then? What did you say?'

'I stood there panting like a dog. 'Twas the brainless ones who get to the top, the ones with no ideas and fewer principles. Empty desk, empty bloody mind. They are the ones with the friends who count, and some are outright crooks. I opened my mouth and started on a lecture. I expect I went on about my duty as an officer, about getting justice for the town, about the *respectable* men who shouldn't be permitted to conceal what they do and defraud the poor. In fact I can't tell you what I said because I 'low I've got no idea. I was too angry to do anything about my tongue.'

'And what did the inspector do?'

'He sat like Buddha until I stopped and then he flung me out of his office.'

'And... then?'

'And then had me declared unfit for service and booted out of the force. On grounds of ill health, you understand. He and his good friend George Farley, along with a lawyer and a few of their mates on the council. And a bent doctor they called in from Plymouth. The truth is, Jimmy, even if I'd had the whole constabulary on the case and assembled a roomful of evidence, it would have ended the same. If it had ever got to court, Farley's friends would have kicked the whole show out. And I would still have lost my job.'

Grant was gasping, leaning forward and now struggling to breathe, face bloated, scarlet. Kitty came and sat and put her arm round him and it was a long time before he could speak, and then, leaning forward, he was looking up at Jimmy and speaking in a whisper.

'So when Mr Farley unexpectedly has a brand new smack on the slip, an investment he can't afford and someone else must be paying for, and he's making his dimwit son its master, you can work the rest out for yourself.'

'*Deliverance* over again?'

Grant was coughing.

'Only this time it has to be a much bigger operation, not just a bit of 'bacca. Something that needs its own boat and a crew of loyal men. Or stupid boys. Or maybe lads he reckons he can bully into keeping quiet.'

'There's nothing anyone can do?'

But the punching, howling cough was back and becoming too much and he could see Grant would not have more than a minute or two more in him before he would not be able to speak. The room seemed to have grown colder and darker, the Raeburn fire a low tinkle and only faintly warm. For a moment the breathing evened to a laborious wheeze.

'Why have 'ee told me, Mr Grant?'

Grant swallowed and his face cleared a little and he was sitting forward again, croaking a few words at a time.

'Jimmy, you're honest, and intelligent and Kitty thinks the world of 'ee. So does Mrs Grant. But you've got yourself, without meaning to, into the middle, of something, that's too difficult to handle. If they've warned you, to stay clear, my advice, is to do, what they say.'

Jimmy was winded. Grant had been brilliant, in complete control. Then without warning he had gasped an unconditional surrender. *Do what they say.* In the silence that suddenly fell, Jimmy's first thought was that Farley had been able to cage even this wild and angry mind and, if that was true, then there was not a living soul who could escape him. He would have no choice but to give in to them too. His second was that Grant's sudden capitulation meant he knew more than he was telling. He wondered how long Grant had been trying to warn him, and asked himself again whether it had been a coincidence that Kitty had found him on the quayside the day he had finally left Alice. He wondered what Grant knew about Billie, about Boy Mutch and about Alice herself. Questions blocked his mind but Grant's hacking and retching was blowing into a rage and Kitty helped him into the back yard and he stood leaning, shaking against the wall, gasping, spitting, humming tunelessly to himself between the squalls. When the coughing subsided he returned to his chair and his wife offered him tea or whisky and he waved her away, shaking his head, unable to speak and closing his eyes. Within a minute he was asleep.

Then Kitty was at Jimmy's elbow and it was the moment to leave. She came out into the street and they walked together along into Prospect Road. It was just days since Jimmy had walked to the bottom of the steps with Alice but it already seemed long in the past. Suddenly Kitty locked her arms tightly round his waist, taking Jimmy completely by surprise, sensing her awkwardness, wondering if she was holding him so close because she was waiting to be kissed. But then he realised that what she wanted was to be able to speak to him without anyone else hearing.

'Jimmy, you see why my pa told you?'

Jimmy looked down and saw her face older, her grey eyes narrowed, shadowed by a nose that was a little long and gave her face its warm, characterful strength. Without thinking he kissed her on the forehead. The skin was slightly pitted, carrying the last imperfections of adolescence.

'If we see each other, Jimmy…'

'Of course we will…'

'If we go on seeing each other, it will make it worse. You were on *Deliverance*, you worked with Roddy, you've been with Alice, you've watched the likes of 'em build Farley's new smack. And now you know my pa's story.'

Jimmy understood there was more besides, the malevolence he had seen in Beaton's eyes at the chapel and on the coper, and what Boy had told him. Perhaps Kitty and her pa already knew about all of that too.

'Farley and O'Connor will think you now know everything, Jimmy. That you know what's going on.'

'And then?'

Kitty looked up at him, her pa's face, tinged with the first hint of impatience, as if he were the slow pupil. But he did not want to make the necessary connections.

'My pa hasn't worked since they threw him out of the police station. Nobody in this town will give him a position.'

Jimmy hesitated, remembering Beaton's plain blackmail and his own stupid swagger in return. Kitty waited a long moment, searching.

'If you go on with me, O'Connor will shut you up.'

A knot of lads came running by, pushing, tripping each other, and for a moment Jimmy wanted to join them, climb on up the hill, eight years old again, taking Kitty with him, back into some careless childhood he could not remember. Then the boys were gone and he was still holding Kitty, feeling more adult than he had ever felt. He found the choice had become clear. For too long he had allowed himself without knowing to be pushed. Beaton and his men had been trying to turn him or terrify him. But the truth was intoxicating. And Grant believed in him. And because of that Jimmy knew he would fight the bullying deeps and currents, open his eyes, strike out for the surface, gasp the air, pull for himself. He would not let them push him under.

'When shall I see thee, Kitty?'

She did not answer but the question filled her wide pupils.

'I'll come for 'ee *tomorrow*, Kitty. What time?'

'After dinner. Half-past two.'

Then Kitty was smiling her heaven and earth smile and Jimmy kissed her again on the cheek. This time he knew the salt was the taste of her tears.

Chapter 18

It was at last a decent July afternoon, blue clear light pooling the shadows, a cool breeze sharpening every detail with its moistness, lifting a little swell and blowing their hair and a skyful of softly detached clouds of pure white. The weather had been no more than decent as June had turned to July and everyone was uneasy, thinking it would give way, the heavy damp rolling in, returning them to the awfulness of the previous year. It seemed a lifetime since anyone had seen the sun. But today the town was wearing its summer colours, trippers in their cotton, white parasols wildly aloft as they swayed and staggered along the planks and jumped ashore from the Torbay steamers; the smacks sepia as a postcard, their forest of cutched ochre, stanchions and bulwarks picked out with palette primaries, lettering glittering gold at quarter and transom. They were riding their chains like schooling horses, rigging chattering, a few being prepared to go out later in the day, unlike the winter when crews found excuses to stay in until Tuesday morning.

Jimmy stood on the port bow and scanned the shore, past Upham's yard, where Farley's new smack was now standing clear and ready to launch. He was not looking at it. He was searching for the brown coat and the bonnet with the ribbon that might be blue or pink or yellow so that you tried to guess the mood she was in. Henry and Eb said it was easier to guess the fish or the wind or the price of the market than a girl's temper.

Over the weeks Jimmy had watched Kitty bubble with excitement, imagined her whispering to herself over and over that *she was walking out with Jimmy Blackbridge*, caught her eyes as they stole up to his face again and again. They seemed to him to have deepened, delicate and yet strong. He had taken her climbing up towards Fishcombe, along the low cliff above the quarries which looked out past the new breakwater and found a place on the grass and Jimmy had found himself explaining all over again about being an orphan. Kitty had said it surely meant he could go anywhere and not care. But it was not like that because if you went you never knew who would be there when you returned. So they talked about the bitterness, everything being stolen when you were too small to know. And how you sometimes clung on to what was only half-good for fear of losing it. And they said that one weekend they would take the bus and see the village Jimmy could hardly remember and try to get some of it back for him. Then Jimmy had kissed her again on the cheek and for a moment there was a feeling that they were becoming a couple and no longer an adult taking a young girl out for the air.

All the while there had been the sense they were being watched, the expectation that heavy boots would pursue them from the quay and Jimmy would find himself with the gutter mud in his mouth. But nothing happened. Nor would Grant talk any more. He dodged Jimmy's questions with feint and parry, constructing brilliant arguments over Ireland or the Pankhursts or the Balkans until Jimmy laughed and gave up. He had begun to believe, with Alice gone and the new smack almost ready and no more contact with Beaton than looking down on his pink baldness from the chapel gallery, that O'Connor and Farley had opted to get on with their business and to leave him to his. It appeared that Grant thought so also.

That July afternoon, *Maryann* had come in with four full trunks, not bad, although the prices were only middling.

Even after all these years Jimmy found the fish market a strange half world, grey light under the tin roof and the men standing arms crossed whose jobs you never discovered. For Jimmy it was a place of death, where what you did accused you. He had never met another smacksman who thought it. You lay your fish out in ghastly silver rows, stretching onto the square grey scrubbed stones outside, and waited for the auctioneer and his knot of buyers to shuffle down. You could guess the market from the number of smacks. Too many meant glut. You had ridden the seas to spill your catch and taken it struggling and gutted and washed and iced, as the hold heaved in the night swell. It was days of snatching sleep two hours at a time, and reaching the net over, hands blown up with wet and bleeding with cold and smarting from the salt until you could not feel the pain. Then it was gone in a rattle. The Dutch auction sank and you took only a couple of pounds home, half to spend on rent and the rest on food.

Today there was a modest number of boats stowing sails and gear but Jimmy knew the fish had been running and that the market would not be much. He found for once he did not care, the warm brightness and the confidence of the calm weeks filling him with optimism. He had been washing out the trunks as Henry sorted the shares at the office when she was suddenly there, arms tight and face buried in his stinking canvas. Yellow ribbon, for sun, for an outing, for good news or because she was sad and needed it? It was easier to whistle up the wind and call the fish. But in that moment Jimmy believed he could do anything.

'Miss Grant.'

'Mr Blackbridge. You smell.'

'Not me. 'Tis either the fish or 'tis you. Fortunately I have handy a bucket of water.'

And then they were running, Kitty screaming as Jimmy had never heard her and at last he had her cornered and threw the bucket at the kids who had collected and took her in his arms and kissed her, on the lips, properly and meaning to for the first time. He had not thought of doing it. Yet today in the sun everything was possible and Kitty was dancing, her grey eyes fixed on his, leading him along in his hobnailed sea boots. She seemed to have grown another inch and to be unable to walk, but was skipping and spinning and standing on tiptoe until Jimmy gave up trying to stay with her. For the first time he believed, as he knew Kitty always had, that they were going to be lovers.

'Jimmy.'

Jimmy turned and found himself facing George Farley. The shopkeeper was standing awkwardly by the end of the fish market, out of place as a schoolboy in his sister's bloomers. Jimmy guessed he had paid one of the harbour lads to tip him off when *Maryann* was in and her catch had sold. It was the first time in years the man had spoken to him, probably since he was cookie on *Deliverance* and he had half lifted Roddy home, drink-singing and no good to walk. He looked smaller and greyer than Jimmy remembered, a man no more than five feet four, his woollen jacket dust-brushed and several inches too big, like a relic from a richer, younger individual. His face had always seemed pointed and rat-like to Jimmy and more so now the thinning whiskers had become a ragged grey. With the light brown of his waistcoat he seemed colourless and insubstantial. Jimmy wondered if his childhood memory was playing false, or the man really had faded. He stood, holding Kitty's hand, feeling robust, able and defiant.

'Mr Farley. Do thee know Miss Grant?'

'Yes.'

Farley had not had the manners to acknowledge Kitty and Jimmy decided he did not need to waste his time on a man who did not how to behave. He turned to go. Farley at last seemed to remember what he had come to do.

'Jimmy. I'd be grateful for a word.'

Jimmy turned back, raised an eyebrow. The man was a toddler, sheepish, swallowing his words, simpering, confused, stuttering.

'If, of course, Miss Grant would be willing.'

'It would depend on the skipper, Mr Farley. We've a smack to sort, a living to earn.'

'I'll wait.'

Jimmy picked up the trunks and took Kitty back along the wet stones between the fish market and the harbour side, to the step where the gaggle of ships' boats jostled on their painters. Kitty was pulling on his arm, her face full of warning and Jimmy nodded that he had understood. Henry flashed a look that said he too knew the score and that they should take no nonsense. Jimmy took Kitty back to where Farley could see and kissed her formally on the cheek. Now her face was closed behind a greyness of fear and defiance.

'Be careful. Please be careful. You know you can't trust him, Jimmy.'

Kitty had whispered it but Jimmy answered with a laugh loud enough the man could not miss.

'I wouldn't trust the man with a kid's ha'penny.'

Jimmy ambled easily alongside Farley through the heavy midday, his boots sounding a satisfying ring on the granite. Farley stopped outside his shop, looking in at the window.

'The boys have been at my stock again.'

He pointed to a crack between two of the panes. A lad, Jimmy remembered, could push a wire through and fish out the sweets below. Farley was fingering the cracked glass.

'I'll need more toffee. Or do you suppose we should make the crack bigger?'

He looked up and smiled.

'We do what we can for them.'

Jimmy had the urge to seize him by his pretty buff waistcoat and his silk tie and his velvet lapels and demand what he knew about the poverty of the children in these streets and the uncertainty every week whether their fathers would return and whether they would eat and the respect they deserved.

'You approve of theft, Mr Farley?'

There was not the slightest tremor in Farley's smile.

'I used to invite the boys in to choose sweets but their mothers wouldn't let them accept. And it's more fun this way.'

Jimmy stepped back as if the man stank. He was tempted to ask if it was fun cheating the Customs or crushing the spirit from Alice Rogers, but instead turned to walk away. Farley put a hand on his shoulder and Jimmy found himself half pushed through the shop door. Alice looked up from the counter and Jimmy saw a book covered with her scrawly figures. Her mouth opened to speak but nothing came. Farley pulled out a pocket watch.

'Finish those on Monday, Alice. Everything else can wait. Go home to your father.'

Alice scraped the papers together haphazardly. Her hair was useless and dull, her skin ghostly in the pale light from the street, her hands flaking dry. Farley had turned her into a skivvy, broken, cold and blue with hurt.

'Thank 'ee, Mr Farley.'

Jimmy was still only just inside the door.

'How is your father, Alice?'

'Still hurting from Billie.'

Alice had still not caught his eye but Jimmy could tell she was prepared for the fight. He was appalled that the stench of Farley's hypocrisy and cant clung even to her. Farley was scanning the street from the window. Jimmy raised his voice.

'Ask Mr Farley why he jumped.'

The shuffling of the papers was the only reply. Alice pushed them into the large accounts book and lifted it off the counter. Farley still did not look round. Jimmy heard her collect a hat and the house door slam. Farley watched her from the window as she walked away.

'She's easily upset, Jimmy.'

'Look what you've done to her.'

Farley turned and Jimmy thought he had at last put a blade through the armour. But the man recovered in a moment. His hands went to his jacket pockets and the look of patronising kindliness faded a degree. He produced a pipe and filled it, pushing his tobacco, making a show of careful concentration as he spoke, acting the part.

'You're walking out with Kitty Grant?'

Jimmy did not answer. It was none of this man's business.

'Don't believe everything you're told, Jimmy.'

'Do thee, Mr Farley?'

Farley got his pipe alight and looked up.

'I expect Mr Grant has told you about our disagreement.'

Jimmy hunted for a reply, but calculated that anything he said would be either a lie or an admission. He took a breath and was assaulted with the velvet smoke and the sweet shop damp and the stifling scent of spices. He tried to imagine

William Grant standing in his place and to hear what he would say.

'What other things might you be expecting, Mr Farley?'

Farley was pulling at his pipe, the smoke filling his space, and then looking up.

'It was clever detective work. I had made a mess of things. Too many good causes and not enough cash in the bank. But it needn't have ended as it did. It could have been sorted out and no harm done. But Sergeant Grant didn't want it that way. Poor judgement on his part.'

'He was a policeman. There'd been a crime.'

Farley looked out into the street. Jimmy observed the performance from a great distance. It was less convincing than the heavy-eyed characters at the Electric Theatre, supported only by the close silence of the shop and coloured by the bitterness Alice had left.

'The police, the law, it's not the way we do things in a small town. A quiet word and matters can be sorted out and nobody hurt. We know how to behave.'

'Kicking a man in the head and leaving 'en to bleed in the street. That's how to behave is it, Mr Farley? And doing what 'ee do to Alice…'

'Kitty is a sweet girl. She doesn't need to come into this.'

Farley had swung round.

'I think you'd better explain what you mean, Mr Farley.'

Farley took his time to reply. Jimmy found himself back in the dark below deck aboard *Deliverance*, his flesh creeping raw sensitive, the skipper leering into his face, weak, drunken and duped, savouring the threat of the injustice he could command. Jimmy knew more than enough of Farley to think no better of him.

'Jimmy, I was only a small part of the business. There were others.'

'O' Connor.'

'Sergeant Grant did his investigation and was ready to bring the affair to a conclusion. But then, you see, he changed his mind. Quite suddenly the sergeant lost interest in the others and was only concerned with me.'

'Perhaps they know'd how to behave?'

'But, the thing is that the chief constable told me he was ready to make arrests, men he had been after for years. But Sergeant Grant decided not to testify against them.'

'I don't know naught about what Mr Grant did. Perhaps he needed thee to give evidence afore he could arrest the likes of them.'

The shopkeeper waved his pipe, a smile spreading through the smoke.

'Of course that's what he's told you, Jimmy. And I understand. To men like Mr Grant I'm not a shopkeeper, I'm a class enemy. I'm a Conservative, a Unionist, a Church of England man. The others in the case, you see, were more his type. Members of the new Labour Party, Catholics, Irish Nationalists. Don't you imagine they met and talked, after Mass. Or at a socialist meeting? They made him an offer, Jimmy. He was happy to sweep men like me aside, to make way for his new socialist Jerusalem. It's Miss Grant's father who should be in prison. You see, he took their money and then he destroyed his evidence.'

'Nobody ever charged Mr Grant.'

'I was able to sort it out. I didn't want anyone to come to harm.'

'You had 'en kicked out of the police force.'

Farley laughed.

'He had himself kicked out, Jimmy. Miss Grant's pious, socialist, Roman Catholic father did a deal with the men he accused and they've looked after him ever since.'

'Why would you sort it out, Mr Farley?'

'Work it out, damn you. I asked the chief constable to let Mr Grant go quietly.'

'While they dropped the charges against you. 'Cause thee's know how to behave.'

'I offered Grant a job, Jimmy. I would have looked after him. He's a sick man.'

There was a silence. Jimmy could not imagine any words sufficient to communicate with the creature who was standing in the light of the window, framed by a halo of his own smoke. Farley took a step towards him.

'Kitty Grant is a good girl. I wouldn't want her to suffer any more, not now, after all this time.'

Jimmy's only thought was how he could prevent himself taking up the heavy iron scales on the counter and smashing them into Farley's face. Once his instinct would have been to hide, to scramble into a woody corner and push himself into the shadowy grain. Now he held the man's eye, shaking with a new energy he understood had come from Kitty's father, his brain sky clear. To stand in the musty shop and bargain would be to give Farley what he wanted, to reveal what he knew, to give him *sea-room*. Why make way for him? Better to let the bastards blunder. They might choose to put him at the bottom of the harbour. But he would take the risk because, *fuck them*, it was the right thing to do. It was better than half-truth, limp-wrist, head-ducking, douse your sails and go quietly. Farley could dangle.

'I'll tell 'em 'ee says so, Mr Farley.'

Farley seemed for a moment nonplussed and caught Jimmy's arm as he strode to the shop door, his words spilling messily, a shred of tobacco dangling in his moustache.

'Jimmy. You got on well together, you and Roddy. Get your ticket, learn your trade. You'll have your own smack. Don't quarrel with me. You don't need to put Kitty Grant through this again.'

'I'll tell her exactly what you said. And anyone who asks, the moment you touch her.'

Jimmy pulled himself free and walked out into the heat-cracked air of the street and up towards Overgang. He was suddenly elated with his fury, shaking off the corruption of the shop. Everyone said the smacksmen were masters at sea but silent on land, their half-life in these streets saved for sleep and family. The town belonged to the soft-handed dealers like Farley, with their perfumed and superficial self-assurance. But Jimmy was not yet ready to let them take him while Kitty and her father stood beside him.

Before he reached the house he saw Kitty in the street besieged by children, screaming, hopping, beaming. Her smile wavered as she saw him but he held out his hand to take hers and her touch was midday sun.

Chapter 19

The following Saturday they launched Farley's smack. At midday Roddy came in to the fish market, stiff in new guernsey and jacket, and took hold of Jimmy's arm.

'I want thee to come to the launch, Jimmy. Bring Kitty.'

Jimmy decided he did not want to argue.

'What'll 'ee call her?'

'*Rosaleen.*'

The name struck Jimmy because he'd not heard it before. But you never knew where the names came from, *Us Dree* or *Addax*, or *Erycina* the Plymouth smack they reckoned would have outraced *Ibex* in the Regatta given the chance. At least they had not called her *Alice*. When he had told Kitty's pa what Farley had said in the shop the old sergeant had shaken his head until he was overtaken with the cough. When Jimmy tried again Grant only asked him if he believed Farley's story and of course he had said no and the man told him again that without Farley's evidence there was nothing to lay on O'Connor. Jimmy scoured Grant's face, the red lines scored under its skin. He was a man who sat you by his range, the room around him furnished with nothing but necessity, and answered your questions until he had no more breath. Farley was affectation and evasion and pushed you like a playing card. It was not difficult. As for Farley's threat against Kitty, Grant smiled as a man who understood more than he was willing to say out loud and told Jimmy that the shopkeeper knew better than to try.

Kitty put on her best yellow ribbon and they were at Upham's at two-thirty, half an hour before high tide. *Rosaleen* had been painted out in white from bulwark to bilge, her name in gold at her bow. She looked as fast a fine vessel as Upham's had built, a match for anything afloat in 1913. They would step her masts once she was launched but they had rigged short flagpoles at bow, stern and amidships and she flew the Union flag as well as the flags of the shipping insurance and of the yard. At her bows and on the truck of the pole amidships were the traditional bunches of flowers and green. A ladder ran up to her rail and everyone was taking a turn on her deck, including several of the women, the climb daunting enough even without a heavy skirt and broad hat. Jimmy helped Kitty up and they walked the length of the caulked pine, oddly bare under the daylight sky without masts or spars or rigging.

Alice was in the bows, arm in arm with another woman and they turned as Jimmy and Kitty walked up. It was Fanny Beaton. Except at her mother's funeral, Jimmy had never seen Alice spend a moment with her aunt before, but side by side they could almost have been sisters. Fanny had perhaps been born ten years after Alice's mother. There were the same curls, darker in Fanny's case, and the same fine jaw. Fanny was watching Alice, hand on her elbow as if she had been instructed to look after her. Alice looked frail, leaning on her aunt but Jimmy could tell she was going to make the effort to be polite. She nodded to Kitty and waved awkwardly along the rail and spoke without looking.

'Have 'ee been on a smack afore, Kitty?'

'No. Jimmy'll show me. She's beautiful.'

'There's no better yard than Upham's. They keep my father busy.'

'Where's Roddy?'

'With Mr Farley I imagine.'

Jimmy saw Alice was on the point of telling Kitty something more but Fanny was pulling at her elbow and they turned with a nod to walk back to the ladder. For a moment Alice looked back into Jimmy's eyes. The cold had gone from them, the mistrust which had bitten so painfully when he had seen her in Farley's shop. In its place was a confusion he took a moment to recognise. It was like the despair you imagined in a man drowning, the waters kissing his face and closing. She didn't speak, but mouthed a word.

'Don't.'

Then, almost at once, she was gone. Jimmy was numb, reeling. It had been just a word. But Alice had said *don't go away just yet*. And Jimmy had said as much in return.

Everyone was gathering and it was the moment to climb down and Jimmy was left dizzy with the sudden disorder in his mind he was unable to compass. He did not know what he should do but only that nothing could be done for the moment. Kitty took his arm and led him to the ladder and looked up into his face and he saw she too had understood. Jimmy counted thirty or more people on the slip around *Rosaleen*, the women edging awkwardly up the slope as the water lapped to the skeg at the foot of the stern post. Smacks were usually launched with a quiet solemnity and Jimmy could not remember so big a crowd. There were now two men aboard, Flush, his face without expression, and Roddy suspended laughably between confusion and pride. Kitty held out her hand and Jimmy took it, still feeling unreal, examining the tidy stitching on her cotton glove, wondering if she had made it. She looked up and nodded, smiling. She was the most generous girl whose heart ever beat.

The men from the yard took off their jackets and stood in their waistcoats, heavy mallets in hand, ready for the signal to knock away the last of the rough timber supports and send *Rosaleen* down on the cradle. Three men were sculling a punt thirty yards off to tow her to a berth for the stepping of her masts and the rigging. All that was left was for someone to break a bottle on her stem. Mr Farley stepped forward. Alice was at his side. It was a moment before anyone realised the man was speaking and even then much of whatever he said was lost. Jimmy heard a few words, 'Empire' and 'gathering storms' and stopped listening. Farley was a pointless smudge in the sharpness of the air, the salty brightness of the slip, the orderly beauty of the new smack, ready to be fitted and to go to work. Others were clearly thinking the same and the chat rose, the men guffawing and noisily dropping their mallets, not bothering to hide their disdain. Even the gulls seemed to send ugly jeers ricocheting around the warehouse walls. Farley began to clap and there was a limp fluttering around the crowd. Jimmy looked up and saw Roddy's face grim in embarrassment. His father's final words had announced that Roddy was to be the smack's master and every man there knew he could not possibly skipper her except in name. The shipwrights shouldered their mallets and moved on the scaffolding. They stopped when they realised that Farley was speaking again. One of them shouted *let's all play silly buggers* and aimed a swing at his mate. Farley waited for the laughter to die.

'Ladies and gentlemen, I have one other announcement to make, one which gives me great pride. You will want to join me in offering our congratulations and best wishes to my son Roderick as he announces his engagement to be married, to Miss Alice Rogers.'

Farley paused, perhaps for applause, but met only dull silence. Then he began again, about Alice, how he had known her since she was a child, how she had made herself indispensable in the business. Jimmy grasped none of it. He thought he heard a brief crackle of clapping and Alice breaking the glass and naming the smack in a voice that could barely be made out and the rumbling creak as the cradle at last slipped away. *Rosaleen* took to the water with a sigh and turned sickeningly as the current took her, a featureless hulk on the water, half born, without masts or sail. In the space where she had been these months was an emptiness Jimmy dimly imagined could not be filled.

Kitty took him home, the harbour gaping and the granite steps cold and blue in the shade. Jimmy heard her voice, talking about the launch and its strangeness. Dimly he was astonished she bore him no accusation but simply waited through his dumbness. He had the disconnected memory that he was beginning to love her as she obviously loved him but he was for the moment completely unable to own the emotion. She put him in one of the chairs by the range and brought tea, sweet as they had on the smacks, while her pa rumbled on about Farley in a way Jimmy knew he did not expect him to take in. Kitty disappeared into the scullery and Grant quietened and fell asleep.

Jimmy's mood gathered into cloud-black bitterness. Farley had blackmailed Alice with the dangled dream of her qualification. Today he had assembled a crowd, announced her engagement and wrecked her hopes of going to college in a single sentence. Yet Jimmy had seen Alice, her drowning *save me*. He found himself holding out his hand, calling out that he would not go away, even if there was apparently nothing he could possibly do.

Kitty sat at the table with her Saturday work but Jimmy stood and told her he needed the air. He did not want to face

Grant if he woke and the certainty that the man would read what was in his mind. Kitty put her arm through his and led him up onto the green above Battery Road where you could look out beyond the harbour and around Torbay and occasionally, on the clearest days, around Lyme Bay to Portland. He knew she sensed how much the wide space comforted him, even if the ground under his boots was dead and the sea far below. He pulled in the salt air, familiar and calming and told himself he was lucky to have a girl so imaginative, so selfless. Yet at this moment Kitty seemed barely real, an object floating in a current. He told himself to settle for his new course and be grateful.

By the time Kitty took him back to her house her parents had gone to Saturday evening Mass. She sat on Jimmy's knees but was far away. There was a long silence.

'Jimmy?'

'Yes?'

'Do you love me?'

'I think so, Kitty.'

She looked without accusation and seemed older than ever and he was grateful she had learned about being in love, that loving was not the same. Jimmy knew she had understood. At that moment, he had too much to decide.

Chapter 20

The next afternoon Kitty gave him room and he remembered that Alice would not have done as much. After supper he sat hopeless in the dull rhythm of the range, his mind blank as Mr Grant slept and his wife closed the scullery door. Then Kitty slipped in and asked Jimmy to take her out to *Maryann*. It took him a moment to catch the spark in her eye.

'Bad luck to have a girl on board, Kitty.'

'You don't believe any of that chawl?'

'No.'

'Then don't tell the others.'

Jimmy weighed up what it would mean. Of course he could not take a girl alone out to the smack, moored as she was almost out at the breakwater. Besides, every man in the harbour would see him. But he told himself it was no different from walking alone on the cliffs or in the deserted boatyard. And Kitty's instincts were right. He needed to undertake some risk, to bring his pulse back to life. Henry would probably say nothing if he were told. Most of all, if he was not going to play with this girl's feelings, he had better find the courage to take a decision, make at least some kind of commitment. Otherwise it was time to quit.

'Don't wear aught green.'

''Cause?'

''Cause 'tis bad luck.'

They clambered into *Maryann*'s boat where it was tied up a little around from the fish market steps. The quayside pubs were beginning to fill and Jimmy felt a dozen pairs of eyes watching them. He smiled at the risk. Now they would achieve something together. It took several minutes to row out and Kitty chattered brightly, asking after the smacks they passed, waving at the few men trying to look as if they were fixing their gear, more often refugees from empty lodgings or yelling children or sullen wives. Every smile, every word carried significance beyond the stillness of this dusk.

They climbed aboard *Maryann*'s gangway amidships on the starboard rail and Kitty made straight for the bow. Jimmy grinned to himself as he made the painter fast that a sailor would have headed for the tiller. But he was growing to love Kitty's girlish enthusiasm. He came up and leaned over her shoulder, hands around her waist, guiding her into the little space between the bowsprit and the port bow, Kitty looking over to the stem and Jimmy showing her the roller and where the trawl warp came when they shot. She insisted on turning the windlass and Jimmy held her hands on the handspikes and felt in his arms her laugh at how freely the heavy mechanism ran. And then she made him name every single one of the ropes, jib sheet and topsail halyard and topsail sheet on the fair leading post and jib halyard, and main halyard and topping lift and the peak halyards on the main rail and so all along the starboard bulwarks to the mizzen rail. And the way she sang back their names made poetry in a way Jimmy had never noticed before. And then she wanted to know all the cleats at heel of mainmast, the topsail sheet, tack and leader, the foresail halyards and the main truss and Jimmy had to explain the foresail traveller and its horse. When they reached the main sheet chock she would not let him say a word but imitated him explaining to a girl how it held the boom and then ran straight to the taff rail, to where the mizzen sheet belayed. Jimmy caught her up, delighted in her wide eyes and laugh, and held her close, his head over her shoulder and his face next to hers and closed his eyes and felt her warmth. But Kitty broke away and stood solid on the grating with the oak tiller in her hand and, without even looking in at the binnacle, reeled off all sixteen points of the compass from north to south.

'I learned 'em when I was a girl.'

'Kitty, why? 'Tis amazing.'

'I thought…'

'What? That one day you'd be lost at sea and you could find your way…'

'I thought if ever I found myself…'

'…in the middle of the Atlantic, looking for the way to America…'

'…on a smack…'

'…with icebergs all round…'

'…with Jimmy Blackbridge…'

'…with *Jimmy Blackbridge*?'

'I'd be able to say the compass and he might…'

'Might?'

'Might believe I think about 'en every day when he's at sea…'

Jimmy slipped his arm round her waist again as she held the tiller, looking up at him with her great grey eyes.

'…and that ever since I can remember I have prayed every night to the Virgin she will bring 'en safe home.'

Jimmy ran his hand through the mousy hair that pushed out under the bonnet and felt the stickiness of the salt and pulled her close to him, knowing that his heart was thumping through his canvas top and not knowing whether he should have brought her here away from everyone. They kissed until the breeze blew cold and Kitty shivered and was clambering forward again, now pointing to the trawl beam and the tow post and the fish hold. Jimmy laughed.

'You've done this afore.'

'They're all *easy*.'

Jimmy showed her where the ropes ran when they shot and hauled and pulled out the fish tackle and the relieving tackle and explained the ice and the coal and the fresh water. Then Kitty was pulling at the hoodway cover. Jimmy stopped her.

'Kitty, it'll be dark below. We don't want to burn the lamp.'

They both understood he was making the proper excuses. Kitty laughed and shook her head.

'And people'll talk and spread rumours and neither of us will ever work again.'

'No, Kitty, your parents will stop us seeing each other.'

'They adore you.'

Kitty tore his hands from the hasp and pushed back the sliding roof, opening the little doors. She turned to go down the narrow companion steps and Jimmy reached after her. Now he was certainly not pretending.

'Kitty. Don't.'

But Kitty had disappeared into the half dark and Jimmy heard a crash as she sent the billy cans flying in the galley. Now there was no alternative. His feet had barely touched the deck at the bottom of the companion before Kitty's arms were round him, her face looking for his in the half-light from the stairs. Jimmy pushed open the aft cabin door and together they got inside, Jimmy leaning on the table in the middle as the door shut. Quickly she pulled her bonnet off and he took her tight in his arms and kissed her, tasting again the salt on her lips but not caring because of their softness and their warmth and the quivering that was in them. Her breath was short on his cheek and he could feel her pushing against him, the softness of her breasts over the whalebone below and he knew his hands were shaking as they pressed into her back and as he held her head and pulled her against him and felt for where the ties were to her dress.

And in the silver from the skylight above, Jimmy's eyes opened and in a snap his mind was clear. He knew the decision that had to be made. Kitty had always given him everything she thought he wanted and would give herself to him now and want to. But taken now, it would shackle them both to a future without choices. He asked himself whether he would ever be able to ask enough of her. More than that, he wondered if he would ever be man enough to shelter her beautiful, deep goodness. He also realised that his memory of Alice still lay in the shadows of the cabin, the fear in her eyes and the pleading in her voice and the unfathomable conviction that despite everything that had been done, they were joined to each other. He could not pretend he was ready yet to give himself to the girl who was holding her breath in his arms.

His voice was as steady as he could make it, his pulse insisting, constricting his throat, wanting more than the world not to hurt this child.

'Kitty. I'm going to row thee home now.'

He felt her eyes screw tight against his cheek and but for her thumping chest she was still, the life draining from her and she hung against him, his hands holding her and stroking the hair on the back of her neck. Jimmy listened to the water caressing the counter as *Maryann* shifted a fraction in the breeze and thought her tiny sob when it came would suffocate him. There was another, and another, each a cry caught, breath-snatched, tear-wrapped, hopeless and hopeful, alone and lost and shared. Then she dropped her head and was gone, feeling her way to the door and through it, a shadow in the dimness, not looking back. Jimmy stood just for a moment, then went and put the galley back as it should be and climbed up the companion. Kitty was leaning on the mizzen mast, her face in her hands, shoulders tight.

'Kitty, 'tis not...'

'Jimmy, I'm so sorry.'

She looked up. There was a smile under her tears.

'You're older than me, Jimmy. You've done more and thought more. And you're right, you're always right. You are the best man there could be. You could have... and I love you so much...'

Kitty sobbed again as she put herself in Jimmy's arms and he was astonished that, even this, she could love. Then he thought once more that perhaps they might yet grow in each other and meet the world and its hurts together and that that would at last be enough. He rowed her home and she dipped her hands in the harbour water and washed her face and there was no more than a redness around her eyes when they had climbed back to Overgang. Her complete lack of bitterness took his breath and he wanted all over again to love her completely.

Her pa was hunched over a pail in the scullery, tremors wrenching through his back, singing his tuneless tune as he dragged each breath and struggled against the next. His hands were clutching the wood of the outside door frame, blue and dry and wrinkled as Jimmy had ever seen a man. Kitty and her ma went on as if it was normal and Jimmy understood that was important. Kitty finally reached a bottle from the top of the cupboard by the range and took her pa a tumbler of brandy and the coughing ebbed away. Jimmy helped the man back to his chair and then kissed Kitty and said goodnight. Neither of her parents had asked what had happened between them but Jimmy had seen that they had looked into their eyes, his and their daughter's, and had assured themselves that nothing had been done that would hurt and he thanked God for good people.

When he returned to the port the following Saturday Kitty was standing on the quay and her embrace was as soft as it had ever been and her voice had no trace of misgiving. They had moored Farley's *Rosaleen* far out, inconveniently beyond the middle quay. Even so, they had already floated her masts and hoisted them aboard, dried them, tarred their heels and stepped them. By the end of the following week they had set up rigging and tackle for sails and trawl and *Rosaleen* was nearly ready to clear port and stretch her canvas. The smacksmen all agreed Upham's had broken every record to get her fitted and that she was a beautiful boat. You could also see they meant it but did not feel it. The joke between them was that Farley had pushed and probably skimped, not to get her earning her keep but to cut a figure against the other Brixham smacks in the August Regatta. It would be typical of the man, smart paint to the bilge, rot below the water.

Chapter 21

Nobody could explain what happened to Henry Buckley in August. For fifty-one-and-a-half weeks of the year the skipper was silent and unalterably just. For four days he was taken by a spirit so competitive it transformed him into a bear, unreasonable, brutal and dangerous. He was not completely without humour, just completely without humour when it concerned the Regatta.

For those four days nothing was too good for *Maryann* and nothing good enough. There were always three or four dozen smacks in the August Regatta. In 1913 there were forty-nine. The fishing had been good and crews were willing to take a few days away from the trawling. They raced supposedly in working tack but skippers who were minded about winning unscrewed and jettisoned everything they could get away with and hauled up towering topmasts and long jibs to carry the greatest press of canvas they dare. They begged sails from smacks that had not been entered and recruited a crew of twelve not counting the cookie. The Regatta committee set out a forty-mile chase to test every point of sailing and marked it by boats riding to their anchors. If your gear was right and crew in order you completed in something over three hours, fighting your way through a fleet that had been known to finish no more than three minutes from first to last.

For years they had all trailed in behind *Ibex*, the beautiful 76-footer built at Upham's in 1896 and so fine in her lines Upham's kept her for themselves. One year she outpaced the entire field by fifteen minutes. Eventually, under her skipper Jack Widger, she had flown so many winning flags between taffrail and topmast head that the committee had persuaded her owners not to enter. In 1913 she was back, her mizzen mast shifted two feet forward, her main boom cut and a cloth taken from her mainsail. You could get quayside odds either way on what old Widger could yet coax out of her.

They brought *Maryann* in on the Wednesday morning and knew they would scarcely touch shore until the Saturday race was over. For once Henry brought his smack up into the inner harbour, propping her over the mud on her precarious legs so that they could scrape the year's rubbish from her hull. It was Jimmy's task and one he detested, balancing above the stink on a plank or standing in the ship's boat, arms over his head for hours at a stretch. Eb was aloft yards above, singing and yelling like a young one, greasing travellers and tumblers, relacing blocks, replacing halyards and sheets where they were running rough. Every year at this time old Horace came aboard and quietly emptied the contents of cabin, galley, hold, tanks and lockers, his eyes sparkling to be back in harness, joking every year they should nail the tea kettle down before Henry threw it overboard. Dusk gathered with the high tide on Wednesday and the skipper halted everyone and yelled them in to heave the spare anchor into the hold and shift the rest of *Maryann*'s iron ballast so they could raise as much sail as they dare.

For years Pentecost Rogers had come down after finishing at the yard, running a shipwright's hand over all the gear that twelve months at sea had worn and grooved and loosened. Jimmy supposed they would not see him this time, but he appeared on the quayside very early on Thursday, drawn but glowing with determination. He told Jimmy that *Ibex* was still the finest ketch in the Channel and they would not be able to hunt her down. But he would do anything under heaven to see them head *Rosaleen*. Farley's smack had been built as a racer and in the demands of a thrash around Lyme Bay for the Regatta cup, old *Maryann* would have to be at her best to catch her.

Henry spent Thursday collecting on promises. Outside Beaton, O'Connor and the *Rising Sun* he had not an enemy in port. They took a mainsail from *Valerian* along with all three of her men. There was a huge tow foresail from *Referee*, together with her 34-foot topmast, which Eb and Pentecost spent three precarious hours in Thursday's failing evening light hauling and fitting up. It was dark when it was done but there was still a long discussion under the white of the naptha on the state of *Maryann*'s new mizzen sail, still only a month old and the canvas not fully stretched. On Friday morning they laboriously replaced it with an older mizzen from *Valerian*, took *Maryann* out of the harbour and were back in an hour bending and rehoisting the new sail again, Henry shaking his beard as if it were all a plot and the old girl had known it all along.

They spent most of Friday running *Maryann* hither and yon outside the breakwater, Eb rolling his eyes as they cracked on in a force five that was gusting closer to six, spars bent and strained like Henry's temper. He spent the morning at the tiller locked in calculation with old Robert Grey, the little Kentishman who had been his skipper back in the early nineties when he was an apprentice. Grey was now nearly seventy, shorter every time you saw him, wiry as a whippet, light as a bird. There was not a shrewder tactician between Ramsgate and Falmouth. His good eye was bleary blue and the other looked over your shoulder. They said he used it to see the future, the skies, the weather and the stars.

Only nine of the eventual crew of twelve were yet in port and Henry roared that the canvas was too slow up and down and if they were going to tack like *Titanic* they might so well scuttle her. The storm came when they broke out the balloon jib and then the spinnaker, sails they very rarely used in the fishing, fighting the immense flying canvas as *Maryann* bucked and gybed downwind. She was unrecognisable, out of order and Jimmy could see in the men's faces the fear that they had let her down. Henry towered in wordless rage as they came about and pulled the canvas soaking from the sea, hauling in the staysail a crumpled pile for the long tack upwind and the hasty re-rig as they went. It took them three runs and four hours to get a performance that had the skipper less than spitting but it was the same every year. Every man knew they had in the end got the job done, and that next day Henry would be icy as a fishmonger's parlour.

By darkness on Friday they were moored out near the breakwater. The last of the other crews had drifted by to put in their token hours with the outsized sails they rarely used at work. Eb had persuaded Henry up the hill for a few hours' kip and called them all for four the next morning. They would spend the early hours at sea with a full crew before the race at ten. Jimmy volunteered to stay aboard overnight. It was more to make Henry go home than because there was anything that could go wrong.

Jimmy sat with Kitty for an hour on the breakwater while Eb took the forward winch apart and fixed it. It was a job that needed doing, but one which Henry had outlawed because it had nothing to do with the Regatta. They watched the dying sun in its ochre haze on the hills in the west and listened to the comfortable evening sounds that ghosted over the water air. At nine-thirty Jimmy rowed Kitty back and walked her up to Overgang. She promised to be down at four-thirty to see them off. Finally Jimmy rowed Eb in and returned alone.

He saddled himself on the long bowsprit, hauled in on its wooden roller. He was keenly alert to the rippling quiet and the moonlight that leached the colours like death. He understood why he had volunteered to stay aboard. It was a catch between breaths, a glimpse of his life from another viewpoint, neither at sea nor on land and in a time that had no past or future. *Maryann* was prepped, polished and primed. She was an open, pure space.

Jimmy could hear Old Aggie as clearly as if she were now leaning on the rail by the topsail halyard. *A spring marrying*. Aggie's was an uncanny magic, plucking the pain you harboured inside and making you listen to its ring. But Jimmy was truly more and more fond of Kitty, her devotion a salve to his wounded belief. Her company was keener the longer they were together, and she was more beautiful the brighter she glowed. Even her voice had dropped a fraction of a tone. She smiled, grateful, truly excited, whatever happened, when he took her in the gusting, unfeeling rain up to the ruins of the fort on Berry Head or to the rugby or when they sat for hours with her pa and listened to his half-joking, half-serious anger at the way things were. Kitty was spirited, opinionated and driven by a practical, human piety. But she accommodated him, always finding a way to put him in the right. His hours with her lacked edges and he found it disorienting, compelling him to decide, when he would rather debate. It stirred a memory of the compass-less drift when his father died, when he had no-one to chart his existence. Inwardly he felt becalmed.

In the darkness he could vividly see Alice at the launch, reaching up in her anguish from the waters. Alice was fine-boned, fingers spidery and oddly crooked. She was a rocky, reef-ridden coast, deadly shifting and deceiving, intolerably difficult to sound. Her anger and her complete unreason had always left him bruised and bleeding. Roddy would not be able to withstand the acid of her perverse intelligence, the winning sweetness to others when she chose, and the damning blindness towards those she said she loved. It would become another pitiless marriage like those of both of their parents. But Jimmy told himself for the hundredth time that it was now beyond him. He watched the lights vanish from the last of the smacks and from the windows around the harbour and wondered if he was becoming one of those wounded men who had loved once and lost and grew old alone. If you learned nothing else from the unrelenting tyranny of trawl and time and tide it was that you accepted what was in your hands now and did not suppose that tomorrow would make your fortune.

Then he heard Alice's voice. He imagined it must be in his head but when it came again it was sounding through the dark from the direction of the breakwater. It was unmistakably her and it was shaking with fear. Jimmy ran aft and dropped over the gangway into *Maryann*'s boat. He began to thread through the press of smacks, sculling silently with a single oar. He passed almost under *Rosaleen*'s counter and dimly saw Flush Beaton disappear below and heard a faint hammering from her cabin. Then Alice's voice came again, cut short by Roddy, shouting drunk.

Jimmy sculled towards the sound, calculating how close he dare risk the broken rocks at the foot of the black sea wall. Twenty yards out he detached three silhouettes from the last of the eastern glow, Roddy gripping Alice by the wrist and pulling her back towards the land and Boy Mutch running ahead. Jimmy let his boat drift, on the point of yelling, trying to guess if it would confuse Roddy and give him time enough to scull in and carry Alice away. But as he watched she broke free and ran, lifting her skirts, brushing past Boy and away towards the land. Roddy began to run after her but stopped, bent winded, waving Boy away. The words between them were too low to hear but finally Roddy straightened and the two of them headed slowly and unsteadily after her. Whatever had happened was over. There was nothing Jimmy could do.

Jimmy turned his boat and sculled back towards *Maryann* with cold on his face. He ducked his head and shuddered, not from the night breeze but because he had watched Alice flickering, black and white, from a distance, as if she were already dead or lost in a world far away. Once more without warning he had the image of slipping over the low rail of the boat and into the shadow, a silent death that was welcome and unwitnessed. But as the blackness began to close he forced himself to breathe, a long, shuddering haul, and found his life returning and his anger. He closed his eyes and took another breath and then sat on the thwart and felt for the other oar and pushed them both firmly into their notches and pulled strongly for *Maryann*, careless of the noise he made. He would heave through the greedy water for all that was good, for Henry and his crew and for Kitty and their love and for her ma and her homely piety and her pa and his holy anger. And yes he would pull also for Alice and he prayed God deliver them all from evil.

Chapter 22

He was woken without warning by Eb stoking the boiler fire. From the light that had already begun to drift from the skylight he could see the cabin clock at half past three and guessed the mate had rowed across in one of the ships' boats they had borrowed for the day and would be going back for the first five or six other men once the steam pressure was climbing.

By four-fifteen they were all together except old Robert Grey. Five o'clock came and Henry would wait no longer, his deep regard for the man the only thing that kept him from losing his race morning calm. Kitty had come out on one of the skiffs, hunched against the morning, kissing all the crew and beaming. She had of course not come aboard and they sent her off to look for Grey with the old smacksman who had rowed her out. *Maryann* slipped her chain and they worked her out on a light, swirling sou'westerly, fair token of a decent blow to come, with clouds aloft, towering immense like witnesses. It was a magnificent crew, hardly a word spoken as they sweated and swagged and sheeted their canvas home, tight as you dared before the race itself. *Maryann* rounded the breakwater and leaped in weightless lines as deft and trim and balanced a vessel as sailed.

At nine they came back in, jubilant at the old girl's performance, confident at least that Henry would not think his crew anything less than matched and uncompromising. They brought her through the crowd of smacks now preparing to go out and tied up at the middle quay and found Kitty waiting in her work clothes, fetched by the lads and their barrows. Grey was not at his lodgings. Kitty had been told he had gone down the previous evening to the *Blue Anchor* on Fore Street as he usually did. The landlord, ungrateful to be woken at seven, told her that Grey had left early, telling the whole place that Henry Buckley would come out the winner and that he'd be there to do it with him. After that nobody knew a thing. Henry gripped the rail, torn by uncertainty as Jimmy had never seen him. Grey's weight was negligible on the ropes, his tactical nous these days only an echo for Henry himself. They had already worked the smack four joyously heavy hours without him and hit every mark. But Grey was the talisman and without him the crew was incomplete, more than simply a fraction below the fullness of its force.

A crowd was beginning to gather around Kitty on the quay.

'Time to be a big boy, Henry. Set your own course.'

It was Beaton and he was standing by Kitty, his arm now around her waist. Henry's voice was its quietest, most crushing.

'You can shut Grey up or worse. I don't want to know. You casn't outrace me.'

'I'll join 'ee if you're a man short.'

Beaton was almost grinning. Jimmy wondered if he was drunk. He should have been a mile clear of the breakwater by now, *Rosaleen* in full sail and crew. The skipper came and stood by Jimmy and Eb.

'I'd rather take Miss Grant.'

Jimmy could hear the angry breath whistling through Henry's beard and saw the cold defiance. The rest of the crew were occupying themselves, silent eyes fixed on their great sea swollen hands. Eb was scanning the men edging the quay, murmuring under his breath.

'Choose one of the lads, Skip. Thee casn't wait no longer. Any man of the likes o' they'd be proud to do it.'

Some of the young men began to edge forward, pulling themselves up, one or two rolling their sleeves, pulling caps down. Their readiness to go was the clearest measure of Henry's reputation.

'A volunteer for Mr Buckley's smack?'

Kitty had pulled herself away from Beaton, straightening up, looking along the line as if she was responsible for recruiting Grey's replacement. Her voice had come clear and confident, hard stone as her face. Henry looked up and down the quay as hands and caps rose slowly into the air. There was a moment of stillness before he called, and his voice was velvet and steel.

'Hop down, Kitty. If Beaton's got his hands on Grey, I'll bloody smash 'en *and do it with a girl on board.*'

Kitty was looking down from the quayside as if she was really going to jump and Jimmy laughed and blew her a kiss because her innocence still charmed him and he shouted to her under the cheering that of course Henry had only said it out of anger and she couldn't possible come. But Kitty was not listening. She was gathering up her skirts and the men were holding her, ready to hand her down and Beaton was gone. Jimmy realised Henry was grinning in command again, striding aft, bellowing to Eb, and the deck was alive. Before he could catch his breath Jimmy was holding Kitty as she jumped and then she was disappearing with old Horace down the companion, looking back with a laugh, hearing the shouts and cheers from the quay and the crew. The news was spreading around the harbour even as *Maryann* leaped into action, her cables loose and sails rattling on their hoops, bow swinging through the wind and the low harbour waves already beating at her foot. All Jimmy could do was bellow in disbelief with the rest of them. *With a bloody girl on board.*

They were a quarter of a mile past the breakwater when Kitty reappeared, long thick trousers turned and crumpled over her bare feet, a guernsey Jimmy recognised as his own rolled up at the sleeves under an oily that reached to her knees. Her hair was tied up under one of Horace's blue serge caps and she looked magnificent. Jimmy would have hugged her right there had she not pushed him in the chest and disappeared forward, Eb shouting her orders as she went, picking out the topsail sheet at the heel of the mainmast and telling her to hold on to the rope if she valued her honour and to heave till she burst when he shouted. *Aye aye* came the reply and it was, incredibly, ludicrously, going to be alright. She was standing in the safest place and when the topsail needed sheeting there would be hands enough to do it. But already there was not a man who was not pulling twice his weight out of sheer devilment. Henry had found his talisman.

By ten to ten they were circling three quarters of a mile off the breakwater, *Maryann* jostling with the four dozen other smacks, the laggards at last coming clear of the breakwater, many of the crews in the red Regatta caps Henry would not tolerate. A decent sou'westerly was catching *Maryann*'s canvas in rough blasts as the other boats closed and began to steal her wind. Kitty had finally been talked away from her sheet and sent below to discover the galley, reappearing over and over with tea for each of the men and being kissed over and over until the skip yelled her back to her station. Now she was at the mainmast again, gripping the topsail sheet in its cleat as if the whole trim of the smack depended on it.

The short first leg ran two miles north-west from Brixham to a marker lying off Paignton. But what mattered above all was to cross the starting line in full cry at the moment the Volunteers in their uniforms fired the gun from Battery Green above the quarries. It called for supreme seamanship. Approach the line a moment too soon and you had to strike your canvas and lose way. Worse, if you overshot, you were obliged under the rules to turn and start again, a quarter mile or more adrift of the field. They brought *Maryann* round and tacked south, away from the line, Henry with the shining chronometer they had presented to him years before and calculating his moment to turn. *Maryann* heeled over, scuppers almost awash as they went through the wind onto the port tack. Jimmy watched Kitty as the deck tilted, saw the fear in her face and heard every man in sight shouting her encouragement until Horace came over and put his arm round her waist and held her tight. He was six inches shorter and grinning like a lunatic. One by one the other smacks began to turn and head back for the line but every man aboard knew Henry would hold out as long as possible so they would be under full canvas and flying when the gun went. By the time they came about onto the starboard tack again there were only three smacks left, *Maryann*, *Rosaleen* and *Ibex*, and they all saw what they had known all along, that this was where the real race was.

Maryann turned before the others. From his station at the jib sheets Jimmy could see forty-six boats, jammed tight half a mile forward, barely moving, one or two already setting off in large circles because they had jumped the gun. *Maryann* was leaping to the wind, Henry finding the fast water that ran north at this time of the tide if you knew exactly where. Looking back Jimmy could see *Ibex* turning and her crew hauling up her jibs so she would be on to them quickly. Only *Rosaleen* was still tacking south in a show of bravado. Jimmy suddenly found himself taking the strain on the jib sheets, and realised he had heard Henry yell and that the gorgeous red-brown sail was cracking into life over *Maryann*'s bow, the deck surging forward beneath his feet. And then they were sheeting the sail home and Kitty had run forward and was pulling alongside him. Now the marker boat came rushing on and Jimmy found himself yelling for everything to stop, until there came the thud of the gun that told them yet again Henry had hit the line almost dead on. Jimmy looked back to Kitty to see if she had understood and saw Eb smack her bottom and get kissed in return.

Then the light went from the deck and *Maryann* faltered and *Rosaleen* came careering through, every inch of canvas straining, stealing their wind and no more than five yards off their port bow. Everyone aboard knew the rules, that windward should give way to leeward and that Beaton had given no room and forced Henry to throw the helm over but there was nothing you could do until the race was over and by then it would be too late. They also understood that Beaton was going to pull any trick to win.

They ran the first reach with the wind inshore uncertain and turned at the first marker, still a dense, bucking fleet, voices shouting across from smack to smack, *Ibex* and *Rosaleen* and *Maryann* barely yards ahead of the others. Now Henry could bring *Maryann* almost dead before the wind, skimming, humming, every inch of canvas aloft and spars bent, the red canvas balloon of the great spinnaker exploding around Jimmy as they let it fly. By the time they rounded the marker boat off the Oar the field was strung out and most of them two hundred yards behind. *Rosaleen* was fifty ahead, *Ibex* dogging her wake, the two smaller smacks flying over an easy sea with their racing lines, *Rosaleen* breaking the rules over and over and crossing each time *Ibex* had an overlap. But Henry was grinning because the duel between them was wasting their advantage and old *Maryann* was still in touch.

Jimmy shouted to Kitty that the next leg would be a good one, *Maryann*'s bluff lines better against the swell than the two smaller smacks. Now they would see who had set their ballast and could carry the most canvas as the wind gusted and freshened. *Rosaleen* was heeled over and making heavy weather, struggling to regain her balance and a racing line and *Maryann*'s crew was silent, standing by as they drew closer, watching the new smack falter, canvas fluttering as her crew decided at last to change their sail plan. *Ibex* came across, establishing an overlap, Widger yelling and giving *Rosaleen* room to clear and *Rosaleen* breaking the rules yet again, changing her course into *Ibex*'s path. The two of them drifted away and left clear water and a clean wind for *Maryann*, gaining every yard.

They rounded the marker off Exmouth almost abreast, within yards of each other, the water fuming and the crews aboard *Ibex* and *Maryann* yelling at *Rosaleen* in between to keep clear. Jimmy saw Beaton at the tiller, looking ahead as if he could not bring himself to take the scorn of the men on either side. Roddy was standing by the binnacle, head stooped like a man naked, every working body on the decks eyeing him for the hollow sham of a skipper he was, every man on *Maryann* shouting encouragement to Kitty so that the crew of *Rosaleen* would see her. Now all three smacks would be tacking over and over on the long, arduous upwind leg and it would be a miracle if they did not collide. But by the seventh tack *Ibex* was fifty yards ahead or more and *Maryann* was behind *Rosaleen*, Beaton abandoning the tiller to Roddy and thundering at his crew to haul the sheets across at each turn so they did not lose way.

From his position in the foresail sheets Jimmy watched Kitty back at the cleat at the foot of the mainmast. She screamed every time they came about and Eb yelled her name and she let the topsail sheet loose. And then *Maryann* came round and old Horace ducked under the boom and made it fast for her. Jimmy was entranced. Not because it was a good joke, but because Kitty was more alive than he had ever seen a girl. Her hair was flying in salt-heavy clumps, her eyes unblinking and her face glowing with the wind and sun and exhilaration. She was seeing everything, Henry towering at the tiller, Eb a roaring giant amidships, every man gauging the other smacks, *feeling* wind and current and the moment when Henry would call his ready about and lee-ho. Then they threw themselves into the routine and *Maryann* kicked on like a thoroughbred. Kitty had watched this mastery of sea and vessel, the pride of men who were gentle and honest, finding joy in their skill and the technicalities brought to bear in beauty and speed and community. It was what gave men grace and silence and assurance, qualities that words would not equal. It was an experience you lived or could never imagine.

They came about for the last time and were off Brixham itself, only the last marker boat and the shorter shoreward leg remaining. Jimmy found Kitty was alongside him, her fine white hands grabbing for the ropes with the rest and her face lost in shrieking concentration as she lifted herself off the deck and put her weight into the haul. They came up towards the final marker and *Ibex* was a hundred yards clear and *Rosaleen* ahead but taking the corner wide, being forced to put in a short last leg, almost losing way as she finally went about.

Suddenly Henry was yelling for them to let loose the sails. They were at the marker, the end of the tack. Jimmy shouted to Kitty over the spray that Henry was mad. Only keep their canvas tight and they would be ahead. But it was obvious Kitty understood not a word and was doing what she was told and Jimmy's stomach dropped as *Maryann* slowed sickeningly towards the marker and the turn. Ahead *Rosaleen* was picking up speed and heading back in on a course that would carry her clear. At the last moment Jimmy saw Henry's plan and pointed and could not believe it. Kitty looked, with every other eye on deck. Henry threw the tiller. *Maryann* was moving so agonisingly slowly and they came round by the marker boat so tight they could have shaken hands with her yelling crew. Then in an instant *Maryann* was jumping, ropes taut, leaping before the wind. Henry had put his smack round so sharply she had made up yards on *Rosaleen* and was now running alongside, half her length ahead. There were twenty yards of sea between them and Jimmy saw Henry hand the tiller to Horace and, standing at the port rail, yell over to *Rosaleen* in a voice as mountainous as the man and full of the anger of the righteous. He was, he announced, coming across and *Rosaleen* had better make way.

Henry took the tiller and they waited, the two smacks inch for inch, *Maryann* with her canvas up and drawing long before the other, *Rosaleen*'s crew still breaking out their big balloon spinnaker but her lines cutting more quickly through, nothing to choose. As *Rosaleen* drew level Henry yelled once more that he was coming across and *Maryann* shifted over. Every man aboard knew Beaton should give way, windward giving way to leeward, the unquestionable rule. And every man could see, as *Rosaleen* pulled a fraction ahead, the two smacks now feet apart, *Maryann* beginning to lose the wind in the other smack's shadow, the water white furious between, that Beaton had no intention of giving quarter.

Then without warning Henry gave the ready about and threw the helm over and *Maryann* lurched to port, almost stopping in the water, her sails collapsing, booms and gaffes rattling and bending. Jimmy caught Kitty as she fell and the two of them slumped into the bulwarks. Over the rail Jimmy saw *Rosaleen* above them for an instant and the look of horror on Beaton's face as *Maryann*'s immense thirty-nine-foot racing bowsprit came raking over, his crew throwing themselves to the deck. And then with a splitting wrench *Maryann*'s spar caught in the other smack's mizzen sail close to the mast and tore back through it, *Maryann* shuddering as she broke free, her bow scraping and crunching around *Rosaleen*'s stern and a great roar clapping the air that Jimmy realised had come from Henry.

Jimmy looked across as he got to his feet. *Rosaleen* was in confusion, her crew picking themselves up, loose rigging flying in the wind, her mizzen in ruins, three or four canvases fluttering, ropes severed and the boom swinging dangerously. At *Maryann*'s tiller Henry was looking intently ahead as if nothing had happened, a grin as Jimmy had never seen spread across his face as he brought *Maryann* before the wind again. The whole crew was reeling in her sheets, her heavy canvas filling with a volley like gunshots and at once they were drawing, leaving *Rosaleen* astern, limping with no possibility of repair. Kitty was shaking her head, still in

Jimmy's arms, asking what had happened and whether it could really have happened and Jimmy could hardly hear what she was shouting.

'They'll disqualify us.'

Jimmy held her face in her hands and kissed her.

'It was Beaton broke the rules and he won't say a word. We could have 'en thrown out a hundred times.'

And the crew were yelling back to Henry, men slapping him on the back and shouting at once and he was pointing furiously ahead. *Ibex* was a hundred and fifty yards or more clear and Eb was snarling through his smile as if there were still a hope of catching her in the final mile and they were back at their stations.

Skipper Widger won yet another flag for *Ibex*'s topmast. *Maryann* crossed a hundred and seventy-five yards behind and came in to cheers from the breakwater where they had seen it all. Henry was roaring as Jimmy had never seen him, tiny old Horace at his side, sparkling, twittering about collisions back in the eighties and nineties but nothing like this one and nobody was listening but heaving in the awkward stay foresail and dropping the main and topsails so they could come in on jib and mizzen and finally bring her up alongside at the cheering quay on mizzen alone.

Jimmy saw the tears in Kitty's eyes as they made the warps ready. She folded herself into his arms, ignoring the shouts from the crowd along the quay.

'One day, on a smack…'

'You were amazing, Kitty.'

'Amazing yourself. I didn't know.'

'Didn't know?'

'How beautiful it was. The canvas and the wind and the way she cuts through and every man knowing her and loving her like she's a queen. And I was so scared and likely I'll never be scared of naught ever because we can do it together and these men will do anything for each other and for us and, Jimmy, *we can do anything.*'

Then the sobs overwhelmed her and she was being hugged by everyone, even Henry himself who was on fire as though he had won the cup by half a clear mile. Kitty looked Jimmy full in the eyes, tears running and he thanked the Lord for this moment that could never be taken away. He was truly amazed. Alice had seemed so much more forceful than Kitty, yet she would have attempted nothing like this. Had she even climbed aboard she would have clung to the companion and complained it was too difficult and the men would have treated her with respect and that would have been all. Kitty had made every man aboard feel her home was with them.

Clamour was running along the quayside and pointing fingers and Jimmy told Kitty the news had spread and she would have to face the crowd and she wiped her eyes and took his hand. Then she hitched up her long oily to climb the rail and there were a dozen hands to help with the low heave onto the iron band that ran along the quayside edge.

But no sooner was she up than it was obvious something was wrong. The hands were still pointing, not at her but at Jimmy. They pulled him up onto the stone and then pushed him away from Kitty, who turned, confused, her mouth open. Jimmy was being bundled away from the edge, eyes following as he went. He was aware of strong hands gripping him and saw a policeman's uniform ahead. Even as his mouth was opening to call out a sergeant stepped up, breathing heavily. He asked Jimmy to confirm who he was and where he lodged.

'In that case, Mr Blackbridge, I'm a-asking thee to come with me.'

Part III

Chapter 23

Through the small, barred window Jimmy could hear the sounds of the Regatta fair on the Common. He was mocked by the chirruping organs of the gallopers and gondolas and the switchback and the shrieking of the steam whistles, the muted chatter of the people as they walked in their little collections up and back. He remembered the cheap confusion of the fairground, the odd dullness of the grass under your boots in the middle of all the gaudy paintwork, the summer air heavy all around, thick with confections of sugar and grease, the hissing of the showmen's engines, the light quivering from the electric bulbs. He could hear the cheers from the races and the wrestling and pictured the men in their rope ring, thudding between entertainment and fury and the crowd watching the lardy scuffle like voyeurs. He could even smell the burning of the chestnuts and the oily smoke.

Four men had marched Jimmy without speaking along the quay and through the staring streets to the police station by the Market Hall. They took everything in his pockets and recorded it in a ledger. Then they led him along a short, newly painted corridor to a cell, four yards by two, beams across one end with a thin mattress and a covered pail for a toilet. Somewhere in the building a clock called the hours, its wheedling bell like a spirit trapped within the walls. It was chiming six when an officer unlocked the door and came in without speaking and put down a jug of water and a plate of thick stew. Jimmy was not able to eat. Panic and anger fought for his mind and he sat on the floor, back against a wall, grateful for the cool, vaguely refusing to lie on the bed because it would seem an acceptance.

He had been alone in the cell at the police station for four hours. He longed for Kitty. He imagined her radiating in every inch, taller, straighter, each gesture slow and graceful and her voice clear, measured in the way that was only possible in the smiling of success. He tried to glimpse her eyes, large again but also narrower with more knowing. He knew in reality she would be with her parents, lost and shaking, her crowning turned to ashes. He wondered if she had been told why he was here.

He assumed it was something to do with the accusations over Billie. Nobody had said anything since the dreadful first days, so that he had imagined Beaton and Farley had given the story up. So far as he was able to recall, they could not hold him in the fetid cell without making a charge. But he had already heard William Grant enough to understand that one face of law was concerned neither with truth nor justice, but was meant to bully. Its layers of secrecy and pointless complexity were intended to be exploited by the few who could afford it. Even if a legal defence were worth mounting, he had not the slightest idea how to organise it.

Finally the light thinned and died and left Jimmy in the summer dark, the stew stinking cold, the bucket worse, the drinking water bitter and warm. The sound of the funfair had become monotonous, drifting louder and softer as the wind wheeled. At last he lay on the damp mattress and slept in the kind of snatches he had taught himself between shooting and hauling, waking each time to find things cruelly unchanged, except for stillness outside, almost tangible after the noise of the fair. Injustice hit him each time like an iron spike and he considered shouting for explanation, fresh air, exercise, the decency of a proper meal. But rather than give them cause he huddled himself closer on the rough mattress and forced himself to draw on the emotion of the day before, Henry's brilliant sabotage of Beaton's *Rosaleen* and Kitty's transformation into a woman who had seized his world and held it, alight with joy.

The next day was Sunday and Jimmy, his disbelief growing with each thin-tolled hour, saw nobody except a succession of station officers who brought food and water. They emptied the bucket on the first visit and then not again all day until the stink rose with the August heat and Jimmy was glad to stand on the bed and draw in the street air through the bars. The evening light crossed the cell and still nobody came. The evening bells set up their complaint and he imagined the congregation at the chapel and tried to pray but found he was only angry. His only thought was that the scene on the quayside had persuaded everyone he was guilty. It was not their fault. He was the orphan. Outside, people hurried past on business he could not imagine, faces set with their own contentments and concerns. He slipped into sleep feeling abandoned and woke in the small hours sweating with claustrophobia that he had never known before and which he was convinced would kill him.

It was not until four o'clock on Monday that he was led out of the cell and along the windowless corridor to a room empty except for a table and three chairs. His limbs were awkward as he moved and he was aware of his smell filling the new space and the stubble of three days without a razor. It was another numbing half hour before the sergeant walked in, the man who had spoken to him at the quay. He sat opposite and alongside him another officer who set out notepaper and inkwell without looking up. The sergeant smiled, a cold simulacrum of geniality.

'Suppose 'ee tell me all about it?'

For a moment Jimmy was so struck with a sense of unreality he considered standing up and walking out. This scene could not in fact be taking place, the table with the scratched varnish where victims had twitched and fidgeted, the bulb with its glass shade, yellowing underneath from the cigarettes, like a tarnished witness to deals transacted below. He was sure that it was against the law to keep him. But the sergeant's stare held him. His face was lean and large, an enormous moustache concealing any expression, grey eyes steady but not still, silvering hair still rimmed where he had worn his heavy helmet. Jimmy guessed that he was a man in his forties, practised in concealing his weaknesses. His voice was deep and without any of the tones of understanding you detected in a normal conversation. Jimmy waited for an explanation or an allegation. Nothing came. There was only the sound of the sergeant's breathing and Jimmy began to wonder how long it would be before they beat him up.

'We're talking about Friday, son. About what 'ee did on Friday night.'

'On Friday night? I slept aboard *Maryann*. 'Cause of the Regatta next day.'

The officer with the pen slowly scratched a sentence and looked up at Jimmy, expecting him to carry on. Jimmy looked from face to face but there was no clue. He tried to read from the tension around the sergeant's eyes whether this man in fact believed he had committed a crime. At least, he thought, this was not about Billie.

'I have a witness, my lad. A statement. So I don't really need to hear what thee has to say. But it would make it quicker for 'ee.'

'Whose statement?'

'Well I should think 'ee could work that out.'

Jimmy considered blurting something about Flush Beaton and how nobody could believe a word he said. Then he thought of George Farley and the hidden influence he had and numbness gripped his feet and hands.

'A lady of repute.'

Jimmy's mind was suddenly falling. What woman in the port would have given the police a statement about him? He was only able to think of Alice. What had they forced her to say? The sergeant stirred his tea and quietly placed the spoon onto the saucer. The performance was starting again, his voice at first quiet, ready for its crescendo.

'Blackbridge, you're a twopenny deck hand and you are in—'

But he was interrupted by a commotion. There was shouting and scuffling in the corridor. With a loud burst of voices Kitty's father pushed his way into the room. Jimmy was on his feet and saw two constables standing apologetically in the corridor behind. The sergeant did not bother to look up.

'Well here's a surprise. Keir Hardy himself has come to investigate another conspiracy by the evil capitalists.'

Grant ignored him and sat down in the chair beside Jimmy, wheezing his heavy whistling breath.

'Obstructing Mr Blackbridge's legal assistance; preventing the visits to which your prisoner is entitled; keeping him in custody without charge beyond the legal time.'

Grant turned to Jimmy, who had sat down once more beside him.

'Do you want to go now, Jimmy, or shall we put it to a judge?'

'Why don't us go now?'

Mr Grant got up and Jimmy again stood. The sergeant was now on his feet too.

'Let's not be hasty, Mr Grant. The boy has remained in custody for his own good. I took a decision in his best interest.'

'Nobody asked me.'

'I have four constables who will swear on the Bible you requested to remain here for your own safety.'

The sergeant had not looked at Jimmy. Grant shook his head, his features fixed, calm. But the sergeant had apparently landed a punch. Grant sat down, the quiet smile unchanged.

'Let's say, Sergeant, you tell me what you want and we cut out all the mess of having you charged with contempt.'

The sergeant considered for a moment but Jimmy could see he was willing to do a deal.

'The boy goes back to the cell and we talk.'

'Jimmy stays. He's a right to know.'

There was a longer pause. The sergeant nodded to the other officer and he collected his writing things and left, closing the door. The sergeant dropped his voice another degree.

'I had to keep 'en here.'

'In that case you should have charged him.'

'I hoped it wouldn't come to that. Friday night, between the hours of ten and midnight, there was a rape. We have the lady's statement. She names Jimmy Blackbridge as the attacker.'

Grant turned to Jimmy.

'Did you do rape anyone on Friday night?'

With Grant in the room the charge was absurd, laughable. Whatever they had made her sign, however much hurt there had been, surely Alice would never let them use her to send him to prison. When they had met on the new smack she had all but cried to him for help. Jimmy felt the muscles in his back and legs tense and for a moment believed he was going to stand up and walk out. There was nothing real here to keep him. Instead his voice came louder than before.

'I was on *Maryann*. 'Twas the night afore the Regatta and I stayed there.'

Grant was looking into Jimmy's eyes. Suddenly it was not comfortable. Grant turned back to the sergeant.

'What else have you got?'

'A statement your boy was seen leaving his boat in the harbour that night.'

'Signed by?'

'Mr Beaton.'

Grant was wracked with coughing and Jimmy looked over for what he could do and was met instead with a look that said everything had suddenly become a lot clearer. Grant at last regained his lungs, his face again suffused with the familiar hot scarlet, his eyes sharpened to their iciest. But Jimmy again saw the two men understood each other far better than he understood either. Grant turned, his face now impossible to translate.

'Jimmy, I suggest you leave us for a moment and let us consider.'

Before Jimmy had time to grasp what Grant had said, to object, to refuse, the sergeant was on his feet, opening the door, calling for a constable to escort him back down the corridor. The cell lock echoed and he sat bewildered, facing the door, waiting for Grant to come puffing in and take him away. The station clock threaded through the hour and then the half hour and Jimmy's optimism began to shrivel. He knew he had caught barely anything of what had been exchanged between the two men but he could not imagine what there was to negotiate. Just after five-thirty the door opened with the evening meal and that was all. Jimmy had never wanted to admit to himself that Kitty's father had been anything other than straightforward. But he had seen him step around every question about himself, and the story Farley had told in his shop now began to sound in Jimmy's head like a bell.

The station fell silent and Jimmy sat on the floor, knees drawn up and hands over his face, desolate, unutterably alone, unable to think or feel. He was slit, scraped clean, frozen and black, caught in a net he could not see.

Chapter 24

It was after eight o'clock by the hidden station clock. Through the window the sky was thick with dusty evening gold. Jimmy had stretched out on the bed and breathed his blood into quiet and slept. He woke with bitterness pushing at his chest like a fist, his face a taut mask. He swung his feet to the floor and the loneliness hit as a hammer. It was like touching the ground for the first time. Every one of the people he had trusted had left him. If he ever emerged from this barred and whitewashed mockery he would quit this town and its mincing people. He put his head in his hands and imagined streets that soared with steel and concrete, people who gave a stranger a chance.

There was the sound of keys in the corridor and an officer's voice. The lock gave its reluctant scratch and the door swung, hanging its beat before it closed. Jimmy did not bother to look up. It was a moment before he realised there was someone standing in the cell. He raised his head and was looking into Alice's face.

He stood without thinking and backed to the wall, accused by his fish-stinking clothes, his unshaven face and oily hands, the stench of the bucket, the grim slop of the most recent meal. He had never been so destroyed. Alice was in a woollen coat, despite the summer warmth, and a bonnet Jimmy did not recognise and could see was expensive. She stood just inside the door, separated from him by four feet, but also by a distance of connection and manners and prospects. Jimmy supposed she had come to broker a deal for Beaton and O'Connor. He told himself to think better of this woman he had once asked to marry but found he could not distinguish her from everything else that was deceitful.

'Jimmy, I'm sorry.'

Her voice filled the bareness of the cell. Jimmy did not reply because it was not much. They were easy words to have offered and he was infinitely detached and there was nothing for him to say. But Alice was continuing.

'Henry came, twice, three times and they sent 'en away. Kitty has been here every four hours, every time they change shift. She was here again first thing this morning and again at dinner time and again after work.'

The tears had begun in Alice's eyes and her mouth had swelled, thickened and red as it always became when she was about to cry. Jimmy recoiled. Alice was able to walk into this hole because she was a Farley and then she stood and felt sorry *for herself*. He supposed it would not be long before she found a way to blame him for the grief this business had caused her.

'Why did you accuse me?'

Alarm now clouded her expression.

'I haven't accused you, Jimmy.'

'Who did?'

'Fanny Beaton.'

Jimmy was surprised but not shocked. Why shouldn't Fanny Beaton accuse him? The Beatons were O'Connor's creatures. Besides Henry and his crew, there was only Kitty in this town with a grain of decency. He waited. Alice went on.

'Friday, the night afore the Regatta, Flush Beaton stayed aboard until nearly midnight...'

'Yes, I saw him. I saw you also, on the breakwater, with Roddy. I heard 'ee shout and I rowed over to help.'

Alice looked up. Her face had drained white and black, a death mask. She did not seem able to see Jimmy.

'Boy Mutch ran to get me. Roddy'd hit Robert Grey outside the *Blue Anchor*. He broke his jaw. He was dragging 'en along the breakwater. He was going to dump 'en at the end.'

'I saw Roddy, and you. I rowed across. But you got away. I saw 'ee run.'

'I went for Dr Young. By the time I got back with him Grey had crawled halfway to the land.'

Alice stopped, halted by the memory.

'I could scarce recognise 'en, his mouth all blood.'

'You told the doctor who did it?'

'No.'

Jimmy reproached himself because he supposed Alice had done what she could. He had heard her that night and remembered the fear in her shriek. But this was still a story about herself. Alice's eyes dropped and she wept. A long minute.

'Beaton went home and found a man in his house. Whoever it was climbed down from a window at the back and got clear. Flush beat Fanny up, threatened to throw her out unless she told 'en who she'd been with. She wouldn't tell him. So he made her write a statement, said she'd been raped, and told her to name you. She couldn't stop 'en.'

'They were always going to find something to put me away. Whatever it took. For however long they want.'

'They can't put you away, Jimmy.'

'Mr Grant can't do naught about it.'

'He's sorted it. Kitty told me.'

'He's gone. Left me here.'

'There are lawyers, police, arrangements to make.'

'Farley.'

'They wanted 'ee out of the way for a few days, Jimmy. Then they'll drop the case.'

'Thee's know all about it, then.'

Alice was silent, looking down at the bare floor. Suddenly she stepped into the cell and sat on the crumpled mess of the bed. Jimmy was bewildered. It was a gesture that spoke more than had been said to him for three and a half days. It could be considered a thin beginning. It was even, generously considered, some sort of apology. But Jimmy was frozen, clinging to his newly-formed resolve. The silence between them became so long he wondered if a significant moment had passed without his realising and she would just get up and knock at the door to leave. When at last Alice spoke again her voice was quieter and firmer and he could not tell at first whether she was speaking to him or to herself. But he knew then this was why she had come.

'Six weeks ago Farley took me to Plymouth. He had an appointment with a jeweller 'cause he said he needed the money. He took a bag with his wife's jewellery, what's left of it. There was a pearl necklace, some sapphire earrings, a ruby brooch, three, four diamond rings, other things. The valuer giv'd 'en a written quotation and they paid 'en in cash, enough to pay his creditors for three months. Then they a-pulled down a tray of cheap new rings, with stones too small to see. Farley picked one out, any one, he didn't care, and then they were all looking at me, asking if I was the *lucky girl*. Farley said I was engaged to his son. It was the first time I knew. I couldn't even look when they tried it on. When we got back from the train Farley walked in to our house and told my father. 'Tis the end of everything. No college, no anything.'

'You know'd it'd happen, Alice. You told me he couldn't pay for 'ee to go to college. You said he only ever wanted 'ee for himself.'

Alice's sobs suddenly came heaving and ugly and Jimmy did not want to look. He felt his feet firm on the cell floor and repeated to himself that Alice had told him nothing but the ruin she had created. She had allowed the Farleys to exploit her self-pity with their pitiless pride. But when he spoke he knew in his voice that his conviction had cracked a fraction, and that it was hopeless to imagine Alice would not have heard the flaw.

'You're sorry for yourself, Alice. That's all.'

Alice wept noiselessly, her head bowed, making no attempt to cover her face or push away the tears. Then she sat silent again before she continued and Jimmy listened for sounds in the rest of the building, outside the door, evidence that she had not come alone, or that the station officers were listening. He could not hear anything.

'After the Regatta I found out what they'd done to you. That's when I decided. I went to Farley and told 'en what I'd seen with Robert Grey. I told 'en to let thee go or I'd a-finish the engagement, publicly, so's everyone'd know. In the end, after he tried to stop me, he told me what this is all about.'

Jimmy looked more carefully. There was no bruise, no injury he could see. But it was obvious that Alice was finding the retelling almost too much to bear. He decided to take the risk.

'This is about *Rosaleen*. Farley's pilfering, just like he did with *Deliverance* afore. And 'cause I know about it they want me dead or away.'

'If that's all 'twas about they wouldn't care if 'ee know'd. They got the police fixed.'

Alice stood and took a step, placing herself next to him, face against the wall, close enough to whisper but without touching. He could feel her breath on his face, smell the camphor in her clothes. Nobody outside the cell would be able to hear her.

'Farley told me *Rosaleen* had been built to go to Ireland, Jimmy, and they think 'ee knows about it. Or've prob'ly worked it out. Farley wouldn't tell me what she's carrying 'cept 'tis much more valuable than boxes of cigarettes. Something too big to take any chances. Farley's behaving as if this is going to solve all his money worries. But he's finished if he's found out. They were going to load her up after the Regatta, still in her racing rig, moor her out by the breakwater when the harbour was jammed and everyone was up at the fair. The plan was to sail afore dawn, with nobody there to watch 'em go.'

'But they didn't?'

'*Rosaleen*'s out of the water for repair, Jimmy. *Maryann* holed her during the Regatta. Didn't 'ee know?'

'They came across us and we tore their mizzen. I didn't know we'd damaged her hull.'

'You holed her at the waterline on the starboard quarter. She was taking on water. They got her onto Munday's slip but Flush wouldn't let anyone touch her. He offered my father double money to mend her but he works at Upham's and anyway he hates Beaton. Now they've bought off two of the men at Munday's. Apparently 'tis worse than they first thought. She's cracked two of her planks, broken a knee, other things. She could be there ten days. That's why they want 'ee out of the way. In case you talk afore she gets away.'

'So I have to stay here ten days?'

'Farley told me you were safer here than being beaten up by O'Connor's men. He said he was the one who fixed it and he did for your own good.'

'He would.'

'I think he was just told to get thee out of the way. 'Twas supposed to be just a few hours until they were clear. Once they saw what was needed doing with *Rosaleen* it had to be much longer. But the sergeant knows he can't keep 'ee here that long. Especially not with Mr Grant on your side.'

'Grant hasn't done naught.'

'Mr Grant has found a way.'

There was a long silence. Jimmy was now fighting back his anger and trying to hold on to some gratitude. Perhaps he was after all in the safest place. Or he had been. Now he realised that he knew far more than he had wanted to. If he was marked before, he was now condemned. He looked up, ready to throw Alice out before she did any more damage. But he found he was looking into a gaze clear and open, and waiting for him to connect with an obvious urgency. Alice knew too well how to read him.

'Alright, why have 'ee come, Alice? They'll all know you've been and they'll already be working out you've told me everything you know. 'Tis much worse now than 'twas, seems so.'

Alice leaned closer still, her mouth next to Jimmy's ear, her nose now in his hair, her hand on his arm. They could have been lovers again. Her whisper was as crystal sure as Jimmy had heard it since their earliest days together.

''Cause I'm going to break Farley, Jimmy. I'm going to tell everyone about him.'

'What's the use? O'Connor always finds a way to shut people up.'

'Mr Grant can get 'ee out of here and Henry can keep *Maryann* clear for a few days. They won't touch 'ee. I've told Farley he's finished if they do. You'll be safe.'

'Meanwhile they'll dump 'ee in the harbour.'

'They can't. They can't do naught to me 'cause Farley won't ever let them. They need 'en and he can't give me up.'

Jimmy wanted to laugh out loud.

'Farley would sell his own son if he had to. And even if thee a-told the whole town, there's not a lawyer or a policeman who'd do naught. Look what happened to Kitty's father.'

There was a pause. Jimmy found he could now not read Alice's face. It was hung between loss and grit and gall. But Jimmy realised that she was also elated with a new resolve.

'Don't ask me, Jimmy. But Farley knows I can finish 'en when I choose. If I start to tell what I know about 'en, O'Connor will drop 'en like a deadweight. I've already told 'ee about Grey and about *Rosaleen*. They'll be listening but they can't stop me, even in their own police cell. There's more. Much more… And when 'tis time I'll tell everyone the rest.'

The last words were spoken loudly. You could have heard them clearly along the corridor, even at the desk that stood at its end.

'When is it time?'

Jimmy wondered why he had asked the question, for himself or for her, and what answer he expected. It even seemed possible that she was losing her reason, talking as if she somehow controlled them all.

'When 'tis time I'll tell everyone. But 'ee keep thee safe, Jimmy. Get clear of town and they won't touch 'ee. Once I've told everyone I'll jump like Billie.'

Jimmy would have shouted, told her not to be self-indulgent, self-important, self-regarding. But he could see that this time she was not asking anything for herself. Just a bitter return against the man who had taken her as his possession. If this was madness it was momentarily of a cold and rational kind. And he could see that, whatever Alice was set on doing, he could not prevent her. Somewhere in the building a drunk began to sing in a low voice and there were shouts at him to shut up. Steps came in the corridor, keys, the officer locking the station down for the night. Alice was speaking again, her voice now small and formal.

'You'm a good man, Jimmy, and you deserve the best. Did 'ee know Kitty a-comes and visits my father every week 'cause he's sick and alone? Kitty does everything. I do *nothing*.'

Jimmy tried but could not find any sympathy. Alice had stepped back again into the world measured by her misjudgements. Kitty's blossoming, and her transfiguration at the Regatta, had perhaps made Alice figure the price she paid for her self-regard. But now her face was ghastly, as if bruised and streaked with blood. For a moment Jimmy thought she was going to faint. Her voice came unsteady and he was not convinced at first it was even directed at him. It was a speech she had made up for herself.

'I can't ask 'ee for anything, Jimmy. I was deaf 'cause I was proud, blind 'cause I only saw what concerned me, taken in 'cause I always thought I deserved better. I always thought I was the one the rules did not apply to. I wrecked what was sweet and chose what was bitter. I was angry at everything I did not understand.'

Now Alice looked up at him and Jimmy saw she was truly not asking any return. These were words she had imagined in her room and perhaps on the short walk to Farley's shop, or when she was given a moment of peace. She had maybe believed they were words she would never speak out loud. He wondered how much had been broken and refashioned in her since that last hour they had spent together, framed in the timbers of *Rosaleen* on the slip. She was still speaking.

'What happened between us was not perfect but I see now nothing can be, and 'twas as right as anything ever could be. I'll do anything in the world for thee 'cause you are the only man I'll ever love.'

The last words were difficult to distinguish because her voice was lost in sobs, her face twisted ugly, as if she had at last discovered that she meant what she had for so long said to herself. He was afraid because nobody could reach inside him as Alice did. She had broken the hardened, embittered peace he thought he had found.

'Will you help me, Jimmy?'

He heard his voice speak, but he was not clear how.

'I'll help you.'

Chapter 25

They woke Jimmy at seven the next morning, barging into the cell with a razor and cold water in a bowl. Half an hour later a constable cracked a tin plate of bacon and bread on the floor. At eight-thirty they led him to a yard in the back of the police station, the blue whiteness of the light confusing, the movement of the air and the oblong of grey sky overhead immense, as if it would be possible to take the wind and float. It was going to rain. Three of the officers, however, were taking off their jackets and ties, rolling up their blue shirtsleeves. Another lad was brought in and Jimmy recognised him from the smacks. He was small, his fair hair lank and Jimmy guessed he was the singer from the previous night. The lad saw the policemen with their sleeves to their elbows and a look of terror came into his bloodshot eyes. For a moment Jimmy wondered if he was right and they were in for a beating. But the constables stood the two of them with their backs to a wall and lined up alongside them, chatting and joking.

The door from the station opened and the sergeant walked out and behind him was Flush Beaton. He was holding Fanny's elbow in the merciless grip Jimmy remembered. Around her right eye was a grey bruise, poorly concealed behind hair worn more loosely than usual. Fanny was taller than her husband but looked hunched, slight and sick. Jimmy thought she had once been beautiful, her dark hair against skin that was now dry but was still smooth and without flaws except for the bruise. Jimmy again saw a memory of Alice in the fineness of her jaw. William Grant stood in the doorway. So this was the *arrangement* he had made, an identity parade in which all Fanny Beaton had to do was select him in a yard of men she had never met and looked nothing like him.

The sergeant waved a hand along the row.

'Right then, Mrs Beaton. Which of these lads do 'ee know?'

Fanny began to walk the line, her husband pushing her, starting with the three constables, making no effort to look at them, staring at the yard's mould-green flagstones. She was struggling not to weep. She came to Jimmy and Flush stopped her. She looked up. Her eyes were grey and she smiled weakly.

'I'm sorry you've been mixed up in this.'

Suddenly she wept, shaking her head, walking on, unable to speak and Flush took her arm again and guided her on past the other lad and gave the sergeant a look that said it was up to him to get the job done. The sergeant stepped forward, took Fanny's arm, guided her back to Jimmy.

'So this is the man, Mrs Beaton? You know Jimmy Blackbridge don't you?'

Fanny looked up at him again, her voice a croak.

'Yes this is Jimmy Blackbridge. But it wasn't him who... who...'

She looked round at Flush who said nothing, his face completely without expression. The sergeant had not taken his eyes from her. His voice was blank.

'In your statement, Mrs Beaton, you said Jimmy Blackbridge was the man.'

Fanny turned and dabbed her cheeks with a handkerchief. Her voice was composed again. It had a hardness that was sudden and a surprise.

'I was mistaken, Sergeant. It wasn't this man. I'm sorry to have caused you this trouble.'

She turned and without looking back walked to the door, waited until Flush opened it and disappeared. She did not acknowledge William Grant. The constables pulled on their jackets and filed towards the door, one of them leading the other lad back to his cell, another offering to take Jimmy. The sergeant shook his head. When they were all gone except Grant, the sergeant came and stood facing Jimmy. He spoke so quietly it would have been impossible to hear from any of the windows.

'You can be on your way, lad, and good luck to you. I'm sorry you've 'ad a *jit* these past days. Take my advice. If your friends a-value your company they'll get you aboard that smack of Henry Buckley's and clear out for the rest of the week and next week as well. I don't want to see 'ee back in my cells again.'

William Grant hunched over the range and raked it, the red coming reluctantly, slow flames in the steam of coal and splintered wood. He had been silent through the wheezing, racking, coughing, rain-danced walk up from the station. The wet had penetrated his jacket and the shoulders of his waistcoat and turned them into a flowering black.

'I knew Fanny Beaton wouldn't look you in the eye and say you'd done it. Thank all the angels, saints and holy ones I was right. God help her when she gets home.'

Grant was tense and his speech was clipped. Jimmy was torn between relief and the tightness of mistrust he could not shake off. He was not comfortable in Grant's house.

'How did 'ee know she wouldn't?'

'I was a copper, Jimmy. I know everybody.'

Grant's smile did not reach his eyes and Jimmy waited, guessing that there was plenty Grant was not saying. He was also aware that the man could read him too. There was a long silence. Grant's hands were restless and his breathing was short and difficult.

'Look. I paid Fanny a visit, after they took you. It wasn't easy. I had to sort my own affairs first.'

Grant looked up again and Jimmy could see he was ready to tell him more than he had before.

'I'm through with O'Connor now, Jimmy.'

It came almost as a relief. Not because Grant had finished whatever business he had with O'Connor but because he had admitted there had been a deal of some kind with him. Jimmy badly wanted to trust Grant again, and this time to know him properly, even if it was ugly. He could see Grant wanted the same.

'What was the deal you had with O'Connor?'

'The house you're in is O'Connor's, Jimmy. We couldn't afford the rent if he charged it, let alone the arrears. What I told you was true. I couldn't lay any charge against O'Connor unless I got Farley on the stand. But then O'Connor made me an offer. I'd leave him alone and he'd see I had enough to bring Kitty up, give her a chance. I half thought I'd double cross him if I could get Farley to sing. I tried to tell myself I might in the end get them both.'

'But you didn't get either of 'em.'

'I was a fool, Jimmy. Farley walked and left me dangling on O'Connor's hook. They'd worked it out. Now I was a bent copper and I had no hope of work again. O'Connor's kept us out of the workhouse. But the price is I have to keep my mouth shut. Never a day I don't regret it.'

'You casn't break with 'en now.'

Grant knelt and gave the fire a vicious push with the poker and watched the flame burst and die, listening to the tinkling crack, his face red with its heat. When he looked up, his face was congested, at once accusing, resigned and determined.

'You're as honest a lad as walks these streets, Jimmy, and I've met them all. There are plenty would do a man no harm but neither would lift a finger if his house was a-burning round him. There's plenty more so bricked in to their own narrow alley they imagine everyone is either like them or would be if they had the means. There are the men who detest the world in private but are sweet reason on the street, chased by the fear they'll be discovered if they raise their voice. There are the men like me, born on the edge or put there by circumstance, who see the world in three dimensions but only from one side and speak the truth but are hated for their unreasonableness. And there are men like you, very few, who see and understand, but know to hold their counsel. I haven't got long left, Jimmy. Now I worry more about my eternal soul than about what O'Connor can do. I've sat here and watched you and Kitty and you deserve better, the two of you. I won't have you under my roof if I go on as I am, refusing even to confess. That's what I said to Fanny Beaton. I've decided to finish this business. And you know what I discovered? She told me she'd decided to do the same because she's had enough of that vicious creature she's married to. You saw what he'd done to her. She told me Alice Rogers has also made up her mind to quit Farley and together they were going to do what they could to bring the lot of them down. That's why she agreed to come to the station and get you out. But I didn't know until she walked out of the door whether she'd have the nerve. God preserve her from that bastard now.'

Jimmy looked down at the man, on one knee at his feet in the fire-crackled silence. He knew that he, himself, was fearful and confused, far from the crystal-thinking individual Grant described. But Grant often only half believed what he said, trying on thoughts to see how far they fitted. Jimmy understood that this was all about Kitty. The man was appealing to him. He wanted Kitty honourably, honestly settled before he died. If Grant split from O'Connor the future would be poverty and a grave within months, leaving nothing. But if Jimmy married his daughter he would provide for her and for her mother and he could go peacefully. So he had gambled. Jimmy wondered whether he would have done the same if he had known exactly what Alice had said to him in the cell. Perhaps he did, or had guessed, and it had made everything more urgent. Jimmy looked away, the heat and weight suddenly rushing him like a squall. Not twenty-four hours before, he had decided there was not a soul in this port to be trusted. Now this man was kneeling at his feet, asking him to marry his daughter.

Jimmy remembered coming to the house with Kitty, Saturday evening, three weeks ago, and wondering if something had shifted. William Grant had been by the range in his best black suit, starched white linen collar cutting in to the red of his neck, hair oiled. Mrs Grant was also in her best brown woollen dress for Saturday Mass and Jimmy had drunk their tea and looked from one to the other. There was a heavy silence, but Jimmy could see a question flickering between them.

'What have I done?'

Kitty had stood behind his chair and cradled his head.

'Nothing.'

Now it was obvious. The word had been edged in a way that only made sense because Kitty had been holding and kissing him and talking almost without stopping ever since she had met him by the harbour steps months before. *Nothing.* It said that she had been sitting in this room each night, talking to her parents about the time when he would ask her and they had all been waiting, hoping each Saturday against Jimmy's return. But he had done *nothing*.

Now he looked into Grant's eyes and saw the complication there again. They both knew he could not yet do what Grant so much wanted. For a moment he imagined himself shaking the man's hand and running to embrace Kitty. But then he pictured himself instead walking away, quickly, without having to go through Kitty's sobbing goodbye. His tongue was useless in his head and his limbs were anchored. He told himself that marrying was a decision that had to be taken and did not make itself, that generations of smacksmen had asked some girl they knew just because they needed to set up a home. They married not for love, or because it was perfect or would be easy. He imagined Kitty's red eyes, the tilt of her face a longing cry and he loved her. The thought he would marry her glimmered. But it was somehow Alice's voice he heard. He focused again on Grant's head, pink in the rising heat of the room, and the hands gripped below. He was the most perceptive being Jimmy had ever known, his mind sharpened by anger. More than anything he longed to ask this man what he should do. But of course he could not. Grant looked up, his eyes narrowed.

'This is what the bastards have done to us, Jimmy. I'm a dying man waiting for a young lad to say he will marry my daughter so I can pay for my funeral. It's been like that for a hundred generations but this is 1913 and we supposedly have the world's finest empire and a government says it is on the side of the poor.'

He paused while he filled his lungs again. His eyes were steady and Jimmy understood the storm was not against him.

'Kitty's a perfect girl. So anxious to please she does not know who she is. In these months with you she has grown up. She is going to grow up much more in what's coming. Perhaps in the end you and she will be happy together. Maybe not. But I'll be bloody damned if I'll let the bastards run our lives and take our decisions for us and make you do what's not meant or right. Just look after her, Jimmy.'

'Of course I'll look after her, Mr Grant. Kitty… I want…'

'You don't need to say it.'

There was a silence. Jimmy longed to make some contribution, carry some of the weight for this man.

'Mr Grant. You don't have to cross O'Connor no more. 'Tis almost over. When 'tis done he can leave us all alone.'

In an instant Grant had looked up and his eyes had cracked into focus. He pulled himself up, sat in the chair, motioned Jimmy opposite.

'What do you know?'

The man's quickness cut Jimmy, even though it was what he needed most.

'Nothing. Only if I stay out, keep clear of the town for a few days, it'll be over. The sergeant said it would be over in a few days.'

Grant took a moment to answer but his head was shaking and his eyes shining.

'You and I are going to nail the likes of them if it kills me and breaks your heart.'

''Twill kill 'ee.'

'I said to you, Jimmy. Whether or not you marry my daughter, I am going to die an honourable man. Now tell me what Alice Rogers said to you.'

Jimmy was light-headed with the man's wretched intelligence.

'They're going to Ireland. As soon as *Rosaleen*'s afloat.'

The smile was already spreading across Grant's face, the satisfaction of a man picking up a trail he had almost lost.

'*Rosaleen. Rosaleen.* Stupid not to work it out. *All yesterday I sail'd with sails, On river and on lake. The Erne, at its highest flood, I dash'd across unseen, For there was lightning in my blood, My dark Rosaleen.* It's really *Roisin*, Jimmy, Dark Roisin. It's a name the Irish Nationalists use for Ireland because they say she's wild and ungovernable. O'Connor was a fool to use the name. So... O'Connor's set up his deal with the Irish Nationalists. I'd take a bet he's shipping guns or explosives. Did Alice tell you anything else?'

'No, except she had more to tell about Farley.'

'Clever girl. Knew the coppers would be listening. Can you see her again, find out anything more?'

'O'Connor would know straight away. I've got to get out of harbour, stay out.'

'Fuck O'Connor.'

But Jimmy told himself he must not see Alice. Not because of O'Connor. She was the one person in the world, other than the man sitting across the range from him, who could see under his skin. The Alice he had seen in the cell had been for a moment changed, a broken mirror and Jimmy did not know whether it would be possible to trust her again. He did not know whether she wanted him or only to keep him from anyone else. He could not shake off the notion that she was playing with him as she had played with Roddy and would probably play with any other man. He would not be able to withstand her acid as she destroyed Kitty with kind words. He could not see her.

He knew Grant was reading him. He would make almost any other sacrifice for this man and his family before death came and it was too late. But he could not see Alice. Whatever would happen with Kitty should complete its course and Alice must not be allowed to wreck it. Already Grant was smiling.

'It won't be long, Jimmy. Sooner than you expect. But when it comes and all that's left is to listen for His call, let you and me not say *we did nothing*.'

Jimmy found *Maryann* half an hour later, in the middle harbour, almost the only smack still at her chain. He stood on the middle pier and Henry shouted up that they had the coal and fresh water and a couple of hours would be enough for the ice and provisions for the crew. Henry and Eb asked Jimmy more with their eyes than with their questions and he told them it was alright and he would not talk about what had happened except that it was over and there had never been any truth in it. They all knew it was to do with O'Connor and that there was nothing more they could have done. Jimmy thanked Henry for what he had done to try to get him out. They told him about the celebrations after the Regatta and Kitty's tearful, triumphant, reluctant progress through the town. She had not been able to go anywhere without being stopped and her hand shaken and women stepping up to kiss her and shaking their heads and saying it was about time. When she had reached the fair, she had been pushed onto ride after ride until at last she had insisted on going to find Jimmy. He grinned with the men but was too confused to enter into the story. Kitty's sheer innocence in all this felt like an accusation.

They hoisted the jib to turn as soon as Horace was back with the beef and weighed anchor with a treacherous, swirling breeze that caught the mainsail as it climbed. *Maryann* slipped past the breakwater alone. Jimmy found himself with his back to the mainmast or leaning on the winch, unable to go below because the cabin was like another cell. Old Horace's voice threaded across the deck, creased as a wind-torn jib, the old songs thrown at the breeze from the tiller because nothing in the world would ever daunt a smacksman. The other men's quiet was like a funeral and Jimmy guessed they had been threatened too. They had probably always known more than they had said about Beaton and Farley, and maybe about Grant also. Henry had set their course for the Cornish waters and Jimmy could see from the stores they would not be back for five or six days and perhaps longer, enough to keep O'Connor's boys away. Eb's face was tight grey and he was avoiding Jimmy's eye. He took the tiller as they came past Dartmouth, a light faint in its castle, and Jimmy went below at last.

That night Jimmy dreamed the *Empress of India* was passing, crashing through the foul night and the smack was bucking and listing and flooding and slipping and he was sinking, water rattling in his ears, leather boots dragging him down like an insatiable lover, weed entangling him as he thrashed. All the time O'Connor's voice clamoured and poisoned like a tocsin. Jimmy struggled to reach the surface because he had to marry Kitty but sensed the life draining from his limbs and the cold invading his lungs until he began not to care. Then he remembered Alice teaching him to swim and light began to break above his head. But when he opened his eyes it was only the cold of the hour before dawn.

Chapter 26

They rounded Land's End in the early hours of Wednesday and flew up into the fishing grounds off the north Cornish coast. By Friday morning the fish hold was stacked, barely ice left for more and they all expected Henry to turn for home. Instead he sent them below and they shot one more time and then made for the sheltered bay of St Ives with its ring of low houses. They sold twelve cases and only made the money they could have made with eight at Brixham. Nobody spoke about it and Jimmy knew they were staying out because of him and felt weighed down like a dead man. They refilled with coal, ice and fresh water and took on enough food to stay out until the Tuesday at least. Then there would be a chance of returning to Brixham on an empty market, where the prices would repay some of what they had lost.

They shot three times more on Saturday night and filled four cases, as if Jimmy's black dog of depression, or Eb's, were a lucky charm. But then the wind turned foul, backing steadily round to the east and they reached around Land's End and found themselves in a lumpy sea off the Lizard, competing all Monday for space with the boats out of Plymouth and the long-liners from Fowey and Falmouth. *Maryann* shot and hauled every four or five hours for the entire two days but the fish hold was barely a third full, so much ice still in the locker it was melting into iron lumps they struggled to smash with the spike. Horace sang only in snatches and Eb lay on his bunk when he would have been smoking at the rail. Jimmy was numb but also grateful for the rhythm of it. He admired the granite patience of the older men, who had fished through plenty of empty days.

They turned for home as the grey light failed on Monday evening. It was going to be a long struggle to make easting, the wind blowing heavier in their faces by the hour. They set every stitch of canvas they could, sheeted iron hard as they tacked as close to the wind as the old girl would wear. Horace cocked an eye at the sky but it was clear to them all that the easterly was set and was going to get worse. They would either have to make Brixham before the gale reached its peak or batten down and ride it out, eking their stores through until the end of the week or more. They also knew without anything said that they would not stay out.

For the second time in two weeks they were in a race, this time in the pitch of night and against time and the rising gale. The heavens wept. They stretched every ounce out of the canvas until *Maryann* was within a breath of cracking her spars. At three in the morning Henry shouted the ready about to tack yet again and they climbed up into rain that was cold and harsh, knowing now they would have to reef up the mainsail, reduce its canvas or risk losing it. Jimmy, of course, had to do it and they hoisted him into the water-filled belly of the sail to do the lacing. One cruel gust now and he would be thrown yards clear. But he had laced the reefing a hundred times and emptied his head as the water seeped salt sore into his cuffs and he felt for the yarn. Three times more they tacked. By the time a gun-lead dawn was drifting up the sky all four of them were on deck, Eb at the tiller, the others leaning on the weather rail, looking for any rattle of her canvas that might give them another inch of speed. It was nearly seven in the morning when they reached at last for Brixham harbour.

The gale was now in full cry from a black sky and they were past the breakwater in an instant and running for home.

They were halfway across the outer harbour when Eb yelled. *Rosaleen* was coming out, forcing her way against the wind across the crazy white wind-whip of the water, heading towards them after taking an enormous tack in the direction of Fishcombe. She was heeling badly in the shrieking easterly and making drunkenly for the murderous, unfinished end of the sea wall. Henry watched them transfixed as they swung across their stern.

'Bloody madmen, idiots.'

Suddenly Eb was running back along the rail, screaming into the wind.

'Boy. No! *Boy.*'

Jimmy looked again. There at the foot of the mainmast, huddled miserably under the straining red of the new canvas was Eb's son, head hung against the slicing wind, fumbling hopelessly as a sheet flew away from him in the gale.

'*Boy. You're fucking not going to make it. You're not fucking going.* Beaton, you *bastard.*'

But already *Rosaleen* was thirty yards astern and Beaton was leaning with all his weight on the reliever at the tiller to put her about for the last time before the breakwater. Roddy was heaving at the jib sheet in a desperate bid to pull the smack round. Boy was lost in the mess he had made at the mainmast and there was no sign of anyone else. Jimmy followed Eb's pointing, gesticulating arm as he bellowed, willing the smack around the rocks, jagged where they had abandoned work on the breakwater. *Rosaleen* barely shot the end, and the top of her masts heeled suddenly as the swell took her. She clawed the yards beyond, turning south dangerously close, where everyone knew that in an easterly the breakwater wall lay deadly in your lee, the waves rebounding and turning the sea to a hungry froth. By now

Maryann was far enough in for them to hear the men on the other smacks shouting as they pointed. *Rosaleen* and her crew were outcasts, insane and alone. It was Tuesday, barely dawn, and a bullying, angry easterly. Every man afloat knew there was nothing in going out but ruin.

Eb could barely speak as they threw the cases into *Maryann*'s boat and hurled it towards the quay. It was obvious to them all that, if it were Eb's decision, he would go out after *Rosaleen*, even if it blew to kill them. The fish market was almost deserted and the porters told them Beaton had spent the week bragging he would work his smack up as soon as she was off the slip, no matter what the weather. So far as anyone knew only Roddy Farley and Flush Beaton were aboard and their faces creased with pity when Eb told them he had seen Boy. Not a man believed even Beaton was idiot enough to go far. Eb's face tightened, his eyes hauled to the harbour mouth for *Roseleen*'s returning masts. Every minute hurt.

Jimmy pulled open the cases so the men could sort the catch but said nothing, his guts drawn down by the weight of what he knew. This was weather to test hardened smacksmen and Beaton had set sail with a shambles aboard. But if he could get *Rosaleen* to Start Point and turn west, there could hardly be a better moment for him to try for Ireland. An easterly gale would have them at Land's End in hours and they could beat across the Irish Sea like the furies. The risk was insane, but if the deal were worth it, the rest of the smacks would have run for safety and the seas would be theirs. They would not see *Rosaleen* back for at least a week.

He went to pull Eb over and tell him and at that moment heard running steps and was almost knocked off his feet. Kitty's arms were round him, her face buried in his chest and then pushed into his, eyes closed, lips soft against his. And then she was spinning him round, tugging him away, out of the fish market, along the quay. And Jimmy was shouting at her to stop and she was not listening but skipping ahead, flashing eyes and silly grin like a dog wanting to be chased. Ten yards from the end of the market Jimmy stopped, hands on hips, the wind now roaring full in his ears, willing himself not to turn and go back and let the girl run on in her childishness.

Kitty held up a finger and walked calmly back. She pushed herself once more into his arms, pulled his head down, her cheek warm against his.

'Idiot. We can't talk there. They'll hear.'

'What?'

'Pa says 'tis up at Aggie's.'

Jimmy went to pull away from her, look into her face for meaning, but she was gripping him too tight.

'Your pa says what's at Aggie's?'

'He said you would find out or you were not the bright lad he took you for. He also said they would go any time and I had to tell 'ee straight away, soon as you a-landed.'

'Who would go any time?'

This time Kitty stood back and laughed. But her reply was still a whisper.

'*I don't know*. But apparently you can work it out.'

Then Kitty was kissing Jimmy and saying goodbye and was gone and he understood that she had played out the scene as she had been instructed and now needed to be away, just a girl late for work, raising no questions, drawing nobody's attention. He set off around the inner harbour, his sea boots sliding, rain needle sharp on his face. From a hundred yards he could see Aggie's shop was open and she was standing in the doorway, waiting.

'Took 'em this morning, Jimmy. Loaded her on the slip.'

'Aye, 'tis guns? Or explosives.'

'Look for yoursel'.'

'But they took it?'

'Not all of it.'

Aggie was pulling him through the back of the shop, past a storeroom he had never seen, filled to the ceiling with splintered and blackened rubbish, out into the yard he knew from the days with Roddy. There were two outbuildings. The door to one had been replaced, a new hasp still shining in the wet, its padlock now open. Aggie ignored it and pulled at the other door, rotting in its frame. Inside was a riot of boxes, the wet soaking up their sides and dripping down through the useless slates above. Just inside the door was a sturdy wooden crate, between three and four feet long and perhaps a foot and a half high, its planks completely waterlogged. Aggie looked up at Jimmy.

'Wet as when they brought 'em. They'd a-kept 'em under the Customs House, in the cellars. Next door to O'Connor's house where young Kitty Grant lives. You can get into those cellars if 'ee knows how. But they fill with water in a big spring tide and a summer like we've had. This box was the worst and I a-made 'em leave it.'

'How? Why?'

Aggie grinned her broadest grin, her few teeth black and yellow, disgusting.

'So's I could show 'ee. And anyone else as I wanted.'

Jimmy ignored the crackling laugh. It was impossible to know when Aggie was telling the truth. He was looking around for a mark or a label. He remembered a box exactly the same on the table in the coper when Beaton had taken him into the cabin. There was a crack of metal on the concrete floor. Aggie had dropped him an axe.

'Go on, then.'

Jimmy looked into her eyes, grey and laughing, everyone's fortune in her filthy hands. There was a black lock, too heavy to break and Jimmy aimed instead at the lid, first hacking off one of the two planks nailed across and then splitting one of the long wooden pieces like firewood. The axe was sharp and it only took a second. He levered the plank from its nails and out from the iron hoops that held the lid together. The box was filled with wet straw. Jimmy reached in and felt cold metal and pulled out a rifle, its barrel shiny blue grey, the mechanism smelling of oil, water oozing down the stock. He straightened, cold in his stomach.

'Ireland. They're taking 'em to Ireland, Aggie.'

'I know that, Jimmy. They had ten cases, a hundred guns. Would've made O'Connor a fortune.'

'They've still got t'other ninety.'

Aggie grinned, the same tobacco stink, stained black and yellow. Everything was as she wanted and she was talking to a child.

'*Rosaleen*'s a Brixham smack, Jimmy. She's got it writ in big white letters on her mainsail. Stands out like she's got *O'Connor* ten foot high for anyone to see. And there's folk watching out for her and her pretty white paint. Folk who know exactly what she's carrying. They'll hang 'em when they catch 'em.'

'You mean you told someone, Aggie? Who? The police? The *Navy*?'

Aggie kicked the box with a laugh and Jimmy did not know whether to despise or admire her.

'Day afore yesterday. Now 'tis time you were after 'en.'

'But the Navy'll be out for 'em already. And we'd be no use against a boatload of rifles. Or O'Connor and his thugs if we ever get back.'

'He'll pay 'ee to shut up. So will Farley. You'll a-name your price, Jimmy.'

'They'll shut us up anyway.'

'No they won't. 'Cause I've got 'em on a hook, Jimmy. Dangling. They won't touch you. Now, be off. They'll hang Boy Mutch if they stop *Rosaleen* afore you do.'

'They don't hang children no more, Aggie.'

'Smuggling arms to the Irish is treason, Jimmy. And I tell you, there's a war is coming. Even I don't know what they might do.'

Aggie laughed her husky laugh again and Jimmy could not tell her reason from her madness. But in that moment, every croak of her ruined voice made sense. She pushed the gun back into the straw, slotting the splintered pieces of plank back into the space, singing a rusty incantation.

'Roddy'll be finished. Farley'll be finished. O'Connor'll pay 'ee what you want. And they can't touch me.'

She pushed Jimmy out of the door.

'And Sergeant Grant'll die in his bed like a saint.'

'Aggie, you'm a witch.'

But Jimmy was now thinking about O'Connor and Farley and whether they would really be willing to pay for tipping them off about what Aggie had done, and for his silence if they could head *Rosaleen* off before it was too late and the law caught up with them. Aggie was waving her hands at him, shooing him like a goose.

'Eb Much'll be waiting. There's no wind'll stop 'en this side of hell.'

'Henry'll never go.'

'You watch.'

They were back in the rain and she shouldered the door shut, grabbing his arm and pulling him back through the shop again. She pushed a brown paper parcel into his hands, tied already.

'Run, you fool. You already lost an hour.'

Jimmy turned to speak but Aggie was grinning, eyes dancing, spittle on her chin, waving him away, laughing.

'A spring marrying!'

Chapter 27

Aggie's package contained enough beef for two days. With the stores they threw together at the quayside they had enough to make it as far as Ireland. By the time they had raised the coal and water tenders they were three and a half hours behind *Rosaleen* and the gale was still gathering. They told everybody they would only go so far as Dartmouth or Plymouth but everyone knew Eb was beside himself for his son and would follow as long as he had to. Henry had not hesitated when they told him. Privately Jimmy was astonished the skipper had agreed to risk his smack in this weather and wondered how much it was out of regard for Eb and how much his loathing of Beaton. They agreed between themselves they would find a way to get Boy off and leave Beaton to do what he wanted. Jimmy said nothing about O'Connor and Farley. He'd work that out if they ever hunted *Rosaleen* down.

Eb was all for hauling up the big jib once they rounded Start and could run the westing down to Land's End but Henry would put up no more than a staysail and they could all see the wooden spars were bent with the strain. Besides, *Maryann* would go better in a storm than the other, lighter smack. Horace went below and the others huddled at the transom, shouting across the midday dark and kicking spray. The glass had now been falling for forty-eight hours and they were in for a full-throated gale for another two days at least. It would be a bruiser. But Jimmy saw the race fury burning in Henry's eyes. Nothing in the world would hold him now.

Jimmy went below to ready them for the storm and found the bottle they used and put the fresh matches and dry lamp cotton in it, corking it tight and wedging it where it always went under the deck. He checked the hatchet in case they should be dismasted and have to cut the spars away before they fell inboard and wreaked the kind of confusion that would kill them all. Then he cleared the cabin of every loose object and tied the lockers shut. The last time he had gone through it all was the day Billie had died, and in every inch and odour he sensed the boy again. That time was grim routine. This time Jimmy finished the job quickly and climbed straight back on deck. He found Eb running the lifeline forward to the winch for them to grip as they crossed the deck.

They rounded Land's End in the early hours of a malevolent morning, Jimmy standing again in the belly of the sail to thread the reefs as they rolled full foaming. They had seen not a single other vessel and stood north-east towards Ireland. Now they were committed to the chase, whatever happened. The waves were fifteen foot, lifting the smack four or five times a minute so that Henry was meeting their peaks head on, the canvas shaking in the troughs, *Maryann* hardly answering to her tiller. The noise pounded Jimmy in his chest and through his boots, the sea roaring and the gale bellowing in the rig, every chain ringing protest and every line a whine. After two hours even Henry was exhausted and Eb took over, his face steel, feet apart on the grating as if he would push the boat by sheer will. Jimmy hardly slept and came up with him and Eb sent him forward to harden the mainsheet, tightening the mainsail, and to haul in the foresail another half foot. Henry was in his bunk and Eb was pushing his luck. Any more and *Maryann* would heel too far and lose speed. Worse, they would lose the mainmast, the sudden gut-splintering ruin that Jimmy had never experienced and prayed he never would. For now the old girl was rising to the seas and there was no smack that could ride a blow better, so long as they did not try her too far.

Eb was silent and Jimmy finally went and slept. After two hours Henry shook him awake. The cabin was canted at an angle, the floor littered with objects from a locker that had burst its ties, water pouring down the companion. Jimmy pulled his oily frock around him in the swirl of the swinging lamp and struggled onto deck. The rain was whipping, stinging malevolent and it was impossible to breathe if you faced the wind. Henry was now heaving the tiller down and Jimmy knew the moment had come when they would have to haul the foresail aback and hold the smack steady in the water before the gale ripped her rigging away or worse. Jimmy could just see Eb heaving himself hand over hand forward, his face a foot above the planking, one hand on the deck, the other gripping the life-line, edging forward like a ghost. Jimmy closed his eyes against the rain and followed, bent double, half crawling, half hauling against the hammering on his head and shoulders. He pulled himself around the great cleats of the mainmast and braced his back against the shaking timber so he could loosen the foresail sheet in the block and let the canvas fly in the wind. Eb fell on the streaming deck and then lurched back to Jimmy and together they hardened the foresail sheet so that *Maryann* finally came to, halted, swinging slowly so that the seas began to take her broadside on. Henry was now at the forehatch, pulling from his mouth the nails they used when there was no longer any defying the evil in the storm, hesitating, the hammer above his shoulder as *Maryann* caught another sea and rose and hung and then crashed down into the shelter of the next.

'The beam. Put out the beam.'

There was nothing more they could achieve with the sails all close reefed, unless they took everything down and lay with nothing but bare poles and their prayers to hold them. But they could unhitch the net and drop the heavy trawl beam astern to steady the old girl. Jimmy pulled himself aft until he was wedged in the stern against the transit rail and reached for the end of the net. He was still grasping at the first of the knots when the others joined him and Jimmy could see Henry cutting the lacing away and so he pulled his own shet knife from his pocket and sliced through the yarn. They pulled the net inboard foot by foot. It took them twenty minutes, fingers and faces wind red raw as the seas threw *Maryann* towards the furious skies and crashed her into the black below. Then the beam sank under the weight of its iron shoes, the capstan's clank barely rising over the din as it paid the thick trawl warp out. Then *Maryann* was calmer, her rise and fall steady with the sea, her bow a couple of points north of east and holding.

They closed the hoodway behind them and Horace had food on the cabin table as if they were lying at a chain in the harbour. Eb was shaking with anger and exhaustion, his face far away. Jimmy caught Henry's eye and saw still the race madness, the glint of the old smacksman. It did not come much worse than this and, to the man who knew his sea, it did not come much better. These were hours in which a skipper's reputation was made. His voice was dead calm.

'*Rosaleen*'ll be hove-to, no more'n half-hour ahead, hour perhaps.'

He had not looked up. Nor had Eb.

'But there's not a man aboard save Beaton and he's insane.'

'Say your prayers, Eb Mutch, and get some sleep. We'll have the beam aboard and be in their wake the moment she drops.'

'You say 'em for me, Henry. I ain't said mine these fourteen year.'

'You're a-doing what 'ee can. Time to forgive yourself.'

Henry's voice was loud against the sea and the rigging but also deep quiet. Eb took his mug to the galley and climbed into his bunk without speaking. Jimmy sat with Henry and Horace, listening to the storm as if to some senseless performance in the wild dark above the skylight, comforted by *Maryann*'s steep rise and fall and the steady set of her bow. Eventually Horace went to lie down and within minutes both he and Eb were sleeping. Jimmy leaned over the table and half whispered, half shouted over the din to the skipper.

'Fourteen year?'

'First son drowned in the middle harbour. Edward. The lad was three years old. Boy was on the way.'

'How?'

'Eb had 'en in his arms and fell in. He pulled himself into one of the wherries but the boy was gone. They found 'en in the mud at low tide.'

Jimmy shook his head, still asking for an explanation.

'Eb was drunk more'n he was sober then. In the cells every Saturday. Brawling, assault, theft.'

Jimmy supposed he should be surprised but found he was not. Eb's silence told of a past he had been afraid to broach.

'He changed. It changed him?'

'Walked away from his cronies, got himself a place as a deckhand and paid for his ticket in two years. Pleaded with me to take 'en on. Twelve years mate now. He'd a-been skipper long since if he trusted himself. He sleeps at sea and eats and makes sense. Ashore he's no good, afraid to go out, hardly speaks. His wife's a saint. But that's why thee and me are hove-to a hundred miles from Ireland, instead of warm and dry at home with Mrs Buckley and Kitty Grant.'

Later Jimmy slept the confused storm sleep, aware towards dawn of the wind shifting towards the north and *Maryann* coming round in answer, the racket heavy and endless, the gale's scream and the rain on the decking, the groaning rig, the whistling, rattling of the chains and the impotent smash of the seas as they ran through. Opening his eyes for a moment he saw Henry at the cabin table like a man completely at peace and yet barely dozing, every splinter of the smack a part of his own body.

Jimmy woke in an empty cabin and heard the clamour of the capstan. He knew at once the storm had conceded enough for them to haul the beam aboard. He pulled himself into an ashen dawn, the wind now a northerly, buffeting heavy and relentless but dry and without the weight of the storm. Jimmy went to release the foresail as Eb unlashed the tiller and with a perceptible lurch they were under way. The beam came up awkward and bad tempered without its net, kicking as the warp grew short, flying out of the foam and threatening to twist and hole them. Then Henry guessed from the look and smell of the sea they were eighty or a hundred miles south of the Irish coast but there was no accurate means of telling. They set a tack which would take them north by north-west, between wind and tide, and was the best they could do. If they could make land around Kilmore, the local men would know if *Rosaleen* had been seen. The wind was dropping and within another hour the sky was ghastly and luminous, racing grey black from horizon to horizon. There was silence between them. Something had to happen now.

Jimmy was at the tiller when Eb came aft from his lookout at the winch and pointed to a steamer through the haze ahead. She was working hard, the wind stretching a heavy black trail of smoke to starboard. Looking again Jimmy could see she was a naval vessel, grey, with a fine wide bridge and two funnels between her towering masts and she was rolling heavily as she came on towards them. She came level with astonishing speed and her engines dropped and churned white full astern under her counter, the sheer grey of her hull as high as *Maryann*'s mainmast, her lifeboats suspended over, a gaggle of ventilator cowls and the two slender raked funnels reaching high above. They could see figures along her rails, a few with binoculars, some carrying rifles. Her wash sent *Maryann* pitching and they fought to bring the wind back on her beam. On the warship's bow Jimmy read HMS *Hawke*. An officer with a loudhailer leaned over the rail of the bridge, demanding to know if they were working alone or if they had knowledge of any other Brixham vessels. Henry yelled back they had been battened down all night and had seen nothing and asked for his position. The voice came back after a pause. It turned out they had drifted thirty or forty miles north-east in the night. The officer advised them to make for Milford Haven and then *Hawke* was gone, turning south-west with a fury of smoke and white water.

The tension on *Maryann* now grew dark and heavy. *Hawke*'s tarpaulins had been pulled down from her turrets and her ratings had been armed. *Rosaleen* would have no quarter. Now Jimmy told them what he had seen at Aggie's. Eb was beyond coherence.

"Tis in the bloody papers. Catholics and Protestants, Home Rulers, Unionists, Nationalists. Aye 'tis bloody war, Jimmy, bloody civil war, and that fucking Fenian O'Connor and his *Rosa*-bloody-*leen* has my Boy running guns for them. Bloody fuck him.'

'Boy's just a cookie. They won't touch him.'

'You saw the likes of them, Jimmy. Schoolkids with bloody rifles and the stuffed duffel on the bridge in a fancy hat. Shoot first and cover the fuck up later. Battle of the Fishing Smack and home to your wife with a fucking medal.'

Jimmy left Eb on his bunk, blue eyes chiselled into a face stone white and furious, and stood by Henry, scanning the sea from the tiller. They had turned up into the wind and set a course north by north-east, too far east for Kilmore and too far north for Milford. Jimmy shouted over the thrashing spray.

'You think we're going to find 'en?'

'Not if they're under way for Ireland. If they are, say your prayers they make safe harbour for Boy's sake. But if they're adrift, the current'll've carried 'em and they'll be hereabouts. Someone'll have seen 'en. We've got the rest of the day and we might as well go on as home. His Majesty's Navy don't know where to look, seems so.'

Jimmy wedged himself against the bow winch and in the lee of the bulwarks, staring into the angry green of the morning, hardly light enough to see more than a hundred yards, seas so high he could mostly see no more than ten. He imagined sighting *Rosaleen* ahead, Beaton cracking the last inch out of her, and the foul tempered race that would follow. Then he pictured *Rosaleen* far to the west of them, making successful landfall and O'Connor venting his spleen on the Grants and perhaps Alice also and nothing good done. Boy Mutch would hang for a crime he was too young to understand. After four hours the wind dropped and a heavy, seething quietness took the sky. *Maryann* seemed utterly silent and Henry went below and Eb stood at the tiller. Jimmy did not move.

The swell was still so high he could see nothing but rolling white-laced green and at first he supposed, confused, he had imagined the patch of brown and black, sliding down the sea ahead. He was on his feet before he knew it. He had been watching for sails, brown red against the grey, perhaps torn, and the distinctive white line of *Rosaleen*'s hull, bright with its newness. He gripped the rail and then he saw it again, this time without doubt. It was a ship's boat. And then he saw Roddy trying to stand, shouting without a sound you could hear. Jimmy ran aft and as he watched again he saw Boy Mutch in the boat's bow, his face barely over the rail, both hands gripping the wood.

Jimmy yelled to Eb and looked for a line to throw but they were past in a moment, almost running the boat down so that Jimmy forgot the line and was along the rail, Eb roaring to him to haul the foresail across as they went about and Henry clambered on deck with Horace behind. In moments they were closing again, the little boat thrown helplessly in the swell, Roddy clinging to its sides because it was impossible to do anything else. This time Jimmy had a painter in his hand and they brought *Maryann* head to wind, the little boat drifting against them, crashing against the sodden planking. Roddy was bellowing, Boy's eyes were terror-stretched in his white face, his hands still locked to the boat's timber. He looked unable to move. Jimmy wondered how they would find a way in the frothing confusion to carry him. Eb was down in a moment and lifted his son with a strength that came from anger and passion. The boat rose again and Eb pushed Boy over, rolling onto the deck. Henry hauled him towards the hoodway and Eb waited for the next wave and scrambled back aboard. Then Jimmy heaved Roddy over, his oilies waterlogged and oozing. He hauled the boat's painter round the rigging and tied it aft. Henry released the foresail and they were sailing again. Jimmy took the tiller, the skipper shouting as he went below for the same course as before. It was no more than five minutes before Horace was back on deck, telling Jimmy he was more use below than an old man.

Jimmy found Boy in Eb's bunk, covered in their rough blankets, his father on the bench and watching him, pushing fingers through the sticky filth of his hair. The lad's hands were clasped, shaking, and so, now, was his jaw. He was too scared even to cry. Roddy was hunched over the table, ghost pale and raw, hands bone white around a mug, eyes-hunted and defeated. Jimmy pictured him at the boat's oars for a desperate hour or more since *Maryann* had come into sight. He looked up and Jimmy saw abject submission.

'Dismasted, Jimmy. Main, took most of the mizzen with it.'

'Did she go down? Where's Flush?'

Roddy shook his head. He must have told the others already but it was apparently no easier a second time.

'Heaved Boy over between us.'

'Why didn't Flush come with you?'

'Refused.'

Roddy looked around the cabin and Jimmy guessed it was as far as he had got. It was Henry who answered, his grin unconcealed by his beard and sarcasm in his voice.

'Salvage. If they abandon her anyone can claim her. And whatever he's got on board.'

Roddy was looking down into his mug, just a lad, far from home. Nobody spoke and the rain began its racket, staccato on the skylight

'Go on, Roddy. Why were 'ee set for Ireland in the worst gale for twelve months? What were 'ee a-carrying?'

Jimmy wanted to hear him say it, a sudden bitterness in his mouth, the desire to see the man bleed his guilt. But Roddy only shook his head, without looking up.

'O'Connor's men came and pulled me out of bed, Tuesday dawn. They'd already got Boy, dragging 'en out of his mam's arms. Just off the slip... *Rosaleen*.'

It seemed to cost Roddy even to pronounce his ship's name, as if she were lost already.

'Flush wouldn't tell me a bloody thing. 'Twas a bloody storm, bloody madness to risk her at all. And he put every stitch of canvas on her, cracking on, spars bent. Us lost a jib afore we cleared the Start.'

Jimmy suddenly thought the man was about to weep, his eyes screwed narrow, the back of his fist against mouth and nose. He was truly broken.

'And you got her this far, the two of 'ee?'

'Flush told me we were rounding Land's End. He threatened me, if us turned back. Told me O'Connor would be a-standing on the quayside. Then he went below and left me, two hours at a time, two hours on, two hours off.'

Roddy lifted a hand and looked at it as if he had not seen it before. Jimmy saw the red calluses where he had worked the tiller hour after hour with a gale in his face and a madman in his bunk.

'Early yesterday it came on much worse. I lashed off the tiller but I couldn't get no canvas down on my own, and I a-screamed down the companion but couldn't get the bastard on deck. In the end I went down to pull him out but he was yelling we had to get ahead, kept swearing they'd be on us. He kept shouting *do 'ee want blood, Roddy?* And there was a crack, probably the topmast coming down and I was halfway back up the companion when I heard the rest go. The mainmast severed below the boom, and I went back to get the hatchet but already she was catch'd up in the rig and a-shearing back aboard. She'd taken most of the mizzen by the time the bastard came up. It was all over. There was canvas and rigging everywhere and the spars vicious, heaving. We just hacked 'em clear and got 'em over the side and we had nothing. Not even enough for a jury rig, nothing.'

'So 'ee jumped and left her?'

Again Jimmy could not tell whether Henry's tone was sarcasm or pity. Roddy looked up as if hoping for sympathy but it was not possible to fathom Henry's face.

'We got off at dawn this morning. We sent the trawl beam over to steady her but she was taking the seas over her deck, sweeping everything. Flush ordered us off before the ship's boat went too. Said we'd be safer off. Said he would stay against salvage, take the risk. But he knew he wouldn't make it.'

Henry shook his head, still grinning.

'Slippery bastard. He'll have a plan.'

'He was insane from the moment we untied. Angry, with me, with everything. He didn't care no more. Didn't care if he lived or died. In the end he shouted at me to clear out, take Boy with me. He said I could tell Fanny… tell his wife… she could do whatever she wanted. And to tell Mr O'Connor we'd been dismasted but he would see no-one found naught.'

The crew of *Maryann* exchanged glances and it seemed at last to dawn on Roddy that the three of them knew more than he did. He looked around the table and finally at Jimmy.

'What's happening? Tell me what's happening.'

Far away came the thin sound of Horace singing at the tiller, his voice lilting against the rattling masthead, and the seas breaking at her forefoot. When Jimmy spoke he was unable to contain the triumph in his voice.

'You'm smuggling guns, Roddy. Your smack *Rosaleen* was built to carry guns for the Irish Nationalists, for the civil war as is coming in Ireland.'

Roddy looked from man to man around the dim cabin and it was as if his face was falling apart. It could not have been more obvious he had not known. Jimmy's voice was steady now.

'Nine cases of 'em, ten rifles in each. Happens I've seen the one they left at Old Aggie's'

'Old Aggie's?'

It was as if Roddy was remembering the long-dim scene from his childhood and Jimmy a lad, carrying the tobacco boxes with him to Aggie's shop, the two of them O'Connor's dupes. Jimmy felt an unexpected gentleness.

'I opened it, pulled out a rifle. This morning a naval cruiser stopped us. They were looking for a Brixham smack. They've got *Rosaleen*'s number, Roddy. Without the storm you'd have run straight into 'em. You'd have swung for it. You'll still swing if they find *Rosaleen* with her cargo aboard. 'Tis your smack. You're her master.'

For a moment Roddy struggled as if he were going to stand up in the swaying space, as if he were going to quit the *Maryann*, set off to find the wreck of his boat. Henry put a great hand on his arm.

''Tis over, lad. You're out. That's something.'

Roddy sat down again, utter loss in his face. Jimmy imagined him beginning to grasp how cheaply he had been bought by O'Connor and the shallow hypocrite that was his father. A week ago Roddy had been master of a new smack, perhaps the fastest and most elegant in the port. He was engaged to the girl he had doted on since he could walk. Now he was lucky to be alive, and when he made home again there would be humiliation and the probability of a criminal trial. He looked like a man who no longer possessed even the space he stood up in.

Chapter 28

The wind dropped over the hours and Roddy did not speak but sat in the cabin enclosed by the silence of the crew. Henry relieved Horace at midday and they ate the last of the food, Boy sitting also at the table, silent and sick. When Jimmy went up to take the helm from the skipper they were still on a broad reach, heading north-by-north-east.

'We need to make Milford, Skip. Last of the food's gone.'

'We can hang on till evening.'

'What are 'ee hoping?'

'Worth a look while 'tis light.'

'*Rosaleen*?'

'Wind's no more'n five or six now. If *Rosaleen* rode out the gale she'll be drifting this way, floundering broadside on and heavy with sea in her cabin and bilges. We'll overhaul her quick enough. Unless Beaton's found a way to scuttle her.'

Jimmy held *Maryann* on her course for two more hours. Henry spent most of it at the forward rail. Boy pulled himself on deck towards the end of that time and vomited heavily over the side, slumping and sitting against a stanchion until his father came and half carried him below. Horace took the helm and Jimmy joined Henry.

'What'll you do?'

'Kill the bastard.'

But Jimmy knew what Henry was after. They could go about now and head for Milford and home. They would lose another day or two fishing. Alternatively they could bet on finding *Rosaleen*. If she were abandoned, or if they could talk Beaton into saying he had come off with the boys – which shouldn't be impossible, given what they knew – the salvage money would be better than weeks of trawling. That and seeing Beaton cut down and Farley's new smack ruined was enough to drive even Henry Buckley for a few hours without food. Jimmy also thought of the money O'Connor would pay to keep their mouths shut, but did not say it.

The first they saw was a dark line, slopping in the swell, a hull flat and unformed as a smack first launched. It was a mile away on their starboard bow. As they closed it was obvious that it was what was left of *Rosaleen*, her white paint flashing in the late grey afternoon above the shouldering sea. Along her decks stood a row of splintered stanchions, blackened like Old Aggie's teeth. Behind them stood the towpost and capstan, the forward winches and the shocking stumps of her masts. Her tiller post still stood in her stern. She must have been swept over and over to have been cleared so completely.

They yelled as they came under her stern but there was no response, nor when they threw out their fenders and came alongside. Jimmy was punched breathless at the damage. He jumped over and made fast, roving off to what was left of her winch and staggering aft, disoriented along her denuded deck to the remains of her transit rail. There, with a force that almost knocked him off his feet, he remembered sitting with Alice on the day he had walked away from her and it had been over.

Both forward and main hatches were battened down but the skylight and hoodway were a mess of ruined wood and open to the sky. Looking down Jimmy could see the water seething at the foot of the steps, broken planks and sodden objects washing backwards and forwards as the swell lifted her. For the first time he began to be afraid of what they would find. Eb had no hesitation but thundered down the steps and landed cursing in considerably more than a foot of water. Jimmy followed.

He struggled at first to make sense of what he saw. There was splintered timber everywhere, the water turning and rolling with sodden clothes, boots, billy cans, a tobacco tin, the case for the foghorn. Coal had cascaded from the bunker and blackened the water. In the galley foul water was oozing up from the bilges where the concrete slabs on the floor had lifted.

Eb was climbing into the mess of the cabin, the broken glass of the skylight over the table and lockers, everything sodden. Jimmy went to follow and stopped, recognising the timber crate that lay half submerged across the door. He also saw the ship's hatchet embedded in the shattered planks of the lid. Reaching into the water he felt the metal of the guns and pulled one up, just as he had at Aggie's. Eb came back across and took it from him.

'So the bastard was clearing out his cargo. Rid her of evidence afore someone found her. Chucking it over the side.'

'But not all of 'em. There's still half a dozen guns in this box. And who knows how many still somewhere.'

Jimmy looked around, half expecting Flush Beaton to step out from the shadow by the boiler and bluster his way out. He had been halted in the middle of the job, the crate opened and half emptied. Eb stepped over and rolled up his sleeves and reached down into the water where the galley floor had been lifted. Then he straightened with a grunt and braced himself, veins in his face straining, kneeling almost into the water and heaved another crate up by its rope handle. It emerged with a gush, shiny black as a sea serpent.

'There's a gap below the platform. Specially made. Space for crates instead of ballast. No chance the laddies on *Hawke* would have found 'em.'

'Nor Roddy or Boy.'

'And you and I'll agree on that in a court of law.'

They left the box in the havoc of the cabin and climbed on deck again, prising the two hatches open but finding nothing in the hold or the lockers below. There was no explanation, except that Beaton had been washed overboard. Jimmy imagined him pounding up the heaving companion, rifles in his arms, or a case he had emptied, the seas crashing across *Rosaleen* and pouring in around him, tearing away sections of her bulwarks, sweeping the ruins of her shattered rig. And then, the last time, making it to the top of the steps and the water charging again and bullying him away, carrying him across the deck with nothing to save him. Perhaps he had been glad it was over. The smack had been ill-fated all along. Now she was a mocking parody, new caulking and paint and varnish a tawdry joke. A grave.

'Serves the bastard right.'

Eb was getting ready to put her in tow, pointing Jimmy back aboard *Maryann*.

'Poor Fanny.'

'Better off without, Jimmy.'

In the end they took the decision to keep *Rosaleen* alongside while they got the rest of the guns out and threw them overboard. They agreed that justice had already been served. Beaton had paid for his crime and the Irish would not have their weapons. Boy was innocent. They judged Roddy guilty of nothing other than Farley arrogance. He allowed himself to be taken back aboard his vessel, vacant as a madman. They made him see for himself what Beaton had done to him. Then they threw him back onto *Maryann* and cleared the rest of the bilge below the galley. They found another case, beside the one Eb had already pulled up. It took a back-breaking labour in the foul ooze to heave it up. Beaton, in the teeth of the storm, as the smack was destroyed around him, had got through six crates and was partway through the seventh and it was a wonder to none of them if he had finally given in to exhaustion. Jimmy thought the man might even have earned some respect if it could be said he had given his life so that Roddy and Boy could keep theirs. If they disposed of the evidence O'Connor and Farley would slip the law yet again, but the police at Brixham would have done nothing anyway. This way Henry and his crew would claim salvage on *Rosaleen*, and without any complication. Between themselves, Eb and Jimmy agreed, with the case that was still at Old Aggie's, they could also put O'Connor very handsomely in their debt.

Then they took a judgement on the weather and rove *Rosaleen* alongside, painters fore and aft, springs crossing between. There was nothing they could use for a jury rig and it was not safe in open sea to leave anyone at her tiller. *Maryann* laboured with the disfigured hulk on her back and it took until the early hours before the inky vastness of Milford Haven closed around them. They came in finally towing *Rosaleen* on a short warp, Eb now at her tiller, protected by the low land that loomed around them in the quarter moon. The last of the clouds cleared and the night put on its disturbing stillness. It was three-thirty before they tied up, *Rosaleen* once again lashed alongside. Then they slept as the dead.

Part IV

Chapter 29

A young November sky hung over the New Ground. The black fringe of its grey was a pledge of yet more rain after another month of wet. They found a space on the touchline just as the band finished. Jimmy held her close inside his oily and she stamped her boots in the mud. He did not think it would rain yet, but it was fine if she wanted to think so and stand so close against him he could feel the stiffness of the whalebone in her corset. The Brixham lads kicked up, waiting for the referee to call them together, while their old Treorchy rivals stood in a ragged huddle and their little bald coach whined on and they eyed their opposition. Jimmy admired the Brixham black and whites for their confidence and style. Nobody was telling *the likes o' they* what to do.

'Who's winning?'

Her voice was so much more confident when she was joking now.

'I am, and very likely I'll send thee home if 'ee asks another question.'

'You're a cruel and heartless man, Jimmy Blackbridge.'

'Aye, 'tis why I can have any girl I choose.'

Kitty lifted her face and he kissed her, the pulse of her lips as much home to him now as *Maryann*'s swaying cabin or the warm chatter of the Grants' range. It was a rare treat to have Kitty up at the New Ground. She had worked every evening and every Saturday afternoon since they had quit O'Connor's house. But today *Maryann* had cleared fifty-seven pair of sole early at the market and Jimmy told her parents he would *buy* her for the afternoon.

'You'll do no such thing, Jimmy Blackbridge. She'll walk out with 'ee and be glad of it.'

'Then I'll a-pay 'ee to do her share, Mrs G.'

'And I'll box your ears for your charity.'

Even so, they had marched up the hill behind the team and its band and Jimmy had made a note in his head that he must make the money back to them. Their cold, dark confinement in the tiny house on St Peter's Hill was better, as William Grant said, than living in the Irishman's waistcoat. The only grace of the house was that it was barely a minute from Captain Schjonemann's, the dry old Dane who got the Brixham smacksmen through their maritime certificates. He gave his lessons in the room that had the best lookout in town, an eyrie from which your eyes flew over the harbour and its flock of drying sails. O'Connor had not waited for the lawyers to make their expensive and time-wasting hash of *Rosaleen*'s salvage. He paid Henry Buckley and his crew off. The sum was a great deal more handsome after Eb had demanded the Irishman meet them and he and Jimmy told him straight in the stinking room at the *Sun* what they knew and what they had done. O'Connor had almost composed his features into a look of respect.

So Jimmy had the money at last to climb the steps to Schjonemann's lookout and the tall old Dane nodded with his famous 'ya ya' and said he would have had his ticket long ago and with a minimum of lessons if he had come earlier. He proposed also to teach him chart navigation as it was practised by the long-haul skippers and Jimmy readily agreed. The calculations and the diagrams lifted him. For the first time in months he felt he was headed with a steady wind, reaching for the calmer water. He was taller, stronger, more red-bloodedly alive, his eyes burning like a lighthouse. He could do anything. He had never felt like it before. Sooner or later he supposed he would be standing at the tiller, the swell rolling through and a homeward breeze, and marrying Kitty would suddenly be the right thing to do and his heart would not beat right until he had asked her. For now, it was waiting while they grew together and the rhythm of his breathing became the same as hers.

Jimmy remembered watching Brixham draw 13-a piece with Treorchy back on New Year's Day, an ugly and bitter grind, a memory that seemed so old it belonged to another person. This time barely five minutes were gone before the home side were on the board. Kitty was jumping with the best of them, shouting *did we win?* and beaming to break your heart because you knew she understood perfectly well. The old boy next to them began to explain and Kitty put her arm through his and listened like a child while the man grew an inch and his watery eyes smiled again like a young one. That, Jimmy thought, was because Kitty was a saint.

Usually these Saturday afternoons, after his hour with Schjonemann, Jimmy spent the time at the Grants' on the navigation exercises. He found he enjoyed the clarity and the tightening of his mind and it stirred a dim memory, or perhaps it invented one, of arithmetic in class with his father. Kitty sat with the sewing on her lap but wanted to learn everything and Jimmy found it was exhilarating to explain, even if she made elementary mistakes that had her pa laughing himself into a scarlet fit. It was not the least of her utter sanctity that she neither minded nor magnified her failures, never cared about asking him again and again and loved him for each success.

It was impossible to talk to Kitty about the things that mattered most to her because they were about money and the struggle to give her pa a decent chance and perhaps at last a decent burial. He was now a stooping invalid, grey as January. The battle to pay a rent and to save against the doctor's bills that would inevitably come was threatening to make Kitty into a weary drudge. Jimmy paid for as many things as he could without stirring Kitty's pa into objection. He knew, as he always did when they were together, that Kitty would listen to whatever he said but that she was too tired and the routine of her life too tightly bound to have much to say in return. Even so, when he looked down he always met the uncomplicated grey eyes with their transparent smile and it was the most dependable thing he had ever known in his life.

Brixham were 16-9 up at halftime and Jimmy took Kitty out of the iron gates and they stamped the circulation back into their feet up towards Berry Head, looking down into the gaping quarries and through the old stone defences, and then on past the squat grey guard house that was now a tea room and out to the odd little lighthouse at the end. Kitty was singing and Jimmy was content to walk with her warmth in his hands, a persistent mystery because the veil between two people thinned but was never torn and you could never really know, only trust. Away below the *Duchess of Devonshire* was steaming in to Breakwater Beach, her paddles turning lacework strands along her elegant hull, the little knot of visitors collecting on deck and making their way to her bow where the plank would be laid to the pebbles. Smacksmen cursed the pleasure steamers that clogged the outer harbour and its approach but the *Duchess* had been a friend since Jimmy had taken Kitty, soon after the return from Milford, and they had climbed across the wobbling gangway and stood in the bow all the way to Torquay. Kitty's face had been alight with the wind and the freshness of it all.

The cheering from the New Ground followed them down the hill an hour later and it was not difficult to guess who had won. They headed for the Electric Theatre. Jimmy swung Kitty through streets now soft-edged from the rain, past Fore Street's Saturday afternoon closed fronts and into the doors of the Market Hall at Bolton Cross. They were not ten yards from the police station where he had been dragged a lifetime before and where Kitty had been born a lifetime before that. The difference was that now he was not, at any level in his being, afraid of the place.

Early on Sunday he went with her to Mass, as they did whenever the furtive priests came over from Paignton. The more he had knelt with her, the women's Latin under their lace a whisper like alley leaves, the more he loved the possibility that something quietly tremendous was being done. God was not only spoken about but at work. The rows of clenched and work-worn hands, and the silent, ruddy faces of craftsmen and smacksmen, wrapped in prayers old as the world, seemed to Jimmy exactly as they should be.

That Monday was blowing an awkward, gusting easterly and many smacks, as usual, took the chance to lay up an extra day. Jimmy went down to the quay expecting Henry to have them away as he always did. Instead he found the skipper in his shore suit, shifting uncomfortably in his Sunday boots. Mrs Buckley had at last insisted he part with some of O'Connor's money. It was, according to the skip, a question of the bus to Plymouth and the purchase of a piano. He looked pained as a dog under his oiled hair and he waved his huge hands and told Jimmy to make himself useful. So he rowed slowly out and put in two lazy hours, new greasing *Maryann*'s massive main sheet block amidships and laughing to himself it was a well-run outfit if that was all he could find to do. Towards nine he was getting ready to drop back into the ship's boat when he heard shouting in the town, somewhere up in Higher Street or Prospect Street where he lodged. He had nothing better to do so he rowed over and climbed the steps. He found a crowd of twenty or thirty men outside Farley's shop.

Farley had fallen like Adam, so completely you could not imagine anyone had ever believed in him. It had taken only two weeks after the loss of *Rosaleen* for the shop's shutters to go up and for Farley to disappear, leaving a smart London address but, according to the gossip, going no further than a cheap lodging house in Exeter. Jimmy joined the edge of the crowd. Most of the men were well-heeled, middle-aged shopkeepers never seen anywhere except at church or behind their counters. On one window was a poster under the banner of Dugdall, auctioneer on the quay. It announced the sale of the contents of the shop that morning at nine o'clock. The place, however, was very clearly locked.

A wiry man was standing on a box and trying to make his voice heard against a tide of scornful shouts. He had the pinched and impatient look of a lawyer or a man from the city and Jimmy guessed he was probably both. He noticed also a tall woman to one side, in a fur-collared and expensive coat. Mostly she kept her back to the crowd, but anyway her expression was impossible to see under the heavy brim and gauze of her hat. Jimmy joked with the men around him that she was a suffragette and she would presently chain herself to Smardon the stationer, who was standing awkwardly by her side. The men, however, were grim faced and obviously thought whatever was going on was not a matter to laugh about.

An unsympathetic silence finally began to fall and the man on the box read out a statement loaded with ludicrous, barbed legal terms, apparently about an *injunction* and a *sequestration* and something to do with Farley's estate. His voice was dry and thin and he was making no effort to conceal a deep disdain for his audience. When finally he finished, he eyed the crowd narrowly for a response, clearly expecting none. Voices came from the back.

'Bloody lawyer. Learn to talk English.'

'Go back to London and mind your own business.'

The lawyer put his nose a fraction further into the air.

'I regret, sirs, that it is my duty to inform you that this business, while not mine, was not Mr Farley's either. He is not legally entitled to offer it for sale.'

'This is bloody O'Connor's doing. Send 'en bloody back to Ireland.'

The man was enjoyably nonplussed for a moment and more voices hissed at him. Jimmy could hear the men at the front trying to explain in a confused way about the money O'Connor had put up for *Rosaleen*. Everyone seemed to think the Irishman was now demanding his cash back. Finally the lawyer held up his hand again.

'Gentlemen, I am not at liberty to say to you on whose behalf...'

Now he was drowned in a chorus of jeers. O'Connor was an Irish Fenian and Farley a crook, a cheat and a fraud. O'Connor got what he did by threats and violence. Farley owed money to every one of them but always got a lawyer to worm him out of paying. The least this bloody lawyer could do was clear off and let them tear the shop up and carry it away piece by shabby piece and at an insulting, knock-down rate. The lawyer climbed off his box, apparently satisfied he had done all he was obliged to. The crowd, however, was not about to move and there were shouts demanding to know who his lady friend was and what she had to do with it. The man exchanged words with her and was about to climb back on his box when she gestured him down. She stepped forward into the small space in front of the crowd and held up a gloved hand. She was already taller than most of the men and in her hat easily commanded attention. There was a reluctant, murmuring quiet. A voice finally bellowed.

'Come on then, love. Give us your name. What's it to be? Votes for bloody women?'

The crowd was enjoying this and as the woman lifted the gauze, Jimmy thought he saw a smile.

'My name is Victoria Farley. I am Mrs George Farley.'

There was a sudden silence. Then came a torrent of angry yells that took Jimmy completely by surprise. Had she no shame? She had upped and left her feckless husband to bring up their insufferable boy and bled his hopeless business dry with her sanitorium bills. Now she had the brass to turn up, dressed in furs and in the company of some expensive London attorney. And the front to claim the scraps that were left. Mrs Farley stood completely still, her gloved hands folded. She did not look, Jimmy thought, either sick, mad, penitent or callous. Finally she lifted her hand again.

'Do I understand that Mr Farley told you I had gone to a sanatorium?'

There was another chorus of jeers. Fancy doctors in some European *schloss*... hydrotherapy, hypnotism... *neurasthenia... galvanism*. Each shout had the crowd hooting, and Mrs Farley smiling with it. When the quiet returned it was more sympathetic. For years everyone had longed to laugh out loud at George Farley.

'Let me assure you, gentlemen, I am quite healthy and entirely sane. I have never set foot either in a sanatorium or a *schloss*. Mr Farley has not sent me a penny since I left Brixham, more than ten years ago.'

This time the shouts were muted and quickly stifled. The woman had very nearly convinced the shopkeepers that she was telling the truth. Hardly any of them was surprised. Farley lied about everything.

'Gentlemen, I am sorry it should have come to this. I believe you are owed an explanation.'

She paused but Jimmy thought from her confidence that she was not in any doubt about what she meant to say.

'For more than ten years I have lived by my own means, without a single reply to my letters. I should have remained in London had I not had word from Brixham that Mr Farley was proposing to sell this business to pay his debts. As my solicitor has explained – in a language, I own, that bears little relation to English – this shop has never belonged to my husband. The premises are rented. It was I who paid for the furnishings entirely from my own money and the original capital was a loan from my own account. You, gentlemen, are men of business, and you may calculate at the sum at which my advance of over £1,500, made more than twenty years ago, interest never having been paid, may today be valued.'

Again she allowed the talk to die away. The men were torn between their disappointment at the loss of the sale and their enjoyment at Farley's exposure. He had, it seemed, never had a penny of his own.

'However I appreciate your position as Mr Farley's creditors. Let me therefore lay a proposition before you. I shall sell the stock of the shop at auction on my own account, as soon as a new date can be arranged. The furniture, however, cannot be sold until my solicitor has enforced my own claim. I fear, as legal matters do, it may take some time.'

Her last words were almost lost in a new chorus of jeers. Now they had got to the point and the woman had no more shame than Farley himself. She had invested in the family business and she ought to bear its losses. If she had wanted her money back she should have thought of that when she walked out. She waved for quiet but now had to shout, her voice rising, her composure beginning to slide.

'Gentlemen, you and I have no quarrel with each other. Our difference is only with the man whom in law I must still call my husband but whom, under a more enlightened legal system I should have divorced long ago.'

Now there were shouts of 'shame' and 'what did he ever do to you?' Under the veil Jimmy could see the colour coming to her face. Her voice was less sure. She stood, however, with no sign of moving.

'Gentlemen, I left Mr Farley ten years ago because he was violent and abusive.'

The uproar in the street was now deafening, sharp-edged and accusing. Mrs Farley's voice was a wail and nobody could make out a word and her lawyer put a hand up to the din and grimly started to push a way out, half pulling, half pushing her through the shaking heads and jabbing fingers. Jimmy could see, in the respectable faces, disgust at things that could not be spoken about in their business-occupied streets. Jimmy began to walk away with the crowd, some going down Apters Hill, others down the steps. He had only an unformed notion of what it was Farley was supposed to have done, except the ruin he had brought to his own son and the drudgery to which he had reduced Alice. He saw Mrs Farley look over her shoulder and decide to walk on with the lawyer, away from the crowd, in the direction of Overgang. Halfway down the steps towards the harbour Jimmy took a decision. He jumped the steps three or four at a time and half ran along behind the fish market and up the steps beyond. As he climbed into Overgang he saw Mrs Farley coming down, leaning heavily on her lawyer's arm. Then she stopped, looking out over the magnificent view across the harbour, pausing to breathe and to collect herself.

CHAPTER 30

She turned but did not answer when he spoke. Jimmy saw a woman in her mid-fifties, not unkind, used to authority but now distracted. There was a breeze from the harbour and she lifted a long-fingered hand to steady her hat, suddenly looking like just another rich tourist from over the bay, taking a trip to watch the men at work. It was infinitely difficult to begin, especially as they were standing just where, before they had moved, William Grant could have seen and heard them from his window.

'Ma'am, do 'ee remember Alice Rogers?'

It was abrupt and Jimmy supposed she would only be able to see his rough oilies, a smacksman without education. He expected her to walk away. Instead the woman lifted her veil to look properly. Her eyes were tight with suspicion. Jimmy had not spoken to Alice since *Rosaleen*'s salvage. She had found a new position in the office at Upham's yard but she had not broken her engagement to Roddy Farley. Instead, she had stood by him as if the two of them had been stranded by Farley's ruin. Jimmy saw them arm in arm. Alice led him like an elderly patient and slipped him hidden by the half dark into the seats at the back of the Electric Theatre. Roddy was out of work for weeks until *Albion*'s mate was brought ashore barely breathing and they had reluctantly taken him on as a replacement, short term.

'I do remember Alice. Does she live in Brixham still?'

'She worked at Mr Farley's shop until it closed. We were engaged to be married. But then Mr Farley announced she was engaged to Roddy.'

'My son is engaged to be married to Alice Rogers?'

'Mr Farley promised her money, kept her at the shop, at his house, late every evening, Saturday afternoon. Then he told her she was engaged to Roddy. He hadn't asked her, hadn't even asked her father.'

Jimmy was spinning his story like William Grant. But the significance of what he was saying was starting to spread through his veins. Now the woman was shaking her head, waving the lawyer away, unable to lift her eyes from Jimmy's.

'I had no idea. Is Mr Rogers still alive? I shall need to speak to him.'

'Pentecost? He's very sick. His wife died last Christmas. And Billie Rogers, he died too.'

Jimmy had no idea why he was telling the woman all of this, except that there was a growing light of recognition in her eyes.

'Billie died?'

'We lost 'en overboard last May.'

'Billie was drowned? I'm so sorry. I hadn't heard.'

Jimmy saw the tremor that passed across her face and waited but nothing more came. The lawyer began to edge down the hill and Mrs Farley made to take his arm.

'What did Mr Farley do to Billie Rogers?'

She turned back again, her head now tilted at the slightest angle. She was shaking Jimmy off.

'I'm sorry. Billie Rogers was a small child when I left Brixham.'

'Billie committed suicide. Farley was giving 'en money and drink, taking 'en to his house. O'Connor's men beat 'en up 'cause he was going to tell. That's why he jumped.'

Jimmy knew he had begun to sound uncouth but accepted that was what the middle-class did to you. So long as the woman did not walk away it did not matter. Mrs Farley turned again, looking into Jimmy's face for a long moment without speaking.

'Billie? *Billie as well?*'

'Yes.'

Jimmy saw that the woman's stony cool was breaking again. She looked away over the harbour, her face lined. When she looked back her eyes were blacker and her voice was sapped.

'I shall visit Mr Rogers. Do you have an address?'

Jimmy waited a beat. He did not want Pentecost Rogers in the way, allowing this woman to dictate what happened while he squirmed in his oily puritanism. In that moment Jimmy also considered walking away. The harbour was blue and sharp in the damp air and the scent of salt and fish fresh against the odour of mothballs from this woman's clothes. He had a future and he could turn and take it. Then he understood he had not stopped Victoria Farley just to find out what exactly her husband had done to Billie or Roddy or Alice. He had come to heal his own wounds. The future would have to wait until it was done.

'I'll bring Alice to see you.'

This time it was Mrs Farley who was silent and looked towards the lawyer who turned away, awkward as if this was women's talk. When Mrs Farley looked back she was working to regain her authority.

'Very well, Mr...?'

'Blackbridge.'

'You may bring her this evening. We are staying with Dr Brett Young, at his house. You are familiar with Dr Young? On this occasion I think it would be better if Alice came without Roddy.'

Jimmy reached Upham's office just as the light was failing. He had called at the dressmaker's and explained as plainly as he could and Kitty had come without hesitation. Alice and the other clerk were closing the books as they pushed the door and she stood awkwardly by her desk while the man put on his coat and left. Her eyes were unwilling to engage, her face without life.

'I don't want naught to do with Mrs Farley. I've had enough of the likes of them. So has Roddy.'

'We'll come with you, Alice. You don't have to go on your own.'

Kitty's firmness was gladdening and consoling. She lifted Alice's coat from the stand by the door and wrapped it around her, holding her in her arms when she was done like a child.

'I casn't. My father…'

'I'll sit with him. You don't have to worry.'

Kitty guided Alice out onto the slip and put her onto Jimmy's arm. With a wave Kitty was gone. Alice's voice was hoarse.

'You are lucky, Jimmy.'

They were shown to a drawing room at the Brett Youngs' house, a fire burning noisily and filling the room with unbearable heat. Mrs Farley came in after a minute, the yellow silk of her skirt and short jacket filling the room with a rustle. She crossed and kissed Alice on both cheeks, leaving the girl stranded, stepping awkwardly away while the older woman held on to her hands, mouthing polite words about her health and about Billie. Alice looked drab, grubby and impoverished, her face patchy because she had wept almost all the way. She was, Jimmy realised, a small child again, uncertain of what the others in the room were going to decide for her.

'Alice has not been well, Mrs Farley. These months have been difficult for her.'

Mrs Farley looked towards Jimmy as if he were a servant and then, remembering herself, nodded.

'I am grateful to you, Mr Blackbridge. Now, perhaps you would leave us to talk? Dr Young's cook will find some tea and something for you to eat. And for you too, Alice, my dear. I am forgetting myself. You'll have come straight from work.'

'Jimmy must stay. What you have to say is difficult and Jimmy is the only person in the world I trust.'

Alice sat awkwardly and turned her heavy eyes to Jimmy. Mrs Farley hesitated and then gestured Jimmy to sit. She offered to call for tea but Alice shook her head and said quietly that she would rather hear what had to be said. Finally Mrs Farley sat, her hands turning in her lap.

'Mr Blackbridge told me you worked in my husband's shop.'

'Mr Farley promised me money to go to college.'

'He made promises to many people. You have been able to find another position?'

'Yes.'

There was a long silence. Mrs Farley began to ask about Upham's and about Alice's father and seemed to expect her to continue but she said almost nothing and Jimmy could see the suspicion that was gathering behind her eyes. Finally Mrs Farley leaned towards her and spoke so quietly Jimmy could barely hear.

'Alice, I want to talk to you about what has happened.'

Now Mrs Farley looked up at Jimmy and Alice lifted her face to him and the resignation in the tears told him it was no longer any good. Mrs Farley gave him directions to the kitchen but as he closed the door he found a chair in the hallway and sat silently. He did not trust the woman in her inappropriate showy silk. A single electric light bulb fluttered feebly in a shade. The oak of the hall doors was comforting, golden and honest in its grain, as dependable a wood as a craftsman could wish in his hands, trustworthy for a lifetime. But the rest of the space chilled Jimmy's skin, encaustic tiles shiny as a tomb, the lifeless chalk white of the walls, the space deadened by curtains in dull oranges and yellows. No-one came for him and after a minute Jimmy edged silently over to the door to listen but the two voices were so low they were impossible to hear. He sat again, dully aware of other people in the house, the cook preparing a meal in a kitchen, the muffled sound of a man and a woman, Dr Young and his wife, talking in one of the other rooms.

Farley had, in some unfathomable way, owned Alice. She had been alone, rejected by her mother who was in love with the man, and cut off from her own father, who was in love only with his principles. And she had, Jimmy now realised, picturing their months together, been confused by her feelings for him. An image struck him suddenly and shockingly, Alice standing in the water, reckless with her nakedness. But it was the opposite of the rebellious spirit he had imagined. She had surrendered her body because it was a dead object without colour or value. She had been unable to share herself. It was unbearably plain now that the girl he had loved had been a shell, the hiding place for a spirit lost deep within. *You don't know me.* It had hurt so much when she had said it. But it had been true.

Jimmy supposed he had sat in the quarter light of the hall for twenty minutes. The longer he remained, the more the heavy memory of those months began to dissipate. It was like a fog in a drying wind. He found himself hoping that Alice was experiencing the same cleansing, enlightening clarity and got up and listened at the door again. This time he could hear Alice, her voice louder. She was telling Mrs Farley she would not do what she wanted and Mrs Farley, her voice firm, insistent, was telling her it was for the best. Finally there was silence, save for Alice's sobbing.

Jimmy opened the door without knocking. He supposed it was ill-mannered but also that he was unlikely ever to come to the house again or meet Mrs Farley. Alice was sitting with her face in her hands, shaking as she wept. Mrs Farley was standing in the middle of the room, her face tight with uncertainty. She was plainly relieved Jimmy had come back. His voice came with a quiet certainty that surprised him.

'Alice do 'ee want to go?'

'I have made Alice an offer. She will want to consider.'

The woman was doing her best to retain her dignity but she hung in the room torn between pride and loss and for a moment there was silence except for the muffled noises from the rest of the house. Mrs Farley looked to Jimmy as if hoping he would take charge and then quickly back to Alice, opening her mouth to speak and then saying nothing. Now all Jimmy wanted to do was to get Alice away, let her talk this thing out of herself, allow it to dry and harden and pass into history. Abruptly she stood up. She seemed taller than she had, like a creature that had been crushed and was beginning the awkward process of stretching into remembered space. It was Mrs Farley who was now more uncertain. Alice held out her hand and thanked her. The older woman told Alice to let her have her decision and anyway to write with her news and to visit if she were in London.

The cold as they left the house was sharp and clean and a liberation. Instead of heading back into the town Alice turned away, for Berry Head.

'Alice? Your father?'

'I don't want to go home yet. And Kitty's with my father.'

Jimmy walked after her as after a person he had just met, whose history he had yet to learn. They passed the orphanage in silence, Jimmy grateful as he always was now that he had been apprenticed to the smacks and not abandoned like other boys in the heavy building above the harbour. When they stopped they were looking out across the dark shrouded bay, the few lights of the town muted and faint.

''Twas about what Farley did?'

'We also talked about Roddy. I told her I won't marry him. But Roddy's breaking apart. He's humiliated by every face in the harbour. He thinks they all know, what happened to *Rosaleen*, what Beaton did, what his father did, everything since he was child. Of course he can't speak about it, even to me. I have always known, since the questions he would ask me when we were small, whispered when there was nobody to hear. And he has known about me too. We've always understood. I can't leave him just when I choose. I'm a-carrying his secret so well as my own. I'm the only one who does.'

Jimmy had the feeling of standing looking over a wall, into a private space. He found he wanted to hold them both, Alice and Roddy, and to bless them with whatever meagre goodness and light he had in his being, and to love them back to warmth and life. Only Billie's tragedy was greater, the boy too young to understand, who had struggled to break away and had only found freedom in his final falling, sinking black.

'What did she say about Roddy?'

'Nothing. She offered me a position in London. She says 'twill be intolerable for me here. If not now, then as time goes on, wondering what they're all saying, like Roddy does. She says I shan't likely ever find a husband here, that I have to go where nobody can possibly know. 'Twas meant well.'

'And you said no?'

'I said perhaps she was right and I was grateful, but I couldn't accept.'

''Cause of Roddy?'

''Cause I'm not ready to leave. Not yet.'

Alice's tone allowed Jimmy no answer. The breeze was sharp off the sea, now cold, the sound of breakers loud in the gusts and the night. Jimmy turned to walk back and in turning felt again as if he were starting out on something new. He had wasted so much anger, so much bitterness when he had never truly known what he had been up against. As they began to walk towards the town he knew that Alice Rogers was the person he used to suppose he knew best in the world. Yet the distance between them was too much to bridge.

When they reached the house Kitty had cooked a meal from what she had found in the kitchen and Pentecost was calm and as full of sense as Jimmy had seen him since Billie's death. As soon as they walked in Alice hid herself behind an angry quarrelsome face, unable even to acknowledge her father. Jimmy felt his own presence an awkwardness, the formality between them all unbreachable. He walked Kitty home and she was quiet and asked nothing of him. He was exhausted but his spirit jumped at Kitty's utter honesty, her quiet joyfulness. Suddenly he wanted only to weep into her hair and her neck and her shoulder, to let the warmth from her body thaw the ice the last two hours had made, the blue paralysis of joints and sinews. Kitty's unchanging love was as sure as anything he had ever known. She might never know him as he longed to be known but he had surely discovered that no-one ever reached into another life and that what you imagined you saw was sometimes no more than your own shadow. Love was will and faith and hope and the only decision was who could best be trusted to carry those things with you. Relief spread through him like returning home, becoming solid again.

They stopped at the foot of St Peter's Hill, in the darkness under the buildings by the quayside, and he kissed Kitty as if he could never let her go. The need to have her next to him was overwhelming. She was without the caveats and corners and broken edges that would make living alongside each other bloody. It was her acceptance that had remade him because it was unconditional and meant. It was, in some way, blessed. Then she broke away and ran up the hill because she was so late and waved as she turned into her house. He called her back. Had she come he would have asked her to marry him.

Chapter 31

Maryann was clear by six-thirty the next morning and running before a gentle November sou'westerly up into Lyme Bay. Jimmy found he was reluctant, torn in a way he hardly recognised. Finally he lay on his bunk thankful once again for the rolling routine, the richly aged smell of wood and fish, the honest odours of the men, the dampness of their clothes and the sweet wet leather of their boots, the sharp dust of the boiler coal, the lingering lard of the galley. He breathed in the silence, filled with the continuousness of canvas, rope, chain and water, yet always the same, a song of life that you did not have to hear unless it was peace you needed.

They had not shot more than twenty minutes before Henry called them up and they watched a grey naval vessel steaming down on them. The frigate came carefully to starboard, standing away from their gear, and hailed them by loudspeaker, requesting them to get the trawl aboard and clear to the west. The area was closed to commercial shipping for twelve hours. Henry yelled back he would haul in three hours and His Majesty could wait. Jimmy was astonished. They had all changed since the days in the Irish Sea. The officer called his instructions again and Henry turned and took his crew below, leaving Jimmy at the tiller until the frigate turned away.

They were on deck again and ready to haul, three hours later. The sea to the south-east had filled with dull metal grey. Jimmy counted eight large vessels and a handful of smaller ones, the sky dirty with their smoke. Eb pointed and to the north of the main fleet, east of *Maryann*, Jimmy picked out a familiar grey profile, tall twin funnels side by side, unmistakable even at five miles.

"Tis our *Empress*, looks so.'

Whatever else Eb was going to say was lost as a plume of water climbed into the air a hundred yards from the *Empress of India*'s bow. Seconds later there was the dull thud of the gun and they all stood along the starboard rail, unable to take their eyes from the old girl, her stern swinging towards them, high masts lurching. It took several minutes and a series of dull chest-thudding reports before there was a flash and smoke began to appear. Now the gunners had found their range, the *Empress* was hit again and was alight, black smoke rising thick into a greasy grey sky.

'The bastards are going to sink her.'

Henry's voice was shot with anger. Eb's also.

'Alright, she's a hulk, no engines, past her time. But you'd get thousands in scrap.'

'And they tell us there's not going to be a war.'

'We'd better bloody haul some canvas aloft, Skip, and clear out afore they try it on us.'

'If they sink her she'll lie across our fishing grounds. Three hundred foot of iron at twenty-five fathom, breaking up across our fishing lane, snagging the trawl every time.'

Henry's voice was quiet this time.

'That's why they wanted us out. We're five mile away. No danger. They just didn't want us to see, looks so.'

They turned back and Eb swore. Suddenly they were witnessing the death of a relative. There was a spitting flash and Eb pointed to one of the Dreadnoughts, towering over its finer, older sisters, making them appear antique, old, frail ladies. The Dreadnought's shell sent up a white fountain just abaft the *Empress*'s beam. The *Empress* rolled and listed extravagantly, sickeningly, the fire racing bright through her superstructure. Then with an obscene, steaming, belching elegance, the old girl turned over and slipped down with a speed that made your stomach burn. It took no more than five minutes, white steam chasing the black of the smoke and by then Henry had thrown the capstan into action and they were hauling. Nobody had spoken.

The drowning of the *Empress* brought an eerie darkness to the cabin and Jimmy could not clear his mind of the possibility that time was running away. The looming naval traffic had grown ever since the review of 1910, when the Channel had been treacherous with vessels steaming for the Solent, peacetime black and white obliterated by battle grey. They had believed the Royal Navy held the seas and war would never touch them. But now they had witnessed the hissing violence sudden and close, and the vandalism of their fishing ground was wanton. War with the German navy would mean worse than a seabed of twisted iron. It would be weeks tied up in harbour, jobs aboard done for the fiftieth pointless time and voices from the quayside telling you to join up for the Empire. If it went on longer, and the last one, against the South African Boers had taken three years, it would be hard to tell the voices no.

Jimmy stood his watch in the bleak blank of the small hours, the memory of the turning, drowning *Empress* in his eyes. He was pacing forward along the starboard rail and turning back for the tiller. He could conceive of his life no more than a few months ahead. But now he wished to make his decisions before they were made for him, and he could not think of a single reason why he should not marry Kitty Grant as soon as possible. Her generosity infected him and she was learning the rules of his humour, how it tested the line between what mattered and what didn't and how laughter gauged thoughtfulness and respect and told you whether people were thinking. Jimmy imagined their home together, a security nobody could breach, Kitty feeding and teaching and adoring their children. The decision had to be now because the world was darkening and if there was war there could not be a better wife. It also needed doing now because Kitty's pa was dying, smaller each time, his skin more transparent, the sockets of his eyes darker and deeper, his lips cracked and breathing a shallow hiss, his strength hardly enough to lift him from his chair. Standing now, forward at the rail, Jimmy could barely keep from yelling and laughing. It was so obviously the correct thing to do, life any longer without Kitty inconceivable.

Then in the quarter shadows of the night deck he thought he saw Billie Rogers. The boy was climbing from the hoodway, looking quickly round to where the rest of them were fighting forward with the wild jib sheets and the tatters of the torn canvas, and for a moment he looked directly at Jimmy, his eyes full and hopeless. Then he staggered across the heeling deck and climbed onto the rail, just aft of the mizzen shroud, holding for a moment to the whining, shivering lines. With the slightest bend he pushed himself out, without looking back, without reflection. Jimmy stumbled back to the tiller, peering astern, scanning *Maryann*'s wake, his heart thrashing, as if he might see a frantic arm, an unasked-for chance to return. And then he stood numbly at the transit rail, coldness seeping inside him, blinking unbelief and confusion and anger at a moment that he had believed had gone and which was suddenly raw again and struggling for life. He refused to go back to that time. But the boy's death was unresolved and unfinished, with all the impossibly difficult circumstances that had surrounded it. The Farley woman had conjured the ghost. But he knew it was also Alice. The secret that had kept them from each other was being broken and the connection between them was stirring back to life. He had an unfathomable sense that she needed him to believe in her. Lifting his head to the shifting, moon-shadowed mizzen above, he could not push back his fear that, through all the bruising, bleeding months, he had not yet let Alice go.

What followed was a grinding, biting November day of poor returns, the cod end hanging limp from the fish tackle and the writhing pile that fell too meagre to allow them to get ahead. Jimmy passed the hours in a growing fury, his heart thumping its punishment, dragging himself on deck for the hauling and the gutting, hands lifeless, eyes exhausted sore, deaf to Eb's bitter litany against the Navy and the government and the grey men who would drag them to war. He blamed the cold but burned with guilt that he was betraying Kitty. The useless certainty dragged him down that, whatever the times and however remorseless her pa's dying, he was, once again, not able to commit himself completely to her until this matter with Alice was resolved.

Chapter 32

Jimmy walked steadily and then quickly up and out of the town, onto the hill and away from the closed net of its streets. All he knew were his footsteps and the pulling of his muscles as he climbed onto the cliff top path and then the deep cool of his breathing as he thudded down and across the muddy, scarred slopes with a gusty wind in his face. It was good to walk these damp-softened miles again. It had been nearly midday when he woke in his lodgings with a head like an anchor and washed, shaved and dressed and walked stiffly in the white sun to Fore Street. There he had bought bread and cheese and the other things for the thirty-six hours before they would go out again. He ate in the kitchen of his lodgings, head buzzing until he could not stand the silence and the hammering of his temples. He had set off meaning to put his head into the warm calm of the dressmaker's, if only for a moment. He was a couple of dozen yards away when he turned back, telling himself it was unfair because Kitty needed the work so badly and because, had he gone in, Kitty would have seen straightaway that something was missing and he would not have known how to explain.

Although he would not admit it to himself, he knew before he had walked a few minutes where he was headed. When he got there he crossed the beach to the water's edge, drawn to the horizon, feeling the strength of the breeze and shivering more with tiredness than with the cold. Then he saw the black, huddled pile. It was at the far end of the shingle, where nobody could have seen it unless they were standing at the waterline. It did not move, even as Jimmy walked towards it. As he stood over, Alice looked up, grey as a woman dying, and he sat and she curled herself into his side, her hand gripping the front of his oily by her face. Neither spoke while the waves crashed and then withdrew, over and over until there was nothing else.

'He hit me, Jimmy.'

'Roddy? 'Cause you talked to his mother?'

''Cause I said I was a-going to tell 'ee what his father did. He shook me like a dog, said it was no-one else's business.'

'He's fucked up, Alice. 'Tis not his fault.'

'Nothing's his fault. Losing *Rosaleen* wasn't his fault. Getting drunk every night he's in port is not his fault, seems so.'

'You've done what you can, Alice. Now 'tis time to get away, make something new.'

'Like going to London, in Mrs Farley's house?'

'You casn't go with her, Alice. The Farleys have always fucked 'ee up. You'll be alone in her house and she'll bring it all back.'

Jimmy had no idea what else could be said. The waves were receding a few inches at a time and the waterline was growing sandy, the sound of the breakers muted, retreating fingers of muddy dribble. Jimmy felt Alice breathing under his arms and heard her voice blank, bled of colour. He told himself she had every right to be sorry for herself. But that was why it was difficult to love her.

'You have to make it into a memory, Alice, something that's past and can't touch 'ee no more.'

''Tis too much.'

'Then tell yourself 'tis something you'll do when you've learned how. Something you've just started.'

''Tis my fault, Jimmy. I *let* 'en.'

'Roddy?'

'His father.'

'Alice, you were a child.'

'I did it 'cause I hated my father. I thought I was special, that 'twas a secret 'cause I was the chosen one.'

''Tis his fault, Alice. You were only a *child*.'

'At first.'

Jimmy had seen it first only as a blur on the horizon, and then as a dark shape coming closer. Now it was here. At first her voice was even, a level account of matters she had thought about in every moment of her life. She did not say everything and Jimmy found himself guessing some of the rest. Farley had used her as a tiny girl, sat her on his knees, touched her even as her mother watched. And later, as she grew and Grace Rogers could bear it no more, Farley made Alice kiss him and put his tobacco yellow fingers on her.

"I can give you everything you ever wanted, Alice. Don't you ever forget. Your parents are kind, especially your mother, but what I give you is special. And because your parents are doing their best, I don't want you to say anything about what happens when you're with me in my house. Not to anyone. They wouldn't understand, in their little cottage, without nice furniture or proper carpets. This is only for you. And if you don't say anything to anyone, nor will I."

Her account reached her adolescence and grew ghastly. Now there were longer silences and Jimmy wondered if he should say that she had told him enough, that the rest would come another time. But each time she went on, her gaze on the horizon as if she were rereading her memories in the heavy sky. As the man's business fell to pieces he raped her again and again, his anger and frustration making him violent. He was careful she never fell pregnant but she always believed that in the end she would and that then Farley would throw her out.

And all along he had used Billie for himself too.

"Tis why Billie jumped. I so wanted to tell you, Jimmy, when it happened. But I couldn't and…'

'Billie'd threatened to tell.'

'They thought he'd told you already. O'Connor wanted 'em to finish 'ee and I told 'em you didn't know naught. But Farley hated 'ee ever since we started together 'cause he thought 'ee would take me away. 'Twas *terrible* then. All along he told me you would die. They'd throw 'ee in the harbour. They would ruin you, make it so no-one would ever work with 'ee. The only reason they left 'ee alone was 'cause I let 'en have what he wanted.'

'He only offered you the money for college to keep us apart. Your parents didn't realise.'

'They know'd all along.'

'They *know'd*?'

'My mam always know'd. I realised long ago my father know'd also but he said nothing and did nothing. And do 'ee know why? After my parents were engaged and my mam fell in love with George Farley, she wanted to break the engagement. 'Twas my father who made her keep her word. And it broke her. She never forgave him, never wanted to go near 'en again. And she stopped caring what she did. With Farley. With Billie. With me. 'Tis why we, you and me, had to come here, to get away from the likes of them. And when Billie died she gave up.'

'She gave up?'

'The kitchen, Jimmy. You never worked it out? Farley always threatened us with a knife. Her too. In the end she did it herself.'

Jimmy felt the abandonment shiver through her and held her as closely as he was able. Alice turned slightly in his arms, as if to shut out her anger at her parents.

'When he saw you were not going to go away, he was sure you know'd everything about him. He couldn't think of naught else. He believed you had a plan. To get me, you'd tell everybody about him. He warned O'Connor. But O'Connor threatened him. He'd *make* 'ee tell what you know'd if Farley didn't shut up and go along with his new scam.'

'The new smack.'

'*Rosaleen*. Once the job was done they'd finish you.'

'But why did Farley give thee to Roddy?'

''Twasn't never like that, Jimmy. He told Roddy he could have me. He made me go through that scene at the launch so you could never get me back. But he never let Roddy touch me. If he kissed me, even at the Electric Theatre, his father found out. There was always someone would tell him. And that's when he was worst. He would take his knife from the kitchen and hold it to Roddy's wrists.'

'Roddy? He's strong. He...'

'How can you understand it? Without his father he had nothing. 'Tis what Roddy believed. We both did. Aye, 'tis what Farley had told us, every day, year after year, since we first learned to walk. More than every day. Sometimes every hour. *She's mine*, Farley said. *And if you forget it I'll kill you.* Roddy know'd, if he touched me, his father would start on him again, instead of picking on poor Billie. And he couldn't have taken that, not any more. He would have jumped, just like Billie.'

The wind was still, the sea on the gravelly sand oddly close and yet distant at the same time. Alice's voice, when it came, was so quiet Jimmy barely heard.

'It was Boy Mutch as well.'

'*Boy?*'

Now Alice hid her face in her hands and sobbed, her frame heaving until at last she allowed Jimmy to hold her close again. It was a long while before she could speak, the breakers tolling their gravelled beat, her voice then strangled, interrupted by more sobs.

'Farley said he'd found me someone to teach. A bright lad and I'd like him. And Boy was clever and funny and Farley made 'en come to the shop and I tried to teach him figures. And then he made 'en come to the house. But... Jimmy, I loved Boy and... but Farley... Boy... I don't know... Jimmy, 'twas too much. And I wanted to tell you. I wanted to go to Boy's house and tell his parents what I'd done. But I was afraid. And then Flush Beaton came, and 'twas all *I'm your uncle* and *I know what's best for you*. And I couldn't bear to think what they would do... And then they threatened Boy, got him aboard *Coronet* and pushed 'en onto *Rosaleen*.'

Alice's tears were falling heavy now. Jimmy told her Boy would be alright. Eb would never let him go. Perhaps she could talk to them, start putting things right. And Alice only nodded. Jimmy guessed from her long silence now that there were others, lads, girls, whose privacy she chose to respect because there was nothing anyone could do. They were like a family, silently grieving for the loss of their own selves. At last Jimmy broke the silence.

'And Farley lost *Roseleen* and it stopped?'

Alice shook her head.

'After *Rosaleen* he began closing his affairs, covering everything up he'd done. But still he took me. 'Twas worst of all then.'

Jimmy held her more tightly, unsure whether it was the right thing to do. Finally Alice pulled away a little and turned to him.

'I don't expect you to understand, Jimmy. But when he was gone I missed 'en. I was lost, walking in a world I couldn't understand. All I wanted was someone who'd carry the secret, would tell me what to do, someone who wouldn't condemn me or control. But it was impossible. I couldn't tell anyone 'cept Roddy. And then all I wanted was to run and never let anything or anyone in the world come close to me again. Until Mrs Farley turned up and I told her and something changed.'

The silence lasted a long while because Jimmy could not frame a response, could not construct anything that was practical or tangible. She had spoken things that were never spoken. His horror was becoming anger, revulsion and nausea, a prickling shock that crept through his flesh and tightened his lungs, filling his stomach with burning acid and his muscles with an urgency of forcible, violent restitution. But there was nothing that could make a difference until the past had hardened and closed over. He supposed it had begun. Her account had been strangely quiet because she had rehearsed it again and again in her head until it was ready to tell.

'What do you want me to do, Alice?'

'Just keep it for me, Jimmy. Be the person who reminds me that I am, that I can be, who lets me be lost without letting me go, lets me be angry without blame and without minding the hurt, teaches me to be a human being and not someone's possession.'

There was another pause, the waves keeping their receding vigil, now a distant hiss and smooth. When Alice spoke at last her voice was again less certain.

'And someone to forgive me.'

'Only someone you've hurt can forgive thee and you haven't hurt anyone in this.'

'I've hurt you. Do you forgive me, Jimmy?'

'I forgive thee, Alice. But my hurt's nothing.'

Jimmy felt Alice move again. She was looking up into his face.

'I'm sorry.'

'I forgive you.'

Jimmy knew there was nothing to forgive but knew it helped her if he said it. He kissed her forehead. It was brief but he knew it complicated what was happening between them. He lifted his face to the horizon and was only aware of waves crisscrossing, a sea he could not navigate. He knew his weakness. He waited until dilemmas resolved themselves, until alternatives turned and sank and some tide of events forced itself on him. But if he committed himself to Kitty, or waited for this thing with Alice to be resolved, it must not be an accident. Pentecost Rogers, Roddy Farley – they were men who appeared never truly to have taken a decision, but allowed themselves to be carried along. It had even taken the stalking breath of dying to bring William Grant to an awakening. Jimmy seemed to himself suddenly older.

He looked down at the straw of Alice's hair. She was solid in a way she had never been. Before he had been in love with a ghost, a phantom he had conjured. Now this woman was flesh and blood, an entire person. They were no longer children playing an imaginary game. Alice wiped the corner of his eye with a finger. Instead of words there was only silence.

'I'm sorry, Jimmy.'

He nodded and that was all.

They walked back together, Alice's arm in his, until they could see the first of the houses on the edge of the town, the muddy labourers' cottages the smacksmen called Cowtown. They made no agreement to meet again, saying that Alice had Roddy to care for and Jimmy had Kitty and her pa. Jimmy agreed to walk on ahead so that they would not be seen together. He found he was without feeling by the time he reached Bolton Cross and saw the clocks at four-thirty and went to the dressmaker's and stood in the doorway until Kitty had finished. He sensed the world in his hands, heavy and dense as the air in the room. When he looked at Kitty she was smiling and generous and he knew she would kiss him and take him home and it would again be sweetness. He struggled to recapture the decision he had taken, days, worlds ago, when he had called her back to ask her to marry him, to feel again the urgency of the unsafe world that was coming and the delight of Kitty's warm and inexhaustible humanity in a cold place.

When at last she packed away her things and they went out into the dark street he was truly delighted to hold her and his heart filled as she called him 'Mr Blackbridge' as she did and he embraced her honestly. She lit him up with her love and her optimism and the way she wanted to know everything that had happened. He told her about the *Empress*.

'She'll lie across your fishing grounds, so they're finished?'

'One of 'em, and a good one.'

'Don't tell Pa. He'll be so angry he'll cough all night.'

'He says there's war coming, and the British Navy can stop it.'

'He says all kinds of things and he's always right. I don't know how my ma stands it. At least you're wrong half the time, Mr Blackbridge.'

'I'm never wrong.'

'There you are. That *proves* it. Anyway, you'd better tell him. He'll be furious if he finds out from anyone else. And 'tis you he loves to hear talk. I believe 'tis what's keeping 'en alive. You know how proud he is of you.'

The Grants had become Jimmy's entire life ashore and he loved them more than he could remember ever loving his own father. But at this moment he felt the pain of a part of him that was not there.

Chapter 33

The Board of Trade had set Jimmy's examination for his mate's ticket on 29 December. In the month before he spent as much time with William Grant, rehearsing what he had to know, as he did with Kitty. They joked the old man had now learned so much navigation he could find himself a mate's berth by January. And the joke was good because he was vanishing, his skin growing a thin paper yellow as they watched and his breathing a quiet rattle, sufficient to maintain a sharpness in his eyes, but useless as soon as he stood. Kitty worked endlessly to save enough to make this last Christmas a good one and the house off St Peter's Hill was filled with a joyful quiet that infected Jimmy and lived with him and he could not explain. He persuaded Kitty to allow him quietly to add to the money she brought home and the conspiracy gave their hours together a sense of things progressing. Jimmy, however, knew he was waiting, everything now suspended. He knew that Kitty was waiting also, not only for her pa but also for him.

Maryann came in on Christmas Eve with the others, more than two hundred smacks lashed in a thicket of painted black and nut grain brown, salt-stained blues and golds and the tan of drying sails. Each was a private world open to the sky, and together they made a makeshift pontoon that you could have walked across far into the outer harbour. It was Wednesday and Jimmy's examination was on the Monday. Henry told his crew not to bother until the Tuesday and Jimmy not at all unless he passed. Jimmy was grateful. He would not have said it if he had not been sure.

Kitty and her ma took him through the dense Christmas Eve stillness to Mass. There were plenty of men he had not seen there before, wiry, wind-brown faces from the smacks. He had always been to the Methodist chapel on Christmas Eve, lifted by the singing past midnight and into Christmas Day so that waking up in the morning seemed like a second chance and the Christmas morning service a third. The Mass was without music, its long reflective readings drawing out the whole history and Jimmy was awed by something grown so aged and immense.

The Grants knew how to take pleasure in what they did and the next day Jimmy was carried by their complete certainty, filling their familiar and also their unaccustomed Christmas roles. He watched Kitty become her parents' little girl again, carrying the heart of the family and doing it with a laughing grace that was almost an irony. Her ma had the sense of occasion and self-mockery that produced a stream of insincere complaint about the burden of it all, so well judged you knew you neither had to interfere nor feel ungrateful. Grant himself could easily have been belittled, reduced to an infant, perched in his chair, often unable to speak. Yet with Kitty everything seemed as normal as the blue grey cold outside and the pulsing range. When they took him outside with the coughing and leaned him against the wall until the surging crimson subsided and the shaking with it, even that seemed right, as it should be.

Mrs Grant shooed Kitty and Jimmy out of the house when it was all done and they walked slowly around the harbour to watch Mr James swim. He swam every single day of the year when the tide was up, but on Christmas Day it was to an applauding audience, spider arms and legs wrinkle fuzzed, a tight purple smile as he climbed up the fish market steps.

When they returned they found Grant relentlessly determined not to drag them down. He demanded draughts and go-bang and then cards to play Pope Joan. Each time the king and queen of trumps appeared they yelled *matrimony* and Grant punched Jimmy and told him it was about time he got on with it. Jimmy proposed to each of them over and over and only Kitty's pa accepted, saying it was because it would save him having to volunteer for the Army and fight the Kaiser. The women shut him up before the politics started. Jimmy was exhausted when he left in the dark of the early evening. It was not so much being with Kitty's family as with the certainty that he had not yet played his role to its end and had still not given Kitty what she wanted.

For an hour and a half in the afternoon, after dinner on Boxing Day, Kitty's pa tested Jimmy, using the book Schjonemann loaned to his pupils. Jimmy knew the examiners would not be as precise but rose to the duel with the old sergeant and watched as the blue eyes grew clearer and the hands more steady and the breathing deeper. Then Grant closed the book and for a long moment there was only the whistle and catch of his breathing.

'She's a good girl, Jimmy.'

'Kitty is the most perfect girl in the world, Mr Grant.'

Grant took his time before replying and when he did his voice was not less insistent.

'Plenty of 'em at the *Rising Sun* would be glad of a skivvy. But a man with a *head* on his shoulders wants a partner.'

'Kitty's not a skivvy. She's a *saint*.'

'Exactly.'

Grant's eyes widened and Jimmy could see volumes in their depth, too far to read. The man's aim had been deadly. He was already continuing.

'On most accounts she bends to your opinion and mine rather than have any of her own. But in love and faith she understands no uncertainty. Could you or I live with a woman like that?'

Jimmy was unable to reply, or even to hold the man's eyes.

'She'll hurt soon enough, Jimmy. There's hard times coming.'

'War?'

'Too much bloody Empire and too few to defend it. But you and me aren't talking about war. It won't be easy when I go.'

'It'll make her a woman.'

'Or a puritan.'

Jimmy looked again into the ice blue and was weighed. He would not have believed Grant was capable of seeing his daughter in this way, especially from the shadow in which he now lived. He considered telling him he was good for years yet, that anything could still transpire. But Grant held up a crooked finger.

'You'll look after 'em, Jimmy, until they can manage. She'll understand what's in your soul. You'll know what to do. Whatever, you look after her for me, until it's time.'

It was the kindest and most damning thing the man could have said and Jimmy once more blessed his cursed intelligence, the sea blue which sifted and understood you and which had always been the man's downfall. He made his promise as the man asked and looked away before his emotion was obvious. He knew then that everything that had been simple with Kitty was coming to an end and that they were going to dislike each other before they could love each other completely.

Grant pushed them out of the house saying he needed to sleep. Jimmy took Kitty up into the fields, thirsty for the sharp, wet air. They climbed past Ranscombe House and into the pastures above the town, slender fields that lay along the hillside like fingers. Jimmy had often looked up as *Maryann* came into harbour and imagined these shapes marked out for a thousand years before the first red brown sail had unfurled below. But time hung on Boxing Day, the harbour a dun mass, the smacks at their chains, the chimney of the ice works for once uncapped with smoke, the shipyards motionless below it and the two ropewalks clinging quiet to their opposite hillsides. They could hear the yell of a thousand voices that told you the boys in black and white had the beating even of the great Cardiff Roxburgh, practically undefeated in the rugby all season. Over everything the gulls were giving their insistent screech and you knew another blow was on the way. Jimmy looked to the north, where the weather was coming and saw the dark green grey of the rain in the sky.

They made their way out towards the headland, sighting the length of the tramway that carried stones to the end of the growing breakwater and was today an empty spine along the white. Jimmy stopped and held Kitty close and smelled the lavender in her coat and the sweetness of the dressmaker's shop in her hair and loved her for them. But with every step the silence between them grew deeper. Jimmy again fought the temptation to do what he always did and leave time to dictate, to let Grant's death provoke its crisis and grief impose its price. He realised that he was hoping Kitty would claim what she wanted. She would make what they shared worth fighting for, more than a small girl's dream, or an inevitable arrangement, or a daughter's duty, or a friendship that pretended to be perfect at whatever sacrifice it demanded of her. He wanted her to throw away her obligations and her certainties. He wanted her to find and make her own boundaries, state her own demands, even if they changed, to name his failings and mean it, and then to love him after they had fought. But her pa was dying and he could not see how any of this would be possible until afterwards, and he was afraid that Grant's death might only make her cling more to the certainties that she had learned.

'Your pa says there'll be war.'

'*The working poor buried for the profit of the rich. Capitalists paid with the blood of the working man. The first industrial war.* You've heard him.'

'He's always right.'

'He says 'tis a kind of sickness.'

Jimmy hunted his head again but could not find the words he wanted.

'He hasn't got long.'

'He's ready to go.'

She had said it without hesitation, as if it were the most obvious reply and Jimmy stopped her and turned her face to his. She was smiling. He prevented himself from shouting.

'He's not *ready to go*. Nobody is *ready to go*. Your pa has plenty...'

Kitty's eye was completely steady.

'Every day he examines his conscience and prays his rosary. The priest came last week and heard his confession and gave him Mass and anointed him with the oil of the sick. We shall pray for him until we die. He's ready to go.'

Kitty's voice was without accusation and Jimmy was silenced, the veil between heaven and this darkening, storm-threatened world lightly tugged aside, death confronted with the love of a daughter and the faith of a saint. Kitty burned with the kind of belief Jimmy had heard Pentecost proclaim but never practise. But at this moment he found it stone hearted and wondered whether he could live with it. He also knew he was picking a quarrel where there need have been none. And that this moment was the worst. He longed for Kitty. But he also longed for her for once to name the injustice that stole what you loved, that had destroyed her pa's work, wasted his mind, was destroying his lungs and would take him from her and leave them in poverty. He knew what losing your father meant. He heard his voice coming from a long way off.

'Don't you ever break, Kitty? Don't 'ee ever shake your fist and shout you shouldn't bloody well have to lose what you love, and there should be something for you, Kitty Grant, now, not tomorrow, not *bloody sometime*?'

Kitty looked at him as if he were a child confused.

'I'm angry about everything that's unjust and secret and stolen and denied. But I'm glad I have what is given to me. And when it goes I'll wait for what comes next. I don't always understand. But I always get on and do what seems best.'

'But 'tis not how 'ee wants it.'

Kitty turned and Jimmy thought there was at last a flicker of shadow across her eyes, the first he had ever seen. They had arrived at last, but everything was a mess.

'You know what I want, Jimmy.'

'Is that 'cause you've decided, or 'cause you've never imagined else?'

Jimmy regretted his words perhaps as deeply as he had regretted anything he had done. But then he hoped they might at last bring on the moment when they could stand together. Kitty turned away and looked along the breakwater.

The wind was rising and pushing at her bonnet, carrying the first spits of rain. Her eyes narrowed against it.

''Tis what I want.'

It was said with forethought and defiance and Jimmy believed he had at last glimpsed the woman she could be.

'Will you marry me, Kitty?'

'No.'

She had not hesitated or looked back.

'*No?*'

'Not while Pa is dying and you're not clear in your head. And if you want someone who will be angry and hate 'ee and think the worst of 'ee and then somehow love 'ee again, but you will never be certain, then you had better marry Alice Rogers. I only want what is good and a life to accept together.'

'And if I bain't good as 'ee?'

'I'm not your judge, Jimmy. Nor need you be.'

Jimmy looked away and saw the clouds along the horizon had grown steadily, a fraying edge of rain dragging across the water and obscuring it. The drops around them were coming more heavily.

'Are you always right, Kitty?'

'No, that's my pa. 'Tis intolerable.'

'But you are right.'

'And that's also intolerable?'

The wind was beginning to carry their breath away, the wet now stinging. Kitty turned. Jimmy was searching for a way to claim her, if only for an instant.

'Will you not marry me, Kitty?'

'Not until you want me the way I want to be.'

'What do thee want, Kitty?'

Jimmy had heard the accusing pain. Kitty seemed beyond age, beyond adulthood and now infinitely unreachable. He winced with his own ambiguity.

'When he goes, how can we help?'

We? Who was he talking about? Why did he lack the courage to tell her, that she had spoken correctly, that she would never be angry and lost and then love him again and so come to the things that only lie beyond pain? Here she was, angry as never before, her piety now a pointed weapon, but it had come only because the bond between them had suddenly broken. Jimmy wanted desperately to recover their closeness, now stronger than before, ready to endure. He felt the tears starting in his eyes. But Kitty's voice came back cold and careful as she turned away.

'We can say our prayers, Jimmy. The prayers of the faithful comfort the dying and those who rest.'

'*No, Kitty.* You and your mam. What will thee do?'

'We've got our work. We have our house. We'll look after each other.'

There was a silence before she continued, her steps now faster as the rain began to pour. Her voice was blue cold, the words chipped.

'I know you'll do what you can, Jimmy. And then whatever becomes of us, I'll love 'ee, and you will love me, as we always have, even if it is never naught more.'

Then Jimmy stopped her, pulled her back, like a child tugging at a parent. His eyes were full now and at last the sobs began to shake her until her hands crept up to her face and she wept hopelessly, burying her head in him, tears running between her fingers. He ran his hands through her hair and kissed her forehead and held her tightly as his own eyes closed and he shook with her. They held each other as if it was for ever in the hanging heaviness and the damning wet until the crying was gone and she looked away and at last they walked on, unable to speak, looking out to the grey green that was now filling the bay and was a full-throated storm bullying in.

Chapter 34

Jimmy finally left the Grants' house at seven, its quiet now dense and taut. His legs carried him down the steps and out into King Street and onto the quay but he was dragging against lead. Even if he stood by Kitty through her pa's death, now it would not be right, but be lost and bottomless. He fought the gale onto the quayside and Kitty's tears filled his mind and his own eyes filled with the wind and he put his head down and wrestled. The rain had turned to a torrent. A wind shrieked from the east down the gaping mouth of the harbour and through the wailing rig of four hundred masts.

Suddenly he was aware there were men hurrying around him and climbing out across the decks tied closely together, dropping into ships' boats and pulling out into the steepling water. A figure came shouldering past and he realised it was Roddy.

'What's on? Roddy, what's happening?'

Roddy turned and pulled Jimmy close, shouting against the wind.

'Glass dropping like a dog's bollock, Jimmy, looks so. We're out to double the anchors and the warps. Some of 'em have canvas drying. We were all at the Town Hall, at the dance. Decided we'd better make a run for it while we can.'

Looking round Jimmy saw all the men, like Roddy, were in their best suits. Roddy was pulling him along and he stumbled, slipping down the stairs and falling into the ship's boat with him. Roddy shouted as he picked up the oars.

'Where's *Maryann*?'

'Somewhere middle of the outer harbour.'

'Come on, man. You look bloody terrible, like 'ee fought the monkey in a bloody dustbin. Are 'ee pissed?'

Roddy was hauling now, throwing himself against the wind and Jimmy could hardly breathe in the gale. You could not see more than thirty yards.

'I bain't pissed. Just can't see her. We moored not far from Upham's…'

'I'll take 'ee out… fix *Maryann* first… come back for *Albion*.'

Around them smacks were coming to life, men lashing ropes as springs fore and aft and dropping anchors for safety. A sail came rattling down in the darkness and suddenly there was a shout ahead and Roddy turned and pulled the boat sharply under the nearest counter. A smack was drifting out of the darkness, no-one aboard. Roddy was laughing, out of control.

'She's a-blown in, bloody broken loose, looks so.'

'Aye, 'tis *Osprey*. Can't anyone get aboard?'

Voices were coming from above them, broken by sudden wrenching crashes as *Osprey* careered into one and then another of the boats tied closely together. It was impossible to imagine what damage she was doing.

'Got to get out o' here.'

Jimmy was suddenly and vividly conscious. Roddy let out a roar and they were off, Jimmy standing, fending them away from the tangle of ropes and the overhanging counters, straining through the black to work out where *Maryann* was lying. They found her surrounded with smacks that had come in after and tied up alongside. Henry or Eb had been the last to leave and Jimmy found everything below deck, the trawl inboard, sails tightly furled and a sea anchor with a long chain already down. Perhaps one of them had seen what was coming and had got back before the rest. He and Roddy checked stays and sheets and rigged a slip rope for safety alongside the mooring chain and then set off for *Albion*. Her mizzen had been left up to dry and was flapping like a caged bird. The trawl beam was still on the rail. By the time they were finished their suits were soaked through, the gnawing chill added to the awkwardness of being aboard, the two of them, and without boots or oilies. They had hardly spoken, the understanding between smacksmen so strong there was no need and the wind anyway carrying their words away. It was not until Roddy had pulled them almost back to the Eastern Quay that he shouted over his shoulder, Jimmy standing in the bow ready to tie up.

'You're a dead man, Jimmy Blackbridge, looks so. Not an ounce of blood left in you. You need company. You're a-coming back with me.'

'Fuck you. I need to sleep.'

'Don't talk shit, Jimmy. 'Tis bloody Boxing Day. No work 'til the middle of next week.'

Jimmy tied the painter to one of the rings along the quay and climbed up onto the road. In a moment Roddy had caught him up and put his arm roughly round his shoulders.

'Don't fucking start, Blackbridge. You're a-coming with me and you're bloody well going to dance. Thee's know how to. You went to the classes.'

'Can't remember a thing.'

'You will. You bloody well will.'

Roddy was pushing him towards Fore Street and Jimmy had no strength left to fight. Better to get it over. He did not have to stay any longer than it took to get away from Roddy. Anyway, the man was right. He needed to forget what had happened with Kitty, if only for an hour. For a moment he felt ready to be rough, alongside Roddy and the other men. The hall was hung with red, white and blue and a band was in full cry, the place jammed with couples, a heavy, pink, sweating man on the stage surveying them in bow tie and tails. It was hard to see in the low light, thick with smoke, but a few couples were gliding gracefully through the crowd and the rest were stumbling rigid and awkward, humiliated or angry or laughing in embarrassment. Just as many were sitting along the walls and in corners, turned away and stealing their privacy. Smacksmen were clattering, dripping back through the door and nobody was bothering to check their tickets. Roddy shoved Jimmy into the fug before anyone could stop them. There was a makeshift bar on a trestle table and Roddy bought two beers without a word and downed most of his in one. Jimmy drank two thirds of his for courage, suddenly lightheaded with the music and the beer. None of this was happening. Roddy's eyes were darting like a ferret, hunting the pack.

'Are 'ee bloody well going to join in or not?'

'Happens I've never danced with a man, Roddy. But you'll have the next one if 'ee wants.'

'Not bloody likely. Rather dance with a case of turbot.'

Roddy pointed to Jimmy's beer. He drained it and Roddy hustled him through the darkness to the far side. The dance came to an end and the man in the bow tie announced the new tango from Paris. Most of the couples crowded off the floor and made for the bar and the seats, complaining they did not know the steps and Jimmy grinned at the few who were left, stumbling into the familiar routine. Suddenly a girl was pushed into his soaking arms and they were hauled out into the open floor, surrounded with laughter and applause. She was dressed in a fashionable printed blue silk dress, narrow at the hip, her blonde hair wound into tight spirals at the ears. Jimmy looked round in the darkness for Roddy, his head still spinning with the unreality of the storm and the crowded, airless, pounding hall. He turned back to concentrate on the steps before he pushed the girl over. She looked up. Under the blonde hair, straightened and much shorter than before, he saw it was Alice.

Her eyes were wide and her lips rose swollen again as if she were ready to cry. Jimmy imagined she might have been watching him since Roddy had pushed him through the door, confused about what it would mean. But when their eyes met he saw a simplicity he had not seen since their first blissful summer. As the music got into its rhythm he too was unexpectedly charged with energy and with the confidence they could at any rate get through this moment together.

'Alice... you here with Roddy?'

The music was turning them round, pulling them through the darkness. It took Alice some moments to reply, speaking in snatches as they danced.

'I had to get out, Jimmy. Two days and only my father. He's raving, asking for Billie, calling me by my mam's name. He's forgotten I exist. I went next door, slept in an armchair, shivering cold. In the end I went to Roddy's and he dressed me up in these clothes, ones his father had for me. Made me come with him. 'Tis horrible.'

'Why does he want me here, then?'

'Roddy? He knows 'tis over, him and me. We talk, that's all, 'bout what happened. He says he'd have hung for what they had on *Rosaleen*, and you saved his life and you've never said a word about it. If he wasn't Roddy Farley he'd tell 'ee he's grateful.'

'I think he's gone. I can't see 'en.'

In smoke-dull light it was impossible to be sure. Roddy might be outside, puking his beer, pissing in a gutter. But it was just as likely he had meant to leave them together, a rough parting well-meant, because he did not have the words. Jimmy held Alice closer and for the first time they danced because they intended to and could make themselves one in its elegance and in the exhilaration of the timing. Alice spoke in his ear.

'Jimmy... what about Kitty?'

'I don't know – until her father dies. It won't be long... I think 'tis over. Nearly over.'

Jimmy knew it was true, now he had said it.

'Kitty... poor Kitty.'

'Kitty's stronger than we are.'

They were now caught in the tango, the steps now easier than before. The rhythm started to lift them, to push them like a current. Jimmy saw all the faces that watched them as they danced.

'I'll take 'ee home.'

'Not home. I can't face my father. The old lady next door said she'd look out for him. I casn't go there.'

Alice was pleading, pulling him back, and Jimmy held her and ignored the eyes that now followed them from the dance floor. He took the handkerchief Alice pulled out from her sleeve and wiped her tears with it.

'We'll go to my lodgings. I don't care.'

Alice said nothing but took Jimmy by the hand and walked unsteadily to the hooks where the coats were hung and they slipped out without a word. The gale had taken possession of the streets and Alice clung tightly to him, her skirts soon sodden with the whipping rain and beating wildly around their legs. They climbed the cascading steps to Higher

Street and then on up the long flight into Prospect Road and here the wind was less in the closeness of houses and laughter jangling loudly from one of the windows. Alice suddenly pulled away, out into the middle of the street and span and pulled off her hat so that the rain flew in her face. She was dancing through the running gush, unbuttoning her coat and pulling it off, waving it like a flag, the blue silk of her dress quickly darkening and glistening in the downpour. Jimmy ran to keep up.

'Alice, you idiot. You're pissed.'

'Let's go and swim. Like Scabbacombe. Like Mr James. Swimming every day.'

'Don't be stupid, Alice. 'Tis blowing force ten and freezing. Harbour's jammed with smacks. Ropes parting. The boats'd smash 'ee up.'

But he was laughing too and suddenly Alice was looking up into his face, eyes burning, her arms wrapped around his neck and they were wheeling down the street. They reached his lodgings and two houses along water was cascading from a gutter and as Jimmy pushed his door open Alice stood under the stream, gasping, hunching her shoulders against the bite. Jimmy pulled her away and bundled her into the house, water pouring from her hair and clothes and her eyes closed. She would not let go of him as they struggled up the stairs and into his room, their boots thumping against the silence. As he kissed Alice he could feel her body in the dark through the thin wetness of the fabric and her shivering starting.

'You idiot, Alice. You bloody idiot. You're going to die.'

Jimmy found his matches and lit a candle and Alice unbuttoned the blue silk dress and dropped it like a skin she had never wanted. The linen underneath was completely sodden and she let it drop too, the wet spreading dark across the boards like blood. Jimmy took the newspaper and the kindling and the fire began to spit. By the time he had the gas blue and the kettle filled Alice was wrapped in one of his towels and kneeling by the fire, fingers shaking red, eyes black and lost in the first of the flames, flickering without warmth. She took the tea as the smacksmen did, the thick condensed milk and the sugar that surged through you and told you that you were going to survive.

'What's happening, Jimmy?'

Jimmy sat beside her, felt the shaking through the towel.

'I don't understand. I don't want to understand.'

'That's what I said to myself at Farley's.'

It was a shock, but she had said it without accusation and Jimmy perceived that even the horror was starting to be possible to share. Alice turned her head on Jimmy's shoulder and reached out to him.

'Hold me.'

What happened next was the moment of most trust and lostness Jimmy had ever known, Alice's wet hair in his hands and her lips pulsing soft warm, wanting to give to him and not take. And when they finished kissing Jimmy took off his clothes amazed at his own calm and Alice pulled him into the dampness of his bed and the agreement was quiet and certain and she looked away at the difficult moment and then kissed him and then it was good again and what happened was very quickly over and they held each other utterly lost but completely certain.

'Did we choose this, Jimmy?'

'*I was not ever thus, nor prayed that Thou shoulds't lead me on. I loved to choose and see my path, but now lead Thou me on. I loved the garish day and spite of fears pride rule my will: remember not past years.'*

The words he knew were Catholic. But they had sung them a hundred times at the Methodist chapel and they had always loved them. He whispered them into her ear and the truth and beauty they contained were almost more than he could bear, a kind of spoken silence.

'It won't stop remembering me, Jimmy. It haunts me, in the night when 'tis too cold and still to live, in the time alone, when I wonder if I belong in the body I see. When I'm old I'll wonder where the child went, the years I should have lived, the hope I've never been able to believe in.'

'*So long Thy power hath blest me, sure it still will lead me on. O'er moor and fen, o'er crag and torrent, till the night is gone: And with the morn those angel faces smile –*'

'*Which I have loved long since, and lost awhile.*'

'Are we going back, to before?'

'No. 'Cause now you know as well. We both know.'

'Are 'ee afraid?'

'*I do not ask to see the distant scene. One step enough for me.*'

At last Alice fell asleep. When Jimmy woke the candle had burned down and the fire was nothing but a glow and he asked himself if it was still good and it still was. He had supposed bitter guilt would fill his mouth and guts but as he ran the corridors of his imagination he found nothing but light. He fell asleep believing he and Alice were already married whatever anybody would say in the morning or any day that came after.

Chapter 35

The three days that followed Jimmy hardly knew himself. He was a fugitive, inside a skin that was not his, at an infinite distance from the people around him. He ached for Alice every moment of each sodden day and sleepless night. She agreed without hesitation he should stand by Kitty until her father was gone. He waited by the Grants' flaking blue door, and when he stamped his boots on the pavement he heard her voice calling him through the window and went to wait in the warmth. He felt then how impossible it would have been were it not for the way Kitty was. She loved you first and without reserve and you could not help loving her.

Grant was cheerful, as he always was when he had gnawed some complexity in his mind. There was paper on the table canvas, covered with diagrams and calculations and straight away he had Jimmy navigating across imaginary waters. The currents were ripping through, tide and wind fighting for control, posing the dilemmas of making your course that were obvious when you were at the helm and Henry on his bunk but baffling when they came at you on lined paper. The arrows from Grant's angular pencil bullied you and other vessels pitched into you, sail and steam, from every point of the compass. Jimmy told him that at least half a dozen of the smacks had already run foul of the *Empress of India*. The Navy had salvaged some of the wreck, but still refused to mark the place with more than a buoy, without a bell, invisible at night or in a fog. It was, Grant said with his hands outstretched in mock resignation, because they believed peace was becoming worthless and war was all that mattered.

'It won't matter to me, Jimmy. But to Kitty. And you. And your young Alice.'

There was a momentary silence, ringing like a bell. Jimmy was gripped by the need to stand up, put his hands out in self-defence, shout denial, walk out taking Kitty with him just to prove the man could not possibly know. Instead he felt himself flinch, his hands suddenly cold, skin prickling, and wondered if he could make his voice obey.

'I will look after them, Mr Grant.'

'You're a good lad, Jimmy. You'll say your prayers, and come to Mass sometimes, and make your confession. May the Lord have mercy on your soul.'

The man had not missed a beat and Jimmy had the sensation that he had raised his hand and pronounced absolution.

On Sunday afternoon Jimmy rowed Kitty across to *Maryann* again. For an hour they retold every detail of the Regatta and her radiance returned. She said she had never stopped thinking about the men and their quiet certainty that there was no-one better at what they did and, whatever its insane danger, there was no better job. She leaned against the hoodway and let Jimmy kiss her so that for a moment they were lovers again and understood. They found Kitty's pa bent purple over the scullery sink, his wife holding him up as the coughing punched cruelly through and his eyes bulged for the air. He took Jimmy's hand in his cold, blotched fingers and Jimmy understood he was wishing him luck for the next day.

A shrugging clerk let Jimmy in to the Customs House at ten the next morning. There were two other lads. Lovell, the Board of Trade examiner, took one of them for his skipper's exam first and twenty minutes later called for Jimmy. The room had an odd, bookish quiet, the noise of the harbour silent beyond the rippling glass. Lovell smiled briskly and Jimmy could see he had done this dozens of times and was not going to make it difficult. After days of Grant's inquisition the exam hardly seemed to have begun before Lovell was standing up and offering his hand and telling him he would make a fine mate and asking, as he filled in the forms with thick, steady black ink, if he had a mate's place to go to.

There on the quayside in her best bonnet and dress was Kitty. Jimmy fell into her arms overwhelmed because he knew what it would have cost her, in lost wages and the patience of Miss Wills, to get away in the middle of a morning. More than that they both knew it was a borrowed moment, waiting for death to do its business and the new part to begin. They wheeled down towards the deserted fish market and for a crazy moment Jimmy thought he was going to take her to his room and they would make love as he had with Alice. Instead they went into Smarden's bookshop and Jimmy bought her a copy of *Deep Sea*, the new novel Dr Brett Young had written about the town. Kitty held it like a Bible because she had never owned a book of her own. The wind was cold so they climbed to the railway station and bought sandwiches and drank the thin, bitter railway tea, laughing at the sunny posters and where they would go if they lived other lives. For a moment Jimmy wished only that they had and that everything would be easier. And yet the thought of taking a train and leaving the town stopped him short. It was Alice, of course.

Maryann cast off at four-thirty the next morning. Henry shook Jimmy's hand and asked if he'd be leaving for another boat. Jimmy could see he did not mean it and told him he was going for his master's ticket first, which was true. He ached hollow for Alice but six days in harbour had been enough for the others and they elected to let the wind take them down to the Cornish waters. They finally tied up in Brixham under an early grey Tuesday dusk and barely had their cases on the quayside in time for the last train. They were clear again before dawn the next morning and Jimmy had scarcely had time to call on Kitty and then Alice, who had been to his rooms and taken and washed not only the sheets and towels but also his spare clothes so that he was aboard the next day smelling of her and hardly able to think of anything else. Then it was the same again, tacking around Land's End and finding the sole running beautifully so that on Sunday they slept aboard in St Ives and only returned to Brixham late on the following Saturday afternoon. They had been out nineteen days with only twelve hours in the port.

Kitty was in the scullery and buried herself in Jimmy's arms as soon as she saw him. She was sickly dry, her eyes raw and lips grey drawn.

'He's had a fever since Thursday. He can't eat, can hardly drink. He's too weak to cough.'

'You've had the doctor?'

'Dr Young says 'tis pneumonia and there's nothing he can do.'

Jimmy climbed the narrow stairs heavily. He pushed at the door and was thrown back by the heat of the fire in the tiny grate, the tang of its coal and the bitterness of sweat and decay. Kitty's ma was sitting on the bed, bowl in one hand, a spoon in the other. It was obviously useless, brown soup smeared down the man's soaking face. But what Jimmy noticed straight away was the silence. There was scarce a trace of the phlegmy rattle. Without it the man seemed gone already. Grant shook himself, almost imperceptibly, and then the eyes were open, not their old sharp blue but steady.

'Jimmy.'

His voice was a rasp but enough to bring out his wife's smile. Jimmy pulled a chair, placing it by the bed. Closer, the smell was stronger, the warm stink of sheets unchanged, of stale urine.

'Kitty said 'ee weren't well. But 'ee looks good. Just taking it easy.'

A smile worked painfully across Grant's face, even while the eyes closed again.

'What took you so long?'

'Navigation, Mr Grant. Trying to remember what I was taught.'

'Next time get a decent teacher.'

'The last one spends his time in bed.'

The eyes were open again and Grant struggled to lift himself a fraction.

'I've been dreaming, Jimmy. On a making tack, current and wind opposed. You've got me wanting to go to sea.'

'When you're better.'

'Rest of my life.'

Mrs Grant gave Jimmy the soup and the spoon and left to make a meal for herself and Kitty. He could tell how delighted Grant was to see him. He thought it odd, given that they both knew he would not be coming to the house much longer. But he was the only friend the man had left, beside his wife and daughter. Jimmy knew him. They talked about *Maryann*. It seemed unutterably mundane and yet, with the ears of his listener, wonderful once again. At last he could see Grant was sleeping once more, his breathing shallow and snatched and the wheezing oozing thick, a gurgling that tainted the air.

Jimmy closed his eyes and dreamed he was walking down the hill and out along Fore Street and around the harbour and it was crowded with smacks, Roddy sitting on the harbour edge and laughing. Then he was climbing up on the other side and he knew he was going to Alice's and, in a moment, he was holding her and she was looking up, her eyes closing and her head rocked back and the veins on her naked neck and shoulders pulsing her excitement.

Kitty came up and Jimmy kissed the top of her head and slipped out. He found her ma sitting at the dining table. She did not look up.

''Tis the waiting that's hard, Jimmy.'

'He's ready to go.'

'We're so lucky.'

Jimmy looked around in the dim light of the little window. There was only an old table, worn and stained around each edge, burned in places in its centre. The four chairs were all different and the two armchairs by the range worn through. On the mantelpiece was a small print of the Virgin that cannot have cost more than a shilling. The dresser's paint was scrubbed almost to nothing, lending it dark edges, its plates and cups the remains of a dinner service, filled out by an assortment of other pieces. The Grants owned hardly anything. The only luxury was a small pile of newspapers, William Grant's lifeline, a gift from one of the men at the police station, gripped with those steely fingers while he laboured for air by the fire. Yet Kitty and her parents were undoubtedly the most blessed people Jimmy knew.

Jimmy slept in the armchair by the range. Every couple of hours Kitty or her ma was down to boil a kettle and to fetch coal to keep the fire burning in his grate. The dawn rose with the bell ringing for eight o'clock Matins and the town silent, the chuff and clank of the morning train sounding from the other side. Dr Young came and spoke to Jimmy as he climbed heavily down the stairs to leave.

'He's had quinine but he's drowning in his own fluids.'

'Today?'

'I'm sorry.'

By midday Grant was restless, his eyes watering, unfocussed, his frame shaking with a useless effort to clear his lungs. He had said nothing for hours. Jimmy took his turn and found his eyes closing and Alice's face filling his mind so he stood and went to the window, longing to open it for the fresh air.

'*Jesu Maria.*'

The man was leaning forward, eyes stretched like a watchman in a storm, transfixed by what he had seen. Jimmy stepped to the door and called. Mrs Grant reached the room first and sat on the bed and held her husband's hands.

'*Confiteor Deo...*'

He was unable to go on but his wife's voice was quietly filling the space.

'*Absolve, Domine, animas omnium fidelium, ab omni vinculo delictorum, et gratia tua...*'

'*Credo Domine, sed credam firmius; spero...*'

Again the man stumbled, his throat parched, his breath too feeble for speaking.

'*Adoro te.*'

His wife joined his hands on his chest with hers.

'*Lux æterna luceat ei, Domine, cum sanctis tuis in æternum, quia pius es.*'

His eyes were closed now and he was laid back on his pillows, his hands white as his wife grasped them. Jimmy found he was holding his breath and heard Kitty reciting her prayers as she sat at the foot of the bed. It cannot have been more than a minute before Mrs Grant gently leaned forward, her face very close to her husband's. Then she sat back, calmly, one hand still grasping his, the other making the sign of the cross.

'*Requiem æternam dona ei, Domine, et lux perpetua luceat ei; cum Sanctis tuis in aeternum, quia pius es.*'

Jimmy saw Kitty sway and went to catch her but instead she slipped to her knees. He felt more privileged and more unprepared and useless than he had ever felt. He had no words, no useful thoughts to carry this man's spirit to his reward. He prayed simply and silently that God would hold this man in his arms as his wife and his daughter would. At last he knelt beside Kitty and held her as the sobs passed through until she turned and smiled the most certain smile he ever knew.

The evening bells were ringing as Jimmy got ready to leave. Kitty had talked about her pa and Jimmy had wanted to say she must keep some of it and not talk it all out and change it, allowing her memories to stay unorganised and real. But her need was overwhelming and she talked about when he was fit enough to carry her onto the steamer and take her to the other side of the bay and how his laugh had filled the whole boat. How he had walked the town in his uniform and had known everyone and had words to say on their business, always acute, mostly kind. And how he had been so angry about the government, and the secrecy and stupidity of class, and about the lawyers and the bankers and journalists and every issue you could think of, and how he had talked it all out, half-joking, half-serious, and had always been right enough for it to matter. Her face was composed, a pooling serenity in her eyes, faith setting her features.

That week the weather blew foul, not hard but unpredictably and they had a continual labour to keep the trawl on the bottom and travelling. The fish quivered in Jimmy's fingers, their pale cold as one with the death he had witnessed. He did not want to talk, but recalled over and over the family in its final prayers, centuries of faith brought to one moment. When he carried the baskets into the fish market on Saturday they told him that William Grant's funeral had been on Thursday afternoon. He left and climbed the hard black steps to Kitty's house, wondering if he would find her in steel calm or red with grief. He opened the door and called and heard Kitty from the kitchen.

'Jimmy. Thank you for coming.'

He knew then, even before he saw her, that it was finished and she would not let him inside. Her hair was tightly pinned back and her skin a dry white as if she had not seen light for months. The black under her eyes made them huge, bruised, her head hollow, lips purple. But again Jimmy noticed the calm.

'I came to see you are alright, Kitty.'

'Bless you, Jimmy. Yes we are.'

Her smile was honestly meant.

'Your mam?'

'She cries and tells herself not to.'

'She must.'

'Yes.'

They stood looking, the inches between them an infinite space. There was disinfectant in the air, a cool in the house for the first time Jimmy could remember. Her pa's memory was being washed clean and what Jimmy and Kitty had shared with it.

'You must tell me, Kitty, if there's anything you need. You know I'll always... anything.'

'I know, Jimmy.'

'Do thee have everything 'ee wants?'

At last Kitty managed something of a smile that was her own.

'Of course I don't, Jimmy. But we've done that now.'

The silence was unbearable. Kitty smiled again.

'Thank you, Jimmy.'

'Thank you, Kitty.'

He stepped forward and she let him hold her arms and kiss her on her cheek. In the end it had been Kitty who had chosen.

Part V

Chapter 36

By the time he was back at the quay Jimmy was shaking. A sudden sun threaded through the black blue above and threw the confusion of the harbour into a sharpness he had forgotten. The sight of the crowded smacks soaked into his eyes, the russet of their canvas and the salt-pitched wood of winches and trawl beams, the striking poppy and primrose and cornflower of stanchions and bulwarks. He saw *Sanspareil* back in working order, new planking on the starboard bow. She had been the latest victim of the *Empress*. Still the Navy refused an adequate buoy and for a moment Jimmy could hear Kitty's pa winding up his complaint and thought how much he missed him already.

Alice had finished work at Upham's.

'How is Kitty?'

'Old and grey. She didn't want to see me.'

'She told me. She's wants to get on with the next part, to have time for her mam.'

Jimmy was for a moment irritated at the girls for fixing things between them as if they had interfered in a private grief. But Kitty had already changed them both. Her graciousness at the end had charged him with an uncertain elation and he took Alice by the hand and swung her along the quayside and past the fish market, every detail cut as if for the first time, the men standing cross-armed in their caps, the girls in their stiff aprons with their baskets, catches glistening in rows on the stones and the buyers moving along in a jaded knot under the open roof. Climbing the steps up to Higher Street Alice was almost running ahead and they had given up trying to talk. Pentecost was still at the yard and they ran into the house and up the stairs and were on the old iron double bed almost without a word and holding each other so tightly against the damp Jimmy was sure he would bruise her. Alice wanted to take longer this time, said she was ready to face at least some of her horrors, and Jimmy was astonished as her eyes half closed and she slipped into a state of longing so overwhelming he could not satisfy her and he felt his own inexperience. And she put his fingers into her once he was done and then she fought whatever it was until at last she squealed and Jimmy could not help laughing with the extraordinary joy of it and the idea that old Mrs Drake would come from next door because a murder was being committed.

Alice leaned up on her elbow so she could look into his eyes. She was not flawless, her teeth already crooked and starting to blacken, her hair thinner than he remembered. She was beautiful the way she had chosen to be and Jimmy could see in the openness of her face and the clarity of her eyes that she was present to him now as she had never been before. The veil that had torn was not the last, but it was something that had been very dense and weighed with fear.

'Hello.'

Alice smiled.

''Tis real now.'

'Not something we invented. Not this time.'

Alice toyed with the hair on the back of Jimmy's neck and the silence began to fill with the questions that were left over, the things that had pulled them down the first time.

'How long, Alice? Until 'ee are qualified?'

Alice's hands shifted and she sat away, cross-legged. Jimmy did not look, aware of her nakedness, wanting it not to be important. He heard in her voice she knew what she intended to do but was weighing how much she should say at this moment.

'I bain't going away. I don't care what people think. I think going to college was not about becoming a teacher. It was a way of a-proving to myself I was worth something, for a few minutes every day, in my imagination. I don't need it now. I want to do this while I can.'

'Do 'ee want to wait, find out what happens this time? Whether we can do this?'

Again the silence, the weighing of the words.

'No, I don't want to wait, Jimmy. I want to make it work, with you, whatever happens. Do thee?'

This time Jimmy found it took him time to answer. Once again he had a decision in his hands, choosing a course, the deciding he had always left to others before. He sat and faced Alice. She concentrated on the stray threads her hands were tugging in the coverlet and the white and brown of her breasts danced slightly as she moved. The muscles in her arms edged and folded, sharp in their painful slenderness. Her bony legs gently framed the fine, surprisingly dark and tousled hair between. She was a continent apart, a risk to know, a mess of unresolved intuition and unruly emotions. For no reason he could name, this time he believed he could trust her.

'Let's not wait.'

Alice did not smile and Jimmy knew they had both spoken with consideration. It seemed that they had done no more than take possession of a decision made too long ago to remember.

Three Saturdays, one after another, Jimmy came into the harbour and found Alice waiting on the middle quay and they went to her father's bed and made love before he came back from the yard. And they lay together again, each Sunday, in Jimmy's room, careless of the scandal because they only wanted each other. Making love transfigured them both. Alice told Jimmy she believed her horrors had begun to visit her less often and with less venom, if only a fraction, both in her dreams and in the silent screaming, cold sweating panic that had gripped her for years at work. For Jimmy it was acceptance and trust and future. He found he was not dogged any more by the not-belonging that had lived with him ever since he had come in to the schoolroom as a child and found his father collapsed against his desk. He was content to savour and weigh the present and transact it as fully as he could bring himself to bear.

The fourth Saturday Jimmy looked along the middle quay but Alice was not there. Instead the quayside boys were waiting and a redheaded lad, the lower half of his face buried in a massive black scarf, sculled expertly out and called for him.

'She said 'ee was to come straight. She wouldn't say what for.'

A coldness crept through Jimmy's hands. His first thought was that Farley had returned. His second was that her father had finally lost his reason or his temper and Alice was lying in her neighbour's house, too bruised to fetch him herself. Eb promised to follow when he was done at the fish market, and Jimmy let the redheaded boy row him back to the steps.

When he reached the door in Higher Street it was opened by Fanny Beaton. Jimmy could not read her expression.

'Alice…?'

'I'll let her tell you herself.'

Jimmy saw from Fanny's look that Alice was upstairs. As he started to climb he heard shouting from the bedroom.

'Her father's with her.'

The voices cut off as he reached the top of the stairs and turned into Alice's room. He expected to find her sitting or lying on the bed, shivering from her father's threats and his fists tightened. He was ready to pull the man off and for an instant imagined hurrying Alice down the stairs and away with him for good. Instead he found her standing by the window, red-eyed and in a shaking fury. It was her father who was sitting on the bed, crumpled as if the air had been sucked from his body, his face blood red and his eyes wide and wild with a fury that seemed to be suffocating him. Jimmy looked from one to the other in the sudden silence. It was Alice who spoke, her eyes fixed on her father, her voice quiet. Yet her words were clearly meant for Jimmy. They were ringing with triumph.

'I'm pregnant.'

Jimmy was bewildered. This was one of the moments you were taught to dread and he struggled to remember how he was supposed to react. Yet this was real, an unreadable tide, Alice, his life.

''Tis yours, Jimmy. Ours.'

Out of the confusion Jimmy's lungs began to fill with the fragrant air you scent as you head landward in springtime and the wind carries the sweetness of the blossom and the wet of the grass. He stepped towards Alice, framed in the whiteness of the window, his arms already reaching. It was her father's voice that stopped him, high pitched and quavering. It seemed to Jimmy to be an echo from some distant lifetime.

'You've ruined my daughter.'

For a moment Jimmy hesitated between ignoring the man or hitting him, shouting at him or trying to reason. Now Rogers was on his feet, stepping closer, pushing out his jaw.

'You seduced her in order to take her from Roddy Farley, so you could have her. A solemn promise is not to be broken. But you've a-taken her and now there's nothing for her but shame.'

Alice took Jimmy's hand and pulled him to her side and screamed over her father so that he winced.

'Shame? Thee's know all about shame. Why don't 'ee tell Jimmy why thee said nothing all these years while Farley did what he wanted with me?'

'All these years I've brought 'ee up in honour and giv'd 'ee everything and made it possible for 'ee to have your education and marry and be what your mam wanted 'ee to be.'

For a moment Jimmy believed Rogers was going to throw his daughter out of the house and that they would have each other and their new baby and be free of this fool. If not, he would take her himself. He turned, was about to seize Alice's hand again and walk out. But Alice interrupted, spitting her words in her father's face.

'My mother? What my mother wanted? Do 'ee remember what my mam wanted?'

'Your mam wanted *whatsoever things are true, whatsoever things are honest, whatsoever things are just, whatsoever things are pure.*'

'Perhaps she did, until you…'

'I married her and she a-brought up my children. And you'm all is left and she will not be dishonoured.'

He turned, his finger levelled at Jimmy's face.

'You've been in the prison once for rape and I am not a-going to give 'ee a second chance to get away. You've heard Alice. She says 'tis your baby. Thee's know my daughter was promised to Roddy Farley. So this is what you do...'

'Her engagement to Farley was over months ago.'

Jimmy was shouting but it was useless.

'Save your words for the court, young man. You'll have plenty of years behind bars to regret what you have done. And you can say your prayers Farley will still accept my daughter and give the child a decent home.'

'Well spoken, Mr Rogers. Well remembered. The very same words, exactly as they were said.'

The voice had come from the doorway and they all turned. Fanny Beaton was standing at the top of the stairs.

'The same words my father said to you twenty years ago. And you shook your preacher's finger and damned us all to hell and told us you would take what was yours. And if you had not ruined my sister so completely it would be you, Pentecost Rogers, who had spent your life in a cell where you belonged.'

'This is nothing to do with you, Fanny. Why did 'ee have to come? Does the whole town know what this man has done to Alice?'

'I promised Alice I would be here whenever the time came.'

Rogers looked from face to face and Jimmy saw the tremor that passed, the slightest stoop that dragged at his shoulders.

'Thee's know what Grace wanted, Fanny. Leave us alone. Let it happen this time as it should have happened afore. Let me pay the price. Then we can all a-go in peace.'

'The only way you can pay the price, Pentecost Rogers, is to confess what thee did.'

Fanny was calm, her skin white. It was obvious she had come hurriedly. Her hair was unbrushed and she was wearing the loose, drab brown she must have been wearing in the house. Her glancing grey eyes had been quick and kindly towards Jimmy, merciless as she turned on Rogers. He was shrinking, the skin of his face around his eyes and mouth shrivelling as Jimmy watched, a horror spreading like a cancer. It was as if he were being pushed back into a grave. Alice's voice came in the silence.

'I know what happened. Fanny told me.'

Rogers shook his head, holding up his hand in a gesture of denial, as if whatever it was this woman had to say could be undone, made untrue. Fanny turned to Jimmy. Her voice had been completely calm and Jimmy noticed she was better spoken than he remembered, an upright, proud woman, more confident in herself now she was widowed. Even though she had put on a good deal of weight it suited her and, despite the differences between them, he thought again how strikingly like Alice she was, her sister's daughter.

'If Alice is pregnant by Jimmy Blackbridge then at last she has a man who will love her. You have never done anything for her in her life, but now you will give her your blessing or I'll stand in every street and smack and pub, and climb your precious pulpit, and tell every man and woman and child in this town what you did and how you knew what the animal Farley was up to and you said nothing, with no other reason than to cover your pious sham.'

'I shall never give my consent to this marriage.'

But Rogers's eyes were vanishing, as if he was unable to make sense of what they saw. Alice turned.

'Fanny, tell Jimmy.'

Fanny paused. Her eyes fixed on Rogers in cold and steady contempt. At last she turned.

'Very well. My sister Grace agreed to marry this man when she was very young. But later she asked to break off the engagement because George Farley had proposed to marry her and she wanted to accept. This man refused to release her and then Grace told him she would not now marry him under any circumstances. So he took my sister to the workshop at Upham's and he raped her. Not once but again and again in the weeks that followed, until 'twas clear she was pregnant. Then he went to my parents and they agreed the marriage for the sake of decency.'

Rogers sat on the bed, un-looking and unhearing.

'It was Farley went to the police. William Grant was the sergeant at the station and he would have locked this man up for so long as the law permitted. But now Grace was changed. She was lost. She told me she was worth nothing any more, that it didn't matter what happened to her. She would not give evidence. I'm ashamed to remember the things I said to her, the way I shook her and bullied her. But she could not, and in the end I thought we were going to lose her. So then they had no choice. They had to drop the case. The wedding was a sham. Five months later Alice was born. But Grace was never herself again.'

'And that's why Farley began to use her, and why she let 'en.'

Alice's voice was quiet steel. Fanny's was now breaking.

'And we know where that has led to, and how Alice has suffered. And others. But it was this man – Rogers – that started it all.'

Fanny was silent for a long moment. Then she turned to Jimmy.

'If only Grace had given her evidence she could have married Farley and God willing they would have been content together and none of this would ever have started. So when Alice told me that she had been engaged against her will to Roddy Farley, I took the decision to do whatever I had to, anything so Alice should not have to marry a man she did not want. I hated going to the police station, when you were arrested, with Sergeant Grant there. It brought back the pain again. I did it because Alice asked me.'

Jimmy wondered now if Grant had always known, when he brought him out of the cell, that it would be a new beginning for him and for Alice, and the unravelling of hope for his daughter. He remembered how Grant had tried to persuade him to decide there and then, confessing his deal with O'Connor, levelling with Jimmy about what had happened. But he guessed Grant had already known it would be no good. He felt the loss of the man as brutally as he ever had and wondered what else he might have kept from him and could never now tell.

Fanny was turning back to Rogers, her voice at last raised as if she might reach him in the other life to which he was retreating.

'You knew what you had done, that you had broken my sister. And you knew what Farley then started to do. To her, and then to Alice, and then to Billie – even though we all knew Billie was his own son. You refused to rouse 'ee from your cant. More than anything you were afraid one Sunday Farley would walk in to your chapel and tell 'em all the truth. You closed your eyes until Grace could stand it no more and took her own life…'

Alice's voice interrupted, now thick with tears.

'...and Billie as well, 'cause there was nothing left for him, 'cause it suited 'ee to let us pay the price for what you'd done.'

There was no response. The man did not acknowledge his daughter. Fanny shouted.

'Have 'ee nothing to say?'

Rogers did not look at Fanny or at any of them. Instead in the heavy silence he got awkwardly to his feet and took a step towards the door. Then he turned, his head slightly to one side, a small man, his expression almost a smile.

'Not one of 'ee has the right to instruct me. *He made me lord of this house and ruler of all my possessions.* My daughter does as I decide. I've heard what 'ee have to say. Alice will marry Roderick Farley. She was publicly promised to 'en and her mother would've wished it. Whatever the faults of the father, Roddy is an honourable man.'

He turned to leave. In that moment Fanny had crossed the room and caught him by the arm. He did not turn, but at her words he stopped, suspended in the act of walking.

'Then let me tell you about Roddy Farley. I am pregnant too, several months further on than Alice. And Roddy Farley is the father.'

Alice's gasp was almost inaudible and was met by Fanny's smile. But her eyes had not left Rogers, his back still turned to them.

'It was Roddy my husband saw leaving the house the night afore the Regatta, when they charged Jimmy with rape. I had an affair with the boy for nearly a year. It continued until I fell pregnant because that is what I wanted. Flush was useless and we could never have had children. Finally I told Flush who it was, because he threatened and beat me till I could take no more. That was the day he took Roddy and poor Boy and sailed *Rosaleen* into the storm. He didn't care if any of them lived or died. And when she was dismasted he sent the lads away because he had decided to finish it. Roddy told me. I only pray God 'twas quick.'

There was a moment's silence as Fanny took another step. Now she stood in front of Rogers and hardened her voice until it was no more than a whisper of hatred.

'Roddy Farley's a weakling but we can forgive 'en because of what his father's a-done to him. Jimmy Blackbridge is as honest and true a man as I have met, intelligent and spirited as Alice. May they be happy together for as many years as you've stole from my sister.'

Rogers turned his face away from the woman who blocked his step.

'May the Lord forgive you.'

Jimmy took Alice's hand again and kissed the tears from her eyes, and then went down the stairs because Eb was at the door. He discovered that he felt no disgust for her father, only sorrow. He had learned from Kitty that there was charity enough.

Chapter 37

Jimmy scanned the horizon and counted fourteen. Twelve of them were smacks and two from the rag-tag collection of Belgian boats that had slipped into the port in the grim September weeks after the German invasion. The closer of the two, probably a couple of miles to the south, could almost have been a Brixham smack if her mizzen were not planted on her transom and carrying barely enough canvas for a flag. The other was one of the luggers built in the old French style that you used to see if you went far enough east, its foremast stepped almost in the bow and its stunted mizzen almost aft of the rudder. They had tied up, one after another in their decrepit procession, the wretchedness of the women and children lifted ashore enough at the time to forgive the rotting, ramshackle mess of the boats themselves. And of course everyone had done what they could, taking in the families, smoking with the men on the quayside. They watched the grey iron hulks criss-cross the horizon and waited for the black and brown speck that would grow into another little boat, with its refugees and their cargo, the quickly snatched stock of lives suddenly destitute, and the empty faces of loss.

The first weeks of the war had been the worst. Jaunty, cheery faces danced across the newsreels, the men from the northern towns who queued to volunteer because the Army paid more than they could wring out of the factories. It would, after all, be over long before they were through their basic training. Good luck to them. But there was nothing for the smacksmen. On the Monday, the day before they declared war, they had been ordered to the market hall at

Bolton Cross and another of the little sandy-faced naval officers had told them that if hostilities began they would be tied up in port until it was over. They could not, he said, with words slowly selected, guarantee the safety of two hundred sailing vessels, each of them a target for German submarines. He spoke as if it was a reasonable thing, something they would all agree about. And in the pinched tightness of his face they all saw it was a kind of surrender without a shell fired and that he knew it. It took a fortnight. Five hundred of the men signed up for the Navy, most of them because they were already in the Naval Reserve, others because they could not bear kicking their lives away on the quayside and doing nothing, a few because they needed money more than their pride.

By then the Belgians were coming in. They brought their stories of women and children taken hostage, shot at the village gates, towns occupied and ransom extorted at the point of a barrel, of the flatlands flooded, the soil of the centuries sacrificed to bog the grey-green advance. And always it was gratitude that England had stood by little Belgium, even though they all knew there was more to it than that. Wet September turned into mild October and they found the newcomers places for their few possessions and put their children to sit on the floor in the schools and still there was no news of the truce. In fact there was no news at all, except the rat-tat of official optimism in the London headlines they knew they should not believe but did. Jimmy and Alice offered to take a family even though, after the chapel wedding, with just Fanny and Henry standing as witnesses, the two rooms in King Street were all they had. But they had been told it was not necessary, with Alice due in October.

Hope had come, a little cry in the night. It was breaking midnight on Saturday and Jimmy was in the other room and had heard the anger in Alice's shrieking and the bitterness as the hours went on, the midwife Mrs Turner coming in and out of the room to make tea, so that Jimmy wondered if it would undo them. But then, almost unexpectedly, the baby was in his arms, the blood still in her hair and her hands old-wrinkled and he went in and sat on the soaking bed and saw that Alice was as amazed as he was.

'Hope?'

To Jimmy their baby had always been Hope but he had only asked Alice in the weeks before and had not dared imagine her refusal. At last she had looked up and said that it might be hope for him but was hard work for her, but had turned away and agreed because it was true that they had found hope in each other. And if their baby was a girl, then everything would be better for her than it had been for Alice. Now she nodded again and held out her arms to take her.

In the hours afterwards Alice had at last come out of her hiding place, where she had gone, turning in and away, as her time had grown close. And then they were wrapped up in each other again, now together with their new child as they had never imagined, every dribbled minute of each eternal day such that whatever had been up until then was no more than *before*.

Kitty sat with Alice through the fever in the week that followed, the Belgians she had taken into the house at St Peter's Hill Catholics of quiet warmth who knew what to do. Hope began to look at them with hazel eyes of unexpected wisdom, and when it came her smile was laughter and joy and a blessing that gave them faith. Jimmy had never imagined a day could be so long, nor the desperation so utterly black as the hours when Hope was gripped with the colic and screamed, her face twisted with disappointment, her limbs seized, groping, scrambling against the unreason and the pain. Then Alice and Jimmy were angry with themselves for their anger at their daughter, but discovered only that they were surrounded with hands to take the child and mothers who had travelled the road before and would take their little girl and rock her until she slept exhausted and give them some moments to still themselves. They talked only, ever, constantly about Hope. The shouting between them was terrible, blood red and black as it had always been. But now there was a lifeline, cords that had joined them with a slender permanence. Slowly Jimmy learned to trust that, whatever was being said, Alice would in the end come back to try again.

The ministry decided in the end that the smacks must go out again, fleeting with a naval escort that waited for them beyond the breakwater but they then saw on the horizon only once or twice in each watch. Either the threat of the submarines had gone or the Navy had decided they could do nothing about it and the need for food would have to come first. Men volunteered to go round to the north Cornish ports and Milford but they were already clogged with smacks from Lowestoft and Yarmouth where the U-boat threat was thought to be much worse. So the Brixham men were corralled in the Channel, a day's sailing from harbour and a sitting target for any intruder who could slip under the Navy's watch. For six weeks Jimmy had been back at sea, only ever able to think about Hope, every creaking, foul weathered hour he was away, and suddenly the threat of being taken by a German submarine was no game but blasphemy.

Nobody had yet expected Jimmy to go into uniform. He was only three months married when war broke out, and the baby was then due. More than that, with his mate's ticket, he was an obvious choice for any one of the dozens of smacks who were now without because their men had signed up. In the event he had barely been aboard *Crystal* six weeks before her master called him up to the bow winch and told him quietly he had decided to do his bit and would be leaving for Plymouth on the Monday and that there was no better man in the port to take his smack on for him. So by the end of November Jimmy was master, without a ticket but with the absolute loyalty of an old, cheerful crew and a salt-beaten old girl beneath their feet that had worked a dozen winters before he was born. The fishing had been more than fair, the *Crystal*'s faithful old crew laughing that Jimmy was a lucky skip. The truth was that he had fished with Henry Buckley for so long he knew the waters like the veined white skin on his wife's belly. Better. He knew every odour and pattern of the surface and the gravel and muck that came up in the tallow on the lead line and the way the gulls were when the water was full. So even though they were confined to the Channel, beating up and down around the buoy that feebly marked the grave of the *Empress*, they were filling their ice for a steady profit.

Alice had said on Sunday, as they were pushing Hope back in the rain from the chapel, that if the war lasted a few more weeks they could begin to put money into the bank. A skipper's share was good enough and more. They had worked out how long it would be before they could part-own a smack for themselves and knew the war would surely long be past and Jimmy back to the long haul as mate. Perhaps Hope would also have brothers or sisters, even if it was at that moment impossible to imagine sharing the immensity of their affection and the small energy they had left with any other living thing.

Now they felt the danger they were living with. It was curious because the trawling was already the most dangerous occupation in the kingdom, the shadow of storm or accident so familiar it was a fifth man aboard. The war danger was raw and much worse, the threat of grey steel that would surge out of the ocean, a monster, heaving them aside in their own waters. The Navy had informed them that a surfacing German U-boat would order the crew of a smack to abandon ship and take to their boat. They would then blow the smack up. The Navy had also informed them that it would never occur because their own command of the seas was unchallenged.

Jimmy had seen the naval escort a couple of hours before, her smoke a distant smudge in the shifting December grey of mist and drizzle. The weather was closing and as Jimmy scanned the water again he could now barely make out half a dozen other smacks and could see it would not be long before even they would slip out of sight. The escort might as well have been back in Plymouth. The possibility that the water alongside would break with the grey iron of a German submarine's tower and guns seemed at the same time remote, an outrage and oddly, terrifyingly immediate.

The trawl had been down about an hour and a half, towing for once off the starboard quarter because *Crystal* was reaching due south with a steady force three from the southwest and a tide strongly against, so that that they had to trim the foresail to keep the beam on the bottom. *Vigilance* was half a mile or so to starboard, the latest in a series of smacks on which Roddy Farley had been able to find work, none for more than a few weeks, his increasingly bitter temper and the known facts of his past with Beaton too much for crews to stomach. *Vigilance* was trawling a parallel course, her gear down perhaps twenty minutes longer than theirs. If the weather closed much more they would have to take care not to come too close.

Jimmy was imagining Hope running along by the rail, a girl of perhaps two or three, the blonde hair that was now just faint silk become wild, uncontrollable curls in the wind. He would catch her up, so heavy in comparison with now, yet still no weight at all. They would talk, which was almost unimaginable. He wondered what person lay behind those hazel eyes and what it would be like to be his daughter and how she would begin to make sense of the world he was helping create for her. The daydream was so vivid he wondered if he had shouted out, warning her clear of the warp and the deadly yards where the bight was bent to the tow post and would whip away the moment they stuck fast. Instinctively he looked across in case the man at the tiller on *Vigilance* had heard him.

That was when he saw it. The water between the two smacks was running foul, the pattern of the swell broken as if the sea were running over rocks. It was impossible. They were at least twenty miles off the coast of Lyme Bay and in fifteen fathoms of water. But the sea off his starboard bow was now churning white and whatever it was lay directly in the track of his trawl. Jimmy had no time to hesitate. He yelled to his crew and put *Crystal* hard to starboard, bringing her jolting head to wind as his men came clattering up the companion, pulling on oilies and at once running to the rail to see. They had the foresail aback in a moment and *Crystal* was hove to, two hours of catch spilling fathoms down but her precious gear safe and no harm done to any of them.

Moments later the surface of the water was split. First one and then two folded masts spiked the air and between them a grey tower, rising steadily as it travelled until it was fifteen feet high and on its flank large black letters, U24. In a moment there was a deck, three times the length of a smack, water sluicing across, a low gun on the foredeck, another aft. The U-boat was making three or four knots and figures were now climbing out onto the tower. Jimmy was numb. He had known these waters since he was a child. This foreigner's eruption was shocking, its climb an outrage.

The thing was now fifty yards from *Crystal* and a voice sounded over a loudhailer. Jimmy shook himself out of his horror. *Vigilance* was heaving to, coming to a standstill. A wall of fog was closing, a curtain of safety and Jimmy yelled for the axe, rammed the tiller hard over and called for the foresail to come across. By the time he was hacking at the trawl warp on the rail *Crystal* was coming about and they were sailing, running before the wind, away from the Germans, perhaps a hundred yards from safety in the fog. The German voice came again, now louder, turned towards them.

Half a minute passed, perhaps more, *Crystal* beginning to hum as she ran, the air moistening and thickening all the time. Then came a sound he did not recognise, a dull thump, thudding the air and before he had time to turn at the tiller there was a whistling splash, twenty yards to starboard. He yelled at his crew to find cover and crouched, shifting the old girl to port, making her as small a target for the gunner as he could. There was a second booming thud and then quickly a third, engulfed by a deafening flash and Jimmy was thrown back, blinded into the transit rail. He opened his eyes and for an instant struggled to make sense of what had happened.

Where the hoodway had been was a gaping hole. Flames were beginning to fly up into the mainsail, the oiled canvas quickly alight, burning strips beginning to drift away and down onto the deck. More flames were creeping up from below, from the cabin or the main hold or wherever the shell had exploded.

Jimmy was on his feet. The ship's boat was already circled with flames but the mate was over in a moment and slicing at the ties with his shet knife. The deckie was throwing the gangway open ready to lower the boat into the sea. Everyone knew that a smack was nothing but caulked timber, canvas and rope, and once alight would burn to the waterline in minutes. Jimmy scanned the deck for the cookie, a lad no more than twelve, and saw him thrown, shivering against the bulwarks, shielded from the explosion only by the metal bulk of the capstan. Jimmy clambered through the wreckage, wincing from the heat roaring up from below. He scooped the boy in his arms and bundled him around in front of the mainmast. They already had the ship's boat slithering over the side and in a moment all four were down, the mate heaving the boat's bow around and pulling away.

It was clear it was now the turn of *Vigilance* and her crew would soon be out in their boat. Their best hope would be to stay together, so long as the Germans would let them go. So they left *Crystal* behind, blazing from stem to stern, and rowed slowly back in the direction of the other smack. None of them spoke. The U-boat was now alongside *Vigilance* and her crew were lowering their boat. Two of the Germans climbed over into the smack, heaving an awkward metal case with them. They made their way forward and one lowered himself into the main hatch. The other handed the case after him. *Crystal*'s deckie turned back from the bow of the boat.

'They're going to blow a hole in her.'

'Timing device, long enough for the likes o' they to clear off.'

'Bastards.'

They watched without breathing, an endless two, three, five minutes. Finally the German reappeared from the hold and the U-boat's engines began to whine up to speed. What happened next was too quick and confused at first to understand. The two men were making their way back across the deck when suddenly they dropped out of sight. A second later, a crack came through the air, then a second and then two more. Jimmy looked over as *Vigilance*'s boat came towards them. There were only three in it, two men and a boy.

"Tis Roddy. The idiot stayed aboard. He's shooting at 'em.'

A man was now on the smack's rail and he jumped over onto the U-boat, waving to the tower, shouting. It was one of the Germans, the other apparently wounded or dead. The U-boat was slowly creeping ahead, the crewman running along the deck and climbing up into the tower. Jimmy saw Roddy climb out of the hoodway, a rifle in his hands and even from eighty yards Jimmy could see he had one of the guns that had been meant for Ireland, though where he had obtained his ammunition was a question probably only O'Connor could answer. Roddy began to make his way forward, keeping low. He got no further than the towpost. Two, three shots crackled across the water, perhaps from the U-boat, perhaps from the German lying on the deck. Roddy went down and for a moment nothing in the world seemed to move. Then the U-boat frothed into life, its engines thrashing the water and it began to gain speed.

'They've shot him.'

Jimmy's deckie was standing, uselessly, without meaning, disbelief widening his eyes, opening his mouth. Jimmy pulled him down.

'They shot 'en.'

'He's there.'

The cookie was pointing and Jimmy saw Roddy's head and then his shoulder. He was struggling to haul himself onto the rail. His right arm was useless, and he could barely pull himself up. Now Jimmy was on his feet.

'Jump, you idiot.'

Jimmy had shouted without thinking. If Roddy jumped he would sink within seconds, his heavy leather boots filling with water and pulling him down. He was pushing at them, scraping with his feet. They were a hundred yards away. Roddy would have no chance, even if he could swim. Jimmy shouted at his mate to row and began pulling off his own boots and oily. He had not swum for more than a year but Alice's voice was clear in his head, that now he had done it he would never forget. Roddy was a fool, proud and without an adult thought in his head. But Jimmy had known him too long and understood what he had suffered and told himself that he did not deserve this.

The water nearly took his breath away, intense cold, salt searing his nose and throat. In a moment he was up and turned and looking into the astonished faces of his crew, waving them away. He would keep Roddy afloat, bring him out until they could reach him. He began heavily groping his way towards *Vigilance*. Roddy was still on the rail, and Jimmy tried to shout to him, to jump before the bloody bomb blew. He saw Roddy's head lift. At last he had grasped what was happening. The next time Jimmy looked Roddy had a foot up and was struggling to heave his weight over the rail. When Jimmy was able to look again Roddy had gone.

Jimmy forced himself to pull the remaining yards, his horizon growing grey and blurred as fatigue set in. Roddy was ahead, drifting alongside the smack, his left arm thrashing hopelessly. Jimmy's breath was coming in short gasps, his arms leaden and foreign as he came up to him, *Vigilance* a black shadow just yards away. He summoned as much of his remaining breath and strength as he dare and shouted at him to stop struggling and then had him, his arm around his chest, pulling him onto his back as Alice had once pulled him, the water over their heads and then spitting, gasping clear again. The water around them was reddening, Roddy's right shoulder a clot of bloody canvas.

'Kick. Kick away. She's going to blow.'

But Roddy was rigid, his left arm still crashing uselessly.

'Clear off, Jimmy. Too late. No good.'

'Shut up. Kick.'

Jimmy was suddenly charged with new energy, horror of the explosion pulsing through him. They were still drifting alongside the smack, the current pulling them, Roddy a deadweight, making it almost impossible. Jimmy freed an arm and pulled with all his strength. Roddy was stiff, unyielding.

'Alice. Yours. And your girl. I did what I could. Nothing left.'

'Kick, fuck you. Nothing's finished.'

Roddy seemed to wake up. His voice was gripped, earnest.

'Piss off. Save yourself. I got naught, no point in going on.'

Now he was struggling, trying to break free.

'Shut up, Roddy. Do it together.'

'Never did naught together, Jimmy. Stupid. We could've.'

They were at last edging away from the black timber, past the bow, inching further.

'Do it now, Roddy, for both of us.'

The man was becoming limp and Jimmy wondered if the loss of blood would make him pass out.

'Do it for Alice.'

'Alice.'

At last Roddy's feet thrashed in the water. And Jimmy thought of Alice in her wildness and complexity and Hope already a pulsing, storming presence. And he knew it had in the end been right. The sudden heaving of the water came apparently without a sound, a confusion of light, a twisting, tearing of the air and the punching, winding, shattering that followed, enfolding him into darkness and falling, quiet, wondering, knowing, accepting, Alice, Hope and what was light and deep and old receiving and being received so that finally it was all very good.

Bibliography and acknowledgements

I first encountered the smacksmen in 1998 when I made a film about the Lowestoft smack *Excelsior*. It was obvious that this was an extraordinary way of working life that had been lost, very nearly without trace. History has been unkind to working people and especially to those, like the smacksmen, who recorded very little. This book is an attempt to reimagine their life. Even for an historian, the temptation was to romanticise. I can only say that, the closer I grew to the community around *Excelsior*, and the more I read from the time and since, the more moving I found the smacksmen's pride in their own mastery and defiance of the odds. There really does seem to have been a profound hope and a quiet humour beating at the heart of their struggle to stay alive and to make a poor living. They were very good at what they did and they knew it.

With skipper Stuart White and his team, we helped restore *Excelsior* to working order and finally went trawling under sail in the North Sea. There are not many alive who have had such a privilege. I had conversations about points of working a smack with Percy Thorpe, who had been a smacksman in the 1930s. I met William Finch, whose father had been a smacksman and whose book *The Sea in my Blood* (Diss 1992) is a detailed account of life aboard. I also worked with Robb Robinson, whose *Trawling. The Rise and Fall of the British Trawl Fishery* (University of Exeter 1996) is the place to go for an academic overview. The film, presented by actor Bernard Hill, went out on Channel 4 as *Fish and Ships* (not my choice, not least because there are other films of that name) and is now on YouTube.

Brixham smacks were slightly smaller than those that worked out of Lowestoft, and sailed with three men and a boy, rather than four. Otherwise they were almost identical and the pattern of their crews' life the same.

Edgar J March, *Sailing Trawlers. The Story of Deep-Sea Fishing with Long Line and Trawl* (London 1953) has been my bible, throughout the making of the film and the writing of the book. March researched his work in interviews with dozens of surviving smacksmen and he too found them uncomplaining, proud of what they had achieved. He sought out the smacks that still survived, many by then rotting in creeks. He painstakingly recorded every bolt and batten, strop and knee, down to the quarter of an inch. His book has many pages of exquisite diagrams and tables of details. It is as close to working a smack as it is possible to be without smelling the cutch and the catch.

Many local details come from the Brixham edition of the *Western Guardian* for these years. I also drew on the censuses and local directories. Other details come from Charles Gregory, *Brixham, in Devonia* (Totnes 1896), republished in 2011 by the British Library. You'll find that a number of the events in this book – the sinking of the *Empress of India* for example – are based on fact. Some of the people, like Dr Francis Brett Young, I have also borrowed from history. I have cheated Brett Young's book *Deep Sea* forward by a few months. Similarly, the appearance of the U-boats in the Channel. But I have tried to tell a story that *could have* happened.

There are a number of local publications that have been helpful. David Parker, *Edwardian Devon 1900-1914. Before the Lights went Out* (Stroud 2016) is as much about the period before 1900 as after, but gives helpful context. John Corin,

Provident and the Story of the Brixham Smacks (Tops'l Books, Reading 1980) is a fine introduction to the smacks, though I discover we differ on some details. Other books are mainly collections of photographs, notably Ted Gosling, *Brixham Revisited* (Tempus, Stroud 2005) and Chips Barber, *Brixham of Yesteryear* (3 parts, Obelisk, Exeter 2006). They offer fleeting impressions of living in these streets.

Two other books give us rare insights into this working-class world. Stephen Reynolds, Bob Woolley and Tom Woolley, *Seems So! A working-class view of politics* (London 1911) was written by Reynolds, a journalist and novelist, with two Sidmouth brothers with whom he lodged for many years. The Woolleys were not smacksmen, although they fished from an early motorboat. *Seems So!* is an invaluable source, not only for working-class views, but also of authentic Devon dialect of the period. William J Slade, *Out of Appledore* (London 1959) is a very rare account of life at sea, written by the skipper of small coasters trading out of a north Devon harbour from the early years of the century.

I am very grateful to the South West Maritime History Society and particularly to John Risdon of the Galmpton and Churston District Local History Group for checking the details of my narrative of life aboard. Any mistakes of course remain my own.

Jessica Osborne generously loaned her expertise as a psychotherapist to check my account of abuse and its many implications on victims' lives. She was also the one who eventually insisted I find a publisher. Historian Julie Hankey read an earlier draft with her usual sharpness and suggested important improvements. Helen Baggott has been an acute and sympathetic editor. Olli Tooley has been a sensitive and wonderfully demanding publisher. I'm very grateful to them all.

Penelope Middelboe says she fell in love when she first read the manuscript. Since we have been married (another spring marrying) she has read the text countless times and shared my passion for the story and its characters. She knows how much I owe her.

My thanks above all belong to the extraordinary men and women who really lived these hard lives and made them yet productive and even beautiful.

About the Author

This is Jon Rosebank's first novel. He grew up in the West Country and wrote his doctorate on the history of Somerset and Devon towns. He was a Fellow of New College, Oxford before becoming a TV producer and eventually executive producer with BBC Documentaries and History. Later he made documentaries as a freelance director, also writing an academic book and a number of articles. He currently writes and presents the podcast *History Café* with Penelope Middelboe.